THE WRONG LOVE
WITH THE RIGHT MAN

Sarah took the bag of confetti Patrick offered, tossing the bits of colored paper into the air. "We're off!" she cried as the ship glided out of the harbor. Her face was radiant, her eyes brimming with tears. "Oh, Patrick, we're off on our adventure!"

It was a romantic adventure, with six magical days in Paris. They were together in the dark, smoky cafés of the Left Bank and in the splendor of lavish Right Bank ballrooms. They danced until dawn, breakfasting on champagne and croissants, making love on scented silk sheets.

"I don't want to leave," Patrick whispered to her on their last day as they picnicked in the *Bois*. "Let's stay. Let's chuck everything and stay."

"You mustn't tempt me."

"Why not? Lucy is grown. My boys are grown. Why not stay and be happy?"

Why not? Sarah thought. But she nestled her head on Patrick's shoulder and only whispered, "We have everything. Everything . . ."

CATCH UP ON THE BEST IN CONTEMPORARY FICTION
FROM ZEBRA BOOKS!

LOVE AFFAIR   (2181, $4.50)
by Syrell Rogovin Leahy
A poignant, supremely romantic story of an innocent young woman with a tragic past on her own in New York, and the seasoned newspaper reporter who vows to protect her from the harsh truths of the big city with his experience — and his love.

ROOMMATES   (2156, $4.50)
by Katherine Stone
No one could have prepared Carrie for the monumental changes she would face when she met her new circle of friends at Stanford University. For once their lives intertwined and became woven into the tapestry of the times, they would never be the same.

MARITAL AFFAIRS   (2033, $4.50)
by Sharleen Cooper Cohen
Everything the golden couple Liza and Jason Greene touched was charmed — except their marriage. And when Jason's thirst for glory led him to infidelity, Liza struck back in the only way possible.

RICH IS BEST   (1924, $4.50)
by Julie Ellis
From Palm Springs to Paris, from Monte Carlo to New York City, wealthy and powerful Diane Carstairs plays a ruthless game, living a life on the edge between danger and decadence. But when caught in a battle for the unobtainable, she gambles with the only thing she owns that she cannot control — her heart.

THE FLOWER GARDEN   (1396, $3.95)
by Margaret Pemberton
Born and bred in the opulent world of political high society, Nancy Leigh flees from her politician husband to the exotic island of Madeira. Irresistibly drawn to the arms of Ramon Sanford, the son of her father's deadliest enemy, Nancy is forced to make a dangerous choice between her family's honor and her heart's most fervent desire!

Available wherever paperbacks are sold, or order direct from the Publisher. Send cover price plus 50¢ per copy for mailing and handling to Zebra Books, Dept. 2548, 475 Park Avenue South, New York, N.Y. 10016. Residents of New York, New Jersey and Pennsylvania must include sales tax. DO NOT SEND CASH.

BARBARA HARRISON
SOCIETY PRINCESS

ZEBRA BOOKS
KENSINGTON PUBLISHING CORP.

ZEBRA BOOKS

are published by

Kensington Publishing Corp.
475 Park Avenue South
New York, NY 10016

First printing: January, 1989

Printed in the United States of America

For dear friends

Edna and Adolph Phillips
Bentley Kolodny
Tania Grossinger

With love

Sarah

Chapter One

Twilight was deepening, a soft rain falling as Sarah Griffith left the Aldcross library and latched the door behind her. She smiled, for spring had come early to the quiet English village, and everywhere was the scent of flowers and trees in first bloom. Spring had always been her favorite time of year. It suited her romantic nature, her sudden and exuberant flights of fancy. She did not mind that her mother scoffed at such fancies. She was seventeen years old and it was spring and the world, on this misty Saturday in 1921, seemed a blessed place.

Aldcross was the only world Sarah Griffith knew. She knew it well, its little train station, its few shops, its school, its ancient church, its neat brick cottages with their kitchen gardens and herbaceous borders. To the south lay modest farms and pasture lands. To the east lay Greenway Hall, the magnificent country estate of Sir Roger Averill and his wife Lady Mary.

Sarah, like many others in Aldcross, was intrigued by the Averills, for they were a glamorous couple, young and handsome and possessed of great wealth. Sir Roger had returned from the war a hero, though it was whispered that he had returned a changed man, a restless and often moody man. There were rumors of trouble at the Hall, of too much drinking, of violent quarrels. Sarah had heard the rumors and she dismissed them, remembering instead the Averills' generosity to the village. Of their generosity there was no doubt. Lady Mary sponsored both the Christmas Bazaar and the Girl Guides' Picnic. Sir Roger subscribed lavishly to local charities, providing a new roof for the vicarage, the new library building, and the funds that each year sent several promising Aldcross boys to University. Sarah's brother was one of those boys; she herself owed her job at the library to the Averills.

Now Sarah gathered up her skirts and crossed the wide square. All the shops were closing, shopkeepers in smudged white aprons sweeping their walks or stacking crates. Through the window of the Three Swans Pub she could see a darts game already in progress, and while she had never set foot inside the Three Swans or any other pub, she knew the talk would be of soccer and gardening and rising prices. There would be grumbling about the government, most of it good-humored. There would be war stories, for many of the village's men had fought in the war and some had died.

Sarah's father, a schoolmaster, had not been called but he had volunteered. He had been gone two years, and she still counted the day he had come home as the happiest day of her life. Her family was whole again, safe in the snug cottage on Winding Lane where she had been born. She had fond memories of her childhood, if not of her entry into adolescence. At twelve she had been scrawny and too tall, all arms and legs and freckles. Her hair, pale and very curly, had sprung free of even the tightest braids. She had had one cold after another, reddening her eyes and

10

her nose.

Sarah had been teased by her young friends, often to the point of tears. But at fifteen she had blossomed. The sharp angles of her body had given way to a gently swelling bosom and tapering waist. Her freckles had faded. Her hair had darkened to a lovely honey color, framing her face in loose waves. Her colds had mysteriously stopped, revealing large hazel eyes flecked with deep blue. Almost overnight she had become the prettiest girl in Aldcross, courted by the same boys who just a few years before had teased and taunted her.

Tom Cutler was the boy Sarah chose. She never wavered, for his youthful dreams had touched her imagination; his slow smile, his clear, earnest gaze had touched her heart. Theirs was an innocent courtship. Together they attended Sunday church services, afterward taking long walks hand in hand through the wood. They went to village socials, and when Tom's father could spare the wagon they went for rides, venturing into the neighboring town of Marbury. They talked and laughed and shyly planned their lives. At evening's end they lingered on Sarah's doorstep, stealing chaste kisses in the darkness.

The memory of those kisses was with Sarah now as she hurried along silent, shadowy Beechwood Road. She felt warm and a little giddy, and she turned her face to the misting rain. Soon she would be home, she thought to herself; there would be supper and then talk by the fireplace and then sleep and then it would be Sunday. She would see Tom again. "Tom," she whispered, wishing the hours away. So engrossed in her thoughts was Sarah that she did not hear the low roar of the motorcar until it was nearly upon her. She jumped back, a cry falling from her lips, and in that moment the car slowed.

Sarah recognized the car at once, for there were only three cars in all of Aldcross, the other two owned by Dr. Burshaw and by Mr. Flurry's Car Hire. "Hello, Sir Roger," she called with a wan smile. "I'm afraid I wasn't paying attention."

"Is that you, Sarah Griffith?"

"Yes, Sir Roger. I'm sorry. I—I wasn't paying attention to the road. I'm sorry if I gave you a scare." She heard the car door open. Sir Roger leaned his head out, the burnished gold of his hair like a beacon in the dwindling light. He was very still, watching her. He seemed to be waiting for something, though she could not think what. "I'm sorry," she said again. "I promise to keep a sharp eye next time."

"Are you hurt?"

"Oh, no, Sir Roger. I'm fine, really I am."

"Well, come in out of the wet. I'll drive you home."

Sarah was startled, for despite Sir Roger's generosity to Aldcross, he had always held himself aloof from his neighbors. None of them had ever been invited inside the vaulted doors of Greenway Hall, and none of them, no matter how bad the weather, had ever been invited to share either his carriage or his car. Knowing this, Sarah was unsure what to do. She took a step forward, then stopped, edging away. "I wouldn't want to impose," she said. "If it's any trouble—"

"Come along, Sarah, enough of that. Come round the other side."

"Yes, Sir Roger." She picked up her skirts and ran toward the car. In her haste, in her confusion, she stumbled, righting herself just before she fell. "Oh, I'm so clumsy today," she said when finally she was seated next to Sir Roger. "I've never had a ride in a motorcar before. I was—" She said nothing more, silenced by a pungent, almost overpowering odor. It's whiskey, she thought, recalling her mother's whiskeyed tipsy cakes. For the first time, she wondered if the stories she had heard about the Averills might be true. She felt a sudden inexplicable alarm and she moved closer to the door.

"Do I frighten you?" Sir Roger asked, an edge to his voice. When Sarah did not speak, he thrust out his hand and turned her face to him. "Well, do I?"

"No, Sir Roger." The words came slowly, for she sensed something was wrong, something more than whiskey. She wondered why Sir Roger had not started the car, why he sat so still, watching her. She felt an uneasy prickling at the back of her neck. She lowered her eyes and took a breath. "It's just that I'm late getting home," she said quietly. "It's late."

"Is it? I hadn't noticed."

"It's almost dark."

"There's comfort in the dark, my girl," Sir Roger replied. "And what a pretty girl you are, Sarah Griffith. All grown up, aren't you? Going about with the Cutler lad . . . I hear all the village gossip, you see. The servants never stop chattering."

Sarah clasped her nervous hands together. She wanted to run from the car, to flee, but she dared not risk such an insult to Sir Roger. How would she explain it? she wondered, her mind straining to put a name to the fear she felt. She glanced through the window at the road, shrouded now in blackness. It was supper time in Aldcross; there would be no wagons passing by, no bicycles. Please let him start the car, she silently cried. *Please.*

"Pretty girls and romance," Sir Roger murmured, as if to himself. Abruptly, he reached into his pocket, removing a silver flask. He lifted the flask to his lips and the whiskey smell grew worse. "What do you say,

13

Sarah? Shall we have a toast to pretty girls and romance?''

"I—I don't understand."

Sir Roger drank again from the flask. He drained it and then tossed it aside. "Are you nice to Tom Cutler?" he asked. "Yes, I'll wager you are. You're all the same."

Sarah's head had begun to pound. She felt trapped, afraid to leave the car and even more afraid to stay. "The rain's stopped," she said, her hand creeping toward the door. "And it's not so far to Winding Lane. I'll—I'll be off now." She turned, trying to push the door open, but she was too late. Sir Roger loomed over her, pinning down her arms, forcing his lips against hers. *"No,"* she screamed. *"No."* She struggled wildly to free herself, kicking her legs and twisting her body until Sir Roger's grip loosened. With her last strength, she threw herself at the door and into the road.

Sarah scrambled to her feet. She started to run, clamping her hand over her mouth, for she felt sick. She heard Sir Roger following behind and she ran faster. She lost a shoe, the combs slipped from her hair, and still she ran, in desperation taking the path through the wood. Tears burned her eyes, blinding them. She stumbled, falling to the damp ground. "Please, no," she cried as Sir Roger neared. Again she scrambled to her feet, but again she was too late. Sir Roger lunged at her, his fingers like claws, tightening on her shoulders.

"Let me go," Sarah pleaded. "Oh, please, Sir Roger, let me go." Terrified, she flailed at him, raking his face. She felt the ooze of blood beneath her nails and she froze in horror. "Please," she sobbed, but the violent force of his blow sent her reeling backward into a clump of trees. Quite suddenly, birds swooped from the branches, flapping and rustling their wings in an eerie sound she would remember all her life.

"Damn you, Sarah Griffith! Can't you see there's no place to run!"

"Don't," she cried as Sir Roger came closer. "Oh, no, please don't. . . . Please don't." But her cries died on the air, for now he was upon her, dragging her down to the dark and tangled ground. She felt her skirts flung up about her waist, her underclothes ripped away. She felt his hands rushing at her body. She felt his hot whiskey breath. In a sliver of moonlight, she saw his eyes, hard and cruel and filled with rage. She saw something else, something corrupt, and then, mercifully, blackness closed around her.

"It's past seven," John Griffith said to his wife Hilda. "Where can Sarah be?"

"Put the blame on Miss Sparrow. It's not right the way she keeps Sarah so late at the library . . . and has her doing all those extra chores to boot. It's just not right. I've made up my mind to have a word with the woman tomorrow after church."

"She's never kept Sarah this late."

"Till now." Hilda bent her head to the oven, inspecting the remains of a shepherd's pie. "Not fit to eat anymore," she sniffed. "I'll certainly have a word with Miss Sparrow. . . . You haven't touched your pudding, John. Would you like a bit of cream on top? There's half a pint left."

"Cream? No, I don't think so. I don't seem to have much appetite. I keep wondering where Sarah's got to." John pushed his bowl away. He looked up at Hilda, the woman he had loved for more than twenty years. In 1900 he had been the young, newly arrived schoolmaster, and she the youngest, prettiest daughter of the greengrocer. He had loved her then, almost at first sight, and he loved her now, though it was true that she sometimes intimidated him. She's always so certain about things, he thought fondly. Whatever the problem, Hilda had the answer. "I expect I'm worrying for nothing," he said.

"Of course you are, dear."

"Still, I'll feel better when Sarah's home. I don't like her going round alone after dark. That road's none too safe at night. Why, only last week Alice Steele fell into a hollow and wrenched her ankle."

"Tall tales!" Hilda laughed. "I'm not saying Alice didn't hurt her ankle, but for a cause I'd look to the sherry bottle. Alice likes her sherry and that's a fact."

John smiled, watching Hilda clear the table. She moved briskly between table and sink, not a step wasted. And that, too, was like her. Everything she did she did well, usually with a smile. Her girlish prettiness was long gone, but she had kept her figure and she was an attractive woman, fair-haired, chatty in a pleasant way. She was known to have an iron will, a will most often displayed in her ambitions for her children, Bertie and Sarah. From Bertie, now off at London University, she expected great things. From Sarah she expected a suitable marriage and educated grandchildren. "Come sit down, Hilda," John said. "Your coffee's getting cold."

"I'm thinking I should fix sandwiches for Sarah. She'll be hungry, and her dinner's ruined. There's the chicken I was saving for Sunday tea. Or I could fry up some bacon."

"Come drink your coffee."

Hilda was about to sit down when she heard a crash in the front hall. "Your bicycle rack's come

16

loose again," she said. "I hope there's no damage done this time. We'd best have a look, John."

He followed her into the narrow passageway that led to the front of the cottage. "It's the hooks," he murmured. "I've told Mr. Clegg they're the wrong hooks, but . . ." John stopped, his eyes scanning the dimly lit hall. In the next instant he sprinted past Hilda, dropping to the huddled figure on the floor. "Sarah . . . Sarah, what's happened? Sarah? I don't . . . I think she's fainted."

"Take her into the parlor. I'll fetch the whiskey."

John lifted his daughter into his arms. "Sarah?" he called softly. "Sarah, can you hear me?" He laid her on the sofa, his hand fumbling at the lamp switch. "My God," he gasped, seeing for the first time Sarah's bruised and swollen face, her mouth encrusted with dried blood. There was blood on her hands, in her tangled hair. Her clothes were torn, her bare legs covered with jagged scratches. John turned away, shocked to his very soul. "Hilda!" he shouted, clutching the back of a chair. "Hilda!"

"You don't have to yell the house down," she replied, bustling back into the room. "I'm here. I've brought whiskey and cold cloths. . . . Look at you, John, you're white as—"

"I must go for Dr. Burshaw. Right now. I must go right now."

"But—"

"I'll hurry," John said, and with a last anguished glance at Sarah, he ran from the room.

All this fuss over a fainting spell, thought Hilda, confused. She carried her laden tray to the table and set it down, her gaze moving to Sarah. It was a moment before she was able to comprehend that the battered form lying on the sofa was her child. The room seemed to sway, and she with it; it was another moment before she was able to catch her breath. She knew she had to be calm. "Best not to think," she told herself. "Just do what has to be done."

Hilda knelt beside the sofa. "Sarah," she called, shaking her. "Sarah, you must wake up now." She rubbed her bruised wrists and put a cold cloth across her brow. "That's the way," she said when Sarah's eyes fluttered open. "That's the way.... You're safe, dear. You're home."

"Mama?"

"It's all right. Sarah. I'm here. Your father's gone to fetch Dr. Burshaw." Sarah's eyes began to close and Hilda shook her again. "You must stay awake," she said, though gently. "You can sleep as long as you like after the doctor's seen you.... Can you sit up? Try, Sarah. Lean on me.... Ah, that's better. Much better ... Take a bit of this whiskey. It will help.... Go on, do as I say."

The smell of the whiskey jolted Sarah to consciousness. All at once she remembered the terrifying chase through the wood, the struggle, the pain. "*No,*" she screamed, knocking the glass away. She remembered the last terrible minutes in the wood and her screams grew louder. She was shivering, rocking back and forth, her hands clenched into fists. Her eyes darted about, wild with mounting panic.

"Stop it, Sarah! Sarah!" Hilda ducked her head, avoiding Sarah's random blows. "Let me help you," she cried. "Please, Sarah. It's all right. You're safe now. You're home."

Hilda's words came to Sarah as if from a vast distance. Home, she thought; I'm home. She saw the old china dog sitting in its accustomed place atop the hearth. Next to the hearth she saw the brass coal scuttle, polished and gleaming. She saw her father's chair, his reading lamp, and her screams subsided.

18

"Papa," she whispered.

"He's gone to fetch Dr. Burshaw. It's all right, Sarah. Everything's all right now." But is it? Hilda wondered, searching her daughter's tormented eyes. A suspicion too ugly to speak aloud was forming in her mind. She tried to push it away; she could not. "I'm here," she said, touching Sarah's cheek. "I'm here, dear."

Sarah fell into Hilda's arms. Dry sobs racked her body, but after a while these subsided also. She clung to her mother, sniffling, and little by little her anxieties quieted. When John burst into the parlor with Dr. Burshaw, she managed a feeble smile. "Papa," she whispered again.

Thank God she's alive, thought John, relief washing over him. She's hurt and frightened, but she's alive. "I've brought Dr. Burshaw, Sarah. He'll help you."

Philip Burshaw had been the village doctor for as long as anyone could remember. He was close to seventy, a tall, portly man with a shock of white hair and a bristling white mustache. His manner was direct, often brusque, though never unkind. He was a good doctor, and in his way a good man. "Well, Sarah," he said now, "let's have a look at you." He bent to her, prying her loose from Hilda. "I won't ask how you feel. Bloody awful, I should imagine. . . . John, let's get our girl upstairs to her bed."

"Yes—yes, of course."

"Hilda, I'll want a basin of hot water and one of cold. And some clean towels. You might fix a pot of tea while you're at it. There's a hard night ahead." Dr. Burshaw turned, watching John carry Sarah out of the room. "Did she tell you anything? Did she say anything about what happened?"

"No," Hilda replied, fighting back tears. "She was

19

hysterical, Doctor. I was afraid she'd lost her senses."

"I wouldn't blame her if she had. Terrible, a thing like this happening in Aldcross. I don't know what we've come to. And it isn't done yet. Sarah will have to name the man."

Hilda's hand flew to her throat. "The man?" she asked.

"You can't make this out to be a road accident, nor any other kind of accident. There's blood and bits of skin under Sarah's fingernails. I'd say she put up quite a struggle. How much good it did . . . Well, we'll see about that. You're not going to faint on me, are you, Hilda? No, I suppose not. You've always been the strong one in the family."

"I don't feel very strong right now."

"But you are. That's what counts, isn't it?" Dr. Burshaw drew an old-fashioned gold watch from his pocket. "I'll be on my way to Sarah," he said. "Have your cry and then bring the things I asked for. Don't be long." With that he left the parlor, snatching up his black bag as he went to the stairs. "I hope you have a fire going, John," he called. "The night air plays havoc with my creaky bones."

John was waiting at the top of the landing. "I don't think Sarah wanted me to stay," he explained, glancing worriedly toward her door. "I got her settled down, but when I tried to talk to her she turned away. I don't understand. Only a moment ago in the parlor she seemed glad to see me. But now . . ." He shook his head, his soft blue eyes bewildered and filled with grief. "Now she won't even look in my direction. . . . I don't know what to do."

"There's nothing for you to do, John. You must leave it to me."

"But will she be all right?"

"Sarah is young and healthy. As for the rest, we'll

20

have to see. Go on downstairs and try to relax. It's no good your hovering about. Go on, and no arguments, John." Dr. Burshaw crossed the hall, opening the door to Sarah's room. "Don't be alarmed," he said. "I know you'd rather be let alone, but you've been injured and you need attention."

Sarah lay curled upon her bed, a feather quilt covering her torn, stained clothing. She did not speak, did not move, though her tortured gaze swept from side to side. Dimly, she saw the small desk, the straight-backed chair, the bureau with its oval mirror. Plain white curtains rippled at the window. A fire roared and crackled on the grate. All these sights she had seen thousands of times before, but familiar as they were, they gave no comfort. There's no help for me, she thought, no help anywhere. Her hands clenched so tightly that the knuckles sprang out beneath the skin. Tears stung her eyes, coursing down her swollen face.

Dr. Burshaw pulled the chair next to Sarah's bed. He sat down, reaching to take her pulse. She flinched and his bushy white brows drew together. "Now, now, Sarah," he said, "I haven't come to hurt you. You've had a nasty time of it, but that part's done. You mustn't be afraid. Try to be calm. . . . I'll tell you what I'm doing as I go along. Is it a bargain, Sarah?"

"I want to sleep."

"And you shall. After I've examined you, and after we've had a little talk."

"No," Sarah cried.

"What nonsense is this? You've always been a sensible girl, for all your fancies. I won't have you falling to pieces now. I won't allow it." Dr. Burshaw grasped Sarah's wrist once again. Her pulse was rapid but strong, and he was satisfied. He dipped into his black bag, extracting a thermometer. "Under

21

your tongue," he ordered, "and no squirming."

Hilda entered the room then. "I brought every-thing you wanted, Doctor," she said, placing a large tray atop the bureau. "The kettle's on for tea." She hesitated, brushing her red-rimmed eyes. "Can I help?" she asked.

"Nothing to do," Dr. Burshaw replied with a wave of his hand. "Go see to John." He waited until the door closed before turning back to Sarah. "No fever," he said, returning the thermometer to his bag. "Now we'll put the quilt aside and get you out of your things."

Color rushed to Sarah's pale cheeks. She held fast to the quilt, consumed by embarrassment and shame, for she could not bear the thought of anyone touching her, looking at her. "No, I can't," she said, shrinking away.

"And I can't very well examine you through your clothes, can I? This is very foolish, Sarah. Why, I've been your doctor all your life. I brought you into the world. Funny little creature you were, too. Wrinkled as a prune!" Dr. Burshaw moved the chair closer to the bed. He saw the fear in Sarah's eyes and he sighed. "You're only making matters worse," he said. "One way or another, I *must* examine you. Now let's put aside the quilt and find your nightdress and get started. . . . I've a pretty good idea of what happened to you, Sarah, if that's what's on your mind. Is it? No need to mince words, you know. Not with me. I've seen this sort of thing before."

There was a shrill clanging in Sarah's head. She closed her eyes, trying to shut out the noise, the pain, the memory. "Will you have to tell Mama and Papa?" she asked, knowing the answer even as she spoke.

"You're not to worry about that now. You're not

the guilty party, after all."

Not the guilty party, thought Sarah. But there'll be talk just the same. Word will get out and there'll be gossip. Mama will be so ashamed. And Papa will be worried all the time. And Tom . . . "Oh, my poor Tom," she murmured. She tried to raise herself on her pillow. She fell back and her hands slipped from the quilt, all resistance gone. She said nothing as Dr. Burshaw discarded her ruined clothing and pulled a nightdress over her head. She was poked and prodded, turned this way and that. Her wounds were cleansed and bandaged; her wrist was taped. A foul-tasting liquid was poured down her throat. Mute, unseeing, she stared into the distance, offering not a word of protest.

Dr. Burshaw's face was grim when at last he closed his bag and sat down. "Who did this to you, Sarah?" he asked. "Tell me."

"I can't," she replied quietly.

"Was it Tom Cutler? I don't believe it was. But if you don't name the man, it's Tom who will be suspected. Is that what you want?"

Sarah lifted her stricken eyes to Dr. Burshaw. "No," she said. "No, it wasn't Tom. I swear it."

"Tell me."

"It was—it was Sir Roger."

Dr. Burshaw's expression did not change, though his jaw tensed, as well as his hands. "Sir Roger, eh? Yes, I see. Can't say I'm surprised." He stood, taking a small packet from his bag. He spilled the powdery contents into a glass of water and gave it to Sarah. "Drink this," he ordered. "Every drop. It will help you sleep. . . . Now, don't fret. Sleep is what you need and sleep you shall have. I'll stay here until you're off. I want to hear some good, sound snoring."

Sarah tilted the glass to her lips and drank. She

23

shivered, drawing the quilt to her chin. "What will happen when—when they know it's Sir Roger?" she asked.

All hell will break loose, thought Dr. Burshaw to himself, that's what will happen. "You're safe now, Sarah," he said. "Safe and warm in your bed."

It was after nine o'clock when Dr. Burshaw came downstairs. He found John and Hilda in the parlor, their teacups untouched on the table. John was ashen, his light brown hair straggling across his brow. Hilda sat straight and still, her hands clasped in her lap, her head bent. "I won't mince words," he said, taking a chair opposite. "Sarah's been assaulted. Raped, to put it plainly."

John leapt up, but almost in the same moment he sank down again, covering his face with shaking hands. "How could this have happened?" he cried. "It's impossible. Impossible, I tell you. Not Sarah. It can't be true."

"Is Sarah all right, Doctor?" Hilda asked.

"Cuts and bruises. Quite a lot of swelling. A sprained wrist. In the physical regard, there's nothing that won't heal in a week or two. In that regard, she'll be right as rain."

"Yes?" Hilda persisted. "Go on."

"Well, she's had a bad shock, hasn't she? Sarah's a young girl, innocent. A thing like this is bound to have an effect. And Aldcross being what it is . . ."

Hilda rose suddenly, pressing her handkerchief to her streaming eyes. "The kettle's on," she said. "I'll fetch hot water for your tea."

Dr. Burshaw watched her hurry from the room. Frowning, he turned his attention to John. "I know this is hard for you, for you both," he said. "But it's best to face the truth and accept it."

"Did Sarah say who . . . Was it Tom?"

"It was Sir Roger."

John's lips parted. He stared at the doctor, his hands falling helplessly to his sides. "Sir Roger!"

"There was a similar incident last year with the nursery maid at the Hall. Not that I was called in, you understand. I wasn't. The Averills had their own physician motor down from London. A week later the poor girl was sent packing. Surely you heard the talk."

"That was just gossip, Philip."

"Gossip? Well, perhaps so, but gossip has its uses. Miss Sparrow and Miss Meade and all the other old tabbies know everything there is to know about the doings in Aldcross. They may embroider the details a bit, but there's never any doubt of the facts."

"My God, this is a nightmare! When I think what Sarah's been through. When I think . . . She trusted him, you know. We all did." John looked up as his wife returned to the parlor. "Hilda," he said slowly, "I've just learned that the man was Sir—"

"Yes, I was listening in the kitchen. Here's your tea, Doctor. I brought a plate of cheese biscuits, too. I'll just set it down and you can help yourself. . . . I can offer you whiskey, if you'd prefer."

"No, better not. I'll want my wits about me when we talk to Constable Jenk.

"Constable Jenk!" Hilda cried. "You're not thinking of bringing the constable into it! Do you want Sarah's name dragged through the mud? Do you want a scandal? And don't tell me there won't be a scandal. Oh, I can hear the old tabbies now, tongues wagging nineteen to the dozen."

Dr. Burshaw's sharp gaze narrowed on Hilda. "A crime's been committed," he replied. "A very nasty crime indeed, and it's not the first time. Are we to let Sir Roger go his way? No, I insist you hear me out. I've known three generations of Averills, all fine men. And I'm including Sir Roger in that category, at least until he went off to war. Something happened to him then. God alone knows what. God alone. But two innocent girls have suffered the consequences. A stop must be put, or there will be a third."

"Fancy words," Hilda snapped. She began to pace, avoiding John's outstretched hand. "Fancy words, and why not? You've nothing to lose in this. Your life won't change."

"Sarah's life has already changed."

"I don't need reminding, Doctor. But how can we fight Sir Roger? The whole village is in his debt. *We're* in his debt, when you come down to it. Perhaps you've forgotten that it's Sir Roger who's paying Bertie's fees and lodging at University. Perhaps you've forgotten about our school right here in Aldcross. It's Sir Roger's money that's keeping our school going. How long do you suppose John will have his position in the school once we put the law on an Averill? And what of Sarah's reputation? In all your fancy words, did you give a thought to that?"

"Sarah is the victim, not the—"

"Yes, she's the victim, but who'll take her part against Sir Roger? You and the vicar and who else? I promise it won't be a long list." Hilda turned away, twisting her wedding band around. She saw John then, and wearily, she sat beside him. "People can't help being what they are," she said, her voice drained of emotion. "People—most people anyhow—are afraid of losing what they have."

"You're a stubborn woman, Hilda."

"I'm a truthful woman, truthful in the way I see

things. I can't speak for John and I don't try. Do I, dear?"

John shook his head. He had listened quietly to Hilda's arguments. He had not interrupted nor even looked up, concentrating instead on his hands, studying the palms, the slender fingers, as if he had never seen them before. In those moments he seemed to age. His face was haggard, all the light gone from his eyes, all the color from his mouth. Deep lines etched his brow, and in his expression there was only defeat. "I should be able to speak for myself," he said. "I should, but it's all so complicated. . . . I want what's best for Sarah and I want—I want revenge. I've been sitting here thinking he *mustn't* get away with what he's done. Yet I know he will. I know it, Philip. We could talk to the constable, we could put Sarah through the agony of questioning. . . . But if we did, what would happen in the end? Who would suffer most?"

Dr. Burshaw lighted his pipe and clenched it between his teeth. "You may have a point," he conceded after a while. "For Sarah's sake, the law may be the wrong approach. There are other approaches, however. I won't go to Jenk, but you can't stop me from going to the Hall."

"I shall go with you."

"John, what are you saying?"

"It's my place to go, Hilda. If I had the courage, I'd go with a gun. . . . Please try to understand. I must do this. Ignoring what's happened won't *change* what's happened. Don't you see?"

"Yes, I see." And in her clear-eyed fashion she saw many things, not least the fact that all their lives had been forever changed. "But don't be surprised to find the doors barred to you," she added. "I know Lady Mary's your friend, but she's an Averill first."

"She's not my friend. We talk about gardening, Hilda, that's all. About the bindweed in the Michaelmas daisies."

"Come along, John," Dr. Burshaw said, rising. "My car is just outside. We'll be there in no time."

Hilda looked away as the two men took their leave. She heard the front door open and then close. Moments later, she heard the sound of a car engine. Now there was silence, silence that seemed to ring with echoes of the past, of children's laughter, of love. She bent her head and wept.

Chapter Two

A silvery moonlight fell across Sarah's face, outlining the tired set of her mouth. She lay still, her hands locked together atop the quilt, her eyes fixed on the door. "I'm awake, Mama," she said when Hilda tiptoed into the room. "I couldn't sleep."

"Would you like some warm milk, dear?"

"No, I don't want anything."

"I didn't mean to disturb you," Hilda explained. "I came to see to the fire. There's a nip in the air tonight." She went to the hearth, scooping coal onto the grate, stirring the flames until they leapt and rushed up the chimney. "That's better, isn't it?"

"What time is it, Mama?"

"Oh, it's late. Past twelve."

"Where's Papa?"

"He's gone out, Sarah. He should be home any time now." Hilda left the fireplace. She hesitated briefly, then went to Sarah's bedside. "I'll sit with you a while, shall I? Just till you drop off again."

"Where did Papa go? Did he go to the Hall?"

"So many questions!" Hilda replied, taking Sarah's cold hand. "It's no wonder you can't sleep. And Dr. Burshaw said you needed sleep. Close your eyes, dear. I'll stay with you. I'll be right here."

Sarah turned suddenly. She thrashed about, pulling at Hilda's arm. "But I want to know," she cried. "Tell me, Mama. Did he go to the Hall?"

"Here now, Sarah, don't upset yourself so. You must try to be calm." Hilda switched on the lamp. She dampened a cloth, pressing it to Sarah's forehead. "I wouldn't be at all surprised if you had a fever."

"*Please* tell me, Mama."

"It's nothing for you to be worried about, but yes, Papa and Dr. Burshaw went to the Hall. There wasn't any choice, Sarah. And it's best to handle things this way, without bringing the constable into our troubles. Not that I don't respect the law, but sometimes it's best this way."

Sarah slumped against the pillows, her face drawn and very white. "Mama," she said in a ragged voice, "it—it wasn't my fault."

"Of course it wasn't! What an idea, Sarah! Of course it wasn't! I know my own daughter, don't I? And Papa knows, don't you worry about that. Why, the thought never entered our heads."

"What will happen?"

"I don't know," Hilda sighed, "and that's the truth. Sometimes the Averills carry on like they owned the village. And maybe they do, with all their gifts and subscriptions. With the Hall. There've been Averills at Greenway Hall for two hundred years and more. . . . When I was your age, it was Sir Gerald running things. And in my father's time, it was Sir Charles. But the trouble didn't start till this generation. Or till the war, I suppose I should say. Wars do terrible things to people."

"I didn't do anything, Mama."

"Of course you didn't. You must stop thinking

30

such things, Sarah. No one's blaming you."

"They will."

"I won't listen to such talk."

"But you know it's true."

Hilda did not reply at once. She could not, for she understood the level of gossip in Aldcross. Most of it was harmless, an idle pastime meant to amuse, but there was a darker side as well, and that she laid to Miss Sparrow and the major's wife, Agatha Greer. Two dried-up old cats jealous of youth, she thought angrily. She looked upon Sarah's face, a lovely face despite its bruises, and fear clutched her heart. "What happened is between us and the Averills," she said. "And Dr. Burshaw. No one else. There's no need for word to go any further."

Sarah turned her head, a small sad smile edging the corners of her mouth. "What about Tom?" she asked. "Tom has a right . . . He'll stand by me, Mama, I know he will. . . . He will, won't he, Papa?"

Hilda spun around. She saw John, pale and shaken, standing in the doorway. "You're back," she said. "I didn't hear you come in."

"Dr. Burshaw's gone home. He'll be along tomorrow morning after church. . . . This morning, I mean."

"It's time you were in bed, too, John," Hilda said quickly, anxious to postpone the inevitable discussion. "You're exhausted."

"No, Mama, please not yet. I want to know."

"Sarah, it's so late. I'll stay with you, but your father needs—"

"Never mind," John murmured. "Never mind about me. Sarah will be worrying. We'd best have this out in the open."

Hilda looked from John to Sarah and back again. "If you're both determined," she sighed. "But sit

31

down, John. Here, take my chair. Go on, or you'll fall over."

John did as he was told, sinking gratefully into the chair. It was several moments before he could bring himself to meet Sarah's desolate gaze, several more before he could bring himself to speak. "Well," he began, clasping and unclasping his hands, "Sir Roger had already left for London by the time we arrived. Lady Mary was there, and their solicitor. I—I suppose they were expecting us. . . . It seems Sir Roger is going off for a rest cure. That's been promised." John passed his hand across his face. "It was a difficult conversation," he blurted. "Most difficult. Nothing was really admitted, you see. Nothing was really *said*. . . . It was more in the nature of delicately phrased suggestions."

Sarah's heart began to thump. Once again she felt a cold shiver of alarm and she huddled beneath the quilt. "Suggestions, Papa?"

"Lady Mary seems to feel . . . That is, she seems to think . . ."

"*What*, Papa? Please tell me."

"I'll say this straight out, Sarah. At least I'll try. . . . Lady Mary seems to think it would be in everyone's best interests if you—if you left Aldcross."

Leave Aldcross, thought Sarah. She started to laugh, a strange laugh rising higher and higher until it was a shriek.

Now John was out of his chair, his hands grasping Sarah's heaving shoulders. "Listen to me," he cried. "You must listen to me. They can't *force* you to leave, Sarah. They can't *send* you away. . . . Sarah! Sarah, listen to me. . . . It was a suggestion, nothing more. *Nothing* has been decided. . . . Sarah!"

She heard her name calling her back from some unknown and chaotic brink. Her shrieks ceased. Her eyes focused, coming to rest on John. "Papa?"

"Yes, Sarah, it's Papa. It's all right." He stepped aside while Hilda put another cold cloth to Sarah's brow. "It's all right," he murmured.

Hilda perched next to Sarah on the bed, stroking her hair. "We won't talk about this anymore tonight," she said. "And you're not to think about it. You'll make yourself sick if you go on this way."

"I'm fine now, Mama."

"No, I don't think you are. How could you be after what you've been through? But it's over and done. That's the thing to remember."

"It's not over."

Both Hilda and John were startled by the weary resignation in Sarah's voice. It was as if all strength and spirit had been taken from her, all hope. John glanced away, but Hilda's eyes remained on her daughter. "What do you mean it's not over?" she asked.

"They want me to leave Aldcross."

"What of it? You're not one of their servant girls to be ordered about. And this isn't the olden times. Now stop worrying, Sarah. There's nothing—"

"We're beholden, Mama. There's Papa's job and my job. There's Bertie." She saw Hilda tense at mention of Bertie. "His chances will be ruined," she continued. "He's worked so hard, but his chances will be ruined."

"That's not your worry, Sarah. If you worry about everything all at once, you'll make yourself sick."

"I understand everything now, Mama."

John forced his glance back to Sarah. He was shaken anew, for in her eyes he saw the death of youth and innocence. My little girl, he thought wretchedly; my little girl. Without a word he turned, making his unsteady way from the room.

"Poor Papa," Sarah said, though her voice was flat, utterly devoid of emotion. "He won't be the same after this."

Impatience flickered across Hilda's face. Never mind about your papa," she replied. "And never mind about Bertie, either. We'll manage. We always have. We come of good, sound English stock, Sarah. We'll manage somehow." She had spoken with far more conviction than she felt. She felt torn, her heart telling her one thing but her honest, practical mind telling her something quite different, something she was not yet ready to accept. "And that's enough talk for tonight. It's sleep you need. I'll stay right here."

"You don't have to stay, Mama."

"I want to."

"Tomorrow—"

"Hush, Sarah. Tomorrow will take care of itself."

The details of that tomorrow were left to Hilda. She bathed and dressed and went to church as usual, her smile firmly in place. After services she chatted with the vicar, describing Sarah's "accident" to the guileless old man. "Oh, the poor thing took a terrible spill," she explained. "Broke her ankle and almost cracked her head. But our Dr. Burshaw has her on the mend now." Hilda repeated her account many times, receiving the commiserations of friends and neighbors and even the thin-lipped Miss Sparrow. She spent several minutes with Tom Cutler, lightly turning aside his anxious pleas to visit. "Now, Tom," she said when all her other arguments had failed, "we ladies have our vanity, you know. Sarah would never forgive me if I let you see her looking so droopy. Why, I'd never hear the end of it! Just be patient, dear. Patience, that's the thing."

Dr. Burshaw observed Hilda's performance, amusement mingling with admiration. Trust Hilda to make a good show, he thought, and certainly he had no cause to change his mind in the days that followed. Through sheer force of will she managed to pull John together, sending him off to his schoolroom each morning. She devised pausible excuses to keep visitors away, and when she relented, a week later, these visitors found Sarah arranged on the parlor sofa, her "bad" ankle hidden beneath quilts. "Sarah doesn't like to talk about her accident," she would explain. "Best to talk about cheerful things, isn't it?" Tom Cutler disagreed, but his protests were stifled by endless cups of tea, endless plates of sandwiches "made just for you, dear."

Sarah took part in her mother's deceptions, but what she thought of them no one knew, for she said very little. She ate the food that was placed before her, drank the tonic that Dr. Burshaw brought, leafed through the books that Miss Sparrow recommended. When the last of her visitors was gone she went to her bedroom, pacing the long nights away. Often during the nights she heard the sounds of her parents' voices, voices filled with doubt, with worry, with questions. She had questions of her own, though they remained unspoken, as did any talk of the future. She would not allow herself to think of the future, for instinctively she sensed that it was to be a future without Tom.

A feeling of apprehension seemed to hang over the Griffith cottage now. John was increasingly distracted, Sarah so quiet she hardly spoke at all. To outward appearances, Hilda was her brisk, smiling self, but she too suffered the strain. There had been no word from the Hall and this troubled her. "It could be a good sign," she suggested to John. "It could be they've decided to let us alone. . . . Or it could be they're just waiting." John never responded to these speculations. He just listened, staring down at the floor and saying nothing. Silently, he wondered when the nightmare would end.

A partial answer came three weeks after Sir Roger's brutal attack. On that day—the day Sarah returned to her job—a note was delivered from Lady Mary. Hilda read it first, picking through the polite phrases and carefully chosen words to the point of the message. "Lady Mary wants to know if Sarah's made any plans," she declared when John arrived home. "Not that it's spelled out, of course. Oh, no," she sniffed. "Lady Mary's too *proper* for that. But that's what she wants to know, all the same. Here, see for yourself."

John took the note, crumpling it in his hand. "You were expecting something like this."

"Weren't you?"

"I don't know," he sighed. "I suppose I was. I tried not to think about it. . . . Where is Sarah?"

"Upstairs in her bedroom. I haven't told her about the note."

"What are we going to do, Hilda? My God, we can't send her away. We can't. . . . Lady Mary is thinking of her family, but it's all so blasted *unfair.* What about *our* family? What about Sarah?"

"Well, the time for thinking is past. We'd best talk about this." Hilda went to John and put her hands on his shoulders, as if to give him strength. "There must be something we can do," she said. "Lady Mary has children of her own. If she can be made to understand . . . Come sit down, John. We'll talk after supper."

They talked through the night, through myriad nights, but they reached no conclusions they dared articulate. Hilda realized, perhaps better than John, the kind of life Sarah would have in the village if the Averills chose to apply their subtle pressures. She realized the irreparable damage that would be done, yet she could not say the words out loud. John, for his part, was too confused, too broken to face the truth. "I won't send her away," he repeated over and over again. "I won't do it."

But finally there was no choice, for one cool and rainy May afternoon Sarah learned she was pregnant. She accepted the news without any display of emotion, her thoughts, her feelings hidden behind an impassive mask. "I've cried all my tears, Dr. Burshaw," she said, her voice like the rustling of dry leaves. She said the same thing, in the same voice, to John and Hilda. To Tom, the boy she loved, she said nothing at all.

"Sarah?" John called, knocking at her door. "Sarah, may I come in?"

"Yes, Papa."

He entered the bedroom and sat down. He looked tired and somehow smaller, as if the last two months had diminished him. His eyes were the eyes of an old man, straying to Sarah, then sliding timidly away. "Well," he said, "I've just come from London."

"Yes, I know."

"The train was on time today."

"That's good, Papa." Sarah closed her bureau drawer. She turned and went to the bed, sitting at the edge. "Was it crowded in London?"

"Traffic is very bad. So many motorcars . . . Sarah, we must talk."

"It's all right, Papa. I'm ready. I know you've seen the Averills' solicitor. You can tell me. Where am I to be sent? Can I live with Auntie Rose in Sheffield? Or do they want me to leave England?"

"It doesn't matter what they want!" John cried, a

moment later dropping his head to his hands. "Silly thing to say, wasn't it? I—I meant that the decision was left to us. I *made* the decision, Sarah. And I made the decision that will be best for your future. You could live with Rose, of course, but what sort of life would you have? Rose and Edward have that little confectionery shop. It takes all their time and doesn't bring much of a living. They have their own children to worry about."

"Then I'm to leave England, Papa?"

Sarah's dry, uninflected voice drummed in John's ears. He stared at her, his heart turning over. "England isn't the right place for a young woman alone with—with a child," he replied. "There are so many young widows since the war, so few jobs. And there are our eternal English ways. It's difficult to rise above one's circumstances here."

"What is the right place?"

"Sarah, the Averills have family all throughout the world, or so it seems. They have family in India and Australia. . . . They have distant relatives in America: the Camerons. . . . You must be someplace where you can make a fresh start, you see. Someplace where your circumstances, your background, won't matter."

America, thought Sarah to herself. She had seen a few Americans in the village during the war—brash, laughing young men who trampled the gardens and took ice in their drinks. "America, Papa?" she asked. "Is that what you've decided?"

"I believe it would be best. There isn't the same class structure there. People aren't judged by their ancestors. They aren't limited by them. Oh, I suppose the rich are a class unto themselves. That's true the world over. But there are opportunities in America. And those opportunities have nothing to do with one's class."

"Or circumstances?" The tiniest smile shadowed Sarah's pale mouth. "Do you mean it won't matter about the baby?"

John flushed. "Well, I—I mean you won't have a whole village or a whole town poking their noses into your business. You won't have people snooping about. Not in New York City."

"New York City? You're telling me the decision in bits and pieces, aren't you, Papa? You're trying to make it easier."

"Not doing a very good job of it, I'm afraid. Sarah, the Camerons live in New York City, although they have interests in London also. The Cameron Auction Galleries began in London many years ago. Now the main branch is in New York, but there's still quite a large establishment in London."

"And I'm to live with the Camerons?"

"There's a daughter," John explained, "not much older than you are. She isn't very well and she needs a companion. . . . I believe you will be happy there, Sarah. Happier than you could be here. And the—the child will have advantages far beyond our means. . . . Sarah, this won't be forever. You aren't being exiled, you know. After a few years things will settle down and then you can come home again. . . . Perhaps you'll come home with a nice American husband." John reached for Sarah's hand. "I'm sorry," he sighed, "I shouldn't have said that."

"It's all right."

"No, it isn't. I've been clumsy. . . . Do you want to talk about Tom?"

Something hard and glittering came into the hazel-blue of Sarah's eyes. "Tom is in the past," she said. "But he would have stood by me."

"I don't doubt it. He's a fine boy. That isn't always

enough. You're both so young, Sarah. Did you consider how you would handle all the complications? What of Tom's plans? He'll get title to those hundred acres when he turns twenty-one. We all know he has ambitious plans for the land. Wants to develop it, doesn't he? Wants to put houses on it. Well, there'll be no development in Aldcross without—"

"—without Sir Roger's approval. Yes, I know that, Papa." Sarah's hands tightened suddenly, her nails digging into her palms. "I hate him," she said, her voice cold, steely. "I'll hate him till I die."

"Sarah—"

"I hate him."

"Sarah, please listen to me. There are some things I must say, things you must try to understand. . . . No, not about Sir Roger. About us, your mother and me." John took a breath, staring into his daughter's eyes. "I'm afraid you hate us too right now, and I don't blame you. I ask only that you hear me out."

"Yes, Papa."

"For weeks we've been dithering about like hens. God knows, I've been the worst of the lot. I failed you and I'm sorry. But during the past few days I began to see things in a clearer light. By the time I boarded the train yesterday, I was certain. I realized that I was prepared to fight Sir Roger on his own terms. With solicitors, with the courts if necessary. My position at the school wasn't important. There are other schools, other villages. And if Bertie lost his chance for University . . . Well, there's the Navy or the Merchant Service. I realized that what was important was your future."

"Papa, you don't have to tell me this. I understand."

"Bear with me a little longer. Please." Sarah

nodded and John continued. "The only question was what was best for your future. For your—for the child. I believe America is the answer. I believe that with all my heart. . . . You do see, don't you?"

"The baby will be an American."

"By birth, yes. It's a better start in life than Aldcross."

Sarah stood. She went to the window, gazing down at her father's small garden scarlet with geraniums. She looked beyond to Winding Lane and the beech trees in full, glorious bloom. Idly, she wondered if there were trees and flowers in New York City. "When must I leave?" she asked.

"The *Royal Star* sails next month. They say it will be a rather festive trip. It's her last crossing." Sarah did not reply. She stood very still and John had no idea what she was thinking. He leaned forward and spoke again. "You need time to adjust to things," he suggested. "When you've thought it over, you'll see it's the best possible solution."

Sarah turned, her stoical gaze lingering on John. "What will you tell people?" she asked. "Miss Sparrow and Mrs. Greer and the rest?"

"You can leave that to me," Hilda declared, marching into the room. "I plan to tell them you've been offered a fine opportunity in America and you snatched it up. I plan to make a great to-do about it. Miss Sparrow won't be twitching her nose at us, not if I have anything to say about it. And I'll have plenty to say!"

John smiled despite himself. He rose from his chair, his legs unsteady, for the stress of this conversation with Sarah had taken its toll. "I'll just leave the two of you alone now, shall I? You must have things to discuss."

"Yes, dear, you run along. There's tea in the

41

kitchen, and I've heated the kidney pie. . . . Well, Sarah," she said when John had gone, "I hope you and your papa had a nice talk."

"He explained everything."

"Good. Best to clear the air."

"Oh, it's clear, Mama."

"He spoke to you from his heart, you know. As hard as all this has been on you, it's been almost as hard on him. He's afraid he's failed you, Sarah. He hasn't. He had a painful decision to make and he made it. . . . I hope you're not blaming him for doing what he had to do."

"There's only one person I blame, Mama. And I don't want to talk about it anymore."

Hilda heard the finality in Sarah's tone. She heard the detachment, the unnatural calm, and she sighed. It's the shock, she told herself, not for the first time. It's the terrible shock of all that's happened. "Sarah, I want you to know Lady Mary's doing the decent thing. She's fixing up the plans with the Camerons, and she's putting money in trust for your baby. You and your baby will have everything you need."

"If you say so, Mama."

"I do say so. It's the truth." Tears gathered in Hilda's eyes and she fought them back. "America's far away, Sarah. I don't like that part of it and I won't pretend. But I know it's for the best. That's what matters. You don't want your baby born under a cloud."

Sarah put her hand on her stomach. My baby, she thought, though the words meant nothing.

June came, soft days and nights bringing closer the sailing of the *Royal Star*. Sarah appeared not to notice. With Hilda, she went to the tea given for her by the vicar's wife and the tea given by her friend Lucy James. She opened the little presents that were offered; she was polite and agreeable, but rarely did she say more than a few words at a time. She kept her distance, avoiding Miss Sparrow's pointed questions, avoiding Tom Cutler's hurt, reproachful glances. "It's the excitement," Hilda said in explanation. "Our Sarah's going off on a grand adventure!" There were some in the village who did not believe this, but again Sarah appeared not to notice. If Hilda noticed, she was too tired to care.

In the middle of June the postman delivered a thick white envelope containing Sarah's ticket and five twenty-pound notes. That same week he delivered an enormous box from London. Folded between sheets of tissue paper were several plain spring dresses, several shirtwaists, and a dark blue traveling suit with a long, fitted jacket and long skirt. There was no card enclosed, though Hilda knew the clothing had been sent by Lady Mary. "Good, sturdy cloth," she commented. And drab as dishwater, she added to herself.

It was the end of June when the Griffiths climbed into Mr. Flurry's hired car for the ride to the station. They left Aldcross on the early train, changing at the junction and taking another train and then a taxicab to Southampton. It was a long trip, made longer by the gloomy silence. John's eyes remained downcast, studying his hands. Hands that can write Greek and Latin, he thought, but that could not save my daughter. Hilda was so uncharacteristically still she seemed not to move at all. Sarah stared straight ahead, seeing nothing, hearing nothing.

"There she is, sir," the driver said, bringing his taxi to a halt. "Just off to the left. The *Royal Star*."

The Griffiths alighted from the taxi and now Sarah

43

lifted her eyes to the crowds, the bustle, the happy chaos of Southampton Harbor. In the near distance she saw the *Royal Star* sitting proudly atop the water like a splendid and omnipotent sea creature. Her eyes roamed from its tall gray smokestacks to its railed decks dressed with long, bright streamers. She saw crew members scurrying to and fro. She saw passengers waving and gesturing and tossing bits of colored paper into the air. Somewhere a band was playing *Rule Britannia*, small children waving flags in time to the music. Ships' horns were blowing, and in reply, almost in counterpoint, came the sound of ships' whistles.

"We're allowed to go aboard with you, I believe," John said.

"Of course we are," Hilda quickly agreed. "We'll get you settled all nice and comfy. . . . I hope Bertie made it down from London all right."

"You shouldn't have had him come, Mama."

"Nonsense! He's your brother, isn't he? Maybe we are keeping secrets from him, but that's beside the point. He wanted to see you, Sarah. And you'll be glad of the chance to see him."

"Come this way," John called, maneuvering Sarah's bulky suitcase through the laughing, jostling crowd. "This is where we board. . . . Sarah? Where is Sarah?"

"I'm here, Papa, Don't be upset."

"Here's the queue," Hilda announced. "My, all these people traveling to America! You won't want for company, Sarah."

But Sarah had taken a step away. She took another and another, holding out her hands to her brother. "Hello, Bertie," she said with a faint smile. She looked into his blue-flecked hazel eyes, so like her own, and a lump rose in her throat. "I'm sorry you had to come all this way."

The Griffiths had their reunion, their first since Christmas. Bertie did not try to disguise his confusion at the abrupt changes in Sarah's life, but his questions went unanswered, stifled by Hilda's talk of "adventure." When finally the *Royal Star* sailed away he stood on the dock, glancing in dismay from his weeping mother to his ashen father. There's more to the story, he thought, wondering if he would ever learn the truth.

Second-class passage had been booked for Sarah—a compromise between first class, which had not seemed quite right to Lady Mary, and third class, which had seemed all wrong. The cabins on this deck were pleasant and clean, if not overly large. The stewards were pleasant also, bringing tea and biscuits within moments of sailing.

Sarah wanted nothing more than to be alone, but she discovered that she would have two cabinmates during the journey. Eleanor Simpson was a chilly young Englishwoman on her way to America to be married. Mary Margaret Culhane was an effusive young Irishwoman, a seamstress whose father worked as a cook in London. "I saved for my trip shilling by shilling," she explained cheerily to one and all. "Da told me to go in third class, but I decided to treat myself. What's life without a treat once in a while? I'm going to America to make my fortune and I decided to go in style. My sister Bridget thinks I'm daft. And maybe I am!"

Sarah could not help being amused by Mary Margaret's constant good-natured chatter. It was Mary Margaret who dragged her to the dining room for meals, who forced her to take walks on the sunny deck, who urged her to join—no matter how reluctantly—in shipboard activities. It was Mary

Margaret who held her hand through the long nights when fear and loneliness made her tremble. And it was Mary Margaret who guessed her secret. "You're in the family way, aren't you?" she asked one afternoon near the end of the crossing.

"How did you know?"

"*How?* I'm the second of nine Culhane children. I've seen my ma your way often enough. I've seen my sister Katie. Twenty years old she is and already she has three little ones. Three little steps. Ah, they're adorable. Angels, they are. But I want more out of life than a baby every year till I die."

"What do you want?"

"First I want to make my fortune. Not that I'm expecting to find gold in the streets of New York," Mary Margaret laughed. "My Uncle Jack sailed to New York twenty years ago on this very ship. He went steerage. Crowded together like animals in a pen. But now he has a fine Dry Goods in a place called Yorkville. I'm thinking that's where I'll get my start. I've a talent with needle and thread, you understand. I'll get my start, put my money safe in the bank, and then I'll go looking for a modern American husband. Not like the Irish lads who want a baby every year, and a baby boy at that. When I think of all the tears my ma cried 'cause she couldn't give my da a boy. Ah, well, that's the old country and the old ways. It'll be the same a hundred years from now."

"Yes."

"And what would you be wanting, Miss Sarah Griffith?"

"I don't know."

"We all need dreams. Daft or not, we need them. Otherwise life's just doing the wash and cooking the meals and hoping there's a shilling left over for a pint

46

on Saturday night. That's the old country, too. It's different in America. They say you can pluck opportunity like fruit from a tree."

Opportunity, thought Sarah. She remembered her father using that word, not once but many times. She had not considered his meaning then and she did not consider it now. She gazed past the rail at the vast blue waters of the Atlantic, lifting her hand to shade her eyes. She felt very much alone, apart from everyone and everything. "I hope you find what you want, Mary Margaret," she said quietly.

Chapter Three

Sarah arrived in New York on a torrid July afternoon. The sun was a ball of yellow fire scorching the sky. The air was so thick, so heavy, she could scarcely breathe. She put her hand to her wet brow, brushing at errant strands of limp, sticky hair. Her hat tumbled off her head and rolled away. She watched it, too weakened by the heat to give chase. With a pang, she recalled the gentle English summers—the fields white with daisies, the soft rustling of trees, the mingled scents of hawthorn and roses and wild lilacs. She thought of Tom, of summer picnics, and her heart filled with sadness.

"Are you Sarah Griffith?"

She looked around to see a slim, dark-haired young woman in a crisp linen dress and matching hat. "Yes," she said, "I'm Sarah."

"I'm Janet Munroe, Mrs. Cameron's social secretary. Welcome to America, Sarah."

"Thank you."

"Well, let's get out of this awful sun. The car is waiting. Don't worry, it isn't a long drive. I'll take your suitcase."

"That's all right. I can manage."

"I insist," Janet replied with a smile. "I'm not very good at first aid, and you look about to faint."

"Is it always so hot?"

"Oh, this is nothing. Wait until August. Come, Sarah, I promise it will be cooler in the car. I had Tully park in the shade."

"Tully?"

"Mrs. Cameron's chauffeur . . . And that reminds me. Slip this on your ring finger," Janet directed, giving Sarah a plain gold band. "You're going to be known as *Mrs.* Griffith from now on. Mrs. Cameron will explain."

Sarah glanced curiously at Janet but she said nothing. She drew a breath, almost choking on the steamy air as she pushed through the crowds to the car. A polished black Rolls-Royce waited in the shade. The driver, wearing the gray and black livery of the Camerons, stood ready, his hand reaching to the door. Now Sarah stopped, glancing again at Janet. "Such a big car," she murmured.

"Comfortable too," Janet laughed. "Here's Mrs. Griffith's suitcase, Tully. We're all set," she added, nodding at the middle-aged man.

"Home, Miss Munroe?"

"Home sweet home." She settled Sarah in the back seat, smoothing her own much shorter skirt. Moments later the car drove off. "There's a lot to see in New York," she commented. "It's an exciting city. But we'll save all that for another time. You must be tired after your trip."

"A little."

Tired and scared and unhappy, thought Janet, her heart going out to Sarah. "Everything will seem strange to you at first," she suggested. "The city, the people, the accents, even the food. Don't worry about it. When the strangeness wears off you'll feel just like a native. America is a friendly place, Sarah."

"That's what Papa said."

"Friends are important. I hope you'll let me be your friend. If there's any way I can help, I hope you'll ask."

"It's kind of you, Miss Munroe."

"Janet."

"Janet," Sarah repeated. "Thank you." She wanted to say more but the words would not come. She leaned her head back, struggling with fatigue and the heat and an odd sense of detachment. She knew she was riding in a car in New York City yet she felt removed from the scene, as if she were a spectator. She yawned, quickly covering her mouth. "Sorry," she said.

"I'll introduce you to Mrs. Cameron and then it's off to bed. You're going to have the room next to Charlotte's. . . . Charlotte is Mrs. Cameron's daughter. She's sort of frail, but she's really very sweet. You'll like her, I'm sure. Mrs. Cameron is a widow, by the way. Her husband Jasper died a few years ago. It was quite sudden—a heart attack. But his spirit lives on." The spirit of a tyrant, she added to herself, knowing that only Elizabeth Cameron had truly mourned his passing. "Have I mentioned Ned? He's Mrs. Cameron's son. You'll like him, too. Everybody does."

Sarah listened to Janet's light, rapid voice going on and on. There were brief descriptions of other Cameron family members, of the Cameron house, of the Cameron Galleries, so many descriptions they all seemed to blend together. She turned slightly, staring through the car window at the city's thronged streets and avenues. She saw the tangled traffic, cars and trucks and carriages fighting for the right of way. She saw the tall buildings with more windows than she

50

could count. "Trees," she murmured as the outlines of Central Park came into view.

"We're almost there, Sarah. The Cameron house is just ahead."

The Cameron house was a five-story limestone mansion, its elegant Beaux Arts facade complete with carved swags and a wrought-iron balcony. It was meticulously tended, the door brasses gleaming, the silk-draped windows shining in the sun. The front sidewalk was swept and hosed twice a day. The trees at the curb were pruned and healthy. "Is this where I'm to live?" Sarah asked.

"You look surprised."

"It's fancy, isn't it?"

"Fancy?" Janet laughed. "As Molly would say, fancy is as fancy does. Molly is the parlormaid. . . . But to answer your question, Mrs. Cameron lives very well. Shall we go in now? Just follow me and don't be nervous."

Tully helped them from the car. "I'll see to the luggage, Miss Munroe."

"Thanks. Ready, Sarah? Stiff upper lip!"

"Yes, I'll try."

The door was opened by Raymond, the Camerons' staid and proper English butler. "Good afternoon, Miss Munroe," he said. "And this must be Mrs. Griffith. Welcome, madam."

"Thank you."

"Tully is bringing Mrs. Griffith's suitcase, Raymond. We'll just go on up. Come, Sarah."

They passed through a long hall with twin cloakrooms on either side and polished black marble floors. Above was a huge crystal chandelier, its hundreds of prisms reflecting the soft light. Directly ahead was a staircase curving gracefully to the upper stories. Sarah trailed her hand over the carved banister. "Where are we going?" she asked.

"To meet Mrs. Cameron. I should explain that the living quarters are up here. Downstairs there's only the ballroom and a smaller reception room."

"The ballroom? There's a ballroom?"

"Fancy is as fancy does," Janet replied with a wink. When they reached the landing she pointed out other rooms—the drawing room, the formal dining room, the family dining room, the library, the morning room that Elizabeth Cameron used as a study. "The family bedrooms are on the next floor and the servants' bedrooms on the floor after that. You'll have the grand tour once you've rested."

A frown wrinkled Sarah's forehead. "But there are so many rooms," she murmured.

"Thirty in all. It could be worse. The Vanderbilt mansion has a *hundred* and thirty."

Like Greenway Hall, thought Sarah, feeling a sudden chill as she was led into Elizabeth Cameron's study.

It was a beautiful room, filled with antiques and flowers and delicate porcelains. The single discordant note was the portrait hanging over the mantel, a portrait of an aged and glowering Jasper Cameron, Elizabeth's late husband. "Mrs. Cameron," Janet said, "may I present Sarah Griffith."

Elizabeth looked up. She was a slender woman, smartly dressed in black silk and pearls, pearl clips at her ears. Her hair was dark, brushed off her brow in two glossy wings. Her eyes were dark also, capable of swift and usually accurate judgments. "Well," she said now, her gaze sweeping over Sarah's bedraggled form, "so this is Sarah. Sit down, my dear. I hope your trip was pleasant."

"Yes, ma'am."

Elizabeth folded her hands atop her desk. "Any

problems, Janet?" she asked.

"I think Sarah isn't used to our summer heat. If her room has been prepared, I'll—"

"In due course. There are things we must discuss first. You may leave us, Janet. . . . But do something about Sarah's clothes, will you?"

"I'll take care of it right away, Mrs. Cameron." She glanced once more at Sarah and then went to the door. "Good-bye for now," she called. "Have a good rest. I'll see you tomorrow."

"Thank you, Janet. You've been very kind."

The door closed softly. Elizabeth turned her head to Sarah. "May I offer you tea?" she asked, gesturing to a silver service. "Lemonade perhaps? Cook makes an excellent lemonade. No? Very well . . . I know this is difficult for you, Sarah. To leave one's home, to come to a strange country is a difficult thing. I sympathize. But we must all learn to put the past behind us. We must make the best of things, difficult or not. Do you understand?"

"Yes, I think so."

"You have a place in my home now. You need only look around to see that's hardly a punishment."

Sarah was unsure how to respond. Slowly, she raised her eyes to Elizabeth, sensing the older woman's strength and assurance. "It's a lovely home," she said at last, not knowing what else to say.

"But you don't want to be here, do you?"

"I was sent here, Mrs. Cameron."

"By that you mean you weren't given a choice?"

"No, I wasn't."

"Well, did you put up an argument?"

"I never had the chance. . . . No, that's not the truth," Sarah admitted, lowering her eyes. "I didn't argue about it because there's no arguing with the Averills. They wanted me far away. There would

53

have been talk, a terrible scandal. In the end, I would have been blamed. Mama and Papa knew that. I knew it, too. And with the baby coming . . ."

"We must discuss that, my dear. For the baby's sake and for yours, you will be known as *Mrs*. Griffith, a widow who lost her husband in a road accident. You will also be known as my distant relative, thus explaining your presence here. You will, of course, call me Aunt Elizabeth." She paused, measuring Sarah's reaction. "Necessary deceptions," she continued. "Only Janet and my children know the true facts. And my attorneys. No one else is to know. I must emphasize that point, Sarah. No one else . . . It's a question of family, you see. Roger and I are related through a grandmother, Lady Milford. That sounds complicated and it needn't concern you, but my wishes in the matter must be respected."

"Yes, I understand." It's the Hall all over again, thought Sarah, only instead of the Averills calling the tune it's the Camerons. Averills or Camerons, it's all the same. "I understand," she repeated wearily.

"I'm glad you do. You seem a sensible girl, my dear. A quality in your favor. I'm impatient with foolishness." That was indeed the truth, reflected in the way Elizabeth ran her household. She bought only the best and she bought to last. Every room in her house was given a dusting once a day and a thorough cleaning once a week. Repairs were made promptly. Clocks ran to the minute. Squabbles amongst the servants were settled without fuss, without rancor. "I don't think we'll have any problems, do you?"

"I was wondering what my—my duties are."

"Duties? You won't be a servant here, Sarah."

"But your daughter. I thought—"

"Yes, my daughter Charlotte isn't well." Elizabeth's gaze went to the silver-framed photographs on her desk. There were three: one of her son Edmund, who was called Ned, one of the daughter who had died of influenza, and the largest one of her daughter Charlotte, stricken with infantile paralysis at the age of sixteen. Charlotte had recovered, but she had been left with a severe limp and with lungs too susceptible to infection. "My daughter has a maid to care for her," Elizabeth explained, "and doctors when she needs them. I am hoping you will be her companion. Charlotte is a rather lonely girl."

Sarah saw the flicker of pain in Elizabeth's dark eyes. "I'm sorry," she said.

"Don't be. Life isn't always fair or kind. People rarely get what they deserve. Good people, bad people, it makes no difference. My late husband used to say . . . Oh, but that's enough of that," she sighed. "I have things to do and you must have your rest." She reached out, pressing a small buzzer affixed to the wall. Almost immediately a young woman in starched uniform and cap appeared at the door. "Molly, take Mrs. Griffith to her room. And tell the others she's not to be disturbed."

"Yes, ma'am."

Sarah knew she had been dismissed. She stood, gathering her wrinkled skirts. "Thank you, Mrs. . . . Thank you, Aunt Elizabeth."

"This way, Mrs. Griffith," Molly said. "If you'll please to follow me."

Elizabeth watched Sarah go. She noted her straight back, the determined lift of her head, and she was pleased. After some moments she picked up Charlotte's photograph, staring into the huge, sad eyes. She sighed again, a mournful sound amidst the serenity of the room.

The room to which Sarah was taken seemed larger

than the entire cottage on Winding Lane. There was a ruffled and flounced white canopy bed, a dainty rosewood nightstand, a ruffled dressing table, a double chest of drawers, and a cushioned armchair covered in bright chintz. A bentwood rocker was placed off to the side of the hearth, near a fluffy oval rug. Nestled in an alcove was an exquisite Queen Anne desk and chair; another alcove was lined with bookshelves holding leather-bound editions of Shakespeare and Thackeray and Jane Austen. There were two tall windows, their silken draperies dappled by the sun. There were flowers everywhere, daisies to match the oil painting above the mantel. "Is this my room?" she asked in surprise.

"Yes, Mrs. Griffith," Molly replied, shaking her coppery curls. "You've plenty of closet space, and your bathroom is just to the left. Would you like me to run your bath, ma'am?"

"No, thank you, Molly. I'm very tired. Sleep is all I want."

"Oh, I know how that is. Sometimes I crawl into bed too tired even to wash my face. Drop right off, I do. . . . Well, I'll leave you to your sleep. There's a pitcher of water if you're thirsty. I didn't bring any ice, you being English and all. . . . Would you like me to help you out of your things, Mrs. Griffith?"

"I can manage."

"I'll leave you then. If you need anything, press that bell there. The other bell's for Raymond. And when you hear a bell ringing in here it means dinner is served. . . . Don't fret, ma'am, you'll get the hang of it."

"I hope so."

"Sure you will." Molly crossed the room to the door. "Sleep well," she called, closing the door behind her.

Sarah sank down on the bed. She unbuttoned her jacket and tossed it aside. She kicked off her shoes, peeled away her thick cotton stockings, wriggled out of her long skirt. She glanced around, wondering where her nightdress might be, but in the next instant she was sound asleep, curled up in her camisole and petticoat.

It was a troubled sleep, beset with images of shadowy Beechwood Road, of a man drawing closer and closer, of birds in sudden flight. There were voices, harsh and angry voices. There were the harsher sounds of ships' horns. She glimpsed Mary Margaret's flame-colored hair and then Elizabeth Cameron's cool dark eyes. She thrashed about, trying to escape those eyes, but they followed her, pursued her, until finally she was jolted awake.

She stretched her trembling hand to the nightstand and poured a glass of water. She drank it thirstily, collapsing against the pillows. Her eyes closed again. Now she fell into a deep, dreamless sleep. She slept through the dinner bell, through Molly's gentle attempts to rouse her, through Elizabeth's brief bedside visit.

It was after seven o'clock in the morning when Sarah awoke. She stared at the ruffled canopy above her bed, frowning, for she could not remember where she was. She turned her head, startled to see a thin, pale young woman watching her. Hastily, she grabbed the sheet to cover her underclothes. To her astonishment, she found her underclothes gone, replaced by a lacy white nightdress. "I don't understand," she murmured, wondering if she were still asleep.

"Mother thought you would be more comfortable in your nightgown," the pale young woman explained. "She had Molly—"

"My nightgown? But it's not my . . . Oh, I remember now. I'm in New York City, aren't I? This is the Cameron house."

"I'm Charlotte Cameron."

"Oh, oh, I see. I'm sorry I slept so long. What time is it? Is it morning?"

"It's a little past seven. There's lots of time, Sarah. Breakfast isn't served till eight-thirty. Are you used to an earlier breakfast? I can ask Molly to bring a tray."

"No, please don't. I can't imagine what came over me, sleeping so late. I'm sorry, Miss Charlotte. I'll be up and dressed in a flash."

"*Miss* Charlotte?" She smiled, her soft gray eyes twinkling with light. "If we're going to be friends, you can't call me *Miss* Charlotte. And I do hope we're going to be friends."

Sarah was touched by Charlotte's simple, forthright words. She looked at her, seeing a frail woman of perhaps twenty, with a cloud of pale hair and smooth, pale skin. Her leg brace was concealed beneath her robe but her cane was in sight, the fine wood inlaid with ivory and silver. "Thank you, Charlotte. That's kind of you to say."

"I meant it. I don't have many friends, Sarah. The girls I grew up with are married now. They're busy with their lives. I suppose they're uncomfortable around me, too. They never quite know what to talk about. It wouldn't do to talk to me about dancing parties, would it?" she smiled again. "Not with this," she added, tapping her cane against her leg.

"There are other things to talk about."

"Shopping. The theater. Traveling. It's been years since I've been out shopping, years since I've traveled. Janet takes me to a matinee every once in a while . . . when she can get away from Mother. I'm not exactly in the swim of things."

"It shouldn't matter. Not to your friends."

"I don't really mind, Sarah. I spent two years feeling sorry for myself and then I got over it. I think what bothered me most was that I never had my coming-out party. Silly, isn't it? But we'd made so many wonderful plans. Then a week before the party—*this*. It was bad for a while. Now it's all right. Oh, I have a hideous limp and I'm always catching colds, but that's the worst of it. When I'm tired my throat gets sort of hoarse and whispery. Then I know it's time to rest. I don't really mind that, either. Janet brings me all the latest books. I love to read."

"So do I."

"There, we have something in common! We'll find other things, I bet. Do you do embroidery?"

"I'm not very good."

"I am. I can help you with the fancy stitches." Charlotte rose, balancing her weight on the cane while she dragged her withered leg. "I must go," she said. "Mae will be waiting to help me dress for breakfast. She'll be in to draw your bath, Sarah."

"I'll do that."

"Will you? Very well, if you prefer . . . You'll find your closets filled with new dresses. Mother had your old things thrown out. She's rather particular about clothes . . . and everything else."

"New dresses?" Sarah asked. "For me?"

"Don't you like getting new dresses?"

"It's just that . . . I mean . . ." Sarah colored, absently putting her hand on her stomach. "I don't know about the sizes," she finished.

"Because of the baby? You mustn't worry. These dresses will do for now, and then there will be more dresses. Mother will see to that. Mother sees to everything." Charlotte limped to the door. She paused, turning back to look over her shoulder at

59

Sarah. "You're very pretty," she said. "I used to be pretty."

"You still are, Charlotte."

"No, but I used to be."

Sarah felt tears spring to her eyes—whether for Charlotte or for herself, she did not know. She left the bed and hurried into the bathroom. Now her eyes widened, dazzled by the gleaming marble, by taps and faucets and drains plated in gold. There were bath salts in crystal jars, bars of soap carved in the shape of flowers. There were more towels than she had ever seen. All at once she recalled Charlotte's words: *Mother sees to everything.*

"You sent for me, Mother?" Ned Cameron asked, entering Elizabeth's study. "I was going in to breakfast. I confess I'm anxious to meet your ward."

"Sarah isn't my ward, she's my guest. I think she will be a great help to Charlotte."

"If that's what you think, it must be true."

"Sarcasm so early in the morning?"

Ned smiled. He had an easy, amiable smile, and if it lacked Charlotte's sweetness, it held a kind of lazy charm. He was an attractive man—sandy-haired, dark-eyed—but it was his charm that people always noticed first. "Really, Mother," he said now. "I was trying to pay you a compliment."

"I doubt that very much."

"You're too suspicious."

"When it comes to you, Ned, I'm not suspicious enough. Have you seen the morning paper?"

"Not yet."

"You've made the society columns again." Elizabeth put on her glasses, reading aloud from the paper folded on the desk. "'Society's favorite man

60

about town, Neddy Cameron, seen dancing the night away with chorus lovely Nola O'Rourke.' There's more about your *chorus lovely*,' but you get the idea.''

"Yes, I'm afraid I do.''

"Well, what have you to say?''

"Mother, I'm twenty-five years old. I needn't explain my every action.''

"Your every action embarrasses the Cameron name. When will you understand that? You led me to believe you were seeing Claire Detwiller. Instead, you've been seeing this O'Rourke person.''

"Nola. Her name is Nola. And you met her once. I brought her here to one of those boring teas.''

"I remember,'' Elizabeth said. "She tried to shake hands with the servants.''

"Nola hasn't had our advantages, Mother. That isn't her fault. Nor is it her fault that she must work for her living. She happens to be a nice girl.''

"What would you know about nice girls?''

The smile left Ned's face. His eyes were cool now, as cool as Elizabeth's. "What hypocrisy, Mother,'' he replied. "In this house is a poor defenseless girl who was brutally attacked by that paragon, Roger Averill. Then he forced her to leave her own home, her own *country*, for God's sake. Yet Roger would be welcome here. Why? Because he has a title? Well, it's true he wouldn't try to shake hands with the servants. Rape is more his—''

"Ned!''

"I'm sorry, Mother. But to condemn Nola for no good reason at all while you forgive Roger his sins . . . Well, you must see what I mean.''

"What makes you think I've forgiven Roger? I most certainly have not. And he would most certainly not be welcome here. I'm surprised you would

61

suggest otherwise, Ned. . . . As for your Nola O'Rourke, I don't condemn her. The point is she's unsuitable. Your behavior is unsuitable. It's time you gave some thought to a wife."

"A wife?" Ned shook his head. "I see no reason to hurry. Father was past forty when he married."

"Your father was devoted to his business, a devotion you don't share."

"I do my job, Mother."

"Not as well as I'd like. Not as well as your cousin Patrick does his. Thirty years old and he's Managing Director of the Galleries. If you don't settle down and start paying attention, you'll be left in the dust."

"No more than I deserve."

"Stop it, Ned! I'm quite serious about this."

Ned sighed, running his hand through his sandy hair. "I have a weak character," he said. "You know it, I admit it, and now let's be done with it. Can I please go in to breakfast?"

"What about Nola O'Rourke? May I assume *that's* done with?"

"If you wish."

"I do."

"Very well then, Mother . . . Now I suggest breakfast and a change of subject. Tell me about Sarah."

Elizabeth stood, taking her son's arm. "She's absolutely lovely. Lots of honey-blond hair and a roses-and-cream complexion, as the English call it. Good bones, too. She's unhappy, of course, but that will pass."

"Are you so certain?"

"Broken hearts mend. I'm certain of that."

"You're amazing, Mother."

"Another compliment?"

Ned laughed. He stepped aside to let Elizabeth enter the dining room and then followed her inside.

Charlotte was already seated at the table, Sarah in a chair opposite. "Good morning, Charlotte," he said. "And good morning to you, Sarah. I'm Ned Cameron, the black sheep of the family. You'll hear awful stories about me. They're all true."

"Pay no attention to my son. He's feeling contrary this morning."

"Mother's right," Ned agreed with a smile. "She's always right. Disconcerting, but there it is."

Sarah listened to the family byplay, saying nothing. She was aware of Ned's eyes on her, eyes filled with curiosity and something like amusement. She glanced away, staring down at the fluted white china plates. Breakfast was served then, consisting of juice, melon, scrambled eggs with chives, and buttery rolls still warm from the oven. There were tiny cherry pastries, tiny pots of cherry jam.

"Sarah," Elizabeth said, "you must eat more than that if you're to keep up your strength."

"I'm fine, Mrs.—Aunt Elizabeth. Really I am."

"Leave the girl alone, Mother."

"I'll do no such thing."

"No, I don't suppose you will."

Ned pushed his chair back, throwing his napkin on the table. "Well, I'm off to work. Can't be late, you know. I wouldn't want to be left in the dust. By the way, Sarah, we serve an English breakfast every Sunday. Eggs, bacon, sausages, kidneys, potatoes, and grilled tomatoes. I've forgotten something. Oh, yes, haddock. No one ever eats the haddock, but it's there nonetheless."

"Did you say you were leaving, Ned?"

"On my way, Mother. Good day, ladies."

Elizabeth's cool gaze followed Ned to the door. "My son has his moods," she said.

"But he was right about the English breakfasts,"

Charlotte laughed. "Perhaps they'll remind you of home, Sarah."

"The most we ever had was eggs and bacon or sausages. And that was only on Sundays. The rest of the week we had oatmeal."

"I've often thought that's why the English are so sturdy," Elizabeth commented. "All that good, plain food. We're spoiled in America. So many rich gravies and sauces . . . Janet," she said as the young woman came into the room, "you're early this morning. Have you eaten?"

"Yes, Mrs. Cameron, thank you. I wanted to get an early start today. I wanted to show Sarah through the house and explain things."

"An excellent idea."

"Don't worry about me," Charlotte said, meeting Sarah's troubled eyes. "I'm embroidering some pillow slips. It will take the whole morning at least."

"Go along with Janet, my dear."

Sarah rose quickly from her chair. "Thank you for all the new clothes, Aunt Elizabeth. I've never had such—"

"I'm sure you haven't, Sarah. Now go along."

"This way," Janet said, leading Sarah out of the room. "Mrs. Cameron didn't mean to be short with you," she explained. "It's just that she likes to spend a few moments alone with Charlotte each morning. She's devoted to the girl. She even gave up the summer place at Newport because Charlotte refuses to go."

"Why does she refuse?"

"I imagine it's because she's self-conscious."

"Doesn't she go anywhere?" Sarah asked.

"I take her to the theater sometimes. To concerts. Dr. Westerland would like her to get out more. He's said so. Perhaps you can encourage her. The park is just across the street.''

"Yes, I'll try."

"Are you ready for the grand tour?"

"Ready."

Sarah was shown through the downstairs kitchens and servants' hall, the ballroom and reception rooms, the family rooms, and even the servants' floor and the spotless attic above. She said little during this tour, awed by the splendor all around her. "Treasures," she murmured as Janet tried to explain the differences in style and period. "It's like a palace, isn't it?"

"On a small scale. Wait until you see the Galleries."

"Papa told me about the Galleries."

"We'll save that trip for another day. Goodness," Janet cried, looking at her watch. "Where has the morning gone?"

"Should I go to Charlotte now?"

"No, not yet. We have one more thing to do. I'm sorry to say you'll have to sit through a formal meal, soup to nuts."

"I'm not very hungry, Janet."

"Oh, it has nothing to do with food, not really. Mrs. Cameron has a great many formal dinner parties. She wants you to feel comfortable at these events . . . and so she wants me to take you through the motions. This isn't any reflection on your table manners, Sarah. Please don't think it is. It's a matter of getting you used to things *à la* Cameron. All right?"

"I suppose it has to be all right."

Janet saw the color rush to Sarah's cheeks. "There was no offense meant," she said quietly. "I apologize if it sounded that way. Perhaps I didn't explain very well."

"I understand, Janet. I'm only a country girl, after all. It's true I'm not used to these fancy doings. I wouldn't want to shame Mrs. Cameron, would I?" Sarah took a breath, her anger fading. "It's my turn to apologize," she said. "You've been kind to me and I'm grateful. If I have to learn about formal dinners and the like, I'll learn."

"That's the spirit!"

"I'm usually quick to learn. Papa always said so. And maybe I have a little head start," Sarah added with a shadow of a smile. "I know not to eat my peas off a knife, not to wipe my mouth with my sleeve."

"I'm glad you have a sense of humor," Janet replied in relief. "All this must be terribly confusing, and a sense of humor will help."

"Yes, I'll remember that."

Two places had been laid at the dining room table that seated twenty. "Mrs. Cameron considers twenty the ideal number for a dinner party," Janet explained. "She always sits at the head of the table, and Ned at the other end. Her guests tend to be a mixture of people from business and the arts, with an occasional politician thrown in. Husbands and wives never sit next to each other."

"Why don't they?"

"It's bad form," Janet laughed. "One of society's many rules. After dinner, the men adjourn to the library for brandy and cigars, the women to the drawing room for demitasse."

"I see."

"Mrs. Cameron's dinners begin at eight and the last guest is out the door by midnight. Sit down, Sarah. Our practice meal won't take nearly so long, but we'd just as well get started. . . . Ah, here's Raymond with the soup course. . . . It feels strange to be doing this in the middle of the day."

"But it doesn't seem like the middle of the day. Not in here." Sarah regarded the gleaming mahogany, the twinkling silver, the candlelight falling upon crystal glasses and gold-banded china. "It's beautiful," she said.

"Mrs. Cameron has perfect taste. She's *the* perfect hostess."

Six courses were served, during which time Sarah was schooled in the use of the various knives and forks and spoons, in the use of the finger bowl, and in proper subjects for dinner conversation. She listened, though her mind kept drifting back to Aldcross and the simple, cozy meals she had shared with her family. She knew it would be late afternoon in Aldcross now; her mother would be in the kitchen, her father on his way home. Home, she thought, pain stabbing her heart.

Janet looked at Sarah, smiling. "Lessons are over for today," she said. "You did very well."

"What? Oh, I'm sorry. I was thinking about something else. Thank you, Janet. Should I go to Charlotte now?"

Janet glanced again at her watch. "Charlotte will be napping. You can go on to your room and have a little rest. Tomorrow we'll visit the Galleries if you're up to it."

"What about Charlotte?"

"She needs a friend, Sarah, not an attendant. Once you've settled in, I'm sure the two of you will be great friends. . . . Can you find your way to your room?"

"Yes, I think so."

"I'll see you tomorrow, Sarah."

"Yes, tomorrow."

Sarah's room had been tidied, the bathroom cleaned and the bed made. She removed her shoes, dropping down on the bed. She drowsed, random images of Aldcross tumbling together in her mind. She did not hear the knock at the door, but moments later she awoke to see Charlotte seated in the rocker. "I always seem to be sleeping," she said, embarrassed.

"You've had a long trip and you're tired. I sleep all the time myself, tired or not. . . . Is there anything you'd like to do, Sarah?"

"Well, I was thinking I should write a letter home. I want them to know I've arrived safely."

"Mother's already seen to that. She sent a cable. I told you Mother sees to everything!"

Chapter Four

"Let's have a look at you, Sarah," Elizabeth said when the breakfast dishes had been cleared away. "You look charming, my dear. That green linen suits you. It brings out your eyes."

"Thank you, Aunt Elizabeth."

"Off with you now. My nephew Patrick has arranged to take you through the Galleries. He's an excellent guide. I know you will enjoy your visit."

"I asked Charlotte to come with us," Sarah said. "But she wanted to stay here and do her embroidery."

"Yes, she hurries to her room every morning after breakfast." To her useless embroidery and her books, thought Elizabeth, more in sorrow than in anger. "It's her way."

"Come, Sarah," Janet called. "The car is waiting."

"Good-bye, Aunt Elizabeth."

"Good-bye, my dear."

Sarah followed Janet into the hall. She paused before the mirror, putting on her new white straw hat and white gloves. "I'm ready," she said.

"Why are you frowning?"

"I was thinking about Charlotte. It's bad for her to spend so much time in her room. Oh, it's a fine room, but still she should get out once in a while."

"Perhaps you'll be able to lure her out," Janet suggested.

"I've been wondering how." Steamy summer air engulfed Sarah as she stepped onto Fifth Avenue. "It should be cooler weather, though. This heat . . . When does it get cooler?"

"Usually in September. You may not feel much like gadding about by then."

Sarah rested her gloved hand on her stomach. My baby, she thought, though the words stirred no emotion in her, neither excitement nor regret nor even fear. She had not wondered at the sex of her unborn child; she had not expressed a preference to herself or anyone else. Once again she felt like a spectator to the events of her own life, watching, waiting, but caring little for the outcome. She sat quietly in the car, turning her head to the sights Janet described. She nodded and a few times she smiled, pretending interest if not enthusiasm. In her mind's eye she saw the narrow lanes and neat white cottages of Aldcross. She blinked, trying to return her thoughts to the present, to the city that was now her home.

"New York will grow on you," Janet said, reading Sarah's troubled expression. "I promise it will."

"What? Oh, I'm sorry, Janet. I wasn't paying attention. But I know you're right. It takes time, that's all. Papa said it would take time."

"You need some diversion. And here it is. The Cameron Galleries. Did you ever visit the London branch?"

"I've only been to London twice in my life. Papa took us to the Christmas pantomimes. It was our special treat."

"Mrs. Cameron would say the Galleries are a

70

special treat. You can decide for yourself. We'll go exploring!''

Tully helped the two young women from the car. They passed beneath a long gray canopy, pausing briefly while the doorman touched his hand to his cap. "Good morning, Miss Munroe," he said. "Going to be another scorcher today."

"Yes, I'm afraid so."

Sarah followed Janet into the Galleries, her apprehensions soothed by the tranquil and elegant surroundings. She glimpsed shining marble floors and wood paneling and many arched doorways, the frames handsomely carved. The slender reception desk was set at a discreet angle to the right of the entry. Seated at the desk was a dignified gray-haired woman in simple blue silk.

"That's Mrs. Watson," Janet explained, waving to the woman. "She's been here forever. Most of the employees are old hands, even the guards."

"Guards?"

"Oh, I think they're really for show. There's never been a robbery here. One poor soul tried to slip a Fabergé egg into his pocket, but he was stopped at the door."

"Was he arrested?" Sarah asked.

"No, he was just told not to come back. The Camerons dislike fusses of all kinds. . . . And here's a Cameron now. Hello, Patrick," Janet smiled, holding out her hand. "Sarah, I'd like you to meet Patrick Cameron, Managing Director of all this."

"Welcome to America, Sarah."

"Thank you." She looked up to see a tall man with dark brown hair and earnest gray eyes that somehow reminded her of Tom's. He was well-tailored and barbered, his silk necktie perfectly knotted. He was smiling and she thought it a wonderful smile.

"Thank you, Mr. Cameron," she said again.

"Patrick. No need to stand on ceremony. Besides, Uncle Jasper was the *real* Mr. Cameron. Ned and I are only pretenders."

"Don't believe a word of it," Janet laughed. "Patrick has brought new life to the Galleries. And Ned does his share, too. It's still very much a family enterprise."

"Would you care to see the family enterprise, Sarah? I've cleared my schedule, so we can poke about and then have lunch. How does that sound?"

Sarah found herself returning Patrick's smile. "It sounds lovely," she said, "if you can spare the time."

"It will be my pleasure. Come, ladies. We'll begin with the display areas. . . . We display items from upcoming auctions," he explained to Sarah. "That gives our clients the chance to get a better look at what interests them. Browsers are welcome also. We have quite a lot of those, especially on rainy days."

"It's like a museum, isn't it?"

"Aunt Elizabeth prefers to view it in that light. But it's a business and it always has been. When people tire of their paintings or antiques or jewels, or when they could do with some ready cash, they call us. We sell these items at auction. There are profits all around and everyone is happy. Our standards are high, of course. We authenticate everything we accept for auction. We have experts in various fields. . . . Ned's field is eighteenth-century antiques." A mischievous twinkle came into the gray of Patrick's eyes. "An excellent choice for Ned," he added, "because it means lots of trips to Europe."

"I see."

I wonder if you do, thought Patrick, leading the women into the first display area. "All these pieces are quite good," he began. "Almost exclusively

72

Queen Anne . . ."

The morning was long but it passed swiftly, for Sarah was enthralled by the beauty she saw at every turn. She lingered at a collection of exquisite French porcelains, gasped at a collection of huge and glittering jewels from an unnamed royal house. In one vast storage area she laughed out loud at suits of armor clustered together as if ready for battle. "Do people really buy these?" she asked.

"They do, indeed. And lances and heraldic shields. For some it's the romance of history. For others it's just fun. For a few it's sheer pretension. We have certain clients who've invented ancestries going back to the Crusades. I don't know that anyone believes them, but the game goes on nonetheless."

"Why?"

"Status," Patrick replied with a shrug. "And that's just a nice word for snobbery. Beware our society snobs. They run the show, or at least they like to think they do."

"It's the same in England."

"I suppose it's the same everywhere. Money is one measure, blood another."

"Philosophy on an empty stomach!" Janet cried in mock dismay. "Does anyone care that I'm starving?"

"Claude should have lunch prepared by now. Shall we, ladies?"

They lunched in Patrick's private dining room, a simple lunch of vichyssoise and broiled sole and fresh raspberries in cream. Sarah was surprised to find that her appetite had returned. She ate everything put before her, accepting a second helping of berries and a second cup of strong dark coffee. She was more talkative, adding her own comments to the conversation. She smiled more often, and Janet noticed a flicker of light in her eyes.

Later, riding home in the car, Janet patted Sarah's hand. "You did very well today," she said. "Could it be you're coming out of your shell?"

"Oh, I think it was Patrick. He reminded me of a boy I know—knew—in Aldcross. Patrick's had a better education and he's older, but still . . . I don't know, Janet. There's something about him that reminds me of Tom."

"Then Tom must be a very nice fellow. Patrick certainly is."

"Yes," Sarah agreed.

"I'm sure you and Patrick will be friends. You probably won't like his wife. Nobody does. But everybody likes Patrick."

"His wife?"

"Evelyn. They have two darling little boys."

Sarah was quiet, for it had not occurred to her that Patrick might have a wife and family. She felt a sudden inexplicable emptiness and she turned away.

"What's wrong, Sarah? What happened to that pretty smile of yours?"

"I'm tired. It's been a long day, hasn't it? So much walking about. So much to see."

"But you enjoyed yourself. I was watching you and I know you had a fine time. . . . Sarah, don't crawl back into your shell. Let us help you."

"There's no shell. I did enjoy myself today and now I'm tired. . . . And I'm the one who's supposed to be doing the helping. I should be spending my time with Charlotte. That's what I'm going to do from here on."

"Not all your time, I hope. You have your own—"

"My own life?" Sarah asked, a hint of defiance in her voice. "No, that's in the past with Tom, and I'd best accept it. Please don't say any more, Janet. I just want to get on with things, to keep my end of the bargain.''

"What bargain?"

"Mrs. Cameron's given me a place in her home. In return, I'll see to Charlotte."

"You mustn't think of yourself as a servant. That wasn't the idea at all. You're—you're part of the family, so to speak."

"So to speak."

"Well, you know what I mean, Sarah."

"Oh, yes—yes, I do."

In truth, Sarah was never to feel herself a part of the Cameron family. She was introduced as family and often treated as such, though there were times when she was treated as a kind of upper servant, running personal errands for "Aunt Elizabeth" and occasionally for Ned. Charlotte alone treated her as a friend, a sister with whom confidences were shared, memories explored. Charlotte opened her secret hiding places to Sarah, bringing forth old dance programs, old corsages faded and dried and pressed between the pages of books, old love letters impassioned by the innocence of youth. She spoke freely of the parties she had attended, the cotillions and assemblies. She spoke freely, if wistfully, of the boy she had hoped to marry. Sarah listened, and in time she was able to speak of Tom, unburdening her heart to the frail young woman who had become her dearest friend.

At the end of July, Sarah managed to get Charlotte out of the house for a car ride around the city. It was a small triumph, followed by others. There were visits to moving picture shows, to tearooms, and even to Central Park, where the two picnicked in the shade of gingko trees. Dr. Westerman heartily approved of these outings. "Sarah is a wonder," he said to a grateful Elizabeth. "A tonic! Charlotte is a different girl and the credit is Sarah's." Elizabeth did not disagree. She made no comment at all, though in her mind the outlines of a plan began to form.

It was August when Sarah suggested a shopping spree to Charlotte. "Fall is coming," she declared, "and you must have a whole new wardrobe. I've been clipping sketches from the fashion magazines. The new styles are wonderful."

"But Madame Yvette always comes to do my clothes."

"Oh, Madame Yvette. Aren't you tired of letting her decide what you're to wear? Wouldn't you like to pick out your own clothes for a change? At the stores you can pick and choose what *you* want."

"Sarah, the new styles are so short. My leg—"

"You have very nice legs. It's just the brace you're worrying about, and you shouldn't. It's something you have to wear for your health, that's all. If you had to wear eyeglasses or a sling on your arm, it would be the same thing. And don't worry that people will stare at you. Most people are too busy with their own problems to give you a second thought. It was a different story in Aldcross. People noticed everything there. But here in New York no one notices anything. I've never seen such rushing and hurrying about. . . . Now, I say we go shopping! Really, it will do you good."

Charlotte was silent, studying Sarah's eager face. "I'll go," she replied after a while, "but on one condition. I want to buy some clothes for your baby. Mother is preparing the nursery. I want to buy the clothes. We'll select them together."

"My baby isn't due for months."

"Time goes quickly. It may not seem to, but it does."

Sarah felt her swelling stomach. "Yes," she said. "Yes all right. A new wardrobe for you and for my baby."

They went shopping, and Sarah would always remember that shopping trip as the time her baby first became real to her. She looked at the tiny booties, the tiny shirts and gowns, and felt a surge of anticipation that soon turned to excitement. For her baby's sake she endured Dr. Westerman's examinations and followed his instructions to the letter. She followed the progress of the nursery, making suggestions that were largely ignored by Elizabeth and then making them again. With Charlotte, she discussed the different virtues of boys and girls and giggled over silly names.

Elizabeth appeared not to notice these developments though, in fact, she paid close attention. Day by day she watched the friendship between Charlotte and Sarah grow; she saw the renewal of Charlotte's spirit, of her interest in life. "You're looking so much better, darling," she said one evening early in September. "So much better."

"Am I, Mother?"

"Come now, you know you are."

"Yes," Charlotte smiled. "I was fishing for compliments. Actually, I feel much better. It's good to get out and do things. And it's such fun to plan for the baby. I'd always planned to have lots of babies of my own. Five or six at least! But now it's enough to share in Sarah's baby. She's very generous, Mother."

"She's your friend."

"I've been wondering if she isn't the only true friend I've ever had. She doesn't care that I'm Charlotte Cameron. My name could be Jones or Smith and it wouldn't matter."

Elizabeth sat in a small gilt chair at Charlotte's

bedside. She glanced about the room, her dark eyes roaming over all the delicate silks and laces, the antique vanity table adorned with crystal bottles, with gold-backed brushes and combs. An Aubusson carpet graced the polished floor, its soft colors in harmony with the portrait of water lilies above the mantel. "I've grown fond of Sarah, too," she said. "Her child will have the very best of everything."

"But no father and no grandparents. I think that's troubling Sarah."

"Is it?"

"She's especially troubled because she hasn't had any letters from her family this month. I can't imagine why they've stopped writing."

"They haven't stopped. I decided to withhold their letters."

Charlotte's eyes widened. She stared in disbelief at her mother, shaking her head. "Withhold them?" she repeated. "But why? Why would you do such a thing?"

"Sarah must put Aldcross behind her, darling."

"Aldcross perhaps, but surely not her family."

"We're her family now."

"We'll never take the place of her own people, Mother. She loves them. She worries about them. I don't understand how you could do such a thing. It's *cruel*. And if you're fond of Sarah, as you say, it's doubly cruel."

"Don't upset yourself, Charlotte. I am thinking only of Sarah's best interests."

"You're not. You're trying to—to manipulate her, the way you do all of us. Oh, it's true, Mother. You allow Ned his little rebellions, but if he crosses the line, you bring all sorts of pressure to bear. And successfully, because he's too weak to resist. You used to do the same thing to me. I remember when I was sixteen and—"

"That's quite enough, Charlotte," Elizabeth interrupted. "I won't be spoken to in that manner. Nor will I have you upsetting yourself over something as foolish as a few letters."

"I want Sarah to have those letters and any others that come to her."

"Very well," Elizabeth replied, unruffled. "She'll have them. But in time you will come to understand I'm right. The sooner she puts Aldcross and all its associations behind her, the sooner she will be one of us. A Cameron."

"A Cameron!" Charlotte relaxed, smiling again. "You'll never make a Cameron of Sarah Griffith. Never."

"We'll see about that, darling," Elizabeth leaned forward, stroking Charlotte's pale hair. "We'll see."

Autumn came to the city, sultry summer air chased away by crisp breezes and cooling rains. Leaves began to flutter from the trees, collecting in little pillows of gold and bronze and umber. Store windows bloomed with new fashions. Vendors appeared on street corners, selling hot roasted chestnuts and hot pretzels. In poorer neighborhoods, ice wagons were joined by coal wagons. Along Fifth Avenue, limousines were more and more in view, for it was the beginning of the new social season.

Elizabeth gave her annual October dinner dance, a gala affair attended by two hundred guests. Charlotte made a brief appearance, but Sarah, due to her condition, was excused. Now Elizabeth insisted that Sarah take her meals in her room and that she spend several hours in bed each day. She was fussed over, her wants and needs anticipated by Elizabeth's well-trained servants. Patrick was allowed to visit once or twice and Ned was encouraged to do so, though he often found reasons for being elsewhere. Janet visited and Charlotte was always close at hand, embroidering a christening gown and cap. When, late in November, Sarah asked to see her shipboard friend Mary Margaret, her request was flatly denied. "Too much excitement," Elizabeth declared. "Excitement isn't good for you now. We want a perfect baby, don't we?"

There were many Christmas parties at the Cameron house during the month of December, but again Sarah was excused. With Charlotte, she crept to the top of the stairs, and like children, they watched the bejeweled guests arrive. They listened to the laughter, to the clink of crystal as toasts were offered, and then crept quietly away lest they be discovered. "I feel as if I'm in prison," Sarah moaned. "If I could just go out and get some air. If I could see the Christmas decorations . . ."

"Mother would have a fit."

"But why? In Aldcross, Dr. Burshaw always prescribed long walks, even up to the last day. There's no harm in exercise. Or is Aunt Elizabeth ashamed of—of the way I look?"

"*Ashamed* is the wrong word," Charlotte replied. "There are certain rules about these things. A lady too obviously pregnant isn't supposed to be seen in public. We all still pretend the stork brings babies! But there's another reason, Sarah. Mother really does want a perfect baby. A Cameron baby."

It was a few moments before the words filtered through to Sarah. "A Cameron baby?" she asked, startled.

"Mother planned the nursery. She's made the hospital arrangements and hired the nursemaid. I

wouldn't be surprised if she's picked out the names."
Charlotte's eyes darkened. She stared at Sarah, taking
her hand. "Mother will try to take over, you see. You
must guard against that. I'll help, of course, but you
must make your position clear from the start."

"I wish I knew what my position was. I've never
known, not from the day I arrived here."

"It's *your* baby, Sarah. That's your position.
Mother will try to run everything. She'll try to bend
you to her will. You mustn't let her."

"Why would she do that?"

"I'm not sure," Charlotte frowned. "I haven't been
able to think that part through. Perhaps it's because
it's her nature. Perhaps it's because she wants a
grandchild. I only know she'll try. And once Mother
puts her mind to something . . . Well, she's a hard
woman to resist. Ask Ned. He wanted to be a writer.
That's all he talked about for years and years. Mother
put an end to it. She just wore him down. When
arguments and appeals didn't work, she turned to
threats. She threatened to cut him off without a
penny. She would have done it, too. That was the last
straw. Ned wanted very much to be a writer, but he
wasn't willing to risk losing this kind of life. So he
went into the Galleries, exactly the way Mother had
planned."

"He could have taken the risk," Sarah suggested.

"Mother knows people's vulnerabilities. Ned's is
money. Oh, not money as such, but the kind of
luxurious life money can provide. Ned likes his fun
and that can be expensive."

"What has that to do with my baby?"

"The question is what Mother has planned for
your baby."

Sarah puzzled over that question during the last
weeks of her pregnancy, though Elizabeth's inten-

tions were of less concern than her own discomfort. It was difficult for her to sleep, to sit, and rising from any position was almost impossible without help. Her walk was slow, clumsy. Her back ached. She was always hungry, but when her trays were brought, she found she could not stand the sight or smell of food. "It won't be long now," Charlotte kept reminding her. "Perhaps you'll have a Christmas baby. Wouldn't that be lovely!"

Three days before Christmas, Sarah was roused from a nap by a loud thud on the stair. She thought she heard a scream, and grasping the bedposts with both hands, she pulled herself up. She made her way across the room and into the hall. "What is it?" she asked as Mae rushed past.

"Miss Charlotte. She's fallen down the stairs."

"My God, *no.*"

"It's bad, ma'am. Terrible bad."

Sarah went as fast as she could along the passage and down the staircase. At the foot of the staircase was a knot of huddled servants, some of them crying. Raymond, his face impassive stepped forward to clear a path for Elizabeth. "The ambulance has been called, madam," he said. "Miss Munroe is telephoning Dr. Westerman now."

Elizabeth sank to her knees beside Charlotte's twisted body. She felt for a pulse, a heartbeat, then gently closed her daughter's eyes. "Charlotte," she whispered.

Raymond ushered the servants away. Sarah watched, tears streaking her white face. She took a step closer to Charlotte, stretching a trembling hand to her friend. "Oh God," she sobbed. "Oh God, why?"

Janet rushed in at that moment. "Mrs. Cameron," she began, unable to finish, for she realized Charlotte

82

was dead.

"Take Sarah to her room and put her to bed," Elizabeth directed, her voice very low. "I will stay with Charlotte."

"Yes, Mrs. Cameron. Come, Sarah."

"No, I can't leave her."

Janet took hold of Sarah's shoulders, turning her around. "Come," she said again.

The walk upstairs seemed endless. Sarah clung to Janet's hand, sobbing incoherently. Janet made soothing sounds but said nothing, for there was nothing to say. She got Sarah into bed, tucked the blankets about her, and drew the curtains. Charlotte's needlework was lying on a chair and she snatched it away, hastily thrusting it under a cushion. "Would you like a fire?" she asked. "The steam is on but perhaps you'd prefer a fire."

"Why did this happen? Tell me why."

"I can't, Sarah. I don't know why."

"She's dead."

"Yes. I'm so sorry."

"But she's dead."

"Try to be calm, Sarah. I—I must get back to Mrs. Cameron. I'll send Violet to sit with you until the doctor arrives."

"But she's *dead*."

Six hundred people attended Charlotte's funeral at St. James Church. Elizabeth, dignified and erect in black mourning veils, emerged from the first limousine and ascended the steps of the church, Ned on one side of her, Patrick on the other. In her pew she stared straight ahead at Charlotte's casket, her eyes lingering briefly on the simple blanket of gardenias. After the Reverend Dr. Withers's eulogy, after all the

83

prayers and hymns, she was assisted back into her limousine for the ride to Woodlawn Cemetery. The burial was private, the grieving family shielded from crowds of reporters and photographers.

Sarah had been forbidden by both Elizabeth and Dr. Westerman to attend the services. She had protested their decision, angrily at times, but to no avail. On the day of the funeral she remained confined to her bed in the silent Cameron house, a nurse hovering about. It was evening when Elizabeth entered her room. She watched the slender black-clad figure approach and new tears sprang to her eyes. "I wanted to be there," she murmured.

Elizabeth sat down, drawing a small breath. "Charlotte is at peace now," she said, her calm betrayed by the catch in her voice. "That is what you must remember, Sarah. You must also remember how happy you made her last months. . . . It was so good to hear her laugh again, to see her interested in things. That was your accomplishment."

"It wasn't enough."

"It was everything. I will always be grateful that she had those months. You must be grateful, too."

"I miss her," Sarah said quietly.

"We all have our memories. Memories can make all the difference at a time—a time like this."

"If my baby is a girl, I've decided to name her Charlotte."

"No," Elizabeth replied firmly. "I'm not a superstitious person, but it's occurred to me that Charlotte had very little luck in her life, despite the advantages she was given. . . . No, the baby will have its own name. A name without ties to the past. Now you must get some rest, my dear. I'll see you in the morning. Good night."

"Good night, Aunt Elizabeth."

She rose, nodding to the nurse as she left. She

walked through the empty hallway, stopping for a moment at Charlotte's closed door, then continued to her own rooms. The lamps had been lighted, the bed turned down. A pot of cocoa sat on a table by the fireplace but she went instead to the cellarette and poured a glass of brandy. She poured a second, a third. Glass in hand she went to the windows, throwing wide the casements to the cold night air. After a while she crossed the room and sank into a chair. Her gaze settled on a group of family portraits, and in that instant tears came to her eyes. So many deaths, she thought, and now there's only Ned. The weakling of the family, with his chorus girls and nightclubs and foolish ideas. But no more. I'll see to that if it's the last thing I do.

Elizabeth remained in seclusion during the next week, leaving her rooms to breakfast with Ned and to visit Sarah, now constantly attended by Nurse Hathaway. Several times she visited the nursery, smiling in approval at the dainty antique bureaus and chairs, the white wicker bassinet skirted with white silk, the enormous teddy bear sitting in a child-sized cane rocker. The nursemaid's bed had been placed in an alcove, dressed with cheerful yellow blankets and spreads. On the walls were framed watercolors of ducks and rabbits and clowns. It was a happy room, and to Elizabeth, it meant a new beginning.

At five minutes before midnight on New Year's Eve she left her rooms to drink a glass of champagne with the servants and to dispense the customary gold pieces, a ritual that was interrupted by the sudden appearance of Nurse Hathaway. "I've telephoned Dr. Westerman," she announced. "I'm afraid there won't be time to take Mrs. Griffith to hospital."

*   *   *

Perspiration drenched Sarah's brow. Her fingers clawed the sheets as yet another wave of pain seared her heaving body. She strained until she thought her heart would burst, falling back on the pillows in exhaustion. "I can't," she gasped. "I can't."

"The worst is almost over," Dr. Westerman said. "I can see the baby's head. Now take a deep breath and push. . . . Bear down, Sarah. . . . Again . . . That's it. The baby's head is coming. . . . Push, Sarah, push. Harder. That's the way. . . . Again . . . All right, Sarah, the shoulders are coming and then it will be over. I want you to take a deep breath and push as hard as you can. . . . Again . . . Once more . . . Congratulations, Sarah, you have a fine baby girl."

"A girl?" She smiled, her pain, her exhaustion forgotten. "May I see?"

"In a moment," Dr. Westerman replied. He slapped the baby's bottom and an angry cry filled the room. "Fine pair of lungs, too," he laughed. "We'll clean her up a bit and then you can meet your daughter."

"Please let me see her now."

"Can't wait, eh? Very well. Let's have that blanket, Hathaway." Dr. Westerman wrapped the blanket around the baby and presented the tiny bundle to Sarah. "Congratulations," he said again.

She gazed at her baby, wrinkled and bald and beet-red and felt such feelings of love she could not speak. Gently, she touched each tiny little finger, and when one of them curled around hers, she wept with joy. "My baby," she cooed. "My beautiful baby girl."

Dr. Westerman washed his hands in the basin, dried them, and then slipped into his coat. "I must give the good news to Mrs. Cameron now," he said, going to the door. "Sarah, I'll let you have a few moments with your daughter. After that, Nurse

86

Hathaway will take charge." He opened the door and walked downstairs to Elizabeth's study. "May I come in?" he asked, peering through the early morning darkness.

"By all means, Doctor." Elizabeth stood away from her desk and switched on a lamp. "The baby?"

"A fine girl. Healthy, so far as I can see. I haven't weighed her yet, but she's a decent size."

"And Sarah?"

"Sarah's very tired. The baby came quickly but not easily. I'd recommend bed rest for a week or two. Apart from that, she's a happy, healthy young mother. Quite taken with her daughter, I'd say."

"We're all most grateful to you, Doctor."

"It's my pleasure. I see altogether too much sickness. A baby, a new life, is always a pleasure. . . . And there were times this past summer when Sarah seemed rather forlorn. I believe this baby will do her a world of good."

"Yes, I agree. May I look in on her now?"

"Of course, though I must ask you not to stay too long. The baby will soon be screaming for food and I'd prefer Sarah to get some rest while she can."

"I quite understand. It's been a busy night . . . or morning," Elizabeth added, glancing at the small silver Tiffany clock on her desk. "Heavens, it's past five. I'd completely lost track of the time."

"If you don't mind my saying so, I think you could do with some rest yourself, Mrs. Cameron. You've been under a terrible strain. You've borne it well, but perhaps a sleeping powder—"

"Thank you, Doctor," Elizabeth said as they walked into the hall. "I appreciate your concern. Certainly it's been a strain. Sudden death always is. But we both knew Charlotte didn't have many years left to her. We knew after her last bout with pneumonia. . . . In that sense, I was prepared. I'd hoped for more time, but it wasn't to be. I'm comforted by the knowledge that she didn't suffer. It was very quick . . . without pain."

"Yes," Dr. Westerman concurred. In five years of treating the Camerons, he had seen Charlotte through numerous colds, three pneumonias, and pleurisy. He had seen Elizabeth's devotion to her daughter during those times, yet never once had he seen her lose her composure. A strong woman, he thought, strong as they come. "I admire your attitude," he said.

"I'm a realist, Doctor." Elizabeth opened the door to Sarah's room and walked inside. "Well, my dear," she said, a smile lifting the corners of her mouth, "how does it feel to be a mother?"

"Oh, it's wonderful. I'm so happy. Aunt Elizabeth."

"You look happy. You're absolutely radiant. And how clever of you to have a New Year's baby. They're special, you know."

"New Year's?" Sarah asked. "Is it New Year's Day? Then it's my birthday, too."

"Your . . . Sarah, why on earth didn't you tell anyone?"

"I'd forgotten until just now. I'd forgotten all about it."

Elizabeth went to the delicately carved and inlaid French cradle that years ago had been hers. She stared down at the sleeping baby, her eyes quiet, thoughtful. "What a charming birthday present," she said after some moments. "Have you chosen a name? I've always liked the name Lucy. It's a pretty name, isn't it?

"Lucy?" Sarah repeated, recalling her old Aldcross friend Lucy James. "Yes," she said, "I suppose that would be all right. . . . But I was thinking of the name Caroline. It's always been my favorite. . . ."

"We have a Caroline in the family, and one is quite enough. Lucy is a much better choice. Wouldn't you agree?"

"I—I suppose so."

"Then it's settled." Elizabeth left the cradle, stopping at Sarah's bed. "Now you're not to worry," she smiled. "Lucy's nurse will be here in a few hours and I'll give her her instructions. She will see to everything."

Sarah felt a vague stirring of alarm. She was troubled by Elizabeth's manner, though in ways she could not describe. "I want to take care of my baby," she said. "I know you hired a nurse and I appreciate it. But I want to be part of things, Aunt Elizabeth."

"Of course you do, my dear. But first you must rest and get your strength back. I understand these things, Sarah. For now, you must leave everything to me and Nurse Porter."

Chapter Five

I understand these things. Sarah learned to hate that phrase as the weeks and months passed, for it served to exclude her from her baby's life. True to Charlotte's warnings, Elizabeth had taken over, setting nursery schedules and rules. Sarah found herself welcome in the nursery only at certain times, and then only briefly. She found she was not allowed to bathe Lucy, to change or dress the child. When spring arrived, she was given no role in the christening plans, no choice in the matter of godparents. "It's as if I don't exist," she protested to Elizabeth one sunny April day. "Nurse Porter won't answer my questions or listen to any of my suggestions. She pays no attention to anything I say."

"Has she been rude?"

"No one in this house is ever rude," Sarah replied, more sharply than she had intended. "But that's not the point. The point is I'm Lucy's mother and I want to spend time with her. I wanted to take her to the park today. Nurse Porter wouldn't hear of it. She said Lucy had already had her outing. . . . I don't see the harm in two outings. Fresh air is good for babies."

"You must remember that Lucy is on a schedule."

"It's your schedule, Aunt Elizabeth."

"Mine?"

"You arranged it with Nurse Porter."

Elizabeth sat back, gazing across her desk at Sarah. "I'm thinking of the day you arrived here," she said pleasantly. "Such a shy, timid girl. You've changed, my dear. You speak your mind now. It's interesting the difference time can make."

"Lucy's made the difference. I feel as if I must fight for her. I feel as if—as if she's being taken from me."

"You're still upset about the christening."

"It's more than the christening, Aunt Elizabeth. It's much more than that." Sarah shook her head, tears glittering in the hazel-blue of her eyes. "You gave me a place in your home," she sniffled, "but I don't know what that place is. I've never known. And now—now I don't even know my place with my own baby."

"You're family, Sarah."

"But I'm *not*, not really. Saying I am doesn't make it so. My family is thousands of miles away. My baby is here but she might just as well be thousands of miles away. I don't have any friends. . . . I don't have anything to *do*."

"There are many activities for young society women. There are teas and charity committees and—"

"Excuse me, Aunt Elizabeth, but I'm not a society woman, either. I'm a schoolmaster's daughter from a small village in England. I'm living in a mansion now and my closets are filled with fancy new clothes, but I'll always be plain Sarah Griffith from Aldcross."

"There's nothing plain about you, my dear. You're quite lovely, you know. You have intelligence also, and the beginnings of a fine spirit. Those are gifts, Sarah, gifts not to be squandered.''

"If I had some work to do . . .''

"Work? No, we can't have that.'' Elizabeth folded her hands atop the desk. She smiled, inclining her head toward Sarah. "I am going to ask you to be patient,'' she said. "I will arrange for you to have more time with Lucy, time which will not interfere with her schedule. That should solve part of the problem.''

"I want to be *useful*.''

"Patience, my dear.''

"What has patience to do with anything?''

"It's the key.''

Again Sarah shook her head. "The key to what?'' she asked. "I don't understand.''

"But I do. I've lived a good deal longer than you have, Sarah, and I understand these things very well. Very well indeed.''

It was a month later when Elizabeth called Ned into her study. "Sit down,'' she said without preamble, calmly rearranging a bouquet of yellow roses. "I trust your trip was successful.''

"Paris is marvelous in the spring. I was tempted to stay on another week or two.''

"I'm sure you were. That Cholly Knickerbocker person devoted almost half his column to your escapades. Something about cancan dancers and splashing around in a fountain.''

"Paris is also fun, Mother.''

"You were sent there on business.''

"All work and no play make Ned a dull boy.''

"Dull! We need hardly worry about that. Your life is a gossip columnist's dream.'' Elizabeth finished with the flowers and then crossed the room, sitting on a silken couch opposite her son. "I don't expect you will ever really grow up," she said quietly. "It will be one sort of escapade or another until you're a very old man. That's what I see ahead for you."

Ned smiled. "Is it, Mother? Lucky me."

"I'm not amused," Elizabeth replied, and clearly she was not. "Your charm won't get you out of this. Over the years I've become immune. We've had this same conversation so many times. You promise to behave, to exercise some discretion, but you never do. You go on as before, embarrassing the family. Even now, with poor Charlotte dead less than six months, you persist in making a spectacle of yourself."

"That's unfair, Mother," Ned said, his smile disappearing. "It's unfair to bring Charlotte into our argument."

"Perhaps. I have no interest in being fair to you, Ned. Why should I? I've given you any number of chances and you've flung them back in my face. Well, no more."

Ned shifted uneasily in his chair. "I don't think I follow you, Mother."

"You will. But first I will remind you of a few things. Your finances, for example, are in a sorry state. You have your salary from the Galleries and the income from your trust, yet still you run behind each month. You look to me to pay your tailor, your garage, your club dues, all the bills you cannot pay yourself. It runs to a sizeable amount during the course of a year."

"I'm aware of that, Mother."

"And of course you are aware that you won't come into your trust until your fortieth birthday, a wise precaution on your father's part."

"Yes, that too."

"I control your trust."

"I'm certainly aware of that," Ned sighed. "Mother, we've been all through this. You used your control of my trust to get me into the Galleries. Your threat succeeded. If you plan to threaten me again . . ."

"Yes? If I do?" Elizabeth watched her son, watched his assurance waver and then crumble, as it had crumbled before. "I dislike threats, you know, I much prefer reason. But you, Ned, aren't reasonable. You want the money, the style associated with the Cameron name, and none of the responsibility. You want life on your own terms."

"Doesn't everyone? Don't you?"

"I take my responsibilities seriously."

"You're leading up to something, Mother. What is it?"

"Just this. Sooner or later, one of your escapades is bound to end in disaster. You've been fortunate so far, but you're bound to become entangled. You'll wake up one morning to find yourself *married* to some chorus girl or cancan dancer or worse. I intend to see that doesn't happen."

"Marriage is the last thing on my mind."

"On your mind, I have no doubt. But can we say what's on the minds of your . . . companions? You are an eligible young man, Ned. A young man who often loses his head to the pleasures of the moment. Only disaster can result from that."

"And what do you propose, Mother?"

Now Elizabeth smiled. "An interesting choice of words," she said. "Because the solution to this problem lies in a proposal. . . . Your proposal of marriage to Sarah."

Ned's mouth dropped open. "Sarah!" he cried, gripping the arms of his chair. *"Sarah?* I barely *know* the girl and you want me to . . . Look here, Mother, is this some kind of insane joke? You can't possibly *mean* it. You can't possibly be asking me to marry a girl I barely know."

"You're her daughter's godfather."

"She *wanted* Patrick."

"Well, she got you."

Ned bolted from his chair, rushing across the room and then back again. "Even—even supposing you could . . . force *me* into a marriage," he sputtered, "how do you plan to force Sarah? She has no trust fund, no damned bills that have to be paid."

"She has a daughter," Elizabeth replied serenely.

"What does *that* mean?"

"Sarah adores Lucy. She will do whatever is in the child's best interests. Marriage to you is in the child's best interests."

"My God, Mother, do you mean you would use *Lucy* to get your way?" Ned fell into a chair, wearily shaking his sandy head. "Yes, of course you would. You would use anyone and anything. I know that. And I think I know why you've chosen Sarah for me. You can control her, just as you control my trust. You have the upper hand with both of us."

"Come now, that's rather dramatic."

"It's true, Mother."

"Not exactly. Sarah is a nice, sensible girl who will put up with your absences, your transgressions, for the sake of her child. She's willing to make sacrifices. That much was clear from the beginning. And that's not something I can say for the eligible girls of our acquaintance. They're spoiled, all of them. Soon enough you would find yourself in the midst of a nasty divorce, the Cameron name dragged through the courts, the mud. . . . That won't happen with Sarah."

"Have you had this planned from the beginning? My God, is that why you brought Sarah here in the first place?"

"The reason was family, nothing more. After she arrived, other possibilities occurred to me. Sarah has a fine character. She proved that with Charlotte. And she's lovely! All that lovely honey hair, those enormous hazel eyes. Quite a pleasing figure, too, as I'm sure you've noticed. Sarah may not be chorus girl material, but she's lovely."

"And entitled to a happy life, a life of her own choosing. Mother, you're being cruel."

"I'm being practical. Sarah needs a husband. Her child needs a name. . . . You need a girl who will put up with you and who will save you from marriage to some grasping social climber."

Ned reached into his pocket, removing a slim gold case. He took out a cigarette and lighted it, watching the gray smoke curl toward the ceiling. "What if I say no?" he asked.

"You will regret it."

"That simple, is it?"

Elizabeth rose, going to her desk. "In this drawer is my checkbook," she said. "If you agree to the marriage, you will receive a check for fifty thousand dollars on your wedding day. You will receive a similar check each year you remain married to Sarah. . . . You will also be given a partnership in the Galleries."

"Equal to Patrick's?"

"Not quite, but it will be a voting partnership. You will have a seat on the Board."

"I see."

"Well?"

"You've told me what Sarah needs . . . and Lucy. You've told me what I need. What do *you* need out of this, Mother? Does the question surprise you? It shouldn't. I'm not entirely stupid. Oh, I know the money means nothing. What's fifty thousand to you? But a *partnership* . . . That means a great deal to you. So there has to be more to this than saving the family name. Something extra that you want for yourself. What is it?" Elizabeth was silent, though her gaze went to the photographs on her desk. Ned followed her gaze. He frowned. "Well, I'll be damned," he said a few moments later. "It's Lucy, isn't it?"

"Lucy?"

"Of course. I don't know why I didn't see it before. You've led a charmed life, Mother, except for your children. You lost Anne and Charlotte, and I'm a lost cause. . . . Now you want a second chance with Lucy. Lucy is the bonus in this miserable arrangement."

"I would suggest you mind your tongue, Ned. My patience is not unlimited."

"Oh, but it is. Think of the patience it took to plan this. For ten months you've been grooming Sarah to be a Cameron. . . . Teaching her how to dress, how to style her hair, how to conduct herself. Now I understand why."

"You're in a fanciful mood today, Ned."

"No. I'm on to the game, Mother. You plan to kill two birds with one stone. I get a wife and you get a grandchild, all courtesy of Sarah, all without blinking an eye. You're amazing! Even now you stand there smiling calmly, as if we were discussing the weather. It's a shame you don't play poker. You'd be the best player in the world. You and your nerves of steel."

"Are you quite finished?"

"I don't know. Under the circumstances, it seems to me I could ask for the moon and get it."

"You're the poker player in the family, Ned, so I

will give you a piece of advice: Don't overplay your hand."

"It's an awfully good hand, Mother."

"Not good enough. Now I'm through bandying words with you. I've stated my terms. They stand. The choice is yours."

"Well, Father used to say every man has his price." Ned stood. He stared across the room at Elizabeth. "All right, Mother," he said, "one son bought and paid for . . . You may find Sarah a more difficult proposition. As you yourself pointed out, she has character."

"And a child."

"God help her."

"There is also the matter of your famous charm," Elizabeth added with a chilly smile. "Use it. Sarah's seen very little of New York nightlife, a subject in which you are expert. Entertain her. Court her."

"I'm not even sure if Sarah likes me. She hides her feelings."

"She's a lady. A new experience for you, Ned."

He opened his mouth to reply, then changed his mind. "May I go now, Mother?"

"Certainly . . . Ned? In time, you'll be glad we had this talk. It's the perfect solution."

"And they all lived happily ever after."

"I beg your pardon? What did you say?"

"Nothing, Mother. Nothing at all."

Sarah sat at her ruffled dressing table, studying her reflection in the mirror. Her hair was fashionably shorter and sleeker now, the waves deeper. The faintest touch of rose-colored lipstick enhanced the soft contours of her mouth. Charlotte's diamonds sparkled at her ears and about her long, slender throat. "Mama would never recognize me," she said. "Not in a million years."

"But you're beautiful!" Janet exclaimed. She recalled the day of Sarah's arrival, recalled her dowdy traveling clothes, and she laughed. "A butterfly emerging from the cocoon!"

"I feel so strange about all of this. Why would Ned want to take me out? Ned, of all people. We've scarcely said ten words to each other. I didn't want to accept, you know. Aunt Elizabeth insisted it would be good for me."

"She's right. New York is an exciting city by night. You should see some of it. You've been cooped up in this house too long.

Sarah's eyes darkened suddenly. "Yes," she snapped, "Aunt Elizabeth is always right."

"Oh, I see. You're beginning to feel the weight of Mrs. Cameron's strong hand. She does tend to take charge."

"I feel smothered, Janet."

"All the more reason to go out and enjoy yourself. You need some fun. Ned is the fellow for that. He's the ideal escort. A bit on the fast side, but I'm sure he'll mind his manners with you."

"I can't imagine what we'll find to talk about." Sarah looked again at her reflection. She shook her head. "Sometimes I feel as if all of this is playacting. As if it isn't real. There are mornings when I wake up and wonder where I am. I expect to see my old room in Aldcross. Then I have to remind myself that I'm living in the Cameron mansion in New York. . . . But it still isn't real."

"Perhaps your date with Ned will help."

"Date?" Sarah looked up, startled. "Oh my, it's not a date, Janet. I mean it's not that sort of thing at all. Ned has dates with—with sophisticated women. I know because I've read about him in the newspaper columns. They call him a 'man about town.' No man about town would want to have a date with *me*. I'm a country girl."

"You were. You're a city girl now. You've come a long way, Sarah."

"I'm not sophisticated, though."

"Thank heavens!"

Sarah discarded her robe and slipped into her dress, a stylish creation of short white silk glittering with crystal beads. "Aunt Elizabeth won't discuss what anything costs," she said, "but I'll wager this dress cost the earth. This dress and all the others in my closets." She picked up her small beaded purse, twirling around. "Do I look silly?"

"Silly? You're *dazzling*."

"That's kind of you to say, Janet."

"It's the truth."

"No, it's more playacting. I'm living in this house and wearing these clothes and going out with Ned, but it isn't me."

"Who is it?"

Sarah smiled, shaking her head from side to side. "I wish I knew," she replied. "I wonder about that sometimes when I can't sleep. I wonder about a lot of things. . . . All week I've been wondering what I'll find to say to Ned tonight."

"You have no trouble making conversation with Patrick."

"Oh, Patrick's different. It's easy to talk to him. Evelyn frightens me a little. She's so . . . glamorous. But Patrick's very nice. I liked him from the start."

"Don't you like Ned?" Janet asked.

"I don't know him, not really."

"Then it's time you did. And speaking of time . . ."

"Yes, I'm ready, Janet."

They left the room, stopping at the nursery. Sarah tapped lightly on the door and a moment later Nurse Porter appeared. "I'd like to see Lucy," Sarah said. "I promise I won't stay long. I'm just on my way out."

"Lucy is sleeping, Mrs. Griffith."

"I won't wake her."

"She was a bit fussy earlier this evening. It took a while to get her settled down. If her sleep is disturbed . . ."

"I've already said I won't wake her," Sarah persisted. "I want to see my daughter, Nurse. Must we have this argument every night?"

"Very well, Mrs. Griffith." The nurse stepped aside, allowing Sarah to enter the room. "But I don't know what Mrs. Cameron will say. You're wearing perfume and she's forbidden perfume in the nursery."

Sarah did not bother to respond. She tiptoed to the beribboned crib and gazed at Lucy, now almost six months old. Tenderly, she stroked the child's fluff of platinum hair. She smiled. "Sweet dreams," she whispered, yearning to take her baby in her arms. "Sweet dreams, my darling." She felt Nurse Porter touch her shoulder and her smile became a frown. "Yes, all right. I'm going." She swept past the nurse, muttering to herself as she returned to the hall. "Well, that's that," she said to Janet. "I've been permitted my usual one-minute visit and that's that. Nurse Porter is a dragon."

"Try to put her out of your mind, at least for now. You have a big evening ahead of you, Sarah. Enjoy it. *Try*."

"I will. You're sweet to worry about me."

"Ned is waiting downstairs. I'll leave you to make your grand entrance. And *smile*. You aren't going to a hanging!"

Sarah turned and walked to the staircase. She was nervous, hoping she would not do or say the wrong thing. She felt no sense of excitement, however, for this evening out seemed to be merely another arrangement forced on her by Elizabeth. She was halfway downstairs before it occurred to her that the arrangement had probably been forced on Ned, too, Poor Ned, she thought, we have something in common after all.

Ned followed Sarah's progress down the stairs, his connoisseur's eye noting every curve of her body beneath the shimmering silk. When she reached the last step, he took her hand. "How beautiful you look," he said. "You're a vision."

"Thank you," Sarah replied, coloring. "I'm sorry if I kept you waiting."

"Some women are worth waiting for. You're certainly in that category." Ned saw Sarah's blush deepen. "Now I've embarrassed you," he laughed. "Aren't you accustomed to compliments? You should be. And starting tonight, you will be. You'll see heads turning tonight, all in your direction."

"You're teasing," Sarah said, her smile at once shy and amused.

"Teasing, am I? You'll take this city by storm. Wait and see."

Raymond opened the door for the young couple. "A pleasant evening to you, Mrs. Griffith, Mr. Ned."

"Thank you, Raymond. We'll do our best." Ned offered his arm to Sarah as they walked to the car. "We're going to the theater first," he explained. "The opening of *Abie's Irish Rose*. Then I'll show you how New York is celebrating Prohibition!"

Prohibition had become law in July of 1920, but it was a law doomed to failure, for bootleggers and speakeasies were everywhere. The Anti-Saloon

League urged people to "Shake hands with Uncle Sam and board the water wagon"; this slogan, too, was doomed to failure, drowned out by the more popular passwords "Joe sent me."

There were thousands of speakeasies flourishing in New York alone, and this flaunting of the law was said to reflect deeper changes in attitudes and values. The popular song of the day was a suggestive little tune entitled "I'll Say She Does," a tune condemned by many, for its lyrics seemed to describe the alarming phenomenon of the modern woman. The modern woman shortened her skirts a full six inches, displaying long-hidden legs in sheer silk stockings often rolled below the knee. She bobbed her hair and plucked her brows. She rouged her cheeks and lips and lined her eyes with kohl. She smoked cigarettes. She danced, not the sedate waltz, but the tango and the Charleston and the Black Bottom. She was irreverent, matching the spirit of the decade that would be called the Roaring Twenties.

To Sarah, who rarely left the quiet Cameron house, it was a new world, a world of energy and abandon and happy chaos. She was surprised by the obvious prosperity of the young theater audience, intrigued by the quick friendship and carefree laughter of the speakeasies. Gradually, her reserve slipped away. At Ned's insistence, she learned to dance the Charleston, learned the current slang expressions. She drank glass after glass of bootleg champagne, giggling when the bubbles tickled her nose. She joined in the songs, the jokes. Compliments were showered on her, and for the first time in her life Sarah allowed herself to believe she was pretty.

Ned watched with interest as this other, more playful side of Sarah emerged. Charming though it was, it did not ease his mind. He liked Sarah, but he felt no spark, no giddy rush of desire. He knew he would never love her, could never love her, for she was at heart an innocent, too guileless and gentle. We can be friends, he thought, perhaps good friends, but what does that matter in a marriage? Sarah will be cheated of the husband she deserves and I'll stand by and let it happen because . . . because every man has his price.

Ned was unusually subdued during the ride home. It was almost dawn, wide streaks of pink and white lighting the dark sky, but he appeared not to notice. He glanced often at Sarah, drawing on his cigarette. "Did you have a nice time?" he asked after one long silence. "I hope you weren't disappointed."

"Oh, no, it was wonderful. The people and the places . . . And me dancing the Charleston! Imagine!"

"You were a great success, you know. Whit Reynolds couldn't take his eyes off you. Nor could a dozen other fellows. I hate to say I told you so," Ned smiled, "but I told you so."

"I had a wonderful time. I think I'm tipsy from all that champagne. . . . Ned, I can't thank you enough for taking me out. It was sweet of you, really it was."

"I hope you . . . like me a little better now."

Sarah turned, lifting puzzled eyes to Ned. "Did you think I didn't like you?" she asked. "I'm sorry. It's just that I didn't know you very well. You're away so much. All that traveling . . ."

"Do you feel you know me now?"

"In a way. I mean, there wasn't a lot of conversation, was there? But I saw how sweet you can be. How different from the man I've read about in the newspaper columns."

"I wouldn't be too sure of that if I were you, Sarah."

"Is something wrong? Did I do something wrong?"

"No, no, of course not. You were utterly delightful. As a matter of fact, I'm hoping you'll agree to go out with me again. Perhaps a quiet dinner . . . Will you agree, Sarah?"

"Oh, it's kind of you to ask," she replied, smiling, "but you needn't worry about me. I've had my night out and I enjoyed it. You've done your part, Ned. I don't expect you to waste—"

"My part? Excuse me for interrupting, but I'm afraid I don't understand."

"Taking me out was Aunt Elizabeth's idea, wasn't it?"

Clever girl, thought Ned; Mother will have to watch her step around you. "Mother suggested only that I take a good look at you," he said smoothly. "I did. The rest is history."

"You're teasing again," Sarah laughed. My brother Bertie is a great one for teasing. You remind me of him."

"Brotherly interest isn't what I had in mind."

A frown wrinkled Sarah's brow. She had no fear of Ned, yet something about his manner troubled her. She stared into his dark eyes and saw that he was troubled also. "What is it you have in mind?"

"A quiet dinner."

"But why? You have so many . . . so many friends."

"Are all the English as suspicious as you are?"

"Ned, I told Aunt Elizabeth I didn't have enough to do. Didn't have *anything* to do. I complained, really. Now I'm wondering if she's forcing you to

105

entertain me. I don't want that. I won't let you do it."

"The answer is quite simple. I enjoy your company."

Sarah was not persuaded. She thought about Elizabeth, seeing her serene smile, her cool gaze, and she sensed the truth. "I don't want to put you in a difficult position," she said at last. "We can have dinner whenever you'd like."

"Next Saturday?"

"Next Saturday."

Sarah and Ned had several dinners together during the following two months. They went to the *Follies* and the zoo and to baseball games at Yankee Stadium. They began to know each other; in their own ways, they grew fond of each other. Sarah told Ned something of her life in Aldcross, wistfully recalling summer picnics and village socials. Ned told Sarah stories of his college days, hilarious stories that made her laugh. It was a comfortable relationship, unburdened by passion, by love.

Elizabeth monitored the course of their relationship all through that summer. With the coming of autumn, she again called Ned into her study. "You've been behaving yourself," she said. "I approve."

"Yes, I thought you would."

"Sarah approves also. She isn't frightened of you anymore."

"Sarah was never frightened of me, Mother."

"Of your reputation then."

"Perhaps."

"You're almost a credit to the family, Ned. Only one thing is lacking. A wife. I believe it's time for a proposal."

"It's too soon."

"Nonsense. If you delay, it may be too late. Some of your friends have taken notice of Sarah. The Reynolds boy sends flowers every week. Peter Melvile is always telephoning with invitations to this and that. She has so far declined, but one day she may not."

"I'm sure you'll find a way to keep that from happening, Mother."

"Sarah isn't a prisoner here. She is free to come and go as she pleases."

Ned laughed suddenly, an explosive sound in the quiet room. He leaned forward, shaking his sandy head. "What an amazing creature you are! Do you actually *believe* anything you say? Do you actually *believe* Sarah isn't a prisoner here? It's an elegant prison, I grant you. But it's a prison just the same. And you, Mother, are the warden. You make the rules, you decide the punishments. . . . You run the whole damned show."

"Mind your tongue, Ned."

"Have I offended your delicate sensibilities? Not very likely. You don't take offense, do you, Mother? That would be a waste of time. It would get in the way of your plans, your never-ending plans." Ned sat back, slumping in his chair. He sighed. "All right," he said wearily. "All right. I suppose I'm as bad as you are, because I don't resist. I'm your accomplice, Mother. And like any well-trained accomplice, I'll carry out the rest of the plan. I'll propose to Sarah."

"When?"

"Today, if you want. It doesn't make any difference now."

"Sarah is in the library," Elizabeth said.

"Not a very romantic place for a proposal."

"It will do."

"Under the circumstances, it will do spendidly."
Ned got to his feet, gazing at Elizabeth. "You're
ruining her life, you know. A man is allowed his
diversions, but a woman must be faithful and true,
no matter how bad the bargain."

"Such melodrama! Where in the world do you get
your ideas? I'm offering Sarah a life any woman
would be thrilled to have. I'm offering her the
Cameron name and all that goes with it. That's
hardly a fate worse than death."

Ned was too tired to argue. He gazed at his mother
a moment longer and then left the room, turning
down the hall to the library. "Sarah," he said,
pausing in the doorway, "may I join you?"

"Please. I was just trying to find a book I haven't
already read."

"Surely you haven't read all these? There must be
thousands of books in here. Father collected books."

"Well," Sarah laughed, "some of them are so
boring they put me to sleep. I haven't read the Greeks
yet. I might give Plato a try."

Ned sank down on one of the deep leather couches.
He lighted a cigarette, watching Sarah roll the oak
ladder from shelf to shelf. "You look awfully pretty
with the sun falling on your hair," he said.

"I'm not supposed to open the drapes in this room,
but it was so gloomy. . . . You're a little gloomy yourself, aren't you? Is something wrong?"

"I wanted to talk, Sarah. I confess I would have
preferred a more agreeable setting. Perhaps we
should go to the park."

"Something is *wrong*. Tell me."

"Come and sit down," Ned said, patting the soft
leather couch cushion. "And don't be·concerned.
Actually, it's something quite nice."

Sarah sat next to Ned. She smoothed the skirt of her

red silk dress and folded her hands in her lap. "I'm ready," she smiled. "I'm *dying* of curiosity."

"I—I seem to be at a loss for words."

"Oh, not you."

Ned glanced away, uncertain how or where to begin. He had struggled with his conscience, making excuses for himself, but now that the moment had arrived he felt only shame. "We've spent a lot of time together lately," he said in a voice so low it was almost a whisper. "I've become fond of you, Sarah. I care about you."

"I care about you, too, Ned."

"No, you don't understand." He looked into Sarah's trusting eyes and he knew he could not go on with the charade. "This is hard for me," he murmured. "Please hear me out, Sarah, because I'm about to tell you the truth."

"The truth?"

"When I walked in here just now it was with the intention of asking you to marry me. Please don't say anything yet. Hear me out. I *am* fond of you, Sarah. I do care. That's a kind of love, I suppose, but not the kind of love a husband should feel for his wife. I knew all that and still I was going to propose."

"But—"

"Sarah, Mother wants us to marry. It was her idea. She wants to save me from myself and she wants to make Camerons of you and Lucy. . . . I don't know if she really meant to deceive you. It's possible she thought you would fall in love with me. You didn't, of course."

Sarah rose. She walked quickly to the windows, staring out at Fifth Avenue. "You agreed to her plan, Ned?" she asked.

"Yes."

"Why?"

"Money," Ned replied. "Mother controls all my money. My trust fund, my salary, everything. I don't come into my trust until my fortieth birthday. Until then, she has absolute control."

"I see." Sarah turned slightly, her hands clutching the sill. "That explains your part in this, but not mine. Why was Aunt Elizabeth so sure I would agree?"

"She felt you would do whatever was in Lucy's best interests."

Now Sarah's hand flew to her throat, for she sensed a threat, a danger she could not quite define. "I have so little time with Lucy," she said, as if to herself. "It's Aunt Elizabeth's doing. She controls the nursery, too."

"Mother is accustomed to having her way."

"Like the Averills," Sarah murmured. Yes, she thought, just like the Averills. They had me sent to America because that was the way they wanted things. They would have done anything to get their way. And Aunt Elizabeth will do anything to get her way. She'll use Lucy, if necessary. Oh God, *Lucy*. "I'm scared, Ned."

He went to her then, taking her head on his shoulder. "I'm so sorry about all of this," he said. "I don't know what to do. I should have refused in the very beginning but . . . I can't help being what I am, Sarah. I'm weak, too weak to refuse Mother's bargain, too weak to see it through as planned. I had to tell you the truth."

"I'm glad you did. It was a warning."

"A warning?"

"Are you still willing to marry me, Ned?"

"Yes, certainly," he said, surprise clear in his dark eyes. "But I want you to understand . . . Sarah, married or not, I won't change. I'll have my—my

110

diversions, my amusements. . . . I'm trying to explain that I won't be a good husband. I'll embarrass you at times. I'll—"

"But are you still willing?"

"Yes, of course. You're a lovely girl, Sarah. Of course I'm willing."

"Then I think we must talk."

Chapter Six

It was early evening when Sarah and Ned joined Elizabeth in her sitting room. "I won't pretend surprise at this visit," she said, pouring sherry into thin crystal glasses. "I've been expecting an announcement from the two of you. A most welcome announcement, may I add."

"We certainly wouldn't want to disappoint you, Mother."

Elizabeth settled herself on an ivory silk divan and she smiled. "But you do want to keep me in suspense," she said. "Very well, I'll play your little game. Shall we talk about the weather?"

"Not at all," Ned replied. "There's no need for games. Sarah has accepted my proposal and we're to be married on New Year's Day."

"New Year's? How charming! I don't believe there has ever been a New Year's wedding in the family." Elizabeth's gaze moved to Sarah. "You will make a beautiful bride, my dear," she said. "Naturally, it will be a small wedding, as befits a widow. But it will be quite special nonetheless. I'll see to that. You must leave all the details to me. And you must start thinking what you would like for a wedding present."

Sarah nodded, meeting Elizabeth's gaze. She felt a great surge of anger and she took a breath, trying to calm the wild beating of her heart. She knew she had to speak now or lose the advantage of this moment. "There *is* a present I want, Aunt Elizabeth," she said, the words coming in a rush. "I want more time with Lucy. I want to discharge Nurse Porter and hire the new nurse myself. That's the best present you could give me. It's the only present I want."

"Why, Sarah, I had no idea you found Nurse Porter so trying. Of course she will be discharged, if that is your wish. As for the new nurse, I will see to it. You have no experience in these things, you see."

"If I'm to be Ned's wife, I ought to have more responsibility. I ought to be able to choose a nurse for my—our daughter."

She's learning how to bargain, thought Elizabeth, her smile slipping for an instant. "You seem determined, my dear."

Sarah took another breath. "If I'm to be Ned's wife, I won't be treated like a child," she replied.

"I admire your spirit. Nurse Porter will be discharged and you may hire the new nurse. The matter is settled."

"Thank you, Aunt Elizabeth." Some of the tension left Sarah's face. She glanced at Ned and impulsively stretched her hand to his. It was a friendly gesture, nothing more, yet the touch of his hand reminded her that soon she would indeed be his wife. She forced the thought from her mind, turning again to Elizabeth. "There'll be different rules in the nursery now," she said. "I mean, with a new nurse there'll be new rules."

"I quite understand, my dear."

"And you won't object?"

"I may disapprove but I won't object. Does that satisfy you, Sarah? I do want to put your fears to rest.

113

I'm afraid you're overly concerned about little Lucy. She's had the best of care. Dr. Westerman assures me she's a fine, healthy girl. You mustn't worry so."

"I wouldn't have to worry if Dr. Westerman brought his reports to me."

"There's a bit of the bulldog in you, isn't there?" Elizabeth laughed. "Please consider all these matters settled. And now I think we've had enough talk of doctors and nurses and nurseries. We have a wedding to plan, my dear!"

Sarah's engagement was formally announced in the *Times*. She sent a clipping to John and Hilda, though her accompanying letter was brief, almost evasive, for she could not put her chaotic thoughts into words. With each day the fact of her impending marriage became more real; with each day she grew more nervous. She was fond of Ned, but the thought of marriage to him, to any man, brought fear to her heart. That fear invaded her dreams, as night after night she saw Sir Roger's shadowy figure drawing closer, felt his hands tearing at her body. They're only dreams, she told herself in consolation, only dreams.

Engagement presents began arriving at the Cameron house, the cards bearing the names of New York's oldest families. All the social rituals of engagement began, too—parties, dinners, a gala supper dance given by Patrick and Evelyn. Sarah was the reluctant center of attention at these affairs. She felt as if she were on display and there was truth in that notion, for she was being introduced to Society. Her appearance was scrutinized, as well as her conversation and her manner. Subtle questions were asked and answered. Judgments were made. In the end they were favorable judgments, the most imperious of dowagers won over by her youthful loveliness and her modest ways.

"You're a triumph," Janet declared one day in December. She wriggled out of her shoes, dropping down on the bed. "You've been accepted, Sarah. I know you couldn't care less, but still it's a feather in your cap. . . . Are you exhausted? I am. There are *so* many details to a wedding . . . even a small wedding."

"A hundred guests isn't a small wedding, not to me."

"Oh, you should see some of these society extravaganzas," Janet laughed. "Six hundred guests, two orchestras, an army of waiters. I'm glad we don't have to go through all that. Six hundred thank-you notes! Can you imagine? Just the thought of it makes me tired."

Sarah finished reading the lists Janet had prepared. She put them aside, sitting in the rocker. "How do you know so much about society?" she asked. "How did you learn? I've tried, for Ned's sake, but I'm always getting the families mixed up. The Vanderbilts are a good example. There are at least five Mrs. Vanderbilts, and I can never remember which is which. . . . Then there are all the customs, the rules. It's more complicated than royalty."

"You do very well."

"But how did you learn?"

Janet hesitated before replying. She looked at Sarah and a moment later looked away. "I was born to it," she said finally. "I lived that life until I was fifteen. That's when my father lost all his money. He died the next year, and Mother and I were left with nothing. There were debts. . . ."

"I'm sorry, Janet. I didn't mean to pry."

"No, it's all right. I don't usually talk about the past, but I will now because I have a reason. . . . You see, those years were very difficult. We moved around a lot, one dreadful flat after another. Our friends weren't our friends anymore. Mother gave music lessons just to keep food on the table. It was a frightening time for us." Janet turned back to Sarah. "And that's why I'm so happy you're marrying Ned," she said. "I realize you don't love him. He isn't your choice, Sarah, but he'll be your *protection*. The Cameron name and the Cameron money will save you from all the terrible things that can happen to people. You and Lucy. Remember that when you're having doubts."

"I don't care about the money, Janet."

"I didn't either, until it was gone. The Camerons are much wiser about money than my father was. What happened to him won't happen to them. You'll be *safe*. You don't know how lucky you are. And to have Mrs. Cameron on your side—"

"On my side?"

"It may not always seem that way, but it's true. Don't you understand, Sarah? You've solved her problems with Ned. Marrying you means he won't disgrace the family by marrying one of his—his unsuitable lady friends. That's worth a great deal to Mrs. Cameron."

"Is it worth all the scheming? Would the sky fall in if Ned married an *unsuitable* woman?"

"Now I've made you angry. I'm sorry."

"It's not you, Janet. It's people meddling in other people's lives, interfering in other people's lives. That's what Aunt Elizabeth does. She pushes us here and there as if we were pieces on a chessboard. I've seen it before," Sarah added, her eyes flashing. "The Averills were the same way. They were generous with their money and that was supposed to make everything else all right. Well, it didn't, did it?"

Janet sat up. She found her shoes and hurried across the room to Sarah. "Don't be upset," she said. "It's my fault for starting this conversation in the first place. I'm sorry. I thought it would help you understand. . . . But I was wrong. I've opened old wounds and I'm sorry."

"The wounds aren't so old, Janet. Every time I look at Lucy I wonder if I'll see Sir Roger—"

"Sarah, don't."

"I love Lucy more than anything on earth but I can't forget what happened. I can't."

"You will," Janet said anxiously, bending over Sarah. "I promise you will, if you don't have idiots like me babbling on and on. . . . You've been nervous lately. I thought I could help."

"You're a good friend, Janet. My only friend." Sarah touched her handkerchief to her welling eyes. "I'm fine now," she sniffled. "I've done all my complaining and I'm fine. I do understand what you were trying to tell me. Mama often said it was money that made the world go round. 'Don't believe what you read in poems or hear in Sunday sermons,' she'd say. Mama was the practical one in the family."

"Are you feeling better, Sarah? Are you sure?"

"Quite sure."

"In that case . . . I'm almost afraid to ask, but are you up to looking through your trousseau? I really hate to ask, especially now. It's just that we've put it off and there isn't much time to alter whatever may need altering. You know the fuss Mrs. Spence makes when she has to hurry."

"Yes." Sarah glanced about the room, looking at the many boxes that had arrived from Paris. "Yes, I suppose."

117

"Shall we start with the large boxes or the small boxes?"

"Let's just have it over with," Sarah replied. She stood, going to a stack of boxes that reached halfway to the ceiling. "We might as well."

The boxes were thrown open, and from their tissue paper folds came clouds of lingerie—long satin nightgowns and matching robes in soft shades of ivory and blue and pink, silken underclothes trimmed with hand-sewn lace, flowing peignoirs with deep ruffled hems. The largest boxes held traveling suits of rich wool, daytime dresses of patterned silk, evening dresses shimmering with silver and jet. There were shoes and handbags and gloves and more hats than Sarah could count. "And here's a parasol," Janet laughed, twirling it around.

"That's for Palm Beach. Aunt Elizabeth says I mustn't ruin my skin."

"You'll certainly be the best dressed woman in Palm Beach."

"They're lovely things," Sarah agreed. "I hope I don't look silly wearing them."

"Silly! What an idea!"

"Well, I'm still not used to all this luxury." Now Sarah laughed, trailing her hand across a frothy lace robe. "Sometimes I feel like Cinderella."

"Does that make me the fairy godmother?" Elizabeth asked. "Or the wicked stepmother?"

A little of both, thought Sarah to herself. She turned, smiling brightly. "Thank you for my trousseau, Aunt Elizabeth," she said. "It's beautiful."

"I'm pleased you like it my dear. Any problems, Janet?"

"A few tucks perhaps. And one skirt has to be shortened. That's all."

"Excellent. If you will wait for me in my study, Janet, I will be right along." Elizabeth removed a pile of gloves from a chair and sat down. "Come here, Sarah," she said. "I have a present for you. Consider it an early wedding present."

"But you've given me so much already."

"This is rather special, as you shall see." Elizabeth opened a Cartier box, revealing a long strand of pearls clasped with diamonds. "Aren't they exquisite? Let me help you put them on."

Sarah bent her head. "Thank you, Aunt Elizabeth. I—I hardly know what to say. . . . First a diamond engagement ring as big as the moon, and now this. It's too much, really it is."

"Nonsense," Elizabeth replied. "All the Cameron women have pearls."

Sarah and Ned were married on New Year's Day of 1923. It was, by Elizabeth's standards, a simple wedding, though the pews at St. James were resplendent with long white satin bows, and the altar adorned with roses and columbine and lilies of the valley. Sarah walked down the carpeted aisle on the arm of an elderly Cameron uncle. She wore a stylish dress of ivory silk crepe, draped at the shoulder and embroidered with a spray of seed pearls. The Cartier pearls were clasped about her slender throat, and atop her head was a small, delicate confection of silk and tulle. She was, everyone agreed, a beautiful bride, properly flustered and nervous.

Ned alone understood her nervousness, for it equalled his own. He watched her approach the altar rail and he felt a sudden impulse to run, to flee the church, the wedding, and most of all his mother. "Steady," Patrick whispered. "It's the bride who's supposed to faint, not the groom." *Groom*, thought Ned in rising panic; my God, I'm actually getting married.

The ceremony was brief, the responses of both the bride and groom almost inaudible. When the Reverend Dr. Withers pronounced them husband and wife they looked startled, and it was a moment before Sarah lifted her head for the traditional kiss. After the ceremony the newlyweds were showered with rice and rose petals. Newspaper photographers rushed forward, cameras held high. Janet, Sarah's lone bridesmaid, cleared a path to the waiting limousine. "Hurry," she said, "it's a stampede!"

There was a reception at the Cameron house, white-gloved waiters serving champagne and caviar and dainty finger sandwiches, a string quartet playing softly in the background. The wedding cake was a wondrous creation, its four tiers decorated with vanilla cream flowers and two spun sugar doves. Sarah did everything that was expected of her, though she did so as if in a daze. Only when Nurse Hill brought Lucy into the room did her eyes light up, and she smiled. "Lucy," she cried, sweeping the child into her arms. "Happy birthday, darling. We'll pretend this party is for you, shall we? Would you like that?" Lucy nodded her curly platinum head and Sarah laughed. "That's my girl," she said. "You look so pretty in your little velvet dress."

"She does indeed." Elizabeth's gaze moved from Lucy to Sarah. "You don't mind if I show off my grandchild?" she asked. "You have your guests to keep you busy, after all."

"No, I don't mind." Sarah put Lucy down, watching her toddle off between Elizabeth and Nurse Hill. She followed the child's progress until yet another group of guests gathered around, offering best wishes. "Thank you," she said for at least the hundredth time. "Yes, I'm very happy."

It was evening when Sarah and Ned boarded the train for Palm Beach. They had a light supper in the dining car and then gratefully went in different directions, Sarah to their compartment, Ned to the club car, where he remained through the night playing poker with a Florida banker and two traveling salesmen from Brooklyn. He returned at dawn, tiptoeing past his sleeping wife. This was to be the pattern of their train trip. They were solicitous of each other and polite in a jittery kind of way, but except for meals, they avoided each other's company. They did not speak the thoughts on their minds, the questions, nor did they confide their doubts. No one suspected they were honeymooners, not even the porter who was said to have an unerring eye.

A limousine met Sarah and Ned in Palm Beach. They were whisked off to The Breakers, a fashionable resort hotel known for its charm and for the absolute discretion of its staff. The suite to which they were shown was huge and elegantly decorated. In the bedrooms a single long-stemmed rose had been placed upon each silken pillow, and the balcony doors opened to breathtaking ocean views. "Well," Ned said when the bellmen had gone, "here we are."

"Yes."

"It's almost time for dinner. Do you feel like dressing, Sarah, or shall I have a tray sent up?"

"Perhaps a tray . . ."

"I'd prefer a tray, too. The food is marvelous, by the way. Have a look at the menu while I check the luggage."

"Yes, all right."

They dined on the moonlit balcony, the ocean rushing and rippling below. The food was indeed

121

marvelous, but they scarcely tasted it. Their conversation was strained, for neither of them knew how the evening would end. Ned lingered over his brandy—hundred-year-old brandy he had brought from home. Sarah stared at the sky. She was so quiet, so still, she did not seem to breathe. It was after ten when the waiter removed the dishes, after eleven when they left the table. "I think I'll have a quick walk round the grounds," Ned said, breaking the uncomfortable silence. "I won't be long. Is there anything you'd like sent up?"

"Everything is already here, isn't it? You go on and enjoy your walk. I'm fine."

Sarah had no idea how long he was gone. She bathed and brushed her hair, then wrote a postal card to John and Hilda. She walked a circle about the room, carefully avoiding the bed. She stretched out on the chaise, rising the next instant. She tried the chair, the small rocker. With a resigned sigh, she pulled the bedcovers back and slipped between the scented sheets. She was tired but knew she would not sleep. My honeymoon, she thought over and over again, fear gripping her heart.

Ned hesitated in the doorway of the bedroom. He watched his young wife pretending to read a book and he smiled, for he understood her apprehensions all too well. "Sarah," he called softly, "am I disturbing you?"

The book dropped from her hands. She looked up, her eyes widening when she saw that Ned was in his dressing gown. "I—I didn't hear you come in," she said.

"What are you reading?"

"A murder mystery."

Ned crossed the room. He sat on the bed beside Sarah and took her hand. "Cold," he remarked. "You

122

don't have to be afraid of me, you know. I won't hurt you."

"I know."

"Do you?" He stroked her bare arm, then leaned nearer, kissing her neck, her lips. Now his hands moved to her shoulders, pushing at the thin satin straps of her nightgown. "You're so beautiful," he murmured, caressing her full breasts, "so beautiful." He said nothing more, for he felt her sudden and violent shudder. Ned drew away, and in her eyes he saw a terrible fear. She seemed to be staring past him, staring at some horror that was real only to her. She was pale, shivering; tears streaked her cheeks. Alarmed, he pulled the blanket around her, covering her nakedness. "Sarah," he said. "*Sarah*, it's all right."

She heard his voice. She blinked, and the shadowy, imagined figure of Sir Roger faded. "Ned . . . Oh, Ned, I'm sorry."

"It's all right, Sarah. I understand."

"But you don't. You couldn't. . . . When you touched me, I was so scared. I was remembering. . . . It wasn't your fault, Ned. You must believe that. It was the memory—"

"I understand. There's no need to explain. Strange as it may sound, I'm relieved. Perhaps now we can go back to being friends. We can look each other in the eye again. We can laugh again. We can have the fun we used to have before the Reverend Withers spoiled everything." Ned smiled, entwining Sarah's fingers in his. "We'll be pals," he said. "That's not a bad thing to be. . . . Sarah, the last few days have been the worst of my life. I've been around, as the expression goes, but in this case I didn't know what I was supposed to do, what was expected of me. Well, we've cleared the air and I'm glad. Aren't you?"

"Yes . . . But the—the marriage bed is my duty."

"If by the marriage bed you mean sex, don't let anyone tell you sex is a duty. It isn't. It's really quite wonderful . . . with the right person. You'll meet the right man someday and all your fears will be forgotten."

"The right man?" Sarah asked, confused. "For me? Ned, we're *married*."

"As far as the world is concerned, we're married. As far as we're concerned, we have an arrangement. That means we'll go our separate ways. I would have in any case, Sarah . . . even if tonight had been sheer bliss. There are a lot of women in my life and that won't change. I won't change. So while I'm going my own way, you're certainly entitled to go yours. We'll be very discreet, of course. Front-page scandals aren't to Mother's taste. . . . You need love, dear heart," Ned added with a laugh, "and I hope you find it."

"I have Lucy. That's enough."

"A noble thought, but wrong . . . as you shall discover for yourself." Ned leaned over, lightly kissing Sarah's cheek. "You *are* beautiful," he said. "Luscious, in fact. Given different circumstances it would be my great pleasure to make love to you. As it is, someone else will have that pleasure."

"Ned!"

"You'll see." He stood, tugging at the belt of his dressing gown. "You won't mind if I go out for a bit?" he asked. "I have friends here and the night is young."

"Have a good time. You've earned it."

"We both have. You'll be all right, Sarah?"

"Oh, yes. I'm fine now, thanks to you."

"Sleep well. I'll be back in time for breakfast, and then I'll show you around town. We're going to get some fun out of our trip after all. I know everything

124

there is to know about fun."

"So I've read in Cholly Knickerbocker." Sarah watched him go. She heard the other bedroom door open, heard the click of a telephone before the door closed. "My honeymoon," she murmured, smiling now.

And despite the unusual circumstances, it was a wonderful honeymoon for both Sarah and Ned. They went sailing and swimming; they sunned themselves on the dazzling beach. Sarah had her first tennis lesson, enjoying it so much that she played every day while Ned went off to the polo matches or to play golf. They dined by candlelight and danced under the stars. Ned disappeared for hours each night but he returned bright and early each morning, and Sarah was always glad to see him. They were indeed friends again, friends who laughed and teased and shared private jokes. Their marriage, such as it was, had begun.

The Camerons arrived back in New York tanned and relaxed. To no one's surprise, Elizabeth was waiting for them in her study. "My dears," she said, her smile serene, her gaze as cool, as shrewd as ever, "how nice to have you home. Three weeks can seem quite a long time."

"Yes," Sarah agreed. "I'm anxious to see Lucy. Is she all right?"

"She's splendid. Having her nap just now. She had a visitor this morning, Amanda Melvile's grandson Jonathan. He's almost exactly little Lucy's age."

"Matchmaking again," Ned whispered to Sarah.

"What's that?" Elizabeth asked.

"Nothing, Mother. We appreciate the tea and the special cakes, but it's been a long trip and we're tired.

Besides, Sarah wants to see Lucy. Can't we tell you about our trip at dinner?"

"Certainly, if you prefer. But there are some papers that need your attention." Elizabeth rose, going to her desk. "Lucy's adoption papers," she explained. "After you sign them, my attorneys will do the rest. . . . Are you ready to be a father, Ned?"

"My fondest wish come true. Please don't glower at me, Mother. Sarah knows I was only joking. I think Lucy is a very nice child." Ned lighted a cigarette. "I'll do my best for her," he said.

"You may begin by signing these papers. You and Sarah, of course."

They joined Elizabeth at the desk. Sarah signed first, relieved that now her child would have a legal father, that now Elizabeth would never have custody. She gave the gold pen to Ned and he quickly signed his name. "Is there anything else, Mother? If there isn't, we'd like to go upstairs."

"I hope you find your rooms comfortable. They've been redone."

"Redone? Mother, for heaven's sake—"

"Not your bedroom, Ned," Elizabeth said. "Your bedroom is as it was. Don't get excited. I had the sitting room and the other bedroom redone. There was altogether too much wood and leather. It looked like a men's club. You can't expect Sarah to live in a men's club.

"We'd thought about taking an apartment," Sarah began. "At least we've talked about it."

"What a perfectly ridiculous idea! You have this house and its servants at your disposal, my dear. You have everything anyone could want right here."

"Except privacy," Ned snorted.

"Including privacy. The servants in this house don't snoop and they don't gossip. Can you say the

126

same for any servants you might hire?"

"No, I suppose not."

"Then the matter is settled."

Ned looked at Sarah. He shrugged. "Very well, Mother," he said wearily. "But can we *please* go upstairs now?"

"By all means . . . Sarah, there is just one thing more. Nurse Hill has been discharged. A disagreement in the nursery, you see. Nurse Benton has taken her place."

Angry color rushed to Sarah's face. "You discharged the nurse *I* hired?" she cried. "How could you? You gave me your word."

"There was rather a nasty disagreement, my dear. I'm afraid I had no choice."

"I'm afraid I have no choice either. Your new nurse will be given notice. I'll do my own hiring and firing from now on."

"I'm just not sure that's wise."

Sarah's eyes blazed. "Wise or not, that's the way it will be, Elizabeth."

"My dear, wouldn't you like to call me Mother?"

"No," Sarah snapped, marching from the room.

The second battle of the nurses began. Sarah won that battle, hiring a sensible Englishwoman named Marple, though as time passed, she was to lose more than she won. Ned was often in Europe during the first three years of their marriage, and Sarah was left to face Elizabeth alone. They argued constantly, about the proper clothes for Lucy, the proper toys, the proper friends. The little girls Lucy met on her outings and brought home were not welcomed by Elizabeth. . . . "Not our sort," that phrase dismissing one little girl because she was the daughter of shopkeepers, another because she was the daughter of Irish immigrants, yet another because she was

127

Jewish. Sarah fought, but to no avail. Elizabeth, her smile firmly in place, her cool gaze seeing everything, would not be swayed.

Sarah's mood was grim as the decade of the 1920s progressed, but the mood of her adopted country was jaunty, for it was a prosperous and optimistic time. There was a wonderful new invention called radio. There were new dances and new clubs where Le Jazz Hot was played. There were new voices, the magical new voices of F. Scott Fitzgerald and Ernest Hemingway. In New York, the Barrymores were together on Broadway, not far from where Mr. Ziegfeld's *Follies* girls pranced the stage in sumptuous costumes and towering plumed head-dresses. In Hollywood, the talking picture was about to be born. Everywhere the grisly doings of gangsters named Bugsy and Legs and Big Al mesmerized a nation. Americans, their minds and attitudes broadened, were having fun at last.

For Ned it was a happy era. Free now of all constraints save discretion, he did exactly as he pleased. During brief returns to New York he included Sarah in his plans, taking her to parties and balls and to the latest clubs. He brought her dresses from Paris, tweeds from London; he brought Lucy exquisite music boxes and porcelain dolls. He tried to spend time with the child, though in his visits he was more a playmate than a father. Kindred spirits, thought Sarah, knowing that Ned would never really grow up.

Sarah became an American citizen in 1926. She had long since abandoned any idea of going home to Aldcross, for her life was in New York and she knew that, too. It was not the life she had planned or even the life she would have chosen, but it was hers. She had Lucy. In Ned and Janet she had friends. She had acquaintances with whom she served on charity committees and whom she entertained at endless luncheons and teas. What she wanted was a job.

"I don't see the harm in having a job," she said to Elizabeth one humid summer day in 1927. "Lucy will be going to kindergarten in the fall. And when she comes home she'll have her music lessons and her drawing lessons. The way you've arranged things, she'll be busy morning, noon and night."

"You're exaggerating, Sarah."

"Not really. But that's a different argument. . . . I want a job. I want something to do."

"We've been all through this before, haven't we? Cameron women don't work at jobs. It's impossible."

"Well," Sarah replied, "I've been thinking about it and I've realized I don't need your permission. Ned has no objections to my working. He feels it's an excellent idea."

"He would."

"So you see there's nothing to stop me."

The two women stared at each other. A moment passed in silence, and then Elizabeth smiled. "I don't intend to stop you," she said. "This has been on your mind for rather a long time. Long enough to convince me it isn't a whim. And, as you pointed out, Lucy will soon be starting school. The only question, therefore, is what sort of job you should have. Now let me finish, my dear. In fact, there is only one sort of job you *can* have, and that is at the Galleries."

"The Galleries?"

"That would be acceptable, if not necessarily desirable. A woman in your position is expected to content herself with home and family and charity work. With cultural events perhaps. But I don't think

129

too many eyebrows would be raised if you took an interest in the Galleries."

"What if they were?" Sarah asked. "Why does it matter?"

"You must remember that your actions—and Ned's—reflect on little Lucy. If she's to have the future she deserves, you and Ned must both observe the rules. Of course, men are allowed more leeway in their lives. That has always been the case, my dear. It's a man's world."

"You seem to function very well in a man's world, Elizabeth."

"I do, indeed. But I am careful to observe the rules. You must be careful also."

Sarah sighed. She turned her wedding band around and around, staring down at the Aubusson carpet. "What would I do at the Galleries?" she wondered aloud. "I've learned something of art and antiques since I've been here, but I'm hardly an expert."

"Quite true," Elizabeth agreed. "And that's why I asked Patrick to join us today. He may have an idea or two."

Sarah looked up. "You asked Patrick? I don't understand. How did you know we were going to have this conversation? You couldn't have known."

"I know you, my dear," Elizabeth replied. "We've already settled our argument about Lucy's lessons, and so when you asked to see me I knew what the subject would be. It isn't exactly a new subject between us."

"No. No, but I still don't see what I could do at the Galleries."

"We'll leave that to Patrick." Elizabeth glanced at the Tiffany clock. "I asked him to come to lunch and he's never late. Your problem will soon be solved."

"I don't like to impose on Patrick."

"It's not an imposition, Sarah. It's a question of family. Family always comes first. . . . Why are you frowning, my dear?"

"I want a real job, Elizabeth, not a favor. A real job with—with a real salary."

"That's understood, although I can't imagine why you would be concerned about money. Surely you have everything you want."

"Yes, and I'm grateful. But everything's been *given* to me. I'd feel better if I were earning my way. Oh, I don't expect to earn enough for all this," Sarah added, her hand sweeping in a wide arc. "But whatever I earn, I won't feel so useless."

"You're much too hard on yourself."

Sarah did not reply, for at that moment a knock came at the study door. She turned, her eyes lighting up as she smiled. "Hello, Patrick," she said. "I'm sorry to take you away from work in the middle of the day."

"I'm not at all sorry. It's been a terrible morning. . . . Hello, Aunt Elizabeth. You must have read my mind. I was hoping someone would invite me to lunch."

"Problems?"

"Those French tapestries I told you about," Patrick replied. "They go on exhibit next week, and we're having a devil of a time mounting them. They're enormous. And of course they have to be handled with such care."

"Do sit down, Patrick. Sherry? Or would you prefer something stronger?"

"Nothing for me, thank you. I'll need a clear head when I return to the wars."

"Very sensible." And very like him, thought Elizabeth. She approved of her nephew, finding in

131

him all the qualities she had sought in her son, qualities of tact and restraint and conviction. She knew Patrick could not be bullied, could not be bought. He made his own decisions and he stood by them, offering explanations on the rare occasions when he was wrong, but never excuses. Elizabeth admired that quality above all, for it reminded her of her late husband Jasper. "I suggest we give a few moments to Sarah's dilemma," she said now, "and afterwards we will have a nice family lunch."

"It isn't really a dilemma, Aunt Elizabeth. At least I don't think it is. Sarah, you'll be most welcome at the Galleries. That is, if you're willing to start at the bottom, so to speak."

"Oh, yes, anywhere. I'll do the sweeping up if you like!"

Patrick shook his dark head, smiling. "That position is filled," he said. "The Cleary sisters do all our sweeping and tidying. There's another position, however. It might be just the thing."

"Tell me," Sarah cried, unable to contain her excitement.

"It would be as assistant to Miss Boyce. We prepare catalogues for all our major auctions, you see, and Miss Boyce puts the catalogues together. She's had a series of assistants in the past few years, none of them to her liking. She's a bit finicky, set in her ways. But she's been with us forever. I think you could learn quite a lot from her."

"It sounds grand, Patrick."

"It's serious work, detail work. We can't afford mistakes in our catalogues. And Miss Boyce doesn't tolerate mistakes."

"I understand."

Patrick turned back to Elizabeth. "I don't know if that's the kind of position you had in mind," he said.

"I'm afraid it's the only position we have that fits the circumstances."

"I had no position in mind," Elizabeth replied. "If Sarah wishes to be a clerk, I certainly won't interfere."

"Well, it's something more than a clerk, Aunt Elizabeth. There's a good deal more responsibility."

"If you say so, Patrick. Sarah, what do you say?"

"*Yes. Yes,* I want the job."

"Then the matter is settled. Congratulations, my dear. You seem to have joined the ranks of the gainfully employed."

Chapter Seven

Amelia Boyce was tall and very thin, her graying hair drawn into a tight bun at the back of her neck. No one knew how old she was, for she had never divulged her age, but she was correctly assumed to be in her fifties, an unmarried woman without family or friends. As might be expected, she was devoted to her work, jealously guarding what little authority she had. This jealousy extended to her assistants, all of whom she had disliked and all of whom she had fired. Her dislike of Sarah was intense.

"It's nothing you've done," Patrick explained. "Miss Boyce has found a home in the catalogue department and she resents intruders. That's how she sees her assistants, as intruders. I have no idea why. But the fact is there's too much work for one person to handle. She's here at all hours, trying to keep up. She prefers it that way. Unfortunately, our insurance company doesn't. Insurance companies don't like extra keys floating around. . . . In any event, Miss Boyce needs your help."

"She doesn't want it."

"Perhaps you can convince her otherwise, Sarah. She's always been able to manufacture excuses for

134

discharging her assistants. In your case, that's not possible. She knows she can't discharge a Cameron."

Patrick smiled suddenly, his wide gray eyes twinkling with light. "Of course that doesn't mean *I* can't," he said. "So do a good job and don't worry. If you have any problems, I'm right here."

"I should think you'd be traveling round the world."

"London twice a year. Ned gets all the traveling."

"Yes, we hardly ever see him."

Patrick was silent, staring at Sarah. "And I hardly ever see Evelyn," he said after several moments. "That puts us in the same boat, doesn't it?"

Something about those words caught Sarah's attention, for she had often thought that Patrick's marriage left much to be desired. She knew that Evelyn's life revolved around clothes and jewels and fashionable parties, interests that Patrick did not share. She knew, too, that when Evelyn was pictured in the society pages, it was usually on the arm of Tommy Trent, an aged and epicene interior decorator. "Strange the way things turn out," she said, as if to herself.

"Strange indeed."

"Well, I'd best get back to work. I've taken enough of your time and my lunch hour is almost over. Miss Boyce will be looking for me."

Patrick rose, walking with Sarah to the door. "You mustn't worry about my time," he said, smiling again. "Come by whenever you like. Your visits brighten the day."

"Oh, it's kind of you, but I won't impose. I don't want special treatment after all. I have to prove myself, not only to Miss Boyce but to Elizabeth. She expects me to fail."

"Does she?"

"I won't, you know. I've made up my mind."

"Of course you won't. You haven't so far, and three weeks with Miss Boyce is a fair test."

Sarah laughed. "I'll bring her round to my side. I'm not sure just how, but I'll find a way. . . . I'm grateful to you, Patrick, for giving me the job and for giving me confidence." Impulsively, Sarah kissed his cheek. "You're my favorite Cameron," she said, flushing when she remembered Ned. "I mean—"

"I know what you mean."

Sarah turned, casting a last glance at Patrick as she hurried along the corridor. She passed the executive offices and then a warren of smaller offices before she reached her door. "I hope I'm not late, Miss Boyce," she said, sliding behind her desk. "I forgot to wear my watch today."

"No, Mrs. Cameron. It's precisely an hour."

"Won't you call me Sarah?"

"Thank you, but that wouldn't be proper. . . . And now I believe we both have work to do."

Sarah bent her head over a stack of inventory sheets, though from the corner of her eye she watched Miss Boyce. She saw the starched shirtwaist, the plain black skirt, the sensible flat-heeled shoes, and all at once she thought of Miss Sparrow. It occurred to her that the two women were very alike, that they had the same attitudes and probably the same fears. "Miss Boyce," she said slowly, "there's something I've wanted to explain. I—I want you to know I'm not after your job."

"I beg your pardon?"

."Not that I could do your job," Sarah added. "I wasn't suggesting I could. It's just that sometimes people misunderstand. When I was hired as the library assistant in Aldcross, the librarian thought I was after *her* job. The idea never crossed my mind,

Miss Boyce, but it made things difficult anyway."

"I see."

"I'm here to learn, Miss Boyce, that's all. If you aren't satisfied with my work, I hope you'll tell me. I hope you'll forget my name is Cameron."

"Forget?"

"I don't want special treatment," Sarah replied.

Miss Boyce's stony gaze appeared to soften a little, though her expression did not change. She studied Sarah, nodding almost imperceptibly. "Your work has been satisfactory," she conceded. "Beyond that, I can only say I will keep an open mind."

"Thank you, Miss Boyce." Sarah looked at her, risking a small smile. "You won't be sorry. I promise you won't be sorry."

Another autumn came, another New York social season. Against Elizabeth's wishes, Sarah excused herself from innumerable luncheons and teas and committee meetings, dividing her time between Lucy and the Galleries. When Ned was home he escorted her to the theater and to noisy, smoky clubs, but he was not home often and most nights she was alone. "You're living the life of an old woman," Elizabeth scolded. Sarah denied it, though she could not deny the growing restlessness she felt. She began taking long, solitary walks, which led in no particular direction. Heads turned, for she was beautiful, beautifully and expensively dressed. She seemed unaware of the attention. She walked on, treading unfamiliar streets and neighborhoods as if in search of something lost.

It was during one of these walks that she glimpsed a mane of flame-colored hair, heard a shout of exuberant laughter. She turned. "Mary Margaret," she cried, running now. "Mary Margaret, it's me."

"And do I know you?" Mary Margaret asked when Sarah came to a breathless halt. "Wait, I think I do. I'll have it in a minute."

"Sarah Griffith . . . Sarah Griffith from the *Royal Star*."

"Sarah! Is it really you? I can't believe my eyes. How fine you look, like you fell into a pot o' gold. Did you win the sweepstakes?"

"I—I got married."

"Married, are you? So am I."

"Oh, Mary Margaret, it's wonderful to see you after all these years."

"What are you doing in Yorkville? No, never mind that now. We've too much catching up to do. I live right here," Mary Margaret said, pointing to a six-story tenement building. "Will you have tea with me and my brood? Have you the time?"

"All the time in the world. My husband's away and Lucy, my daughter, is busy with piano lessons. I won't be missed."

"Then follow me," Mary Margaret laughed. She shifted a bag of groceries to her other arm and turned toward the doorway. "It's three flights up," she explained. "I'm always telling myself it's good exercise, but when I'm struggling with groceries and Mike Junior and the twins, it's a torture."

"Three children?" Sarah asked.

"And unless lightning strikes, another on the way. That's what I get for all my fancy talk about making my fortune. It's babies I'm making, just like my ma before me."

Sarah kept pace with Mary Margaret as they climbed the stairs. She heard dogs barking and children crying and, from one of the flats, the angry sounds of an argument. The air was rank, a mixture

138

of cabbage and wet diapers and dwindling coal fires. The halls were dim, though she could see tile floors so grimy and stained they would never be clean again. "Have you lived here all along, Mary Margaret?"

"We lived with Mike's family in the beginning. When Mike Junior came, we moved here. Dear knows it's no palace, but there are worse places. And we're saving our pennies. We want to have a house someday. Nothing fancy, you understand. Just a nice little house we can call our own . . . Ah, here we are. Mind your step, Sarah. Mike Junior's always leaving his toys and things on the floor."

They entered into a small, spotless kitchen. Sarah glanced around at the battered coal stove, the ice box, the double sink with its rusting, exposed pipes. Open cupboards lined the wall above the sink. Cheerful yellow curtains draped the single window, almost hiding the fire escape beyond. In the center of the room was an old table and six rickety chairs. "It's so cozy," she said, not knowing what else to say. "It has the feeling of home."

"Not your home, I'll wager," Mary Margaret smiled. She put the groceries on the counter and then took a step forward. "Mike Junior," she called. "We have company, Mike Junior. Come show your handsome face. . . . Sit down, Sarah. Make yourself comfortable . . . as comfortable as you can in those chairs," she added with a laugh."

"Oh, they're fine." Sarah laughed, too, watching a sturdy fair-haired boy of four or five bound into the room. He wore a clean white shirt and mended knickers, the pockets stuffed with jacks; in his hands he held a scuffed rubber ball. "Well, who have we here?" she teased. "Would you be the famous Mike Junior?"

"Yes."

"Say a proper hello to Mrs.—Mrs.?"

"Cameron."

"Say a proper hello to Mrs. Cameron."

"Hello, Mrs. Cameron." The little boy ran to Mary Margaret, tugging at his long stockings as he went. "Can I go out and play now, Ma? Can I?"

"Did you take good care of your sisters?"

"They're sleeping. It's their nap. Can I go out now?"

"Go on. But take your heavy sweater. . . . And remember to stay close to the house," Mary Margaret cautioned. "Don't wander away and don't go into the street. Now give your poor old ma a kiss."

Sarah saw the easy affection between mother and child. She thought of Lucy, who had been taught to curtsy to her elders, to always say please and thank you, to behave, but who rarely held out her arms for a hug. "Mike Junior is charming," she said when the door banged shut. "Such a bright, happy smile."

"Ah, he has his father's smile. That's the smile that talked me into marriage." Mary Maragret filled the kettle and put it on the stove. "But it's your life I want to hear about," she said, sitting across from Sarah. "Remembering the way you were on the ship, and seeing you now . . . I still can't believe my eyes and that's the truth. I saw you walking by, you know. I thought you were some rich lady out slumming. I couldn't help laughing. Imagine that rich lady being my Sarah Griffith! Or Sarah Cameron, it is now. Tell me about your husband. Is he a millionaire?"

"Oh, I—I don't really . . . I mean, I'm not sure," Sarah stammered, color rising in her cheeks. "It's Ned's mother—my mother-in-law—who has all the money."

"I'm being nosy and I apologize. That's my worst

fault. Once I get started, I babble on and on. Mike says I'm going to wear out my tongue. I wouldn't be at all surprised."

"I don't blame you for being curious, Mary Margaret. I didn't expect my life to turn out this way, either. It just seemed to happen."

"Well, that's love. Comes along like a thunderbolt and there's nothing you can do about it. Nothing in this world . . . Tell me about your Ned while I fix our tea."

Sarah described Ned and Lucy and the Cameron family, though she avoided the subject of her marriage, for she knew Mary Margaret would not understand. She chose her words carefully, just as she did when writing to John and Hilda or when speaking to Patrick. Never once had she admitted that her marriage was a sham. It was her secret—hers and Ned's and Elizabeth's. "With Ned away so much and Lucy in school," she finished, "I took the job at the Galleries. I got off to a rough start, but things are better now. I suppose that's all there is to tell."

"Are you happy, Sarah?"

"Oh, yes," she replied, averting her eyes, "very happy."

"I'm glad. Ah, it must be nice for Lucy, having so many advantages."

"Too many advantages," Sarah said sharply. "My mother-in-law spoils her. We argue about it, but nothing changes. If I win one argument, I lose the next three."

"I know how that is," Mary Margaret sympathized, clearing the table. "I've had a few rows with my own mother-in-law. She's a nice woman and all, but she's forever telling me what's best for my children. It helps that we're not living in the same flat. Still, she's here for supper every Wednesday and we're at her place every Sunday. I guess there's no escaping the grannies."

"No."

"And where are you living? Is it near here?"

Sarah colored again, thinking of the Cameron mansion filled with treasures, with servants. Her glance went to the rusting pipes below the sink, and her blush deepened as she thought of faucets and drains plated in gold. "The house is on Fifth Avenue," she said softly. "I want you to come visit, Mary Margaret. You and your family. We mustn't lose touch again."

"The O'Connors on Fifth Avenue! Ah, it's not you I'm laughing at, Sarah. It's the idea of my brood trooping through your house. Mike Junior bouncing his ball on the fine carpets. And the twins pulling all the china off the tables. Five minutes in your house and there'd be a shambles. No, it's best we do our visiting here. It's safer."

"Lucy has a playroom. The children can't possibly do any damage in the playroom."

"Well, there's something else." Mary Margaret dried the teacups and returned them to the shelf. She looked back at Sarah. "My children will have to understand there's both rich and poor in this world," she said. "But they're too young now. They'd see all the things they don't have, can't have, and they'd wonder why. I'm thinking that's a bad idea."

"Yes, you may be right," Sarah reluctantly agreed.

"Mike works on a loading dock. He works hard, and his wages support us and his mother, too. I'm proud of him, Sarah, but we're not Fifth Avenue people. We'd be out of place." Mary Margaret glanced across the room. She smiled. "Here comes the rest of the brood," she said, pointing to two nearly identical little girls. "Here's Katie and Erin. Three years old last August." The girls ran to her. She bent down, enfolding them in her arms. "So you're awake, are you? It's about time. Say hello to Mrs. Cameron."

"Hello," they chorused.

"Hello there. Aren't you adorable!" Sarah exclaimed, seeing long reddish-blond hair and freckles and huge blue eyes. "How on earth do you tell them apart?"

"It was hard at first. Now I can see the differences. . . . Well, you've met the whole family except for Mike, and he'll be home soon. You have to stay for supper. I want to show you off to Mike."

"I appreciate the invitation, but I couldn't impose."

"There's no imposing in the O'Connor household, Sarah. We always have room for one more."

"I'll stay if you let me help."

"You can help the girls wash up while I get supper started. All right?"

"Perfect."

"Supper won't be anything fancy," Mary Margaret called after Sarah. "Just good, plain home cooking."

It was a typical O'Connor supper—leftover stew, homemade biscuits, chocolate pudding. The twins squabbled; Mike Junior spilled his milk and splattered pudding on his shirt. Mary Margaret was up and down at least a dozen times, tending to her children, her husband, her guest. Mike, a big, friendly Irishman, his napkin tucked under his chin, amiably related the happenings at work.

Sarah relished every moment. She felt the warmth, the closeness of family, and she knew there was more love in Mary Margaret's shabby kitchen than in the

143

whole Cameron mansion. How lucky they are, she thought, how very lucky.

The wine-colored days of autumn grew shorter; the air grew colder. Winter approached, and with it the Christmas season. Beribboned holly wreaths decorated windows and doors all over the city. Store displays sparkled with toys and dolls and shiny red sleds. There were more people rushing through the streets, there were more cars. There were more parties, including those at the Cameron house, where Elizabeth was hostess at two dinner parties, a supper dance, and a champagne buffet. It was said that she was in particularly good spirits, an observation that troubled Ned. "Mother has something up her sleeve," he remarked to Sarah on Christmas Eve. "I've been watching her. She's wearing a very pleased expression these days."

"Well, she keeps hinting about some surprise she has for us."

"I'd rather have a migraine than one of Mother's surprises."

Sarah lifted her gaze from the dressing table, staring at Ned's reflection in the mirror. He was thirty-two now, the boyish contours of his face beginning to settle into maturity. Late nights had not taken their toll on his looks, though there were times when his smile seemed weary, a trifle strained. "You and Elizabeth have been arguing again, haven't you?" she asked. "Is it Nola O'Rourke?"

"Mother found out I bought an apartment for Nola. That's another black mark against my name. Another stain on the family honor."

"Would you marry Nola? . . . I mean if you could?"

"No." Ned shook his sandy head, staring back at Sarah. "I'm quite happy with things as they are. . . . I wish you were happier."

"I'm all right."

"You're lonely."

"Everybody's lonely once in a while."

Ned stood, pacing Sarah's rose and ivory bedroom. His glance fell upon the dainty gilt chairs, the silk chaise, the hand-carved antique bed that was meant for two. "I'm afraid this marriage has been a poor bargain for you," he said. "I know Mother's made a few concessions in regard to Lucy, but I also know what you've sacrificed. It's a very poor bargain."

Sarah left the dressing table. She went to Ned and caught his hand in hers. "There was more to it than a few concessions," she replied. "My fear was that Elizabeth would take Lucy away from me. *Legally*. And she could have. I had no husband, no money of my own. I wasn't a citizen. I wasn't even of age. It was a helpless feeling, Ned. I'd met Elizabeth's friends—lawyers, judges, senators, the lot. I realized she could do anything she wanted. . . . If you look at it in that light, it wasn't a poor bargain at all."

"But what about you, Sarah? What about your life?"

"I have Lucy and I have my work."

"That would be fine if you were an old woman."

"Oh, you sound like Elizabeth," Sarah laughed. "You mustn't worry about me, Ned. I knew the way things would be. You warned me, remember? And you've been so sweet to me. Really, you have."

"I should be home more often."

"Why? I enjoy seeing you, of course, but your being home more often wouldn't change anything. Ned, we have to do too much pretending as it is. Let's not pretend to each other."

"Don't you get tired of pretending, Sarah? Doesn't it bother you? I'll bet you didn't tell your friend Mary Margaret about our arrangement."

"She wouldn't have understood. She and Mike are nice, ordinary people. Honest people. Our arrangement would have seemed—"

"Sordid?"

Sarah flinched, as if from a blow. "Don't," she said quietly. "We were forced into this, Ned, each for our own reasons. I know it's wrong. We both know, but there it is. I don't talk about it. I can't. How can I explain such an arrangement to people like the O'Connors? Or to my parents, for that matter? How can I explain Elizabeth?"

"There's no explanation for Mother. She just *is.*"

"Please let's drop the subject."

Ned saw Sarah's distress and silently he cursed himself for his thoughtlessness. "Yes," he said after a moment, "we'll talk about Christmas instead. There are some things under the tree," he added, taking a Cartier box from his pocket, "but I want you to have these now."

She opened the box, exclaiming over a pair of magnificent diamond and onyx clips. "Oh, they're wonderful! I'll wear them tonight. Help me put them on."

Deftly, Ned affixed the clips to the draped neckline of Sarah's black velvet gown. He twirled her around, smiling. "You're gorgeous, dear heart. A vision."

Together they walked to the door, crossing the hall to Lucy's room. "Darling," Sarah called softly, "are you awake?"

"I was waiting for you, Mummy. Is Santa Claus here yet?"

"Soon. You know he won't come till you're asleep." Sarah straightened the blankets, tucking them about the child. "Would you like a story?" she asked. "Perhaps a bit of *Alice in Wonderland*?"

Lucy shook her head from side to side. "Then Santa Claus won't come," she said. "Do you think he'll bring my tea set? I asked Santa for a real china tea set. Do you think he'll bring it?"

"I can almost guarantee he will," Ned replied. "And a few other things, too. But only if you've been a good girl. Let's see. . . . Have you stolen any elephants lately? No, you wouldn't do that. Have you painted stripes on the moon? No, you wouldn't do that, either. Have you bootlegged gin across the border?"

"Ned!"

Lucy clapped her hands together. "You're silly, Daddy," she giggled.

"He certainly is," Sarah smiled, perching at the edge of the bed. "Isn't it nice that Daddy makes us laugh? Aren't we lucky?"

"Grandmama says we're lucky because we're Camerons. Camerons are special."

Sarah looked at Ned. He shrugged and she turned back to Lucy. "We'll talk about that another time," she said. "Right now it's time for sleep. Here's your Raggedy Ann."

"Thank you, Mummy. Good night. Good night, Daddy."

"Sweet dreams, darling." Sarah switched off the lights, walking with Ned to the door. "'Camerons are special,'" she repeated as they entered the hall. "Elizabeth is at it again, putting absurd ideas into Lucy's head. . . . God, I wish we could move away from here. Away from *her*."

"Don't let it upset you, Sarah. Mother will never change. And I'm afraid we're stuck."

"I know."

Ned took his wife's arm, leading her to the stairs. "Come," he murmured. "It's Christmas Eve."

A charming old-fashioned kissing ball of mistletoe and boxwood hung over the arched entrance of the drawing room. Directly opposite was a towering Christmas tree, its graceful branches bedecked with porcelain angels and white velvet doves and garlands of twinkling crystal beads. Hundreds of presents were arrayed around the tree, many more in two polished antique sleighs. Poinsettia plants were massed on the windowsills. The chandelier blazed with light. "Quite a show," Sarah commented, surveying the festive scene. "And no expense spared." Her glance moved to the people gathered in the room—to Patrick ladling eggnog from a silver punch bowl, to a dozen Cameron cousins and in-laws, to Evelyn chatting gaily with Elizabeth. Her glance settled on Patrick and she smiled.

"Have you found a friendly face?" Ned asked.

"Patrick. He's over there in the corner."

"Hiding from Evelyn, no doubt. Well, shall we join the party? It's almost time for Mother to play Lady Bountiful. She's so good at it, one would think she invented Christmas. . . . Ah, here comes Raymond with the champagne. Won't you have a glass, Sarah?"

"I'm in an eggnog mood tonight."

"Run along then. If Uncle Langley gets to the punch bowl first, it will be drained dry."

Sarah made her way across the room, stopping to exchange brief holiday greetings with the cousins she had not seen in a year. "At last!" she laughed when finally she reached Patrick. "It's so difficult to get away from Cousin Amanda."

"And her monologues . . . You look lovely, Sarah, as always. I hope this is a happy Christmas for you."

"Oh, they're all the same. It was different in Aldcross . . . but that's another story."

"Eggnog?"

"Yes, thank you."

Patrick filled two cups, giving one to Sarah. "Now let's find a quiet spot," he said, taking her arm. "You can tell me about Aldcross. You never have, you know."

"I put all that behind me a long time ago . . . at least I tried. Sometimes there are memories. They sort of sneak into my mind."

"And your heart?"

"Sometimes."

Patrick gazed at Sarah, gently brushing a strand of honey hair from her brow. He was about to speak when he heard Elizabeth calling the guests to gather around the tree. "We should join the others," he said in a reluctant voice. "Aunt Elizabeth is ready to offer the ritual toast, followed by the ritual giving of presents."

"What were you going to say before she interrupted?"

"It doesn't matter. Let's join the others."

Sarah took her place beside Ned. She listened to the toasts and watched the servants help Elizabeth distribute the presents, but her thoughts remained with Patrick. Several times she looked in his direction, blushing when she caught his eye. "Strange," she murmured to herself, wondering at his odd expression, at her own odd behavior.

"Sarah?"

She blinked, as if awakening from a dream. "Elizabeth, you startled me."

"Did I?"

"I'm sorry. I—I wasn't paying attention."

"Perhaps you'll pay attention to this," Elizabeth

149

replied, placing a large box in Sarah's lap. "Merry Christmas, my dear."

"Thank you, Elizabeth. Shall I open it now?"

"We all open one present on Christmas Eve. You know that's our tradition." Sarah tore away the satin bows, the wrapping paper, her eyes widening as she saw a long cape of dark and luxurious sable. She held the soft fur to her cheek, speechless with surprise. "My I assume you like it?" Elizabeth asked.

"It's very beautiful . . . too beautiful. Really, it's too much."

"Nonsense. You must put it on, my dear. We're anxious to see how you look."

"Allow me," Ned said. He helped Sarah to her feet, draping the sables about her shoulders. "The verdict is in," he laughed. "You look sensational."

Evelyn flew to Sarah's side. She ran a practiced hand over the furs, nodding eager, unrestrained approval. "Perfectly matched skins," she exclaimed. "I'd just die for skins like that. . . . Patrick, come see."

"I have a clear view, Evelyn."

Sarah felt everyone's eyes on her. She sank back onto the couch, ducking her head. "You're very generous, Elizabeth," she said. "Thank you."

"I've saved the best present for last," Elizabeth declared. She went to the tree and snatched the cover from a large watercolor sketch. "This is Broadmoor," she explained. "Our new home . . . Our summer and weekend home," she added when the murmurs had quieted. "It has absolutely everything. Stables and tennis courts and a swimming pool. Aren't you pleased, Sarah? It will be ideal for little Lucy. She can have a pony!"

"Where is Broadmoor?" Sarah asked.

"In Old Westbury."

"And how far away is that?"

"Perhaps two hours by train. Of course, the trip is shorter by car. . . . I realize you won't be able to spend the whole summer with us, my dear. You have your work, after all. But you can come out on weekends."

Sarah's hands clenched in her lap. Quickly, she looked at Ned. He was pale, his mouth a taut line, but he said nothing and she knew he would not risk a protest. "Do you mean I'm to be separated from Lucy during the week?" she asked.

"You must remember that Lucy will be busy with riding lessons and swimming lessons. And with her friends. The Whitney children live quite near, at Wheatley Hills."

Once again Sarah felt everyone's eyes on her. She felt her own cold fury and took a breath, trying to compose herself. In the next moment she rose, sweeping wordlessly out of the room. Ned rose also. He heard Sarah's footsteps descending the stairs and he gestured to Patrick. "If Evelyn doesn't mind," he said, "I could use your help."

"I don't mind at all," Evelyn laughed. "Patrick is adept at soothing ruffled feathers."

"Please excuse us, Aunt Elizabeth."

"Certainly."

The two men left the room, hurrying down the stairs. "Sarah has every right to be angry," Patrick said as the front door slammed shut. "Just what is it you want me to do?"

"Go after her."

"I? Isn't that your—"

"There isn't a thing I can do for Sarah now. I could have spoken up to Mother. I didn't. Nor will I, not when it comes to her plans for Lucy. It's dangerous to cross Mother on that subject and I'm a coward . . . as Sarah knows all too well. Go after her, Patrick.

You're the only one of us she respects."

"Very well, if that's what you want. Where will you be?"

"At Nola's. Sarah has the telephone number."

"How cozy."

Ned shrugged. "I play the hand I'm dealt," he said. "Unfortunately, Mother owns all the cards."

Patrick did not reply. He opened the door, stepping into the sharp December cold. He saw Sarah two blocks away and quickened his pace. "Sarah, wait." He began to run, catching her just as she turned the corner. "Please, Sarah, no more of this," he said. "I'm not used to chasing women through dark streets."

"You shouldn't have left the party. I'm all right."

"I don't think so."

"Did Ned send you?"

"He feels badly that he didn't intervene with Elizabeth. He really does, Sarah. He feels guilty."

"Oh, it wouldn't have done any good anyway. Lucy will be six next week, and for six years Elizabeth's made all the decisions. It started at the very beginning. She decorated the nursery and chose the nurse. She chose Lucy's toys, even her friends. Then she chose the Brearley School, not to mention all those tutors in special subjects. . . . Now she's chosen Old Westbury, wherever that is."

Patrick found his handkerchief and dried Sarah's tears. "I know it's been hard for you," he said quietly. "There must be times when it seems impossible."

"Elizabeth chose Lucy's name. Did you know that? I couldn't even name my own daughter." Sarah's voice broke. She dropped her head to Patrick's shoulder, clinging to him. "And Elizabeth chose my husband," she sobbed.

"Come along, Sarah. Come with me."

"Where? I don't want to go back to that house."

"We're going to my apartment at the Galleries," Patrick replied. "There's a private entrance and a private elevator. No one will see you. You won't be disturbed."

"But you won't leave me?"

"No . . . No, I won't leave you."

Chapter Eight

"This used to be storage space," Patrick explained, unlocking the door to his apartment above the Galleries. "But I often work late, and so I had the space made into . . . well, you might call it a retreat. I can do my work in peace, without distractions." He stepped aside, allowing Sarah to enter. "You're the first person I've brought here."

"I'm honored."

"You should be."

Sarah looked around, seeing deep, comfortable armchairs and couches, dark oak wainscoting, and a Persian carpet in shades of red and gold. There was a splendid Hepplewhite desk, its red leather top burnished with age. Over the mantel was a portrait of two handsome little boys and their floppy-eared dog. "It's a wonderful retreat, Patrick," she said. "It's homey. I suppose that was the idea."

"Yes. Sit down, Sarah. I'll get you a brandy."

"I'm sorry to ruin your Christmas Eve."

"You haven't ruined anything. I certainly didn't mind leaving the party. It's been the same party every year for as long as I can remember."

"What about Evelyn?" Sarah asked.

"She's going to a late supper party at Tommy Trent's. Needless to say, I won't be missed. I won't see Evelyn until morning, when we give the boys their presents. Then we go to church. Then Evelyn's parents come for dinner. Tradition," Patrick sighed. "It's forbidden to break tradition." He brought Sarah a drink, sitting opposite her on the couch. "Take a sip," he urged. "You'll feel better."

Sarah raised the glass to her lips and drank. The brandy burned but it did not soothe, and she set the glass aside. "You're so different from the others," she said.

"Different?" Patrick smiled. "I grew up in a house very like Aunt Elizabeth's house. Like Ned, I went to Groton and Harvard, and like him, I belong to all the right clubs. I married the girl I was expected to marry. I joined the family business. . . . I should add that I did all those things quite willingly. There were no rebellions, great or small."

"Because you didn't feel the need."

"Because I accepted a way of life. And for the most part, I enjoy it. What I'm trying to say is that you mustn't see me in a special light."

"But I do, Patrick."

"Yes, I know."

Sarah was quiet, staring at the portrait of Patrick's sons. "Why does Elizabeth want to keep me apart from Lucy?" she asked after a while. "Why is Lucy so important to her?"

"It's not hard to understand. She's loved only two people in her whole life—Jasper and Charlotte. Now she's lost them both. She went to pieces after Jasper died. That was the only time I ever saw her composure slip. And then Charlotte, perhaps the final blow . . . But in Lucy she has another chance."

"For love or for power?"

"A little of both, I suspect," Patrick replied. "Aunt Elizabeth gets tremendous satisfaction from running other people's lives. Jasper gave her a free hand with the children, and with almost everyone and everything else. She's *accustomed* to running people's lives, Sarah."

"She doesn't run yours."

"No, we had that out years ago. We've had a kind of wary truce ever since." Patrick finished his brandy. He went to the small bar and poured another. "Would you like me to speak to her about Old Westbury?" he asked. "The house is a fact now, but that doesn't mean Lucy has to spend the entire summer there. Aunt Elizabeth might agree to a more flexible schedule."

"I can't ask you to fight my battles for me, Patrick."

"You can ask anything at all and it will be done."

Sarah was not sure how to respond. She looked at Patrick and saw that he was serious, and she smiled. Relief washed over her, for suddenly she felt safe, protected. She felt as if she had found a haven and the thought made her blush. "Thank you," she murmured, quickly looking away.

Patrick watched the play of emotions on Sarah's face. His own face was impassive, though his wide gray eyes smoldered with an ardor kept too long in check. He was conscious of the pounding of his heart, the stirrings of his body. I want her, he thought, admitting what he had tried so hard to deny. I've always wanted her. "Perhaps—perhaps I should put you in a taxi," he said, his voice hoarse. "Unless you'd like another brandy."

"I don't want another brandy. And I don't want to be put into a taxi. I want to stay here, with you."

"If you stay . . ."

"Yes? If I stay?"

"Sarah, this is very complicated. Being here alone with you is very complicated."

"Why?"

"Do you really want to know? Think before you answer, Sarah."

"I don't need to think." She lifted her eyes to Patrick, holding his gaze. "We feel something for each other," she said. "I—I told myself it was only friendship. That isn't true and there's no use pretending."

"Sarah—"

"I remember all the excuses I found to visit your office," she went on, the words tumbling in a rush. "I remember all the times I wore a new dress when you came to dinner. I remember how sad I always was when dinner was over and you went home. . . . Oh, Patrick, I wouldn't let myself see the truth but it was there from the start." Tears misted her eyes. She turned, staring straight ahead. "Now it's out in the open," she sniffled, "and I hope you're not sorry."

"Sorry!" Patrick cried, hurrying to her. "I'm in love with you. I think I've been in love with you since the moment we met. I couldn't say anything, I didn't have the right. I still don't have the right. I don't want you to be hurt."

"Do you want me to leave?"

"I'm talking about choices," Patrick replied slowly. "We can both leave here now. We can try to forget what's been said. If we don't . . . If we stay, our lives will never be the same again. . . . Because I want you, Sarah. I want to make love to you."

She felt her heart rising and swelling, as if it would burst her chest. Her legs weakened. A sweet tingling ran along her spine. "Patrick," she whispered, her arms twining about his neck. "Patrick."

Desire leapt within him. He seized her, covering her mouth with his. He kissed her lips, her hair, her throat. His hands grasped the buttons at the back of her gown, and as it slipped away, he kissed her breasts. "My darling," he murmured against her naked flesh. He swept her into his arms, carrying her to the bedroom. In the dim and shadowy half light he stripped away the rest of her clothing. His own clothes were thrown to the floor and then he was beside her on the bed, his hands seeking, urging, demanding. "I love you," he murmured again and again until she could not remember when he had begun speaking.

She felt no fear, no hesitation. Her awakened body moved against his, and for her there was nothing but this moment, this love. "Patrick," she cried out, stirred almost to frenzy by his touch. She clung to him, lost in a rapture that was the only truth. Again she cried his name and it was a cry of joy, for he was everything, he was all.

It was after four when Sarah arrived home. She let herself in and quietly tiptoed up the two flights of stairs to her rooms. A thin band of light showed beneath her door. She paused, taking a breath, then plunged inside. "I thought it might be you," she said. "I apologize for the late hour."

"And do you apologize for your behavior?" Elizabeth asked.

"My behavior?"

"Really, Sarah, to storm out of a party the way you did is quite unacceptable. I can't imagine what possessed you. Such a thing has never happened in this house. It must not happen again. You have a position to uphold."

"It was only a party, Elizabeth." Sarah removed

her cape, dropping it on the chaise. "But I'm sorry if I put you in a difficult position."

"We'll say no more about it, although I do hope Ned isn't proving himself a bad influence. His casual attitudes and unfortunate habits leave much to be desired."

Sarah glanced at Elizabeth, wondering if there was an accusation behind her words. "I—I don't understand," she said.

"You look radiant, my dear. I confess I was worried about you. You were gone a long time, after all. But I see I needn't have been concerned. The morning air must agree with you. It *is* morning, you know."

"Yes, I know." Sarah sat down. She sighed, clasping her hands in her lap. "Must we play games, Elizabeth?" she asked. "I had to get away from here and I did. I had to clear my head, to try to make sense of things. Where I was doesn't matter. I didn't expect to be gone so long. I certainly didn't mean to worry you. I suppose I lost track of time. It was thoughtless of me. I apologize. . . . That's really all there is to say."

"Is that all you wish to say?"

"Yes."

"Very well. You were a girl when you came to this house, Sarah. You're a woman now. You're entitled to your secrets."

"I have no secrets," she replied too quickly. She felt the color flare in her cheeks, angry color, for she knew she had fallen into Elizabeth's trap. "Think what you like," she sighed again. "I'm tired. I don't want to argue."

But the brief exchange had confirmed Elizabeth's suspicions. She settled her cool, dark eyes on Sarah. A moment passed, then two. "Tired or not, you must listen to me," she said finally. "Ned has a taste for outside diversions. He's a man, and as long as he is discreet, he's forgiven. Women are seldom forgiven. I'm told the world is changing. That may be. Still, women will always be held to a higher standard." She rose, going to the door. "A woman with a child," she added, "must be especially cautious about her reputation . . . or be willing to accept the consequences."

Sarah could not speak, for now she had no doubt that Elizabeth had guessed the truth. She heard the door close. Then she heard the silence, silence so loud she wanted to scream. She began to pace, but a moment later she flung herself on the bed. Elizabeth's words echoed in her mind, and with them came the first twinges of conscience. I love Patrick, she thought. That's my reason, that's my excuse. After all the years of loneliness. of being afraid, I won't let myself feel guilty. I won't.

"Sarah?" Ned poked his head inside the room. "May I visit a while?" he asked, smiling.

"Yes, of course."

"Don't worry about Mother. She's retired for what's left of the night."

"Good."

Ned sat down. He lighted a cigarette, watching Sarah through a haze of gray smoke. "It's been quite a Christmas Eve, hasn't it? I can hardly wait till New Year's. On second thought, I can. The Harringtons give very dull parties. . . . Are you all right, Sarah? You seem so far away."

"I'm fine."

"Yes," he said, drawing on his cigarette, "I believe you are. . . . You and Patrick, eh? Now don't start blushing and hiding your face. I'm happy for you, dear heart. And for—"

"My God, does everyone know where I spent the

160

evening? Will I see the story in tomorrow's *Times*?"

Ned laughed. "Mother has a sixth sense about these things," he replied. "I can't claim any special powers. I just always thought you and Patrick were inevitable. You're both nice people, Sarah. Oh, Patrick can be as ruthless as all the other Camerons, but only when he's pushed. That doesn't count. Like you, he has character. . . . And then you've both been shortchanged in your marriages."

"I'm not comfortable talking about this, Ned."

"Why not? We're friends, aren't we? Pals? I *am* happy for you, you know. It's terrible to go through life without love. It's wrong. That's something Mother doesn't understand. She'll try to wear you down. Pay no attention." Ned stood. He went to Sarah, lightly kissing the top of her head. "You may think I'm meddling," he said. "That isn't it at all. I want to save you my mistakes."

"You're sweet, Ned."

"I'm concerned. Mother will come at you with all her weapons, including threats. Be warned."

Sarah had cause to remember Ned's warning in the next weeks and months. Her meetings with Patrick were carefully planned, sheltered from prying eyes, but still Elizabeth always seemed to know. Sarah endured the wounding sarcasm, the oblique yet pointed remarks, the threats. She said little, though often she fled to her rooms in tears. Her sleep was increasingly troubled, her dreams haunted by Elizabeth's cool, dark gaze. She was distracted at work, guarded with Lucy. She grew quieter. She wrote fewer letters to John and Hilda, choosing her words too strictly. Once, lying in the warm circle of Patrick's arms, she began to weep.

Patrick felt her pain as if it were his own. He guessed the unspoken source, and early in 1929 he invited Elizabeth to lunch at the Plaza. "I'm so glad you could come," he said as she sat down. "I've been looking forward to seeing you," he added, resuming his seat.

"Oh? You could have seen me at home. I haven't barred my doors to you. Not yet."

Patrick smiled. "What an odd thing to say, Aunt Elizabeth."

"The appropriate thing, under the circumstances. I needn't define the circumstances for you."

"No, and we needn't spar with each other. This isn't a battle of wits. It shouldn't be a battle at all." The waiter appeared then. Patrick glanced at the menu, ordering a simple lunch of consommé, lamb chops, and endive salad. "I want to talk about Sarah," he said when the waiter had gone.

"I assumed as much. The last time we met privately it was to discuss Sarah's time with Lucy. What case are you pleading today?"

"Not pleading, asking. I'm asking you to stop reproaching Sarah. Please, Aunt Elizabeth, let me finish. Your criticisms aren't going to alter the situation. They merely add a burden of guilt. An unnecessary burden, in my opinion. Sarah and I aren't hurting anyone. Ned couldn't care less, nor could Evelyn. There's no betrayal involved. There's certainly no scandal. We aren't flaunting our relationship in public. Far from it. There's nothing to which you could object."

"I object to adultery," Elizabeth replied, returning Patrick's stare. "I object very much."

"Did you expect Sarah to lead the life of a nun? Is that what you want? I can't believe it is. You loved Uncle Jasper. You were devoted to him. Why must Sarah be denied love and devotion and sharing?"

"Sarah has a husband, Patrick."

"In name only."

"That is not my concern."

"The marriage was your concern, Aunt Elizabeth. It was your doing, even though you knew there was nothing more than fondness between Sarah and Ned."

"Many successful marriages begin in such a manner."

"This one begins *and* ends right there." Patrick fell silent as the soup was brought. He took up his spoon, then set it aside, frowning. "I'll tell you what I think," he said quietly. "I think your position has very little to do with adultery, with moral principles. I think you want to keep Sarah under your thumb because that keeps Lucy under your thumb. You're determined to make that child yours."

"Am I?" Elizabeth smiled. "You aren't usually so fanciful, Patrick."

"I'm never fanciful."

"Love does things to people, if love is the correct word. . . . Do try the consommé. It's excellent."

"What about Sarah, Aunt Elizabeth? Can we come to an understanding?"

"I'm sorry, but I won't encourage your liaison."

"You're deliberately missing the point. I'm not asking you to encourage anything. I'm asking you to be kinder to Sarah, stop treating her as if she were a fallen woman."

"Isn't she?"

Patrick's expression was unchanged, though anger flickered in the gray depths of his eyes. "You force me to play your game, Aunt Elizabeth," he said. "And a nasty game it is, too. But I came prepared. I have weapons of my own, you see."

"I'm afraid I don't see at all."

"You're quick to judge, Aunt Elizabeth. You're

quick to apply your high moral principles to Sarah and everyone else. It's a shame you didn't apply them to Jasper."

"Jasper!"

"Jasper Cameron, the soul of integrity and a pillar of his church . . . Or so the story goes. I know another side to the story. . . . I know how he ruined his daughter's life."

"What nonsense, Patrick. He loved Charlotte. He never—"

"I'm talking about Anne. Poor, forgotten Anne. Only I haven't forgotten. I remember when she returned from a holiday in Rome. She returned with a young Italian husband by the name of Mario Cirelli. He was an artist, I believe."

"He was a fortune hunter," Elizabeth replied coolly.

"Almost the very next day Jasper had the marriage annulled and Mario deported as an undesirable. Then he arranged for Anne's abortion."

Elizabeth was so still she might have been carved in stone. "Where did you hear such filthy lies?" she asked after a moment. "I demand to know."

"I heard the whole sad story—the truth—from Anne herself. She was afraid to confide in Ned. They were close in those years and she didn't know what he would do. Charlotte was ill. That left me. She told me how she begged Jasper not to annul the marriage. How she begged to keep her baby. Instead, Jasper dispatched them both. . . . Anne was never quite the same after that, was she, Aunt Elizabeth? She wasn't very interested in living. . . . I remember how frail she became. And when she came down with influenza the following year—"

"Stop it, Patrick. I won't listen to this."

"I think you will, Aunt Elizabeth. Because if you don't, others will. What a tasty bit of gossip for all your friends. I'm sure your friends remember Jasper's stern moral posture, even now. A word from him was enough to get people crossed off lists all over town. Wasn't it Mrs. Melvile who had to go crawling to Jasper after Mr. Melvile got publicly drunk at the Cotillion? I have a feeling she and the others would be *delighted* with this tasty morsel."

Elizabeth glanced about the elegant dining room, struggling to keep her composure. She started when the waiter brought the second course. She looked at the chops and, for a moment, thought she was going to be sick. "You wouldn't dare spread such lies," she said, though her voice wavered.

"Truths, Aunt Elizabeth . . . Mario Cirelli is indeed an artist, by the way. He enjoys a modest reputation in Europe. I've been thinking of sponsoring a showing for him here in New York."

"What do you want?"

"Stop tormenting Sarah," Patrick replied with an icy smile. "Stop interfering in her life."

"Very well. You've won this battle, Patrick. I wouldn't be too certain about the war."

"Think before you declare war, Aunt Elizabeth. I already have all the money I'll ever want. I have a wife who is utterly disinterested in my comings and goings. I like my work at the Galleries, but should you find some way to force me out, there are a hundred other things I could do. And besides, who else is there to run the business? Ned?" Patrick laughed, shaking his dark head. "No, the only way you can strike at me is through Sarah. But then Jasper will be exposed for the hypocritical bastard he was. . . . Do try the chops. They're excellent!"

Winter lingered in the city. A brief February thaw was followed by more snow, by high winds and cold, soaking rains that pounded windows and rooftops. The sun disappeared, swallowed whole by implacable black clouds. It was said that winter would never end, but in May the skies cleared at last and the air became sweet. Mufflers and boots and sweaters were packed away for another year. Parks and playgrounds bloomed with children, their shouts of laughter carrying on the breeze.

It was a happy time for Sarah, not least because Lucy's school vacation had begun. "I have a wonderful week planned for us," she said one warm day in June. "And it starts now. Do you know where we're going? Coney Island! It was Uncle Patrick's idea. He's bringing Josh and we're all going together. You'll love Coney Island."

"Why, Mummy?"

"It's fun. There are rides and amusements. There are stands where they spin pink cotton candy on a stick. Won't that be fun, darling?"

"Grandmama says Coney Island isn't our sort of place."

"Grandmama has never been there." Sarah gazed at Lucy. She was a pretty child, seven years old and tall for her age. Her curly hair was more golden than blond; her eyes, like Sir Roger's, were deep green. Sarah knew that she was spoiled, though not as spoiled as some of her friends. "I'm sure you'll have a very good time, darling, our sort of place or not. Now come along. Uncle Patrick will be waiting outside." She bent, straightening the ribbons on Lucy's pinafore. "Off we go," she said.

Patrick's car, a sporty, low-slung Pierce-Arrow, was parked at the curb. He sat behind the wheel, his son Josh at his side. "Here they are, Dad," Josh said.

Patrick opened the door. He caught Lucy up in his arms, smiling at Sarah. "All ready?"

166

"Ready."

"Josh, we'll put you in the back seat with Lucy."

"Okay, Dad." Josh, slender and dark and twelve years old, vaulted himself to the back of the car. "There's room," he said when Lucy snatched her skirts away from his gangly legs. "There's lots of room. Don't be a pain."

"Your manners, Josh," Patrick warned.

"Yes, sir."

The car pulled out, merging into the flow of Fifth Avenue traffic. Sarah looked at Patrick, studying his handsome profile, then lifted her face to the sun. *Patrick and Lucy and I all together on a beautiful day,* she thought, feeling a great contentment, a great joy.

"This is nice, isn't it?" Patrick asked, as if reading her mind. "We ought to play hooky more often."

"Do you suppose the Galleries could get along without you?"

"There are times I don't care. Times like now. Coney Island here we come!"

Coney Island was a six-mile stretch of beach and boardwalk on the Atlantic Ocean. Once an area of elegant hotels and restaurants, the extension of a subway line had transformed it into a summer escape for the city's poor. Summer weekends saw hundreds of thousands of New Yorkers thronging the beach and the many concession booths, but on this weekday in June the crowds were pleasantly small. Sarah and Patrick and the children roamed about at will. They rode the Ferris wheel and the roller coaster, Lucy shrieking with delight as the cars rose to perilous heights and then plunged straight down. They rode the Loop-o-Plane and the Whip and the much tamer carousel. At the booths they played Skee Ball and ring toss and beano. They visited the fun house, laughing at their distorted images. They stuffed themselves with food, with hot dogs and corn on the cob and exotic little potato cakes called knishes. "Can we go back to the fun house, Dad?" Josh asked as they strolled the boardwalk. "And can we go to the penny arcade?"

"Aren't you tired? What about you, Lucy?"

"Oh, no, Uncle Patrick. I'm not tired. This is the best time I ever had in my whole life."

"And you want more. Very well, but we old folk are going to have a rest." Patrick took a dollar bill from his wallet, giving it to Josh. "You and Lucy enjoy yourselves," he said. "Just remember there are rules. You're to stay with Lucy every moment, Josh. Hold her hand. The fun house and the arcade are fine, but no more rides. Now let's find a landmark so we'll know where to meet. . . . Do you both see that big wooden Indian by the archway? Good. We'll meet at the archway in one hour. It's three o'clock. We'll meet precisely at four. Understood?"

"Understood, Dad," Josh replied, looking at his wristwatch. "Four o'clock."

"Don't be late."

"We won't."

"Lucy," Sarah said, "I want you to mind Josh. Don't wander off."

"I won't, Mummy. But can we go to the waxworks? Josh says its a chamber of *horrors*. With dead people and *every*thing. Please can we go? I won't be scared. I'm brave."

"Well, I'll leave that up to Josh. He's in charge, and I know he'll take you out of there right away if it's upsetting."

"Yes, I will, Aunt Sarah."

"Then go along. . . . *One hour*," she called after them.

168

"Don't worry," Patrick said. "They'll be fine. Josh is a responsible chap. And I'm glad, because now I'll have you to myself for a while. Let's walk on the beach."

"Can we build a sand castle?"

"I didn't bring my pail and shovel," Patrick laughed. "Next time. Perhaps I can interest you in a shell hunt."

"Oh, I love seashells," Sarah exclaimed. She kicked off her shoes, sinking into the warm sand. She began to run. The breeze whipped at her light summer dress, the surf lapped at her ankles, and she felt such a sense of freedom she wanted to shout. "Catch me if you can," she dared, running past Patrick.

I'll always remember this moment, he thought, struck by Sarah's beauty as she whirled away. He could not take his eyes from her, from her hair shimmering with sunlight and her lovely face rosy in the wind. "Sarah," he murmured, and then he, too, began to run.

"Come on, Patrick. You can do better than that."

They ran faster, laughing, breathing in the fresh ocean air. When they could run no more, they collapsed on the beach. "I wish we could stay here forever," Patrick said, gathering Sarah into his arms. "I love you, my darling."

"And I love you."

"No regrets? No second thoughts?"

"Never. Never in this world."

Patrick felt the beating of Sarah's heart against his own. He gazed at her, and moment by moment his gray eyes became more intense. He lifted his hand, tracing the lines of her mouth, her neck. He undid the tiny pearl buttons of her dress, caressing her breasts.

"Patrick," she whispered.

Their clothing seemed to slip away. They lay naked beneath an outcropping of rocks, fire raging within them. Their bodies, their mouths pressed close. Waves crashed upon the shore and somewhere in the distance a bird called, but the lovers heard only their own cries, cries of passion, of sweet and boundless joy.

Elizabeth left her study and walked to the stairs. She saw Lucy skipping up the steps, Sarah following behind. "I was beginning to worry," she said. "It's almost six."

"The children didn't want to leave," Sarah explained. "We had to agree to one last ride on the roller coaster."

"I hope it is the last. Those rides are dangerous."

"Well, the last for now."

"Lucy, come give Grandmama a kiss. . . . That's my good girl. Now let me look at you." Elizabeth frowned, for the child's hair was tousled, her pinafore stained with mustard and ketchup and crusted sand. "What do you have in your pocket?"

"Seashells, Grandmama. They're pretty."

"Run along upstairs to Miss Marple. She'll wash them. I hate to think of the germs you've brought back."

"Go on, darling," Sarah said. "I'll be up in a moment." She watched her daughter skip away, then turned to Elizabeth. "I wish you wouldn't harp so on germs," she sighed. "You'll make Lucy afraid. The world is filled with germs, you know."

"Exactly my point. Lucy must be protected."

"We can't protect her from the world, from life."

"That remains to be seen. Come into the study, Sarah. I'd like a word with you."

170

"Is anything wrong?"

"No, nothing. Do sit down, my dear," Elizabeth said, gesturing to a chair. "You must be tired after your long day."

"A little."

"Then I will be brief. I'm driving to Broadmoor in the morning, as planned. I want very much to take Lucy with me."

"You aren't going to break your promise, are you? You promised Lucy and I could have this week together. I've made plans, too. I've changed my schedule at work. And I've been looking forward to this week, Elizabeth. We haven't had a whole week together since Easter."

"There's no need to upset yourself. I raised the subject only because Gertrude Whitney is having a children's party at Wheatley Hills. I thought it would be nice for Lucy. But if you would prefer to go ahead with your plans, I won't argue."

"Yes, I would. Elizabeth, we've had sort of a—a truce these past months. Things have been better and I'm grateful. Please let's leave well enough alone."

"As you say, my dear."

"May I go now? Lucy and I are having our dinner together tonight, and I'd like a bath first."

"Of course . . . Sarah, are you quite certain you know what you're doing?"

"Doing?"

"I am all in favor of family outings, but there are situations in which children are best not involved. Situations of a personal nature," Elizabeth added with a smile. "Children are so impressionable. And they can be so brutal in their judgments."

"I don't know what you mean," Sarah replied, though she knew very well. "If you have something to say, I wish you'd say it straight out."

"A word to the wise, my dear. A word to the wise."

Chapter Nine

Summer ended and the new school term began. Sarah felt a familiar sadness, for once again she was reminded that Lucy was growing up, that time was passing too quickly. She stood at the window, watching as Lucy ran to the car, and tears filled her eyes. Another year almost gone, she thought, though somehow it did not seem possible. The car drove off and she turned from the window, starting when she saw Ned. "Oh, I didn't hear you come in," she said.

"I had an idea this might be a gloomy morning for you. I was right. Here, take my handkerchief and dry your eyes."

"Thanks. Are you all packed?"

Ned shrugged. He sat down, stretching his legs before him. "I'll do it tonight," he replied. "I do so much packing there's no trick to it anymore. . . . Savannah, Charleston, and New Orleans. That's the itinerary. I'd rather it were London, Paris, and Rome," he laughed, "but duty calls me to the southland."

"It's pretty there, isn't it?"

"Very. You should see for yourself, dear heart. When are you going to start traveling?"

"I won't leave Lucy. If I could take her with me . . . But Elizabeth would never allow it."

"No, the warden is strict about out-of-town trips." Ned lighted a cigarette. "How are things between you two?" he asked. "Any better?"

"Sometimes. Sometimes not. Elizabeth seldom says anything directly. She prefers to veil her sarcasm and her threats."

"You sound resigned."

"I am, Ned. I've had long enough to get used to it. I know now that a truce is the best I can hope for. Our truce is broken from time to time, but still it's better than nothing."

"Never mind about Mother. She's a depressing subject. Tell me your good news, your really good news. Is there a promotion in the works for you? Patrick said something to that effect."

"There may be," Sarah smiled, "but not right away. I have quite a lot to learn. First I have to digest all those books," she said, her arm sweeping toward a stack of illustrated texts. "And then I have to take courses at NYU. Strange as it may seem, I have Miss Boyce to thank. She decided I had an affinity for porcelains. She sent a memorandum to Patrick, suggesting he take me into the training program. He's agreed. On a trial basis, you understand."

"That's wonderful, Sarah. I'm proud of you."

"Well, it hasn't happened yet. There's *so* much to learn. And the thought of going back to school at my age—"

"Your age!" Ned cried, hooting with laughter. "Twenty-five is a marvelous age, dear heart."

"I feel older."

"But you're not. You're at a marvelous time in your life. This is the perfect time to start expanding your horizons. It's a big world out there, Sarah. So

173

many things to see, to do. You haven't even seen Paris!"

"Someday."

"Promise you won't wait too long."

"You're sweet to worry," Sarah smiled again. "But those things aren't awfully important to me. Oh, I'd like to travel, to see a bit of the world, but other things are more important now."

"Still a country girl, eh?"

"I'm hopeless."

Ned dropped his cigarette into an ashtray. He rose, taking Sarah's hands. "I told Mother she'd never make a Cameron of you," he said. "She'd planned to turn your head with jewels and furs and parties, just as she did Evelyn. But *you* have character."

"Evelyn?"

"Our Evelyn was a quiet, modest girl from a very rich and very stern family. Her parents didn't approve of display of any kind. They were positively grim about it. The only jewelry Evelyn had was a strand of pearls and a small cameo brooch. Then Mother took over. She turned that quiet, modest girl into a silly clotheshorse."

"Why?"

"She wanted leverage with Patrick. She thought she could use Evelyn. She was wrong, of course. Evelyn just got sillier and sillier, helped along by Tommy Trent and that gang. . . . Hasn't Patrick told you any of this?"

"He doesn't talk about Evelyn."

"No, I suppose he wouldn't. A gentleman of the old school," Ned chuckled, "though in a fight I'd want him on my side."

"He'd be there."

"I know. Shall we go down to breakfast? I warn you, Mother is in a difficult mood this morning."

174

"More difficult than usual?"

"Much. Both Patrick and her broker have her worried about the market. Patrick's begun selling off some of his stocks. He says he sees danger signals. Mother doesn't care to admit he may be right."

"Do you think he is?"

"I'm not sure," Ned replied, walking with Sarah to the door. "The market's been slipping but it's still sky-high. And God knows, *everyone's* in the market. My barber told me he made five thousand dollars last month. He went ahead and bought more shares. . . . I decided to sell what I had. I'd already earned six times my original investment. What the hell? That's enough. I'd hate to be done in by my own greed."

"President Hoover says the economy is sound."

"Perhaps it is. Then again . . . Something is wrong on the Street. I'm not sure what, but something."

Something was indeed wrong, for a week later the Wall Street panic began. Thirteen million shares of stock were sold on Monday, market losses exceeding ten billion dollars. Even the bankers, with their vast pool of money, were unable to stem the tidal wave of selling. The next day, a day that would forever be known as Black Tuesday, the market crashed.

There was bedlam on the trading floor as desperate men shouted and cursed and wept. According to a Stock Exchange guard, "They roared like a lot of lions and tigers. They howled and screamed. They clawed at one another's collars. They were like a bunch of crazy men. Every once in a while, when Radio or Steel or Auburn would take another tumble, you'd see some poor devil collapse and fall to the floor."

It was a disaster, the toll stupendous. The selling off of twenty-three-million shares let loose a panic that would destroy thirty billion dollars in market values. Great investment trusts were suddenly bankrupt. Great corporations, the very backbone of American business, were struck a mortal blow. And now the market's big men went down with the clerks and tradesmen and shopkeepers who had risked their last dollars on the golden dreams of Wall Street.

Elizabeth received the news in a late afternoon telephone call from her broker. She reacted with steely calm, though ever after she refused to discuss the subject; to the end of her days she would never admit to having lost three million dollars in the Crash. Various Cameron uncles and cousins lost a combined total of two million dollars. Half of Ned's trust fund was lost, as was half of the trust established for Lucy. Sarah was aware of these losses but she knew they meant little when compared to people who had lost everything, for the Crash ushered in the Great Depression.

The Depression deepened month by month, year by year. Fourteen million men were unemployed in 1932, one out of every four American workers. Millions more had only part-time work to sustain them and their families. Average factory pay plummeted to sixteen dollars a week, national income to half of what it had been. Homes were foreclosed, farmers were forced off their lands, factory closings ran into the thousands, and bank failures were rampant. Beggars were seen in the streets. Breadlines and soup kitchens were everywhere, feeding people who were literally starving.

President Hoover, his optimistic outlook unchanged, continued to proclaim the soundness of the economy. Almost no one believed him. Franklin Roosevelt was elected in a landslide, and to the strains of "Happy Days Are Here Again," a new era in American history began.

Sarah climbed the three steep flights to Mary Margaret's flat, stopping once to transfer her package to her other arm. She wore a simple gray wool dress and matching coat, and a small, simple black hat. She wore no jewelry, for in the midst of hard times she was troubled by her own good fortune. She saw Mary Margaret standing at the open door and Sarah smiled. "Sorry to be late," she said. "I had to look over some papers in the office."

"So they have you working on Saturdays, have they?"

"No, this was something that couldn't wait."

"Well, come in, come in. You'll catch your death in the drafty hall. The kids are with their grandma and Mike's out. We can have a nice chat. . . . Ah, Sarah, I hope you didn't bring us more presents. You know how Mike feels about charity."

"Charity! Don't be foolish, Mary Margaret. I brought a few things for tea, that's all." Sarah entered the flat, ducking her head to avoid the lines of wet laundry. "You've been busy today," she laughed.

"What you see here is for wages. There's a new restaurant over by the park. A café, they call it. I went and had a talk with the manager. To make a long story short, he agreed to let me have the laundry job. It's tablecloths and napkins and aprons. And it means four dollars a week. Mike isn't happy, but this time I had to go against him. Food on the table is food on the table."

"Has he found anything yet?" Sarah asked.

"He had three days work at McShane Construction last week. We were hoping it might turn into something permanent. . . . But there isn't much building being done these days. Now Mike's hoping to find a couple of days work at the freight yards. He heard they were hiring. Day labor is the best he can do. Nobody's hiring permanent anymore.''

"I know." Sarah set her package on the table, removing a loaf of bread, a pound of sweet butter, a pound of sliced ham, a big chocolate cake, and a tin of Earl Grey tea. "I know, Mary Margaret," she said, "but I may have good news for you. There's a job opening up at the Galleries. One of our workmen is retiring next month. The job is mostly unloading crates and carting things around and hanging some of the larger works in the exhibit areas. It's not as easy as it sounds, because the men have to be very careful. . . . Anyway, the job is Mike's if he wants it. It pays twenty-five dollars a week.

"Twenty-five dollars?" Mary Margaret's blue eyes narrowed on Sarah. "You're a dear friend," she smiled, "but what's the real salary?"

"Mary Margaret . . ."

"The real salary, my girl, and no blarney."

"Eighteen dollars a week," Sarah sheepishly admitted.

"For unloading and carting around?"

"For unloading and carting around *very* valuable things. That's the real salary. And it's a real job. The man who's retiring is Frank Chernak. He's real, too."

"Eighteen dollars a week," Mary Margaret said, fumbling for a chair. "I never thought we'd see eighteen dollars a week again. Are you sure Mike can have the job? There must be men beating down the doors."

"No one knows about it yet," Sarah explained. "I asked Patrick to keep an eye out. Just this afternoon he told me Frank was leaving. It's not the best job in the world. . . ."

"But it *is* a job. That's what we've been praying for, Sarah. Any job at all. Mike says to trust in God and Mr. Roosevelt, but I knew he was worried we'd have to go on the Home Relief. He's a proud man, Mike is."

"Well, if you can manage for one more month, neither of you will have to worry. And remember my offer of a loan still stands."

"Mike won't take charity, or loans either."

"Will he take this job, Mary Margaret?"

"Ah, he'll jump at it." Tears came to her eyes and she quickly brushed them away. "I can't tell you how thankful I am," she sniffled. "From here on, we'll trust in God and Mr. Roosevelt and Sarah Cameron. . . . Now I'd best put the kettle on before I start bawling."

"I'll get the cups."

"Stay where you are or you'll be getting a face full of laundry."

"I don't mind."

"I do. Sarah, you'll thank Patrick for me, won't you?"

"Of course, though he was glad to help. That's the way he is."

Mary Margaret glanced over her shoulder at Sarah. "I'm sticking my nose in," she said, "so I won't be offended if you tell me to go to the devil, but is this Patrick fella someone special?"

"Special?"

"To you, I mean. You get a funny kind of look when you say his name. A dreamy look. And when you talk about him, you light up like a fireworks show."

Sarah felt her cheeks burning. She lowered her eyes, wondering how she could possibly explain.

"It's—it's complicated, Mary Margaret," she said at last. "I wouldn't expect you to understand. Sometimes even I don't understand."

"Do you love each other?"

"Yes," Sarah replied in a voice hardly more than a whisper. "You see, it was Elizabeth who wanted me to marry Ned. I went along for Lucy's sake. To give her a legal father. But Ned and I . . . I'm fond of him, Mary Margaret. I do love him, but as a friend. We've never really had a marriage. . . . I'm telling you this because I don't want you to think I'm . . . betraying my marriage. There isn't any marriage. I don't want you to think—"

"Such talk, Sarah. Nothing on this earth could make me think bad of you. Dear knows, I'm not sitting in judgment. You're my friend."

"You aren't shocked?"

"I had a feeling things weren't right with you and Ned. You always said nice things about him but there was no joy to it. There was no twinkling in your eyes, like when you talk about Patrick."

"Silly, isn't it? I'm past the age of girlish twinkling."

"And what has age to do with love? You can't blame yourself for being in love."

"Under the circumstances, a lot of people would disagree. What would your neighbors say if they knew you were entertaining a scarlet woman? What would Mike say?"

"You're no scarlet woman," Mary Margaret chided. "So that's enough of that kind of talk. As for Mike," she continued, setting out cups and spoons, "he'd try to march you off to Father Coyne. Mike thinks the church has all the answers. Well, I'm a Catholic, too, and I have my own ideas on the subject. The priests are good men, but they don't live in the world. And for all they hear in the confessional, they don't know what the world's like. The hurt, the suffering. The troubles we hold in our hearts. No, we have to find the answers ourselves."

Sarah smiled. "That's heresy, Mary Margaret," she said.

"Maybe lightning will strike. Still, it's my honest opinion. I'm not saying I wouldn't be happier if you and Patrick were husband and wife, but I'm not sitting in judgment, either."

"Thank you for that."

"I won't say anything to Mike. If I do," Mary Margaret laughed, "he'll have us saying an extra rosary for your soul. With all the rosaries we're saying these days, my knees are worn out."

"You haven't lost your sense of humor."

"Laughing is better than crying, Sarah. Tell me now, is there a chance you and Patrick will be able to marry someday? I'm sticking my nose in again, I know. It's just that I want you to have the life you deserve."

The smile left Sarah's face. Slowly, she lifted her eyes to Mary Margaret. "In the beginning it didn't seem to matter," she said. "It gets harder as time passes. Harder to lead our separate lives, harder to pretend it doesn't hurt. But we both have responsibilities. And I have Elizabeth looking over my shoulder every moment of every day. . . . It isn't the way I'd choose to live, if I had a choice. I don't. I love Patrick. I can't give him up. . . . Perhaps you should say that rosary after all."

It was evening when Sarah returned home. She went directly to her rooms, too weary to face Elizabeth. The hall was silent, but she saw the light shining beneath her door and she sighed. "Elizabeth . . . Oh, it's you, Janet. Thank heavens. I'm so tired of Elizabeth lying in wait for me. I feel ambushed. . . . Janet, what's wrong? You look awfully sad."

"My wedding's been postponed. *Again*. If I ever walk down the aisle, I'll need a cane. It took Hal three years to propose. Then his mother got sick and that was another year gone. Now he's lost his position at the bank and God only knows what will happen. Our whole future is up in the air."

Sarah threw her things on the bed and went to Janet. "I'm very sorry," she said. "I wish there were a way I could help. Is there?"

Janet shook her head. "Banks don't have much need of loan officers these days," she replied. "They're not making any loans. And Hal's heard rumors that Manhattan Savings will be closing its doors permanently. . . . It's ironic. One of the things that attracted me to him in the first place was his safe, secure job. A bank officer. What could be safer than that? I hadn't counted on this damned Depression. Oh God, listen to me. There are people starving, people sleeping in doorways, and all I can think about is Hal's job."

"It's more than his job. As you said, it's your future."

"I suppose I'll go on being Mrs. Cameron's secretary. I'll grow old in the service of dinner parties and thank-you notes and opera balls."

"Janet, it isn't as bleak as all that. Elizabeth knows lots of bankers. She could put in a word for Hal."

"I've already asked her. She said she doesn't like to interfere."

"Doesn't like to interfere! Why, she does nothing *but* interfere. Well, never mind about her. I'll speak to Ned. Better yet, I'll speak to Patrick. He's quite friendly with the Jennings family. They have something to do with banks."

"Yes, they own them," Janet said, laughing despite herself. "The old man, Philip Jennings, is a bear. The son isn't too bad. Of course you know the grandson. Tony Jennings is in Lucy's dancing class."

"A charming little boy. Though Lucy doesn't share my opinion. She says he purposely steps on her toes." Sarah crossed the room to her desk, scribbling a note. "I'll speak to Patrick first thing Monday morning."

"I appreciate your concern, Sarah. I'm afraid it won't do any good. The Jennings banks only hire men from the right Ivy League schools and the right clubs. Hal worked his way through Columbia and he doesn't have a club yet." Janet slumped deeper in her chair. She sighed. "It's hopeless," she said. "Maybe I wasn't meant to get married."

"That's silly. You must give Patrick a chance to help."

"Sarah, I'm thirty two years old. I'm an old maid."

"Oh, you're no such thing. Hal is the same age you are."

"It's different for a man."

Yes, thought Sarah, it's always different for a man. "We're going to get you married, Janet," she declared. "It's about time *someone* in this house got what they wanted."

Janet and Hal were married in the Cameron house three months later. Ned served as best man; a beaming Sarah was maid of honor. Flowers bedecked the drawing room mantel, and white velvet bows trimmed the twenty small gilt chairs rented for the occasion. Janet scarcely seemed to notice, so intent was she on Hal. Her eyes never left his face as she spoke her vows, repeating the words firmly and without hesitation; this was in contrast to Hal, who was subdued and more than a little dazed. "Well, we've done it," he said when the Reverend Dr. Withers pronounced them husband and wife. "Tied the knot, eh?"

"Thank God," Janet replied, linking arms with her groom.

The guests came forward to offer congratulations. Sarah watched the happy scene, but after several moments her gaze strayed to Patrick. She saw his smile and she drifted toward him, lightly brushing her fingers across the back of his hand. "You haven't kissed the bride," she said.

"I wish you were the bride. I wish we had been standing up there."

"We don't need a ceremony, Patrick. We have so much."

"Is it enough for you?"

Sarah had been pondering that question ever since her conversation with Mary Margaret, three months before. She had searched her heart, her feelings, looking into the deepest part of herself. And finally she had understood there was only one answer. "Yes," she said, "it's enough. It's everything. It always will be. . . . Now go kiss Janet. This is her day."

Patrick went off to join the group around the newlyweds. Sarah turned, wandering through the open doors into the library. She paused before the display of wedding gifts. There was a silver tea service from Elizabeth, a Haviland china service from Patrick and Evelyn. There were various crystal vases

184

and bowls and goblets; there were the inevitable silver pickle forks. "Why do people send pickle forks?" she asked as Elizabeth entered the room. "They're useless."

"We use them in this house all the time, my dear."

"Janet and Hal won't be living on such a grand scale."

"Not everyone is as fortunate as we are."

"Oh, yes, we're very fortunate," Sarah replied, sinking into a chair. "We have riches galore. We have everything money can buy. Lucky us."

"Would you rather be selling apples on street corners?"

"Of course not. I just wish money weren't the only measure of our lives. . . . People in Aldcross were forever pinching pennies but they were happy nonetheless. They had their families and their gardens and their dogs. They had their simple pleasures."

"You forget they also had their gossip. . . . Gossip which would have driven you from Aldcross, if you hadn't left of your own accord." Elizabeth sat down, folding her hands in her silken lap. "The wedding seems to have made you nostalgic, my dear." she said. "Perhaps it's time you took a trip back to Aldcross. I'm sure the old wounds have healed by now. And a trip back might finally convince you of how far you've come. All your romantic notions aside, you have an enviable life."

"We've been through this before, Elizabeth. I won't travel without Lucy. Even if you allowed me to take her, I obviously couldn't take her to Aldcross. If I did, she'd realize we've been lying to her."

"Not lying, my dear. Not exactly."

"What else would you call it? She had to be told Ned was her adoptive father, and we told her. But all the other things we told her were lies. Her natural father wasn't an Aldcross boy named Tom Griffith. I wasn't a widow when I came to America. Her natural grandparents aren't dead. Lies, Elizabeth. I pray they don't come back to haunt us.''

"You certainly wouldn't want her to know the truth.''

"No, I wouldn't burden her with that. I won't have her life scarred by the knowledge that her father was a . . .'' Sarah's voice faded away, for even now, almost twelve years later, she could not bring herself to speak the word. "Lucy mustn't ever learn the truth,'' she said wearily. "And so a visit to Aldcross is out of the question.''

"For Lucy, yes. Not for you. You needn't fear going off on your own. As I understand it, that's precisely what you'll be doing once you've completed your courses at the University. Another year, isn't it? Then there will be many trips. Traveling will be part of your new responsibilities.''

"I won't be traveling far, Elizabeth. My trips will be limited to the East Coast. That's already been decided. I won't be away more than two days at a time.''

"Patrick is very accommodating.''

"In fact, he's very strict about business matters. I'll be sent to examine only the smaller, less important porcelain collections. And I'll be under close supervision in the beginning. That's company policy.''

"I'm well aware of company policy, my dear. I thought Patrick might make an exception in your case.''

"No exceptions, no special favors. That was the bargain.''

"Indeed.'' Elizabeth's cool gaze swept over Sarah. "It's to your credit that you've kept the bargain,'' she

186

said. "It would be so easy to take advantage of . . . the situation."

Color rushed to Sarah's face. "Just once I wish you would say what you mean."

"I thought I had, my dear," Elizabeth replied with a smile. She rose, a dark, slender figure in lavender silk. "We really must return to our guests now. Come along, Sarah."

The gilt chairs had been removed from the drawing room and the reception had begun. It was, by Sarah's design, a lively affair, with waiters serving cocktails and hors d'oeuvres, and a pianist playing the popular songs of the day. Guests mingled freely, their voices rising and falling in conversation, in laughter. Janet was the radiant center of attention. She seemed to glide about the room, calling elated greetings to her friends, now and then throwing her arms around a startled Hal. "Over here," she called when she saw Sarah. "Come join the party."

Sarah threaded her way through the crowd. She plucked a martini from a passing tray, raising her glass to Janet. "A long and happy marriage," she said.

"We're off to a wonderful start, thanks to you," Janet replied. "Thank you for the wedding, Sarah, and for everything else."

"Oh, I was glad to do it. You're a lovely bride. Where's your groom?"

"He's huddled in the corner with Patrick. Talking business, I suppose. Hal's so thrilled to be working again. He's determined to make a success. We're taking only one week for our honeymoon, but I don't mind. I don't mind anything today."

Sarah smiled. She reached into the pocket of her raspberry crêpe dress and extracted a tiny box. "A wedding present from Ned and me," she said.

"Actually, the present is parked outside at the curb. These are the keys."

"A car!" Janet cried. "Sarah, I can't believe it!"

"It was Ned's idea. But we picked it out together. A white Packard roadster."

"You're a love, an absolute love. I'm going to miss you, you know. Twelve years. When I think of all we've been through in these years . . . I practically watched you grow up."

"A slight exaggeration," Sarah laughed, "but you're allowed to exaggerate on your wedding day. . . . It's true we've been through a lot," she added, her face growing serious. "I don't know what I would have done without you to talk to. Let's not lose touch, Janet. Let's promise."

"I'll call you the moment we get back from Vermont. Mrs. Cameron won't welcome her former secretary as a guest here. . . ."

"Janet—"

"She won't, Sarah. At least not until Hal is a senior vice-president. That's all right. You can visit me instead. You'll be our first guest when we get back. I'll try out my cooking on you."

"Fair enough." She turned as Ned came up beside her. "Are you enjoying yourself?" she asked, reaching to straighten his tie. "You look happy."

"I am. I love other people's weddings. I love seeing the net dropped on some other poor devil."

"*Ned.*"

"Misery loves company. Not that you're misery, dear heart. You're a peach. You too, Janet."

"Thanks."

"He's impossible," Sarah laughed again. She sipped her drink, putting the glass down when she saw Lucy's governess standing in the doorway. "Excuse me," she said, hurrying across the room.

"Miss Marple, I didn't expect you back so soon. Is Lucy ill? Did something happen at the birthday party?"

"Perhaps we could step into the hall, Mrs. Cameron?"

"Yes, of course. What is it? What's wrong?"

"Lucy is quite well," Miss Marple replied calmly, "but I'm afraid there was an unfortunate incident at the Harringtons. The party was proceeding in fine fashion. Mr. Harrington came in to give Frances her present. He stayed with the children a while. Talking to them, you know. Then he went to his study."

"Yes?" Sarah asked anxiously. "And then?"

"Well, it seems he shot himself, Mrs. Cameron. There was a loud noise. One of the maids ran to see about it. There were the most terrible screams. Mrs. Harrington ran to the study then, and some of the children. It was chaos. The maids were screaming, the children were crying. Poor Mrs. Harrington collapsed."

"My God," Sarah murmured. "My God. Is John— is Mr. Harrington—"

"—dead?. Yes, I'm sorry to say he is, Mrs. Cameron."

"My God. Did Lucy see anything?"

"She didn't see, but naturally she heard the talk. When the children stopped crying, they started chattering like magpies. It was little Alice Morgan's opinion that Mr. Harrington killed himself over money. I took Lucy away as quickly as I could. It was difficult. . . . The police, you see."

"Yes. Yes, I see. Is Lucy upstairs?"

"In her room, Mrs. Cameron. I asked Violet to bring warm milk with just a drop or two of brandy."

"Thank you, Miss Marple. I'll go to her now. . . . I'd appreciate it if you'd tell Mr. Cameron what's

189

happened. There may be something he can do for the Harringtons."

"I'll tell him straightaway."

"Thank you." Sarah rushed to the stairs, wondering how she could explain such a tragedy to an eleven-year-old. She thought of John Harrington, of Elsie and their two little girls. "So sad," she murmured to herself. "So awful." Lucy's door was closed. She knocked lightly and went inside. "Lucy? Are you all right, darling?"

Lucy lay atop the covers of her flounced canopy bed. She still wore her red velvet party dress and long white stockings, though her patent leather Mary Janes had been kicked aside. She lay quietly, staring up at the ceiling. "Mr. Harrington died," she said.

"I know. Miss Marple's just explained. I'm very sorry."

"He killed himself. He had a gun and he killed himself."

Sarah moved a wicker rocker next to the bed. She sat down, stretching her hand to Lucy. "It's a terrible thing, darling. We can talk about it, if you like, but you mustn't dwell on it."

"Alice said it was because of money. Did Mr. Harrington lose all his money? Was he poor?"

"Well, there's a Depression on. That means a lot of people have lost their money and their jobs. Mr. Harrington was a stockbroker. Business hasn't been very good for stockbrokers lately. I'm sure he was worried. He was under a strain, darling. Perhaps he didn't see any way to help himself. . . . His friends would have helped, of course," Sarah added, stroking Lucy's cheek. "That's the wonderful thing about friends. . . . You can help by being a friend to Frances and Emily."

"They were crying, Mummy."

"I know."

"Are we going to be poor, too?"

Sarah glanced around the room with all its dolls and toys and games, with its antique chests and Brussels lace. She smiled. "No, Lucy," she said softly. "You mustn't worry about that. Your daddy hasn't lost his money or his job. The Galleries are busier than ever. There are more people now who have things they want to sell and more people hoping to come upon a bargain. . . . But even if we *did* lose our money, we'd still be fine. That's what I want you to understand, darling. Money is important because it pays the bills. Because it makes us feel good. But it's not the most important thing in life. With or without money, you'd have your friends and your family and all the people who love you."

"Can we give some money to Frances?"

"Leave that to your daddy. He'll see to it that the Harringtons have anything they need."

"I want to do it, Mummy."

"I'm sorry, but you can't. You can't just shove money at people, Lucy. That hurts their pride."

"What can I give Frances?"

"Yourself," Sarah replied. "Be her friend, darling. Don't ask nosy questions. Don't pry. Listen to her if she wants to talk, and be her friend. All right?"

"Yes, Mummy."

Sarah bent, kissing Lucy's brow. "You're a sweet girl to be so concerned," she said. "Now you must have a rest. Finish your milk, and then I want you to nap. I'll be back a little later. We'll have our dinner together. Would you like that?"

"Yes."

"Remember there's nothing to be frightened of. We're all fine."

"Yes, Mummy, I'll remember."

"That's my good girl." Sarah rose, walking to the door. "Sleep well, Lucy," she said, going out into the hall. She turned and went to her rooms. Ned was seated in a wing chair by the hearth. He looked tired; in the flickering light of the fire he looked every one of his thirty-seven years. "Ned?" she called. "I suppose you've heard."

"I've heard. . . . I went to school with Johnny Harrington. What a hell raiser he was in those days. I was an angel compared to him. Then he met Elsie and they were married. They had the kids. He got so damned *serious* about everything. All he ever talked about was money, investments. Then there was the Crash. Good-bye money. Good-bye investments. I knew he was in trouble. He wouldn't admit it, but I knew. . . . Christ, I should have seen this coming."

"You can't blame yourself, Ned."

"I haven't the courage to blame myself. That would lead to soul searching, and that's hardly my style. I've always ignored life's harsher realities, Sarah. Shut them out. Today's events won't change that, not for long."

"Is there anything I can do?"

Ned shook his head. "I'll stop by and see Elsie," he said. "And then I'll find a willing companion and get roaring drunk."

"Well, if that will make you feel better . . ."

"It may." Ned laughed, a dry, bitter sound in the quiet room. "I'll drink to the Great Depression."

Chapter Ten

The Depression dragged on, its casualties mounting, though by the end of 1934 President Roosevelt
and his numerous "alphabet" agencies had begun to
turn the tide. The WPA created jobs, while the
NRA boosted wages and shortened working hours.
Other agencies were formed to stem the avalanche of
foreclosures and to insure depositors against bank
failures. Despite protests from board rooms and
executive suites, the SEC was formed to regulate the
reckless excesses of Wall Street. It was a massive
assault on complacency, aptly termed the New Deal.
If the New Deal offered hope, the tabloids of the
thirties offered distractions. In 1934 Gertrude
Whitney sued for custody of her ten-year-old niece
Gloria Vanderbilt, and the sensational trial was
headline news across the country. For months the
tabloid press trumpeted allegations of neglect, of
wild parties, of pornography, of lesbianism, and this
public humiliation of the very rich entertained the
millions still enduring hard times. The next year
brought scandal of a different kind—the love affair of
American divorcée Wallis Simpson and the Prince of
Wales, soon to be King Edward VIII. It was called the

love affair of the century, and to people wearied by the grimness of everyday life, it was indeed the stuff of dreams.

To Sarah it was a reminder of her British roots, for she had grown up in awe of the monarchy and its traditions. She followed the story, often clipping articles to send to John and Hilda. She studied the pictures of the English countryside and she thought of Aldcross, wondering if she would ever see the quiet village again. "I wonder if it's changed," she said to Patrick one chilly winter evening in 1935. "Mama writes that everything's the same. It doesn't seem likely, does it?"

"You're homesick."

"Homesick! Fourteen years later?"

"You never used to read the tabloids. You started when the Prince became big news. Don't deny it," Patrick laughed. "I've seen you sneaking looks at his pictures. I think all these stories are reviving old memories."

"Childhood memories," Sarah agreed, snuggling closer to Patrick on the couch. "God, King, and Country, that's how we were raised. And of course the Royal Family could do no wrong. It was a simpler time."

"A happier time?"

"In some ways . . . I remember the peace and quiet of English country life. I don't miss it anymore, at least not very often. I've come to love the city, Patrick, because I see it through your eyes."

"My darling, there's so much I want to show you. I'd like to sweep you up in my arms and carry you off. I'd like to say the hell with everything but us. That's my fantasy, Sarah."

"And mine."

"I want to show you Europe. . . . Paris, the city of

194

lovers. That's the place. That's where we'll go."
Patrick lifted Sarah's hand to his lips. "Someday," he
murmured. "Someday sooner than we think."

"*I* think we shouldn't worry about someday,"
Sarah smiled. "We have now."

"Stolen moments."

"Stolen moments are very romantic. If we were
together all the time, you might get tired of me."

"Never, my darling. And we *will* go to Paris. I'll
work it out somehow. . . . You can take a side trip to
Aldcross and see your parents. Do you suppose they'd
recognize you?"

"Am I so different?"

"You know you are," Patrick replied, ruffling
Sarah's honey hair. "You were a frightened girl with
no real place in the scheme of things. Now you're a
beautiful woman with a degree in fine arts and an
important place in the Galleries. The country girl
has turned into an executive. Going to meetings,
going off on business trips. If I had predicted that for
you fourteen years ago, you would have laughed."

"I would have been scared to death. More scared
than I already was."

"You certainly found your courage."

"No," Sarah said, "I'm still scared of Elizabeth.
The Vanderbilt trial proved how unwise it is to
underestimate rich, powerful women. I've always
been terrified that Elizabeth would try to take Lucy
from me. I think she would have tried, too, if I hadn't
married Ned. I know she would have. Now that
Lucy's thirteen, I don't worry about custody
anymore. Instead, I worry about Elizabeth's plans for
Lucy's future."

"Plans?"

"Oh, Patrick, you know Elizabeth. She just takes
over. She *decides* things. We've had our battles in the

195

past, but I have a feeling the biggest battles are ahead. Decisions become more important as Lucy gets older. It's one thing to give in to Elizabeth on the question of party dresses or playmates. It's quite another thing to give in on schools or beaux. Lucy must be allowed to have a say."

"You needn't start worrying about beaux yet. There's plenty of time."

"Time goes quickly, Patrick. It seems like only yesterday your Josh was a gangly thirteen-year-old, but come fall he'll be entering Harvard."

"Don't remind me."

'That's what I mean. Time goes quickly. And it's never too soon to start anticipating Elizabeth. She probably has Lucy's college all picked out. Not to mention her husband. She's already made several references to Lucy's debut. She wants to have a huge supper dance to celebrate the occasion. . . . No, Patrick, it's best to be on guard against Elizabeth's plans and schemes."

"Can we be on guard tomorrow? I can think of better things to do tonight."

Sarah smiled. "What did you have in mind?" she asked.

"This." Patrick slipped the robe from her shoulders, caressing her naked breasts. "I love you, my darling," he murmured. "I'll never have enough of you. Never, as long as I live."

Elizabeth traveled to Europe in the spring of 1935, her first extended trip since Charlotte's death many years before. There was a lavish party aboard the *Normandie*, and when finally the ship sailed, all the Camerons seemed relieved. Three months, thought Sarah, giddy with relief. Three whole months.

She was busy during those months, for she had her own travels—to Philadelphia, to Boston, to Baltimore—but now she took Lucy with her. She delighted in their time together, showing off her daughter to everyone and anyone. She felt free, liberated, and her happiness was so great it was contagious. Each hour was dear to her, each moment. When she saw Lucy's carefully fostered reserve slipping away, she almost cried with joy. "I have a present for you," she said on their last night in Boston. "I hope you like it."

Lucy untied the ribbon and opened the box. "Silk stockings!" she exclaimed. "My first silk stockings!" She threw her arms about Sarah, jumping up and down. "That's just what I've been wanting, Mother," she said. "Thank you."

"You're quite welcome, darling. I'm not sure your grandmother would approve. It might be best to save them for special occasions. Tonight is a special occasion," Sarah added. "We're going to the fanciest restaurant in Boston, and you can have a sip of champagne. Tonight we'll be two ladies out on the town. All right?"

"It's wonderful, Mother. I've had such a wonderful time with you."

"Hurry and get dressed. You'll find a new dress in the closet, also. Something more appropriate for a grown-up lady."

"Oh, wait till I tell Alice. She'll be *so* jealous. . . . Do we really have to leave tonight, Mother? Couldn't we stay?"

"I wish we could, darling. But I have to get back to the Galleries. Do you remember that drafty old house we went to this morning? The one near Harvard? Well, in that house was the most exquisite porcelain collection. It's terribly valuable, Lucy, and I have to make certain it gets to the Galleries in good condition. It's being packed tonight. Tomorrow we're off to New York."

"It didn't look valuable," Lucy said. "It was all dusty and dirty."

"I know. The Ludlows didn't realize what treasures they had. Most people don't. They stick things away in attics and forget about them. Believe me, darling, this collection is *very* valuable."

"Uncle Patrick will be happy."

"Yes, I imagine he will. And since you were with me when I discovered the collection, you can come to the auction."

"Really, Mother? Oh, I'd like that. . . . But Grandmama won't let me."

Sarah's eyes flashed. "It isn't Grandmama's decision, darling," she said. "One way or another, you'll be there."

And four months later Lucy was indeed present at the black-tie auction, sitting with Janet and Hal in the rear of the crowded room. Patrick took the gavel himself, for the Ludlow Collection, a group of fifty-seven French and Chinese porcelains, had stirred enormous interest. Sarah had estimated the worth of the collection at half a million dollars, though by the time Patrick gaveled the auction to a close, well over a million dollars had been bid and recorded, a staggering sum in Depression-era America. It was the largest single total in the Galleries' history, and to Sarah it was a mark of achievement. "We did it," she cried, rushing onto the podium. "Patrick, we did it!"

"You did it," he laughed. "I suppose now I'll have to give you a raise."

There was a champagne reception following the auction. Ned made an unexpected appearance, presenting Sarah with a bouquet of roses. "For the woman of the hour," he said.

"I thought you were in Chicago."

"I took the early plane. I couldn't miss your triumph, dear heart. And what a triumph! I hope you're properly impressed, Lucy," Ned smiled, tweaking one of her golden curls. "Your mother is a great success. The pride of the Cameron family."

"Lucy brought me luck," Sarah said. "She was with me on the Ludlow trip."

"Yes, Daddy, I was. It was fun."

"Profitable, too."

"Was Elizabeth here?" Sarah asked. "I didn't see her."

"A last minute headache," Ned replied, winking. "But tonight's happenings won't go unnoticed. The story will be in the *Times*. I want to be there when she reads it. Even better, I want to be there when she's forced to congratulate you. She'll do it, of course, but she'll be a bit green about the gills."

"Ned," Sarah said, glancing swiftly at Lucy.

"I speak the truth, dear heart. Mother's been waiting for you to fall on your face. Well, she waits no more. You've proven yourself and I'm damned glad."

Sarah saw the confusion in Lucy's eyes, the questions. She turned, putting her hands on the child's shoulders. "Lucy can't always tell when you're joking, Ned," she said, a small frown wrinkling her brow. "We'll have to figure it out another time. It's getting late. It's past your bedtime, miss."

"Can't we stay a little longer, Mother?"

"I'm afraid not. You'll be leaving for Broadmoor first thing in the morning. You need your sleep. . . . Now go get your hat and coat. Oh, and don't forget Daddy's roses. I'll say our good-byes."

"Just five minutes more, Mother?"

"Now, darling."

Ned watched Lucy walk away. He looked at Sarah then, shaking his head. "Perhaps I was wrong to say those things in front of Lucy," he conceded. "But sooner or later she's going to see what Mother is. And she should, for her own protection."

"She's still a child, Ned."

"An intuitive child. She's already sensed the tension between you and Mother."

"I can't talk about it now," Sarah said. "I want to get her home. Will you tell Patrick I've gone? He'll make my excuses to the others."

"Take the car. I'll find a taxi."

"You're sweet," Sarah smiled, kissing Ned's cheek. "And I'm on my way." She skirted the edge of the room, slipping past the elegantly dressed and bejeweled guests. "Lucy?" she called when she reached the foyer. "Oh, there you are, darling."

"I have your cape and your purse."

"That's very thoughtful." Sarah gathered up her things, walking with Lucy to the door. Outside the air was cool and clear, the sky a mosaic of twinkling stars. "What a lovely night," she said. "Wouldn't it be nice to walk and walk and walk?"

"But Tully is here with the car, Mother."

"Yes, so he is. Good evening, Tully."

"Evening, ma'am."

"Well, we'd best get started or we'll turn into pumpkins. In you go, Lucy. Mind you don't crush the roses."

"Can I have them in my room?"

"If you'd like." Sarah rested her head against the cushioned backseat. She closed her eyes for a moment, sorry that the evening was over, sorry to be going home. "Did you enjoy yourself, darling?" she

200

asked after a while. "You weren't bored?"

"Oh, no, it was exciting. . . . I don't understand, though. Why does Grandmama want you to fall on your face?"

"That's just an expression," Sarah replied quickly. "Your daddy was making a joke. Really a very silly joke."

"No, he meant it. I was looking at him and he meant it."

"The truth," Sarah said, choosing her words with care, "is that Grandmama would prefer I didn't work. She would prefer me to be more like—like the mothers of your friends."

"Why?"

"Grandmama believes a woman's place is at home. She's not altogether wrong, Lucy. Family must come first. But I would rather work than spend my time going to teas and playing bridge. That's where we differ. . . . I'm sure Grandmama doesn't want me to fail. She'd simply prefer me to stay at home."

"Is Grandmama mad at you?"

"Angry, the word is angry. And no, she isn't. Why do you ask?"

"I don't know," Lucy said shrugging. "Sometimes . . ."

"Sometimes what?"

"Well, sometimes you say one thing and Grandmama says another and then she's so stern. She smiles, but it's a pretend smile." Lucy raised her big green eyes to Sarah. "Then I get a funny feeling," she concluded.

"How do you mean? What sort of feeling?"

"Just funny."

"Do you feel worried? Or afraid?"

"No, Mother. Well, maybe a little worried . . . Because nobody is happy."

Sarah was astonished by the sharpness of Lucy's observation. *Because nobody is happy.* Silently, she repeated the phrase to herself, admitting its truth. I wonder if there's ever been any happiness in that house, she thought. I wonder if it was different when Jasper was alive. "You must understand," she said quietly, "that people have disagreements. I have many disagreements with Grandmama and she with me. And when you're older, you and Grandmama may not always see things in the same light. That's perfectly natural. It's not wrong to have a mind of one's own."

"Oh, no, Mother, I'd be scared."

"Scared of what, darling?"

"Grandmama. If I argued with Grandmama, she'd be mad. Angry, I mean."

"And what if she were? Lucy, this is hard to explain, but we all make people angry from time to time. That's the way life is, and you mustn't be afraid of life. . . . You can't be rude or thoughtless, but you can certainly have you own opinions. When you're older, you'll know what's worth arguing about and what isn't."

"Can I ask you if I'm not sure?"

"Of course," Sarah replied, smiling at Lucy's earnest query. "You can ask me anything at all."

The car glided to a halt and Tully came around the side to open the door. "Will I go back for Mr. Cameron? He didn't say."

"No, you've had a long night. Go on to bed, Tully."

"Thank you, ma'am. Good night to you. Good night, Miss Lucy."

"Good night." She followed after Sarah, cradling the roses in her arms. "Oh, look at the moon," she said. "It's so fat."

"A harvest moon. Make a wish, darling. Everybody is allowed one wish on the harvest moon."

Sarah entered her bedroom. She threw her cape and purse on the chaise, turning to face Elizabeth. "I had a feeling you'd be waiting for me," she said. "The auction went very well, if that's what's on your mind."

"It isn't. Lucy is on my mind."

"Surprise, surprise."

"I don't care for your tone, my dear."

"Sorry." Sarah sat down. She looked at Elizabeth, seeing a woman little changed by the passage of time. She saw the same dark, cool eyes, the same dark hair swept in two shining wings off the brow, the same placid smile. She knew Elizabeth was close to sixty, yet age had left no particular mark. There was no lessening of purpose, of determination. Clearly, there was no lessening of will. "What's troubling you about Lucy now?" she asked.

"You kept her out quite late."

"It was a special occasion, Elizabeth."

"For you perhaps. Lucy needn't have been involved. But we won't go into that again. My concern has to do with the future. I hope you plan to exclude Lucy from future auctions, from events in which she has no place."

"I don't think I follow you," Sarah said.

"I'm afraid you're setting an improper example for Lucy. Please, my dear, allow me to finish. You've chosen to have a career, and that's fine. But your choice mustn't influence Lucy. Her future doesn't lie in that direction."

"It may."

"No," Elizabeth replied firmly. "There you are wrong. I've made concessions in your case, Sarah. You've gone your way and I haven't interfered. It was a question of circumstances. Lucy's circumstances are entirely different. She will have the life she was meant to have."

"And what life is that?"

"Lucy will make her debut and then she will take her rightful place in society. Of course, she will marry well. I need hardly tell you she can have her pick of the best families in New York. I foresee a brilliant match."

"My God, Elizabeth, she's thirteen years old! It's a bit too soon to reserve the church."

"Your sarcasm aside, it's not too soon to think about such things. These are the years when Lucy must be guided. Molded, if you will. Children learn by example, my dear. That's why I've been so vigilant in the matter of Lucy's friends. The parents of her friends set an excellent example. On the other hand, the example of your career leaves much to be desired."

"I disagree."

"You always disagree. It took you a while to find your voice, but once you did, you wasted no time putting it to use. I admire your spirit, Sarah. I've said that before. People of spirit must also be careful to exercise common sense."

"Meaning?"

Elizabeth smiled. "You would be wise to trust my decisions," she replied. "I know the ways of the world."

"I don't like your view of the world, Elizabeth. It's cynical."

"In time you may come to share my view."

"No, never."

"You're a romantic. . . . Despite everything that's happened to you, you continue to look kindly on humanity. Another admirable trait, my dear, but foolish. It interferes with sound judgment."

"Where Lucy is concerned, my judgment will have to do. And it's my judgment that she should have some voice in her own life. I won't let you manipulate her, Elizabeth. I've given in on clothes and tutors and Broadmoor. I'm ashamed to say I've allowed you to choose her friends. But when it comes to her future, her *life*, I won't compromise."

"There's no reason for melodrama," Elizabeth replied, unruffled. "I'm thinking only of Lucy's best interests."

"As *you* see them. *She* may see them differently. If she does . . . "

"*If.* A small but important word, my dear. Lucy is a nice girl, an amenable girl. I don't doubt she'll see things my way." Elizabeth rose, crossing to the door. "You must be tired," she said. "I won't keep you any longer. Sleep well."

"Is that an order?"

Amusement flickered in Elizabeth's dark eyes. She opened the door, glancing over her shoulder at Sarah. "You know," she laughed, "we really would do much better if you stopped regarding me as your enemy."

Sarah was not amused. She heard the door close and wearily leaned her head back, recalling the struggles of the past, pondering the struggles yet to come. There was no question in her mind that she and Elizabeth would always be on opposite sides, not exactly enemies but adversaries. She thought of

Lucy, innocent, indeed amenable, and a frown creased her brow. "Oh, Lucy," she murmured to herself, "what are we going to do?"

Lucy's fourteenth birthday was marked by a large party at Broadmoor. Fifty girls and boys were entertained with sleigh rides over the snow-covered grounds, with skating on the pond, and later with mimes and jugglers who performed in the huge playroom. It was a children's party, though the last one, for during the next year Lucy left childhood behind. Her dolls and toy animals were packed away, banished to a corner of the attic. Short, frilly dresses disappeared from her closets, replaced by simpler styles. Fashion magazines began to appear in her room, as did movie magazines. She spent hours on the telephone each day, talking to her friends in the secret language of adolescents. She declined a party for her fifteenth birthday, choosing instead to take six of her friends to a Broadway matinee.

"I hardly recognize Lucy these days," Sarah would joke, and there was some truth in that, for the little girl had become a young woman. She was taller, more graceful, soft curves rounding the lines of her bosom and waist. Her voice was lower, a bit breathless. Her curly golden hair was side-parted and worn at shoulder length. Her eyes, like Sir Roger's, were a deep and perfect green.

Around the time of her sixteenth birthday, she had begun to think about her debut. "I want something nice," she earnestly explained, "but not too splashy. Do you know what I mean?"

"Yes," Sarah replied, "and I agree. We don't want a circus, do we, Elizabeth?"

"You must leave the details to me. I had in mind a

party of four hundred. Although if we decide to have the party here, the list will be pared to three hundred. . . . It shouldn't be a difficult decision. Hotel parties are in vogue just now, but home parties have such elegance."

"Let's leave that particular detail to Lucy," Sarah suggested.

"Lucy will have quite enough on her mind, my dear. Gowns and guest lists and all that sort of thing. A year really isn't very much time."

"The world was created in six days."

"We're not creating the world," Elizabeth replied. "We're planning a coming-out party. Of the two, we have the harder task."

And as the year progressed, Sarah was forced to agree. The Cameron house was thrown into chaos, strewn with fabric samples, sketches, misplaced guest lists, hastily scribbled notes, and with people who seemed to come and go at will. There was the dressmaker, an excitable woman trailing two seamstresses and a fitter in her wake. There was the hair stylist Mr. Claude, an excitable man fussing over an endless array of ribbons and combs and plumes. There were florists and caterers. There was a constant stream of deliveries, a constant stream of telephone calls.

Such chaos overshadowed more ordinary events, including Lucy's graduation. All the Camerons attended the ceremonies and a small luncheon afterwards, but thoughts soon returned to the myriad details of the coming-out party. "You're exhausting yourself," Sarah said as Lucy flopped down on her bed. "Today should be a special day for you, darling, but you're too tired to enjoy it."

"Oh, I just wanted to get it over with. Gran is keeping me so busy with these other things. Lists, millions of lists. If I see another one, I'll scream."

"Have you told her how you feel?" Sarah asked.

"It wouldn't do any good, Mother."

"It's always good to speak up for yourself."

"I try. But then she makes me feel ungrateful and that's worse. I know a lot of work goes into the kind of party Gran's planning. She says it will be the party of the year."

Sarah's glance moved about the room. She saw a muslin-draped dressmaker's dummy, crumpled dress patterns scattered around its base. Every chair was piled high with sketches and notebooks and pages torn from fashion magazines. The desk was littered with papers, the vanity table with headbands and odd bits of ribbon. "I hope it's worth the effort," she said. "Is it what you want, darling?"

"It's what Gran wants."

"Lucy, have you given any thought to what you're going to do with your life?"

"I suppose I'll get married."

"Of course," Sarah smiled, "but you won't be getting married right away. What will you do with the years between now and then? I don't like to press you. It's just that I don't want you to lose sight of the possibilities."

"Possibilities?"

"College, for example. There's still time to enroll you in a good college. . . . Lucy, the only view of life you've had is the Cameron view. College would give you the chance to meet different people, to see things in different ways."

"I know, Mother."

"Won't you consider it?"

"I have. I'm not sure I'm smart enough for college."

"Not smart enough! You've always done well in

school. Why, you even skipped a grade. There's something else bothering you. What is it?"

"Well, I *have* thought about college. But I don't see how I could do it now. Gran's planned more than the coming-out party. She's planned the whole season—dances, dinners, receptions." Lucy raised herself up on her elbow, turning wide green eyes to Sarah. "I couldn't start college and do all that too," she explained. "College will always be there but . . . well, Gran says a girl has only one deb season."

"When you were a little girl and you quoted your grandmother, I let it pass. You're not a little girl anymore, Lucy. You can't let other people make your decisions. If you want a season, that's fine. If you don't, you must say so."

"I don't know what I want. Anyway, it's too late to change the plans now. Gran would have a fit. . . . I'm not like you, Mother. It's hard for me to say no to Gran. I guess I'm a coward."

"You're nothing of the sort, darling. You're just a little unsure. That will change. When I first met Elizabeth I was scared to death. It was a long time before I was able to speak up. I still hesitate sometimes. But when it's important, I get my point across. So will you, when it's important."

"Did Gran tell you the party is going to be here?"

"I suspected as much," Sarah replied. "Your grandmother loves to play hostess. And naturally, she does it well. It will be a wonderful party, darling."

Lucy smiled. "Did you have a coming-out, Mother?" she asked. "You never said."

"No, we didn't do those things in the country. We certainly didn't do them for schoolmasters' daughters. We had a simple life. It took years for me to get used to all this. To the Cameron splendor. I've never exactly fit in, you know. At heart, I'm still a country girl."

"Oh, no, you're elegant."

Sarah laughed, remembering the dowdy clothes she had brought with her from Aldcross. "You should have seen me the day I arrived in this house," she said. "I was a mess! Elizabeth must have been horrified. She sent Janet right out to buy me a new wardrobe. I had to learn about fashion, step by painful step. That's one problem you won't have."

"I couldn't do what you've done, Mother. Oh, I don't mean about clothes. It's everything else. You came to a strange country and started a whole new life. You made a career for yourself, even though Gran was against the idea. . . . I've thought about that. I've tried to put myself in your place. I couldn't." Lucy looked away, absently pulling at a lock of her golden hair. "I'm not a useful person," she said. "I just sort of take up space."

Sarah's brow wrinkled. She reached out, turning Lucy's face to her. "You're in an odd mood today, darling. What's wrong?"

"I don't know. I should be the happiest girl in the world, shouldn't I? And sometimes that's how I feel. But there are other times when I feel something's missing. I can't explain it, Mother. I probably shouldn't try. I'd sound whiny and spoiled."

"You're tired, Lucy. That's part of it. Why don't we go off by ourselves for a few days? We can go anywhere you like. . . . Doubts and confusions are normal at your age," Sarah added quietly. "I think you need to talk them through. And I'm a good listener. If we had some time to ourselves—"

"My dear," Elizabeth interrupted, walking into the room, "have you forgotten that we're all going to Broadmoor in the morning?"

210

"No, I haven't forgotten. But the sky won't fall in if we change our plans."

"Don't be too certain. Lucy has her final portrait sitting this weekend. Fredrick Lee is already at Broadmoor making preparations. You know the artistic temperament, Sarah. There would be such a storm, the sky might indeed fall in."

"It's all right, Mother," Lucy said. "I'll go to Broadmoor. I don't mind."

"But—"

"The matter is settled, my dear. Lucy's portrait must be finished by the time of the party. Surely you understood that." Elizabeth did not wait for a reply. She turned to Lucy, holding out a sheaf of papers. "I've had to alter the guest list," she explained. "I realized we had to save room for the European contingent."

"What European contingent?" Sarah asked.

"The du Rochemont boys. Sophie du Rochemont is one of my oldest friends. And of course there's Derek Hayward from London. His mother and I went to school together. There are a few others, all of them expected to be in New York at the time of the party. They'll add a nice touch to the occasion, don't you think?"

"You don't want to know what I think," Sarah said. "But you could at least have consulted Lucy. It's *her* party."

"Rest assured it will be a party to remember. Lucy, I will leave these lists with you. I have my own copies."

"Thank you, Gran."

Sarah knew there was no point in continuing the conversation. She stood, smiling over her shoulder at Lucy as she left the room. She was halfway to the stairs when she heard Elizabeth calling her. "Yes, what is it?"

"I wanted a word with you, my dear."

"Another time, Elizabeth. I'm going to the office."

"Now? It's rather late in the day."

"I have a lot of work to do. And I'm obviously not needed here. I thought today would be so special. But it was only a graduation. What does a graduation matter when there's a debut to plan? You have your priorities, Elizabeth, and so far you've managed to pass them on to Lucy. Congratulations."

"I know you resent my influence. . . ."

"I resent more than that," Sarah replied, starting down the stairs. "I resent what you've done to Lucy."

"Done to her!"

"Perhaps you haven't noticed, but she isn't a very happy girl."

"She's at a difficult age, my dear."

"That's part of it, not all." Sarah reached the bottom of the landing. She spun around, her eyes fast on Elizabeth. "Lucy said she feels as if something is missing. Well, something *is* missing. She has no sense of herself, and for that I blame you. You've given her a life of great luxury. You've given her everything but the chance to express herself, to think for herself, to be herself. She's never made a decision on her own. She's never been allowed to make a mistake."

"I've tried to spare her."

"Spare her what? Living? You can't do her living for her."

"Neither can you, Sarah. All your talk of college and careers has confused Lucy."

"I want her to know there are choices. My God, there's more to life than money and this house and you."

"Lower your voice. The servants will hear."

212

"No, I won't. I don't care who hears me. I just don't care anymore, Elizabeth. You've made Lucy your— your puppet. There's no doubt that one day she's going to cut the strings. She'll make the break. What worries me is *how*. She's been so sheltered, so controlled, she's almost bound to do something rash. And then we'll all be sorry."

"More melodrama? Come into my study, Sarah. We can finish this conversation in private."

"The conversation is finished, Elizabeth. The damage has already been done."

Chapter Eleven

"I see you're still composing guest lists," Ned said one autumn afternoon in 1939. He walked into Sarah's bedroom, tossing a newspaper on her desk. "This will take your mind off the forthcoming gala," he added. "Have a look."

Sarah picked up the newspaper. Her hand flew to her throat as she read the stark black headline, "Hitler Invades Poland." Another war, she thought. Dear God, another war. "I suppose it was only a matter of time," she sighed. "I've seen Hitler in the newsreels. If you watch his eyes, you can see he's insane. What's more insane is all those enormous crowds cheering him. I don't understand it. . . . And everyone said the last war *was* the last war."

"You have to expect there will always be a madman waiting in the wings. For this generation it's Hitler, king of the master race." Ned sat down, stretching out his legs. "Be glad you have a daughter," he said. "If you had a son . . ."

"Yes, I know."

"You can also be glad you're here. America may not get involved."

"But England will, if there's war. Hitler wants all

of Europe, and England will fight. Oh, Ned, I wish Mama and Papa were here. And Bertie. Bertie has sons."

"Well, we shouldn't really get ahead of ourselves. Nobody's declared war yet. It may not happen at all."

Sarah looked again at the newspaper. She felt a chill and she rubbed her hands together. "I remember how it was during the last war," she said. "I was terrified Papa would die. Aldcross lost so many men."

"Don't look back," Ned said. "It never does any good. Let's change the subject, shall we? Tell me about the party plans. I couldn't get very much out of Lucy."

"Lucy doesn't know very much. Elizabeth's handling everything. Oh, she makes a show of asking Lucy's opinion, but then she does exactly as she pleases. These lists of hers are driving me crazy. And with all these names," Sarah continued, rustling the typed sheets, "she didn't bother to include Janet and Hal. Imagine!"

"I can imagine the argument you had."

"There was no argument. I just stole some invitations from her desk and took care of things myself."

Ned laughed, shaking his head from side to side. "You're marvelous," he declared. "Who else did you invite?"

"Mary Margaret and Mike. I'm sure they'll decline, but at least they'll know they're welcome. I invited Miss Marple. And Miss Boyce."

"Amelia Boyce! Somehow I can't picture her at a fancy dress ball."

"She was delighted to be asked. She's already accepted."

"Does Mother know?"

"Oh, yes," Sarah smiled. "After I sent the invitations I told her all about it. She had a fit, as Lucy would say."

"Bravo, dear heart. Still slugging it out with her. Winning some, losing some, but still slugging it out." Ned rose. He walked to the windows and parted the silken draperies, staring across the avenue at the park. "I often wonder what would have happened if years ago I had told Mother to go to hell. No games, no speeches, just a simple, straightforward go to hell . . . But there was too much money on the line, and I was too used to having money. Don't let Lucy fall into the same trap."

"What do you mean?"

"I care about Lucy," Ned replied. "In my more sentimental moments, I think of her as my own daughter." He turned from the windows, looking at Sarah. "That's why I've been paying attention," he said. "I have the feeling she's ready to assert herself to Mother. Ready, though not quite able. Something's holding her back. Perhaps she needs a little push."

"I've tried, Ned. I've urged her to speak her mind."

"I'd urge outright rebellion."

"We might regret that," Sarah laughed. "I think we'd all better keep quiet until the party is over. We won't be under such stress then."

"One can hope." Ned glanced at his watch. "Damn, I'm late. The club is having a finance meeting and I'm on the committee. Now that the big bad Depression is behind us, we're raising the dues. I'm sorry we can't continue our talk," he said, hurrying to the door, "but duty calls."

"I understand."

"I'll have to get a taxi. I sent Tully on an errand. Damn, damn, damn."

"You could walk," Sarah suggested with an

216

amused smile. "It's only a few blocks."

"Walk? Yes, I suppose I could. Very sensible, dear heart. What would I do without you?"

Ned waved, disappearing into the hall. Sarah took up the newspaper and carried it to the chaise, settling back to read the dispatches from Europe. Her smile faded, her mood changing as again she thought of Aldcross, of England and another war. She glanced through the rest of the paper, skipping the society pages, the fashion sketches. With a gasp she stopped at the obituary pages, for there she saw the notice of Sir Roger Averill's death. She saw his picture staring back at her and she flung the paper away. She tried to stand but her legs were suddenly weak. She felt the pounding of her heart and she drew a breath, calming herself. "It's over," she murmured in wonder. "The nightmare is over." Released at last from her fears, her memories, she wept.

"Mother?" Lucy called, hesitating in the doorway. "Mother, are you all right?"

Now Sarah jumped to her feet. "I'm fine, darling," she said, hastily drying her eyes. "Really I am."

"I knocked, but you didn't hear me. . . . Why were you crying?"

"Oh, sometimes women cry for no reason. At least I do. I get into a certain kind of mood and tears begin to flow. It doesn't mean anything."

"But you're all right?" Lucy persisted. "Are you sure?"

"Quite sure. What have you been up to today? Did you have another fitting?"

"My gown is almost finished, Mother. I was thinking that your pearl choker would be perfect with it. Or maybe just the double strand."

"Of course, darling. Come, I'll give you both necklaces and you can decide later. You may want earrings, too. Let's see what we can find."

Lucy smiled, tilting her curly head to one side. "Do you remember when I was little and you let me play with your jewelry?" she asked.

"You used to play dress up. It doesn't seem that long ago."

"We had such fun when I was little. Everything was easier then."

Sarah heard the wistful note in Lucy's voice. She went to her, gazing into the deep green of her eyes. "You mustn't be afraid to grow up," she said softly. "Your whole life is ahead of you, darling. You can make it any kind of life you want."

"Sometimes I *am* afraid," Lucy admitted. "Gran expects so much of me."

"Never mind what she expects. All that matters is what you expect of yourself." Sarah smiled. Gently, she ruffled Lucy's golden hair. "You're still very young," she said. "The answers will come, in time. I promise they will."

"I want to believe that, Mother. I'll try."

"Good girl! Now come along and we'll go digging in my jewel box."

Lucy followed after Sarah. She stopped near the chaise, bending to retrieve the newspaper from the floor. Sir Roger's picture caught her attention, and frowning, she stared at it. "He looks familiar," she said, as if to herself. "His eyes . . ."

They're your eyes, Sarah cried silently, panic gripping her heart. For one terrible moment she was unable to move, but in the next moment she snatched the paper out of Lucy's hands. "I—I think he was a distant relative of Elizabeth's," she managed to say. "Come along, darling, he was nothing to us. . . . We have the party to think about."

*　　　*　　　*

It was a little before nine on the night of the party when Sarah descended the stairs to the reception hall. She wore an elegant Chanel gown of dark blue velvet, a starburst of diamonds at her shoulder. Her honey hair was brushed into a sleek chignon and secured with a diamond clip. She was smiling, though her eyes moved warily from side to side. "Lucy is still dressing," she said as Elizabeth came forward. "I hope everything's all right."

"I'm sure it is. You look lovely, my dear."

"Thank you. I'm *so* nervous. Ned is, too. He's upstairs pacing back and forth. This is worse than a wedding. . . . What time is it, Elizabeth?"

"We've plenty of time. Our guests won't begin arriving until nine-thirty. The waiters are ready to serve. Mr. Duchin and his orchestra are ready to play. Everything is under control. Would you like to see the ballroom? I'm quite proud of what we've done in there."

"I admit I'm curious," Sarah replied. "You've kept it such a secret."

"Not a secret, my dear, a surprise. I think you will be pleased. We want the proper setting for Lucy, after all."

"Yes, I suppose." Sarah glanced toward the stairs, then crossed the wide hall to the ballroom. Her lips parted as she looked about, for the room had been transformed into a fantasy of silver and white. Around the periphery of the room were slender white marble columns of varying heights and atop them silver urns of calla lilies. One wall was banked with calla lilies and silvered leaves. There were small groupings of tables and chairs, the tables dressed with silver cloths, the dainty chairs painted silver and upholstered in white silk. Fluted silver medallions had been affixed to the French doors, catching the blaze of light from two magnificent crystal chandeliers. "Elizabeth, it's exquisite!"

"I'm glad you approve, my dear."

"Oh, I do. I do." Sarah looked to the far end of the room, where the eighteen-piece Duchin orchestra was tuning up. "Hello, Eddy," she called. "I'm beginning to feel better," she said to Elizabeth. "You really have created something very special."

"Is that a compliment? I believe that's the first compliment you've ever given me."

"Well, God knows we've had our differences."

"Indeed," Elizabeth replied, amused. "Perhaps now you will concede I have only Lucy's best interests at heart."

"We disagree about her best interests, but I realize you're—" Sarah paused, for she heard a sudden rustling on the stair. She turned, gazing across the hall. "Lucy," she cried, rushing to her daughter. "Oh, darling, how beautiful you are. You take my breath away."

Lucy smiled, radiant in a bare-shouldered gown of white chiffon. The bodice was shirred, dipping slightly to reveal the gentle swell of her breasts; the skirt was full and seemed to float about her. A narrow sash of silver lamé encircled her tiny waist, and silver ribbons were threaded through her upswept curls. She wore Sarah's pearls, their glow matching the glow of her porcelain skin. "Do you like my gown, Mother?" she asked. "It's not too showy?"

"It's perfect, darling."

"It certainly is," Ned declared, walking down the stairs. "You're a vision, Miss Lucy. You'll have to beat off your admirers with a stick."

"I don't have any admirers, Daddy."

"Oh? Who are all those moony-eyed boys I see swarming around?"

"Friends."

"A likely story!"

"Come, my dears," Elizabeth said. "We must take our places. . . . Sarah, you will stand here, at the head of the receiving line. I will stand next to you. And Lucy will stand closest to the ballroom. No long conversations please. Exchange a word or two with our guests and let them continue on. After the last guest has been received, Ned will lead Lucy onto the dance floor."

"For a moment I thought you'd forgotten me, Mother."

"Mind you don't forget your duties tonight."

"They're engraved on my heart."

The music began then, and several minutes later the reception hall began filling with the crème of New York society. Sarah, Elizabeth, and Lucy greeted three hundred guests, the women bejeweled and expensively gowned, the men wearing white tie and tails. Three hundred smiles, thought Sarah, sighing in relief when all the guests had finally entered the ballroom. She watched Ned offer his arm to Lucy. She heard the orchestra segue into "The Most Beautiful Girl in the World," and tears sprang to her eyes. Through her tears she watched as Ned and Lucy waltzed across the polished floor. "I was wrong, Elizabeth," she sniffled, struck by the splendor of the moment. "It was worth the fuss."

"Of course it was, my dear. I knew you would see things my way."

"Well, not everything. I just want Lucy to be happy."

"How can she not be happy? She's a Cameron."

Sarah laughed. "You're a remarkable woman, Elizabeth," she said. "Nothing will ever change you. You're as eternal as the sea."

"I don't suppose that's another compliment."

"No," Sarah replied, "I don't suppose it is, either. Shall we join the party?" The waltz ended and she saw Jonathan Melvile claim Lucy for the next dance. Ned left them, coming to her side. "You looked very handsome out there," she said.

"That's one of my duties. Would you care to dance, Sarah? *That* would be my pleasure."

"And mine. Excuse us, Elizabeth."

"Well," Ned said as they took the floor, "how does it feel to be the mother of a debutante?"

"I've grown used to the idea. After seeing this room, seeing the way Lucy is tonight, I'm almost won over. Not that I'd want to go through it again," Sarah added. "Once is enough."

"This isn't the end of it, you know. The next extravaganza will be Lucy's wedding."

"I may encourage her to elope."

"And spoil Mother's fun?" Ned asked, his dark eyes twinkling. "Would you do a thing like that?"

Sarah laughed again. "I would be tempted. Especially if it would spoil Elizabeth's fun. . . . Goodness, I don't want to think about Lucy's wedding yet. She's still my little girl, Ned. Our girl."

"There's an old saying: A son is a son till he takes him a wife, but a daughter's a daughter for all of her life."

"I just want her to be happy. She mustn't be pushed into anything." Sarah looked at Ned, returning his smile. "Perhaps you should have a talk with her," she said. "You're still the most important man in her life."

"I plan to, once all this deb business is finished and once I've found the proper words. I can't come right out and say Mother's a bitch. I'll have to be more subtle than that, although subtlety has never been my strong suit. As you may have noticed, I'm the impetuous sort."

"That's part of your charm."

"Ah yes, my famous charm. I'll try to put it to good use."

"You always do."

"Touché," Ned replied with a laugh. He danced Sarah to the other side of the room, stopping in front of Patrick. "I'll leave you here, dear heart," he said. "It's time for me to make my rounds."

"Rounds?"

"The dowager rounds. The old girls enjoy a bit of flirting. Of course, I tell them they're irresistible. It's a game. . . . Harmless, and it passes the time."

"You're being very obliging tonight," Patrick said.

"Well, it's Lucy's night. I'm willing to play the game for her sake. What the hell? Why not?"

"Can I help?"

"Thanks, Patrick. I'll yell if I need reinforcements."

"Ned surprises me sometimes," Sarah said, watching him walk away. "He's more responsible than people think."

"Yes, but he wouldn't want it to get around. He prefers to be known for his pranks. A blithe spirit to the end." Patrick took Sarah's hand, smiling into her eyes. "I'm in rather a blithe mood myself," he said. "Shall we dance?"

"I was hoping you'd ask." She felt the familiar warmth of Patrick's arms, and for a brief moment she nuzzled her cheek to his. "I love you," she whispered.

"I love you too, my darling. Let's run away together."

"You mustn't tease."

"I'm serious. Come spring we're going to have a week in Paris. It's all arranged. I won't listen to arguments, Sarah. Now that Lucy has been launched, there are no arguments that matter."

"Paris."

"Paris in the spring."

Sarah's heart began to race. She felt a sudden elation and she smiled so brightly that light seemed to fall from her. "Oh, I want to say yes, Patrick. I *want* to."

"Then say it. We may not have another chance anytime soon. I don't know what will come of all this talk of war. Nothing, I hope. But with all the uncertainty, let's take our week while we can. We deserve that much, Sarah. At least that much. You've given your life to Lucy. You can give yourself a week in Paris."

"Yes. Oh, yes, Patrick, I will. Come spring we'll be dancing down the Champs Elysees!" Paris, thought Sarah, tingling with excitement. For years she had dreamed of such a trip; a thousand times she had imagined what it would be like. "We've never even had a whole night together," she murmured. "Now we'll have a whole week. And in *Paris.*"

"The city of lovers."

"It's too good to be true. Pinch me."

"I'd rather kiss you," Patrick laughed. "But I can't, not here. Maybe later we can sneak out onto the terrace. A little hanky-panky in the moonlight."

Sarah laughed also. She gazed across the room boisterous with voices, glittering with jewels and silks and brilliant light, and abruptly the laughter died in her throat. She froze, clinging to Patrick. "No," she gasped. "Oh my God, no."

"What is it, Sarah? What's wrong?"

"He's here. My God, he's here. He's alive."

"Who's alive?" Patrick followed Sarah's anguished gaze to the doorway. He saw Elizabeth standing there, and with her a tall, handsome young man. "That's just another guest," he said, his frown

224

deepening. "Do you know the boy?"

"I know him."

"Well?"

"He's Sir Roger Averill," Sarah said in a quick, ragged voice. "Sir Roger Averill of Greenway Hall." Her hands fell to her sides. She was absolutely still, as if carved of stone. "And he's alive."

"You must be mistaken. Listen to me, there's—"

"He's alive," Sarah repeated. She took a step forward. Patrick tried to stop her but he was too late, for she spun away, dodging and ducking the crush of dancers as she rushed to the door. Her mind was reeling, her expression a mixture of the shock and angry confusion she felt. She wanted to scream, to order the unexpected visitor from the house, but when finally she reached him she spoke only one word. "You," she cried, and it was an accusation.

"Sarah," Elizabeth said, "I would like you to meet our distant cousin, Sir Colin Averill. And this is my daughter-in-law, Sarah Cameron."

"It's a great pleasure to meet you, Mrs. Cameron."

"You're—you're *Colin* Averill?"

"Yes, Mrs. Cameron. I must apologize for coming late. I've just recently arrived in New York, you see, and I haven't quite got the hang of things yet. I walked from the hotel and found myself quite lost. . . . Please accept my apologies."

"I'm the one who should apologize," Sarah replied. "I—I thought you were somebody else." She stared at Colin, seeing Sir Roger's chiseled features and fine golden hair. "The resemblance is so strong," she murmured.

"Colin is said to resemble his father," Elizabeth interjected. "We were all very sorry to hear of Roger's death."

"Thank you, Cousin Elizabeth. It was sudden, as

225

you know. A hunting accident . . . I've come to New York to settle some of Father's affairs. I'd received your invitation months ago and I thought I'd just stop in and say hello."

"We're delighted you did, aren't we, Sarah?"

"Yes, delighted . . . Oh, Patrick, I don't believe you've met Colin Averill, Sir Colin."

Patrick smiled, extending his hand. "How do you do?" he said. He glanced swiftly at Sarah's pale, strained face and then turned back to Colin. "Let's get you a drink," he suggested with a heartiness he did not feel. "If you will excuse us, ladies."

"By all means," Elizabeth replied. "Now before you jump down my throat," she said when they had gone, "there is a simple explanation to this."

"How could you do such a thing?" Sarah demanded. "How could you invite him here?"

"Don't make a scene, my dear."

"A scene!"

Elizabeth led Sarah away from the door, drawing her into an alcove. "All right," she sighed, "to answer your question, the invitation was a courtesy. The Averills were most gracious when I was last in London. Naturally, I invited their boys to Lucy's party. I didn't expect either of the boys to be in New York. I couldn't have foreseen Roger's death, after all. But now that Colin is here I'm not sorry. His title lends a certain cachet to the evening. It's true he's only a baronet, but any title is an advantage in such a situation."

"You play dangerous games, Elizabeth. You play with our lives."

"Nonsense. Colin knows nothing of his father's past actions. And there is nothing to connect you and Lucy to the Averills. . . . I realize this may be awkward for you, Sarah, but you can't blame Colin for Roger's old sins."

"Old sins cast long shadows."

"There are no shadows. Colin isn't Roger. He's a lovely boy."

"You don't have to tell me about Colin. I knew him when he was still in diapers. His nursemaid used to take him for rides in his pony cart. He wouldn't remember, but I do. Anyway, that's not the point. The point is he's an *Averill*. My God, Elizabeth, he's Lucy's half brother."

"A matter of no concern to anyone. Colin will be gone tomorrow. Meanwhile, Lucy will have had a baronet at her party."

"*I'm* concerned."

"You worry far too much, Sarah. You worry when there is no reason. Certainly there's no reason to worry about Colin."

"Well, perhaps not."

"Of course not. Now come rejoin the party. And do try to smile. This is Lucy's night, my dear."

Lucy stood on the terrace, her wide chiffon skirt billowing in the breeze. She watched the moon disappear behind puffy black clouds and she lowered her gaze to the garden. Tiny angel lights had been twined through the shrubbery, glimmering like fireflies in the darkness. She watched the lights, and after some moments she smiled.

"A penny for your thoughts."

Lucy glanced around, her smile brightening as she saw a broad-shouldered young man with jet-black hair and laughing blue eyes. "Oh, it's you, Tony," she said. "Why aren't you dancing?"

"Why aren't you? The belle of the ball isn't supposed to be hiding."

"I'm not. I wanted a breath of fresh air. It's so pretty out here. It's pretty inside, too, but there are all those people. I needed to be by myself for a while."

"How long is a while? You promised me a dance, you know. Nice girls keep their promises."

"You'll step on my toes, just the way you used to in Mr. De Rham's dancing class."

"That was to get your attention," Tony replied, leaning his tall frame against the terrace rail. "Besides, I was twelve years old."

"You were fresh. And from what I hear, you still are."

"Never listen to gossip, missy."

"You broke Anne Schyler's heart."

"Broke her heart!" Tony threw his head back, roaring with laughter. "First I'd have to *find* her heart," he said. "No easy task. Anne's a devious little creature. She also happens to talk too much. . . . But for your information, we had exactly one date. One date and one kiss . . . Are you jealous?"

"Jealous! Why should I be? I don't care what you do."

"No? Come on, Lucy, admit it. You know you have a soft spot for me."

"The only soft spot is in your brain . . . or your ego. I suppose you think all you have to do is smile— the way you're smiling now—and every girl in New York will fall at your feet. Anne and Meg and Wendy and Julie and—"

"I think the lady doth protest too much. I think you'd like to be kissed."

"Don't you dare, Tony Jennings."

"Wouldn't you like to be kissed?"

Lucy tossed her head. "Not by you," she said, mustering all the hauteur of her seventeen years.

"Okay, we'll just stand here. . . . Stand here and get

228

wet. Lucy, it's starting to rain. We'd better go inside. Here, take my hand."

"Can I trust you?"

Tony's smile widened. Quite suddenly he bent his head, pressing his mouth against hers. A moment later he stepped back. "Well, so much for trust," he said laughing. "But I couldn't resist. I've wanted to do that ever since I was twelve."

"Oh, you're impossible! Harvard certainly hasn't improved your manners."

"It's true, all true. I should be shot. No, shooting's too good for me. A dagger through the heart, that's what I deserve."

Lucy could not help laughing. "I wish it weren't so hard to stay angry with you," she said as they entered the ballroom. "But it is."

"In that case I think we should have our dance."

They glided across the floor to the lilting melody of "Isn't It Romantic." It was their only dance, for dozens of eager young men awaited their turn with Lucy. She was indeed the belle of the ball, alternately flirtatious and shy as compliments were showered on her. Toward the end of the evening, Josh appeared at her side. "Have you come for a dance?" she laughed. "I'm not sure I can fit you in."

"There's someone I want you to meet, Lucy," he replied. "Assuming I can tear you away from your beaux.

"Maybe. Who is it?"

"Some distant relation of Aunt Elizabeth's. He's English. *Sir* Colin Averill, if you please. But he's really all right. I think it's time he met the star of the show."

"Do I have to curtsy?"

"I hope you're joking."

"I am," Lucy replied. "All the champagne's gone

to my head." She walked with Josh to one of the small tables. Instantly, Colin rose. She looked at him and felt herself blush, for she thought him the handsomest man she had ever seen. She felt strange, almost giddy. She reached her hand to the back of a chair, clutching it while she caught her breath. "Hello," she murmured.

"Lucy, this is Sir Colin Averill. My cousin, Lucy Cameron."

"How do you do," they said together. Colin smiled, taking the hand Lucy offered. "It's so nice to meet you, Miss Cameron."

"Please call me Lucy."

"Thank you. I've been enjoying your party, Lucy. Have you strength for one more dance? I'd be honored."

"Of course, Sir Colin."

"Oh, Colin is good enough," he said quickly. The *Sir* sounds a bit foolish in America, doesn't it?"

"I think it's charming. Like something out of a fairy tale. Do you have a castle?"

"Well, a large country house anyway," Colin laughed. "Castles are drafty. . . . Shall we try this waltz, Lucy?"

She moved into the circle of his arms as if she had been there many times before. She scarcely felt the floor beneath her feet, scarcely heard the voices rising and falling all around. Certainly she did not see Sarah's anxious glance in her direction. She gazed, enchanted, at Colin, so thoroughly absorbed he might have been the only person in the room. "You're—you're a wonderful dancer," she stammered.

"I have a wonderful partner. You're very lovely, you know. But you must be tired of hearing that by now. I noticed all the chaps flocking around. You've stolen their hearts."

"Oh, no. I mean, they're boys I've known all my life."

"Surely that hasn't been such a long time."

"Seventeen years," Lucy said. "I'm seventeen. Most of the boys here tonight are older."

"Then I qualify. I'm twenty." Colin gazed into her deep green eyes. "And I've never been happier than I am right now," he added softly. "Does that seem a silly thing to say?"

"It doesn't seem silly to me."

The waltz ended. A fox trot began and Colin drew Lucy closer. "I'd planned to return to England tomorrow," he said. "If I stayed, could I see you again? Perhaps I shouldn't ask. I'm afraid I made rather a bad impression on your mother. I arrived late, and I must have sounded like a perfect idiot babbling on about how I'd got lost. It wasn't a very promising start."

"Mother was just nervous about the party," Lucy explained. "Whatever it was, I'm sure it had nothing to do with you, Colin. Mother isn't that way."

"That's a relief, because I *do* want to see you again. Suddenly I want that more than anything in the world. May I see you tomorrow? Could we dine together, Lucy?"

"I'd love to."

"I'll telephone you in the morning. Not too early."

"I'll be waiting," Lucy said, her eyes shining. "I won't move from the telephone until I hear your voice."

"It's odd how one's life can change in a moment. I meant only to stop in and say hello to Cousin Elizabeth. But then I saw you and I knew I had to stay. . . . I'm awfully glad I did."

Lucy smiled and her beautiful face shimmered

with light. From across the room Sarah watched. She spoke a few curt words to Elizabeth, words that brought the older woman to Lucy's side.

"I'm so pleased you're enjoying yourselves," she said, "but we're about to have the last dance. Lucy darling, you must give that dance to Jonathan. He's your supper partner."

"Yes, Gran."

"Colin, if you don't mind, some of the gentlemen are anxious to hear more of the situation in Europe. Can I spirit you away?"

He looked at Lucy, bowing slightly over her hand. "I'm yours, Cousin Elizabeth," he replied.

At midnight the lights were lowered and the Duchin orchestra played "Good Night Sweetheart," ending the dance. The guests adjourned to the reception room, where round tables had been set with crystal and silver and silver-bordered white china. The place cards were edged in silver, and near each place was a remembrance of the evening, a silver trinket box from Tiffany's.

Ned offered a toast to Lucy and then supper was served, a light supper of salmon and Cornish hen and brandy soufflé. Lucy picked at her food, for she had little appetite. She listened to Jonathan's college stories, dutifully laughing at his jokes, but her thoughts remained with Colin. A dozen times she looked across the room to where he sat, smiling and blushing when she caught his eye. It was a while before she noticed that other eyes were watching her—the worried eyes of Sarah and Ned and Patrick. Something is wrong, she thought, but at that moment Elizabeth rose and the thought was lost. She rose also, starting toward the door to bid good night to her guests.

Limousines lined the avenue outside the Cameron

house. Sleepy chauffeurs came to attention, rushing forward with umbrellas and opening doors. It was after three when the last limousine pulled away. "Thank heavens," Sarah said, draping her arm about Lucy's shoulder. "The night is finally over. Did you have a good time, darling?"

"It was wonderful, Mother. Thank you. And thank you, Gran," she added, kissing Elizabeth's cheek. "I'll never forget this evening."

"I should hope not! You were a *great* success. Now you must run along to bed. Very soon the telephone will start ringing off the hook."

"Are you coming, Elizabeth?"

"I want a word with the caterer's men. Go on with Lucy, my dear."

Sarah and Lucy went to the staircase. "I was so proud of you tonight," Sarah said. "I'm always proud of you, but tonight was special. You were a perfect hostess, and it couldn't have been easy with all those handsome fellows crowding around. They seemed very devoted, even our English visitor Colin. Did you enjoy his company?"

Lucy heard the abrupt change in Sarah's tone. She looked at her and beyond the fixed smile she saw apprehension. "You don't like Colin, do you?" she asked.

"Oh, I'm sure he's a fine young man. But I wouldn't want you to—to get any ideas about him. His life is in England. Your life is here. Do you undertand, darling?"

"Yes, I think I do."

"You aren't going to see him again?"

Lucy hesitated before replying. She had never lied to Sarah before but now the lie came readily. "Colin is leaving for London in just a few hours," she said. "I won't see him again."

Chapter Twelve

It was a little past two in the afternoon when Lucy rushed down the steps of Rockefeller Center to the skating rink. Nervously, her eyes scanned the people gathered at the rail. She saw Colin and she smiled, quickening her pace. The brisk winter wind blew her hair about her flushed face. Her hat flew away and still she ran, a few moments later coming to a breathless halt. "Oh, Colin," she said, "have you been waiting long? I hurried, but there were so many phone calls and then I couldn't find a taxi and then—"

"It's all right," he laughed, catching her gloved hands in his. "I would have waited forever."

"Really?"

"Cross my heart."

"You're—you're not sorry you changed your plans?"

"Not a bit," Colin replied. "It was a problem with the hotel, but I've moved to the Plaza and now everything is splendid. I've settled in for an indefinite stay. My time is yours, Lucy. . . . The truth is, you're all I've been able to think about. I didn't sleep a wink last night. I kept watching the clock, counting off the hours until I could telephone you. . . . I'm sounding like a lovesick schoolboy, aren't I? Forgive me."

"There's nothing to forgive, Colin. I feel the same way. I didn't sleep either. And every time the phone rang I prayed it would be you. It's so strange. Yesterday afternoon I didn't even know you existed. But today I feel as if I've known you always."

Colin gazed into Lucy's eyes. Gently, he lifted her hand to his cheek. "What would you like to do today?" he asked. "Where shall we go?"

"I thought we could go to Greenwich Village. It's sort of quiet and pretty. There are little cafés."

"Greenwich Village it is. Do we walk or ride?"

"Oh, it would be a very long walk. It's miles away."

"A taxi then," Colin declared, taking Lucy's arm as they ascended the steps. "I wish I could offer you a golden coach."

She smiled, radiant in the sunlight. "We don't need a golden coach," she said.

And to passersby observing the young couple it was obvious that they needed nothing but each other. Hand in hand they strolled the winding streets of Greenwich Village, browsing in quaint galleries and dusty bookshops. They peered over the shoulders of sidewalk artists, and later, in a small candlelit café, they sipped demitasse and talked of their lives, their dreams. "I read history at Oxford," Colin was explaining now. "History's always fascinated me, although I'm not sure if it's going to be my career. I know only that I *want* a career of some kind. Father never actually worked at anything. He had his friends and his clubs and his social engagements. When he went to the country he did quite a lot of shooting. . . . But that's not the life I want."

"It would be nice to live in the country," Lucy said.

"In a cozy house with lots of books and comfortable chairs and a dog sleeping on the hearth. I can see you in a house like that. You'd have a study where you'd do your work. Perhaps you'd write essays on historical subjects."

"Boring essays no one would read."

"I'd read them, Colin."

He smiled, reaching across the table for Lucy's hand. "You're wonderful," he said. "And you've painted a wonderful picture of my future, but I think you've left something out. A wife. I'd have a wife."

"Yes." Lucy felt the color creep into her cheeks. She nodded, lowering her gaze. "Yes, you'd have a wife."

"She'd bring me cocoa on cold nights and insist I wear a sweater in the damp. She'd fuss about my driving when we motored up to London for theater and shopping. . . . I'd love her very much," Colin added quietly. "I'd try to make her happy."

"You would. I know you would."

Colin stared at Lucy, touched anew by her earnestness, by her fresh and innocent beauty. He wanted to leap across the table and take her in his arms, but almost in the same moment he heard a voice warning that everything was happening too fast, that danger lay ahead. His face clouded. He withdrew his hand from hers and lighted a cigarette. "Perhaps we should go," he said.

"What's wrong, Colin?"

"I don't know. I have the feeling we're getting into deep water."

"I can swim," Lucy replied with a shy smile.

But can you? thought Colin, a frown shadowing his brow. "You're so young," he said. "So young and so sweet. I'd rather die than see you hurt. Last night was something out of a dream, Lucy. I saw you and I knew I had to see you again. I never stopped to think. . . . Now I'm wondering if I've done the right thing. Your mother's concern—"

"Is that what's bothering you, Colin? You mustn't worry about Mother."

"But you've had to lie to her."

"I didn't like doing it," Lucy conceded. "I didn't see any choice. Besides, I know Mother will understand once I explain things."

"It was wrong of me to put you in this position. Your mother's concern is really quite sensible. I *am* a stranger, after all. My home, my people, are thousands of miles from here. Have you thought about that, Lucy? Have you thought about the miles separating us?"

"There are no miles separating us, not now. We're together in this pretty little café. Together, Colin. Isn't that a lovely word?"

"A confusing word. I've been confused since we met. Confused and distracted and in a daze." He smiled, his expression clearing. "I don't know what to make of it," he said. "Or perhaps I do." Again he took Lucy's hand, and despite his misgivings, he laughed. "I'm bewitched, that's the answer. You're a sorceress!"

"I wish you would stop fidgeting," Elizabeth said, settling her dark gaze on Sarah. "I realize you're tired after last night's festivities. We're all tired, my dear. But you might at least make an effort to pay attention."

"The subject isn't very interesting," Sarah replied sharply. "If you want to have an elevator installed, go ahead. You don't need my permission, or Ned's."

"You may both be asked to vacate your rooms

during the installation."

"A terrible tragedy."

"Sarah, your attitude is most unpleasant."

"Oh, for heaven's sake, Elizabeth, can't you see I'm worried about Lucy? It's past six and she isn't home. She hasn't even called. I can't shake the feeling that it has something to do with Colin Averill."

"How absurd. I told you I took the precaution of phoning his hotel. He's checked out, Sarah. Colin is on his way to England."

"Do you suppose that's the end of it? You saw them together last night. What if she's gone to say goodbye? What if they start writing to each other? What if he *comes back?* I'll never forgive you for having him here. It was stupid. Worse, it was dangerous. You and your dangerous games."

"I resent your implication. I couldn't possibly have known Colin would be in New York. The invitation was merely a courtesy."

"Mother is always courteous," Ned interjected, sipping his drink. "She wreaks havoc left and right, but in a *courteous* manner. Of course that makes it all right."

Elizabeth turned, her gaze sweeping to her son. "Your sarcasm is no longer amusing," she said. "I'll tell you what it is. A shield. A shield for your own weakness. Are you finally taking an interest in your family, Ned? Are you finally willing to speak? It would be nice to think you've found your courage."

"It's true I haven't your courage, Mother. But then I haven't your arrogance, either. You do as you wish, and to hell with everybody else."

"That's an odd statement, coming from you. Haven't you done as you've wished all these years?"

"I haven't hurt anyone. I haven't risked hurting anyone. But you—you were so intent on dressing up

238

the guest list, you never considered the consequences."

"Consequences?"

"Well, the effect on Sarah. She certainly didn't relish coming face to face with her past. And the effect on Lucy had Colin remained in New York."

"I repeat, I couldn't possibly have known Colin would be here."

"He shouldn't have been invited, Mother. But you had to do things your way."

"This entire conversation is ridiculous," Elizabeth replied, her serene smile unchanged. "Lucy's debut was a great success. Colin has returned home. No harm has been done. . . . As for Lucy and Colin starting a correspondence, that too is ridiculous. Lucy will be busy enough with her local admirers."

"Oh, let's stop talking about it," Sarah said. "I thought I'd heard the last of the Averills when Sir Roger died. I thought it was over. But it won't ever be over, will it?"

"Sarah—"

"No, I don't want to talk about it anymore. I'm getting a dreadful headache."

"Shall I have Violet bring the aspirin?"

"Don't bother her. I'll feel better when I see Lucy walk through the door. I can't understand why she hasn't called. I hope nothing's happened."

"You're being foolish, my dear. Of course nothing's happened."

Ned turned away from the windows. He crossed the room, sitting next to Sarah on the couch. "Lucy isn't all that late," he said. "You know how bad traffic can be."

"Yes, I know. For once I agree with your mother. I *am* being foolish. I can't help it. My nerves are on edge."

"That's only natural. You had a nasty shock last night. But everything's all right now, I'm sure. Cheer up, dear heart. The worst is over."

"Is it, Ned? I have such a funny feeling."

"Women's intuition, eh?"

"Maybe. It's as good an explanation as any." Sarah glanced at her watch. "Six-thirty," she said, rising. "If you'll excuse me, Elizabeth, I'm going to my room. I have some reports to finish for the Galleries. And please don't tell me I work too hard. Work can be very soothing."

"So I have heard. But before you go, I'd like to settle the matter of the elevator."

"The elevator? Oh, I don't care about that. You'll do what you want anyway." Sarah left the study. She walked along the hall, pausing when she heard footsteps on the stair. "Lucy, is that you?" she called. "Lucy?"

"Yes, Mother. I'm so sorry I'm late."

"I was worried," Sarah said as Lucy reached the top of the landing. "I see I needn't have been concerned. You look marvelous, darling. You're shining like a Christmas tree."

"Am I, Mother?"

"What's put you in such a happy mood?"

Lucy shrugged. "I guess I'm still thinking about the party," she replied. She linked her arm in Sarah's, and together they continued up the stairs. "I wasn't a bit tired today, Mother. Were you?"

"I'm afraid I didn't sleep very well. All the excitement . . . But everyone had a wonderful time, and that was the idea. Tell me about your day, Lucy. You must have had quite a lot to do."

"Oh, just the usual things," she said, avoiding Sarah's gaze. "Shopping, and then I stopped at Schrafft's. I walked for a while. Somehow I wound up at the movies. I know I should have called, Mother, but I lost track of time. The party's left me in a daze."

Sarah smiled, considering Lucy's account of the day's events. She had no real reason to question it, yet doubt gnawed at her. "Didn't you see any of your friends?" she asked.

"I will tomorrow. I'm having lunch with Alice and her cousins from out of town." Lucy looked quickly at her mother. She felt the burden of her lies; she felt ashamed, but she knew she could not risk the truth. I'll explain everything when the time is right, she told herself. Mother will understand. Gran will be furious, but Mother will understand. "It's going to be a busy week. I—I should have asked if you had any plans."

"That's all right, darling. I have a very popular daughter and I'd best get used to it."

They entered Lucy's bedroom. Lucy removed her coat and gloves, suddenly touching her hand to her head. "Goodness, I've lost my hat!"

"Didn't you take it off at the movies?"

"The movies . . . Oh, yes, that's exactly what I did, Mother. Silly of me to forget it. I'll call the theater in the morning." Lucy sat down, glancing at the telephone messages arranged on her desk. "Tony phoned three times," she said, shaking her head. "I'll bet he phoned to tease me about last night. He kept calling me the belle of the ball."

"Tony Jennings? I think he's charming."

"Yes, I guess so. But he's not . . . serious. He's always laughing and making jokes. He says he's going to be a playwright when he's finished at Harvard. A playwright!"

"Well, what's wrong with that?"

"It's not a serious profession, Mother. It's not like

being a lawyer or . . . a historian."

Again Sarah smiled. "The world would be a dull place if everybody were serious all the time. The Jenningses won't approve of their son going into the theater, but it's a fine ambition nonetheless. I hope Tony isn't forced to change his plan."

Lucy dropped the messages into the wastebasket. She turned and walked to a long wall of closets, opening the center door. "I have to find something to wear tomorrow," she said. "Which dress do you like best?"

"You have so many. . . . But I think the jade wool. It's almost the color of your eyes."

"The style is all wrong. It makes me look too young."

"You *are* young," Sarah laughed. "Enjoy it while you can. Be happy."

"Oh, Mother, I'm very happy," Lucy said, spinning around. "I wish you knew. . . . I wish I could explain. . . ."

Sarah frowned, going to her daughter. "Explain what, darling?" she asked. "Is there something you want to tell me?"

"Just that I'm happy. So very happy."

Colin watched Lucy running toward him, her golden hair fanning out beneath a small, stylish hat, her face rosy in the wind. His breath caught and he, too, began to run. "Lucy," he murmured, taking hold of her slim shoulders. "Lucy, I've been counting the hours."

She smiled at him, gazing up into his clear blue eyes. "That's what I've been doing," she said. "We have the whole afternoon, Colin. It's all arranged. My friend Alice Calloway will help us. If there's any question, Alice will say I've spent the time with her."

"This is getting terribly complicated for you, isn't it? The truth would be so much better. And fairer."

"No, not yet."

"I'm certain I could change your mother's impression of me."

"It isn't only Mother," Lucy replied. "Mother's easy. She just wants me to be happy, and I am. But Gran . . . Well, it's different with Gran. We mustn't spoil things, Colin. Please."

"Don't fret. I wouldn't dream of spoiling things. Actually, secret meetings are rather romantic. Where shall we hide ourselves today?"

"I bought a guidebook," Lucy said. "We can pretend we're tourists out to see the city."

"Splendid," Colin laughed. "Where do we start?"

"If we're tourists, we start with the subway!"

Lucy and Colin rode the subway to Chinatown. There they explored the narrow streets, the joss houses, the tiny restaurants and colorful shops. Inside the shops they looked at paper flowers and paper fans and wonderful kites shaped like dragons and butterflies. Colin found a small silk butterfly in shades of deepest green. "To match your eyes," he said, giving it to Lucy.

They continued their walk, stopping in a dimly lit restaurant on Mott Street. Their waiter, a silent black-clad man with a long black pigtail, brought course after course to the table. There were spicy noodles and little spareribs in ginger sauce and fried dough cakes and covered dishes of shredded chicken and exotic Chinese vegetables. Lucy and Colin devoured every morsel. They drank pots and pots of tea. They talked for hours, coming to know each other as they shared the smaller, more intimate details of their lives. When finally they left the restaurant, they were surprised to see it was night. "Where has the time gone?" Lucy said, her eyes searching the dark sky. "Oh, Colin, I don't want to go home."

"And I don't want you to go. It will seem a lifetime until tomorrow. I'm lost without you, Lucy. I just wander about, or else I sit staring into space. This morning I found myself grinning for no reason at all. Grinning like an imbecile."

"This morning I walked into a wall. It's true. I walked into a wall as if it weren't there. See," Lucy laughed, pointing to the bridge of her nose, "a bump."

"It's charming." Colin bent, kissing the patch of raised flesh. "Does it hurt?"

"Not anymore. It stopped hurting as soon as I saw you."

He gazed at her for a long moment. "I—I suppose I should get a taxi," he said.

"Yes. I hate the thought but I have to go home."

They held hands during the ride uptown. Lucy nestled her head on Colin's shoulder, glancing now and then at his handsome profile. I love him, she said silently to herself. I love him and I'm the happiest girl in the world.

The taxi came to an abrupt stop five blocks from the Cameron house. Colin opened the door. "Careful," he said with a smile. "Mind your step or you'll have another bump."

"A matched set," Lucy replied, taking his hand.

"Are you quite certain you don't want me to have a word with your family?"

"This isn't the time, Colin."

Again he gazed at her. All at once he took her in his arms, covering her mouth with his own. "Lucy," he murmured letting her go. "Tomorrow?"

"Yes," she said breathlessly. "Tomorrow."

She turned and hurried along the avenue, her step so light she seemed to be floating on air. Moments later she was home, floating up the stairs. Surely she spoke to Raymond, to Sarah and Elizabeth; she could not remember, for the thought of Colin sent her world reeling. She lay upon her bed and remembered only Colin—his smile, his voice, his touch. She slept, and in her dreams he was there.

The next day, Tuesday, Lucy and Colin went to Battery Park. They watched the ships sailing into the harbor, gaily colored flags fluttering in the breeze. They watched the play of sunlight on the churning river. Hand in hand they walked the path by the sea wall, laughing as birds swooped and soared against the pale sky. They talked, never running out of things to say to each other, never tiring of the discoveries they made. Indeed it was a time of discovery, of all the sweet surprises of first love. "I love you," Colin murmured later in the taxicab taking them uptown. "I love you," he murmured when they alighted from the taxi. "I love you," he murmured when he kissed her good night.

"I love you," Lucy replied each time, all the while feeling such joy she thought her heart would burst.

On Wednesday they again traveled downtown, taking a ferry ride across the bay. It was a cold, damp afternoon, but they hardly noticed the bleak weather. They stood alone on the windswept deck, gazing at each other while the Manhattan skyline blurred and then receded from view. They heard the cry of gulls, the hollow clang of buoys, and it seemed a kind of music. They were in a world all their own, a world without sorrows or terrors, without end.

Now Colin slipped his arm around Lucy, drawing her closer. "I wish we could stay here forever," he said. "Just the two of us on a funny little boat going back and forth."

"We'd get hungry."

"We'd live on love." He looked at her, a small smile edging his mouth. "I do love you, you know. I haven't the right, but there it is. . . . I really *haven't* the right, Lucy. That's the awful part of it. I'll be returning to England soon. Oh, not right away and not because I want to. Because I must."

"Take me with you, Colin."

"That's all I've been able to think about. I've tried to think what's best. For you, I mean."

"You're what's best for me," Lucy said. She met Colin's clear blue gaze, touching her hand to his cheek. "I've never been happier."

"You're seventeen. *Never* isn't a very long time at seventeen."

"Listen to the wise old man of twenty," Lucy laughed. "Mother was married at seventeen. Did you know that? Married and widowed and on her way to a strange country. I don't have her courage. At least I didn't until I met you. Now I feel very brave. I'm *filled* with courage."

"You may need it. There's something else to consider, you see. There may be war in Europe, and if it comes to that . . ."

"There isn't a war yet."

"But to take you away from your family, Lucy. To take you from safety to a place where there may be war . . ." Colin turned, staring past the rail at the rippling water. "How could I do that to someone I love?" he asked softly. "I'd—I'd have to join my regiment. You'd be alone, amongst strangers. I've family, of course, but they'd be strangers to you. It's impossible. . . . Impossible," he sighed, "but still I can't bear the idea of leaving you behind. . . . I've made such a bloody mess of things. I knew I would. A little voice kept warning me. . . ."

"I hope you've finished," Lucy said, laughing once more. "Because now it's my turn. I've thought of all these same arguments, Colin. I've thought about what it would be like so far from home. I've even thought about a war. And none of it matters. *We* matter, you and I. We love each other. I know it happened quickly, but that doesn't matter either. It *did* happen and that's all that's important."

"Perhaps I should speak to your father, Lucy."

"He's in Chicago. Another business trip."

"Your mother then."

Lucy was silent for a moment, her pale brows drawing together. "Mother doesn't think I know my own mind," she replied finally. "And I didn't, until I met you. . . . The other problem is that Gran would find out. She'd separate us, Colin. She'd interfere. If it were just Mother . . . But it's Gran too."

Colin clasped Lucy's hands in his. "You're trembling," he said. "Does she frighten you so much?"

"I'm only frightened that she'll ruin what we have. Gran has her own plans for me. I think she wants me to marry Jonny Melvile."

Colin saw Lucy's distress. He took her head onto his shoulder, stroking her golden hair. "Are you sure of your feelings?" he asked. "Very sure?"

"I love you. I'm sure of that."

"No questions, Lucy? No lingering doubts?"

"No."

Colin stepped back. He reached into his pocket and removed a square velvet jeweler's box. "I did a little shopping this morning," he explained. "I hope you like it."

Lucy opened the box, her eyes glowing as she beheld an exquisite emerald ring. "Oh, Colin, it's *beautiful.*"

"To match your eyes. May I put it on?" He plucked the ring from the box and placed it on her finger. "Will you marry me, Miss Cameron?"

"Oh, Colin." She flung her arms around his neck, pressing so close she could feel the beating of his heart against hers. "*Yes,* I'll marry you," she cried. "Yes, yes, yes."

"Now what do we do?" he laughed. "We can't just sneak off."

"We can! We can elope!"

"You're utterly charming, my love, but you're not of age. Don't we need licenses and permissions?"

"Not in Maryland. Colin, let's elope today, right now."

"Would that make you happy? You're certain you don't want a big, splashy wedding?"

"I want to be your wife. That's big and splashy enough for me."

"How can I resist you? We're off to Maryland, wherever that may be."

"It isn't far," Lucy said, her voice quivering with excitement. "We can take the afternoon train and find a justice of the peace and be back in New York by midnight."

"And what of your family?"

"I'll wire Mother from Maryland. Everything will be fine. Everything will be wonderful."

You're wonderful. I still say you're a sorceress." Colin wrapped her in his arms. His pulse was racing, for he too felt the excitement of the moment, the sheer joy of knowing Lucy would soon be his wife. Again he heard the warning voice but it was quieter now, barely more than a whisper, and he chased it from his mind. "Lady Averill," he murmured.

"What?"

"In a few hours, you'll be Lady Averill."

"We want to be married," Colin shyly explained to the Baltimore taxi driver. "But the thing is . . . well, we don't quite know where we're supposed to go. Is there a registry office hereabouts?"

The driver, a stocky gray-haired man named Homer Dale, grinned into his rearview mirror. "So you want to get yourselves hitched," he said. "And you don't want to wait."

"Why, no," Colin replied. "I understood there was no waiting period in Maryland."

"You understood right, sonny. What you want is a JP."

Colin glanced uncertainly at Lucy. "JP?"

"Justice of the peace," she translated. "Yes, Mr. Dale, that's exactly what we want. Could you take us to a justice of the peace? Somewhere nice? Perhaps in the country?"

"Well, I don't know about the country, but yeah, I can take you someplace nice. Run you four . . . five bucks on the meter. That too much?"

"That's fine," Colin said. "Do you suppose we could stop for flowers on the way?"

"Flowers?" Homer Dale grinned again into the mirror. "Sure. You kids just settle back and leave it to me. I'll get you where you want to go, and with flowers for the little lady. A bride has to have flowers."

Bride. Lucy rolled the word over and over in her mind, savoring it as she might some rare, exotic treat. She gazed at Colin, and once more she imagined the life they would have together—a life far from New York and Elizabeth and the Cameron house. For a split second her confidence wavered. I'll miss Mother and Daddy, she thought to herself. She thought about her friends, knowing she would not miss them, but then, from out of the blue, she thought of Tony Jennings and, grudgingly, admitted that she would miss his roguish charm. These doubts, if doubts they were, vanished when she looked into Colin's clear, earnest eyes. "I love you," she whispered, her own eyes misting with happy tears.

"I love you, my darling. For always and always."

Homer Dale, listening to the tender exchange, nodded his approval. He was glad to be a cabdriver today; it was what he often told his wife. . . . Maybe there wasn't much money in driving a cab, but you sure saw a lot of life. And sometimes the good things in life, too, like these kids. They were good kids, he decided, even if the boy was a Limey. "Hey, sonny," he said now, bringing the cab to a screeching halt outside Simpson's Fine Flowers, "you come along with me. Just let me do the talking. I'll see you get a nice bouquet. With ribbons, maybe," he added, warming to the subject. "We'll surprise the little lady here. Okay?"

"Thank you, Mr. Dale. You're most kind."

Lucy smiled as Colin followed the driver into the florist shop. She leaned forward, watching the sudden activity through the plate glass window. She saw a clerk scurrying back and forth, saw Homer Dale shake his head no, then yes when a length of white satin ribbon was produced. She saw the clerk get busy with clippers and paper lace and bits of wire. A few minutes later she saw Colin open his wallet and place a bill on the counter.

Proudly, he carried the bouquet from the flo-

250

rist's, nestling it in Lucy's hands. "It isn't very grand but—"

"Oh, it's *beautiful,*" she cried. And so it was, a small, old-fashioned nosegay of pale pink roses and white violets, the buds circled with paper lace and long, scalloped ribbons. "It's *beautiful,* Colin. I love it."

"We haven't a proper wedding ring, Lucy. Shall we stop at a jewelers?"

"We can use this," she replied, slipping the magnificent emerald into his hand. "We can always get a wedding band in New York. . . . And besides, I'm in a hurry to become Lady Averill."

Homer Dale's ears pricked up at this. "Lady Averill?" he asked. "Hey, sonny, you one of them dukes or princes or something?"

"Just a baronet," Colin said, a smile lighting his eyes.

"A baronet, huh? Well, I don't know what that is, but it sounds okay to me. A baronet. Wait'll I tell the missus."

Now Colin and Lucy smiled at each other, their fingers laced tightly together. They did not speak during the rest of the drive, for no words were necessary. They sat very close, sighing, giggling with excitement and exultation and love. It was ten minutes later when they heard another screech of brakes. Lucy looked around to see a neat white clapboard house with neat green shutters and a white picket fence. On the lawn beyond the fence was a handsome scrolled sign reading: Samuel Taylor, Justice of the Peace.

"How lovely!" she exclaimed. "Oh, Mr. Dale, it's perfect!"

"Thought you'd like it. Old Sam's okay, too."

They alighted from the taxi, Lucy smoothing her

wrinkled skirt. She glanced back at Homer Dale and, on an impulse, ran to him. "Won't you come in with us?" she asked eagerly. "You can be our witness. Won't you? Please say yes. Please . . . You can even leave the meter running," she laughed.

There was a moment's hesitation. "Nah," he said then and, in perhaps the grandest gesture of his life, turned the meter off. "It's on me. You can pay the four bucks that's already rung up, but the rest is on me. Like a wedding present."

"A wonderful wedding present, Mr. Dale."

The three of them passed through the gate and went to the door. It was opened instantly by a white-haired woman with a twinkling smile. "Come in, children, come in," she said, holding the door wide. "Sam," she called, "wedding party's here." She led them into the parlor, a cheerful room comfortably furnished in soft pastels. "I'll get the book," she added, crossing to the other side of the room.

"Not so fast," Samuel Taylor said. He stepped from behind a small, polished lectern, looking speculatively at Lucy. "How old are you, miss?"

"Nineteen," she lied without hesitation.

"That so? Quick, when were you born?"

"January 1920," she replied, again without hesitation, for she had prepared herself. "I'm nineteen."

"That so? Homer, would you say this pretty little girl is nineteen? Looks younger to me."

"Aw, that's 'cause you're old, Sam. She's okay and they want to get hitched. I brought them here special. You want me to take them to McGruder's?"

"Will you vouch for her?"

"I'm the witness, aren't I? That's as good as vouching."

Samuel Taylor finished polishing his glasses, then took another long look at Lucy. "I reckon," he said finally. "Come over this way and we'll sign all the papers."

The papers were duly signed and stamped. The young couple, following Mrs. Taylor, found their places in front of the lectern.

"Dearly beloved, we are gathered here in the presence of God and these witnesses to join Colin Arthur John Averill and Lucy Griffith Cameron in holy matrimony. If there be anyone here present who knows why these people should not be joined in wedlock, let him speak now or forever hold his peace. . . ."

Lucy gazed into Colin's eyes and he into hers. In a world all their own, they were oblivious now to the words being spoken. They were nervous, Colin dropping the ring, Lucy stumbling over his many names. They repeated their vows softly, and slowly, as if afraid of making a mistake. They barely heard Samuel Taylor pronounce them man and wife, but when at last they realized they were married, they flung their arms about each other, almost crushing the small bouquet when they kissed.

"Congratulations," Homer Dale said, thumping Colin's shoulder. "Could I . . . you think maybe I could kiss the bride?"

"Oh, you get a great big kiss," Lucy exclaimed, laughing and crying at the same time. "A great big kiss!"

Mrs. Taylor brought out a bottle of sherry and five glasses. Toasts were offered to the newlyweds; Colin, in his grateful reply, invited everyone to visit them in England. "After the honeymoon, of course," he added to the laughter all around.

It was dark when the Taylors bid them good-bye. Lucy felt, rather than saw, Mrs. Taylor's shower of rice. She bent, gathering some of the tiny kernels for a keepsake, and in that moment her bouquet flew off in the wind. Colin frowned, thinking that the superstitious old ladies in Aldcross would call it a bad omen.

Lucy only sighed. "I'm sorry, darling. I didn't mean—"

"You mustn't give it a thought," Colin replied quickly, sweeping his bride into his arms. "We'll get another. We'll get a thousand more!"

They waved to the Taylors and then started along the narrow path. Homer Dale opened the taxi door for them. "Where to?" he asked. "I can tell you some nice honeymoon spots."

"We're going to have our honeymoon in England," Lucy explained, heady at the idea. "Right now we have to get to the train station. Oh, and we have to send a telegram."

"Telegram, huh? Letting the family in on it?"

"I expect they'll be . . . surprised," Colin murmured, looking again at Lucy's radiant face. "Your mother and everyone."

"Mother will be *thrilled*," Lucy declared, "once she sees how happy I am. Oh, I can hardly wait to get home. Let's hurry, darling. I can hardly wait to show you off. Sir Colin Averill of Greenway!"

The telegram was brought to Sarah on a silver tray. She opened it, all the color leaving her strained and anguished face as she read the message. It was a moment before she was able to catch her breath, several moments before she was able to stand. She stumbled across the room to the door, her shaking hand fumbling at the knob. She stumbled through the silent hall, fighting off the blackness that threatened to engulf her. She threw open Elizabeth's door, thrusting out the telegram with a stricken cry. "You," she gasped. "You did this."

Elizabeth looked up from her dressing table. "What's happened?" she asked, staring in alarm at Sarah. "What is it?"

"This." Sarah waved the telegram aloft. "Read it."

"But what—?" Elizabeth left the dressing table. She grasped Sarah's hand and helped her to a chair. "Sit down, my dear," she said. "I'll get you a sherry."

"Read the telegram."

Elizabeth took the wire. She began to read, and for only the second time in her life her composure fled. Her face seemed to crumble, to wither; suddenly she looked all of her sixty-three years. "Married," she said, making her unsteady way to the couch. "I don't understand. I simply don't understand. Colin was supposed to return to England. That was his plan. To return to England the very next day . . . I telephoned his hotel. He'd checked out."

"There are other hotels."

"But he was supposed to return to England."

"Obviously he didn't," Sarah snapped.

"No. No, he didn't. I don't understand."

"Oh, what is there to understand? They're *married*. Lucy and Colin are married."

Elizabeth put her hand to her head. "My lawyers," she murmured. "My lawyers will see to everything. Lucy is a minor. The marriage . . . will be annulled." She picked up the telegram, reading it over and over. "They're coming directly here from the train," she said. "That means they won't—there won't have been a honeymoon."

"Do you really believe that makes it all right? Just because they haven't slept together? They're in love, Elizabeth. And they're about to have their hearts broken. My God, it's a nightmare. . . . I'm afraid to

255

think what this will do to Lucy."

"You don't intend to tell her the truth?"

The truth, thought Sarah, her mind creeping back through the years to a misty spring evening. She remembered the darkened road, the wood, the eerie rustling of birds. She remembered the abrupt silence, silence shattered by her own cries as strong hands tore at her clothing, her flesh. "So many years ago," she said wearily. "Old sins cast long shadows."

"Sarah, answer me. You don't intend to tell Lucy the truth?"

"I don't see any other choice. I could invent reasons for an annulment. But if I did, Lucy and Colin would just wait until she was of age and then run off again. It would just make matters worse. . . . They'll have to know the truth, Elizabeth. Terrible as it is, they'll have to know."

"There are things we can do. I'll have Colin sent away. I'll telephone Mary Averill and—"

"Don't be a fool. What good will come of sending Colin away? England isn't the moon. He could take a boat or a plane anytime he wished and be right back here. Or Lucy could go to him. The point is they'd find some way to be together. And that's why they must know the truth."

Elizabeth clasped her hands tightly in her lap. "I feel you're making a mistake," she said. "Colin can be dealt with."

"And Lucy? How do you propose to *deal* with Lucy?"

"That's more complicated, of course. We would have to keep a close eye on her. We would have to arrange to keep her busy. A trip, perhaps. A cruise. The two of you might take a cruise. When Lucy returns she can spend the summer at Broadmoor. She can entertain her friends there," Elizabeth continued, gathering strength with each word. "Think of it, Sarah. Swimming parties and picnics by the pond. Summer dances. It's the perfect solution."

Sarah's eyes flashed. She rose, pacing the length of the room. "You forget Lucy isn't twelve years old anymore," she said. "You can't move her about at will. Nor can you imprison her, the way you tried to imprison me."

"Whatever was done was done in your best interests."

"Best interests! I suppose it was in Lucy's best interests to invite Colin here. I suppose it's in her best interests now to let her pine for a young man she can never have. That's what she'd do, you know. Send her on a cruise, pack her off to Broadmoor, and still she'd be yearning for Colin. And what would you do then? Rush her into a loveless but socially acceptable marriage? No, Elizabeth, I won't have it."

"The truth will be painful."

"Yes," Sarah quietly agreed. "But lies aren't the answer. We've done a lot of lying and the result—the result is in that telegram. What's happened mustn't ruin Lucy's life. She must put Colin out of her mind and go on. Perhaps the truth will help her do that. Once she's over the shock, the pain, she can make a fresh start. At least I pray she can."

"Lucy is a sensible girl."

"She's young, Elizabeth. The pain is always so much worse when one is young. It was for me. Now there's another Averill, another young girl. . . ."

"Will you . . . tell her everything?"

Sarah gripped the windowsill, swaying slightly as she gazed into the foggy gray mists of night. "I don't know," she said, her voice a whisper. "I don't even know where to begin."

"I think you should leave it to me."

"To you!" Sarah whirled around, fixing angry eyes on Elizabeth. "You've done quite enough already," she declared. "Stay out of this." She walked swiftly across the room, her anger mounting. "Stay out of this, Elizabeth," she said at the door, "or I swear I'll kill you."

Chapter Thirteen

The clock was striking twelve as Sarah stepped out of the library into the darkened hall. She heard Lucy's soft, breathless voice on the stair. She heard Colin's reply, and then the sound of muffled laughter. She tensed, for this was the moment she had dreaded. "Lucy," she called quietly. "I'm over here, darling."

"Mother, we were afraid you didn't get our telegram. The house looked so dark and still. It looked like everyone was asleep. You did get the telegram?"

"Yes, hours ago. Come into the library. You too, Colin. We must all have a talk." Sarah followed them inside and closed the door. She saw their faces shimmering with happiness, with love, and quickly she glanced away. She reached for a chair, sinking into it. "This is very hard," she murmured. "Very hard."

"Mrs. Cameron," Colin said, "I want to apologize to you. Our running off must have been a terrible shock. We hadn't planned it. It just seemed to happen. Now that it has, I want you to know I love your daughter with all my heart. I'll do everything I can to give her a happy life. . . . If there are questions you'd care to ask . . . I mean, you know so little about my background."

"I know a great deal, Colin."

"Don't be angry, Mother," Lucy said. "I couldn't bear it, not tonight. Maybe we were wrong to elope but—"

"Sit down, darling. Come sit here on the sofa. Colin, I think perhaps we could do with a drink. There are glasses and brandy on that table by the windows. Would you mind?"

"I'd be delighted."

"Mother, look at my ring," Lucy eagerly insisted, holding out her hand. "Isn't it beautiful? Colin says it matches my eyes. He surprised me with it when we met today. It was so romantic. We were on the ferry and fog was swirling all around. . . ."

"Why didn't you tell me you were seeing him, Lucy?"

"I'm sorry. I really am, but I didn't think you'd approve. The night of the party it was clear you didn't like Colin. He said he'd made a bad impression. I had a feeling it was more than that. I was afraid to take the chance, Mother. I knew I loved him. I just knew it. . . . You'll think I'm silly, but it was love at first sight."

"You've known each other less than a week."

"That's not important. Are there timetables to love? Are there schedules? We'll have the rest of our lives to—"

"Don't, Lucy. I can't listen to this." Tears glittered on Sarah's long lashes. She turned her head, staring blindly into space. "There are things you don't understand," she said. "Things I have to explain."

"What things? Is it Gran? You won't let her make trouble? Promise me you won't. Oh, *please*,

Mother," Lucy cried, her hand closing on Sarah's. "Promise me."

Sarah did not reply, for Colin had appeared with their drinks. She took the glass he offered, lifting it to her lips. A moment later she set the glass aside. "Sit down, Colin," she said. "We must talk."

"Yes, of course. Where shall we begin? Perhaps first I should assure you that I'm well able to provide for Lucy. I have a house in London and a larger house in the country. I—"

"Have you ever told Lucy where your country house is?"

"It's in Greenway, Mother."

"No, darling. Greenway Hall is the name of the house. The name of the village is Aldcross."

Lucy glanced in confusion at Colin, then turned back to Sarah. "Aldcross?" she asked. "But that's where you're from, isn't it? Is it a different Aldcross?"

"The same one. I never spoke of the Hall or the Averills," Sarah said slowly, "because there were . . . unpleasant memories."

Again Lucy glanced at Colin. "What are you trying to say, Mother? If you had some kind of quarrel with the Averills . . ."

"You must listen to me," Sarah interrupted. "You both must listen carefully. What I have to tell you will be difficult, but it can't be avoided now. I had hoped . . . well, it doesn't matter what I'd hoped. . . . The point is I grew up in Aldcross and I knew the Averills. Sir Roger, Colin's father, was a fine young man. He was a great war hero, but the war changed him. War does that sometimes. When he returned, he started drinking. He wasn't himself. There were times when he didn't seem to know what he was doing. Colin, you were only a baby then. You wouldn't remember."

"Excuse me, Mrs. Cameron, but I don't quite see—"

"Please let me finish."

"Father was ill after the war. He went away for a rest cure."

"Yes, I know, Colin. He went away following a—a certain incident in Aldcross." Sarah reached out, tightly clasping Lucy's hand. "Darling, there's no easy way to say this. I'm afraid I haven't always been honest with you. I tried to spare your feelings. The truth—the truth is that Sir Roger was your father."

A terrible silence settled over them. Colin sat frozen in place. Lucy stared straight ahead, her face blank. Her lips moved again and again but no sound came. Again and again she twisted her fingers, pulling at her handkerchief until it was in shreds. "My father," she said finally, and it was as if the words had been torn from her throat.

"I'm sorry you had to find out this way, darling. I'm so sorry for you both."

"My father." Lucy turned. She looked quickly at Colin and just as quickly looked away. Her thoughts broke into little pieces, shattering like glass. "Then Colin and I are—"

"Colin is your half brother."

"I—I didn't know, Lucy. I didn't know anything about it. I was never told."

"There wouldn't have been any reason to tell you," Sarah said. "Until today there was no reason for either of you to know. When I got your telegram . . . Of course the marriage will be annulled immediately. I've already spoken with Judge Wayland. He's a friend of the family and we can rely on his discretion. . . . I'm sorry," she said again. "I wish I could help. I wish there were something I could do."

"There's nothing to do, Mother?"

"No, darling, there isn't." Sarah studied Lucy's pale, closed face. After some moments her gaze moved to Colin. She saw the tears in his eyes and she took a breath. "I'll leave you alone now," she murmured, rising. She went to the door, casting a last glance at the stricken couple. Tears filled her eyes, too, and quietly she entered the hall. She stiffened suddenly, for Elizabeth was seated in a small chair nearby. "I told you to stay away," she said.

"How is Lucy? I have a right to know."

"How do you suppose she is? All her romantic dreams have come crashing down on her head. . . . It's late, Elizabeth. Go on to bed."

"I'll wait."

"Wait for what? This is no time for a discussion. Lucy and Colin are saying their good-byes. After he leaves, she's going directly to her room. She can do without your pearls of wisdom tonight."

"You blame me, don't you?"

"There's more than enough blame to go around, Elizabeth. What difference can it make now? It's done. And I'm too tired to argue. We've had seventeen years of arguing. It hasn't accomplished much, has it? You're always going to be the way you are."

"And you, Sarah?"

"I'm always going to be the way I am. Let's call it a draw and have it over with. *Please* go to bed now. Ned will be home in a few hours. He's taking the morning plane. We'll talk then, if you wish. . . . Judge Wayland will be here at noon."

"You've been most efficient."

"Good night, Elizabeth."

She stood, gathering the folds of her robe. "Good night, my dear," she said. She walked to the stairs, her step slower than usual, her back not as straight.

"I'm sure we'll all feel better in the morning."

Sarah wandered to the other end of the hall. She stopped at a polished oak chest, absently rearranging a bowl of chrysanthemums. She saw that her hands were shaking and she let the flowers drop. She wandered to the window seat, perching atop the silken cushion. Five minutes passed, ten. A half hour later she heard the library door open. She watched Lucy and Colin pause on the threshold, watched their sad and tentative gestures. With a weary sigh, she got to her feet. "Lucy, are you all right? Colin?"

"We're all right, Mother."

"I was just leaving, Mrs. Cameron. I—I wonder if I could have a word with you before I leave?"

"Yes, certainly." Sarah went to where they stood, glancing from Colin to Lucy. "You must be exhausted, darling," she said. "Run along to your room. I'll be up in a moment."

"Yes, Mother." Lucy turned her head. "Good-bye, Colin," she murmured. "I love you."

"Good-bye, Lucy." He watched her go, and when he could watch no more he looked away, his eyes blue pools of misery. "I don't quite know what to say," he sighed as he and Sarah started toward the stairs. "I realize this has been painful for you. . . . But I have so many questions. I've always had a certain picture of my father, you see. I didn't think he was a saint, but I never imagined he was a . . . May I ask you a question, Mrs. Cameron?"

"It's time to bury the past," Sarah replied.

"I'm not sure I can. Not without knowing . . . I suppose I'll have to ask it straight out. Were you . . . assaulted by my father?"

Sarah grasped the banister, hesitating before she answered. "Colin, you've been hurt tonight. I don't want to make things worse than they are."

"But I must know. I'm his son and I *must* know."

"Then the answer is yes. I was on my way home, walking on Beechwood Road. Your father offered me a ride in his car. I accepted. . . . He had been drinking, Colin. I don't believe he knew what he was doing. He was an angry man. There was violence in him in those years. A result of the war. As you said, he was ill."

"Did my mother know?"

"Lady Mary made the arrangements for me to come to America. She did the best she could, under the circumstances. Your mother is an honorable woman, Colin. She had her own family to consider—you and your brother Harry. And given the nature of Aldcross, she did the only thing possible."

"You're very kind, Mrs. Cameron. I'm deeply sorry for what my family did to you."

"It was long ago," Sarah said when they reached the downstairs hall. "You mustn't allow yourself to dwell on the past, because if you do, it will eat you alive. Feel the anger, the pain, and then put it behind you. You're a young man, Colin. You must think of your future. It's not true that people love only once. The wonderful thing about life is that we get second chances. Thank God we do. It may be small consolation now, but you *will* meet another girl. You'll meet the right girl and you'll love her. . . . Unless you allow the past to stand in your way."

Colin bent, lightly kissing Sarah's cheek. "Goodbye, Mrs. Cameron," he said.

"Good-bye, Colin. God bless." The door closed and there was silence. Sarah exhaled a great breath, her head pounding as she climbed the stairs. She thought about Lucy and the pounding grew louder. My poor girl, her heart cried, my poor little girl. Quietly she entered Lucy's room. She drew a chair to

265

the side of the bed and sat down. "I wish I had some magic words to make it all better," she said. "You probably won't believe me, but I know how you feel, darling."

"No one knows how I feel. . . . Has Colin gone?"

"Yes."

Again Lucy held out her hand, staring at the fiery emerald. "I forgot to return his ring," she said.

"I'm sure he wants you to have it."

"It doesn't belong to me anymore."

"Lucy, Colin was your first love. First love is very special. My first love was named Tom. I still think about him once in a while. I remember him, but I stopped loving him many years ago."

"I'll always love Colin."

Sarah stroked Lucy's pale, cold brow. "You'll love your memories of him," she said gently. "That's not the same thing. . . . Darling, I know how much it hurts now. I also know it will hurt just a little less with each week, each month. The heart is kind of amazing. It breaks, but if you let it, it heals."

Lucy raised her anguished eyes to Sarah. "Not my heart, Mother."

"Yes, your heart too. In time, there'll be another young man. There will. . . . Because the only thing worse than a broken heart is an empty heart."

"Why did Gran invite Colin here? Why did she do it?"

"It was a courtesy. She never dreamed he'd actually be in New York. . . . Elizabeth always observes the amenities."

"No matter who gets hurt," Lucy replied bitterly.

"Sometimes people don't stop to think."

"I hate her."

"Lucy . . ."

"I *hate* her."

"All right, darling, don't upset yourself. . . . You might feel better if you cried. Don't try to be brave. Don't try to pretend."

"But that's what we've been doing all these years, isn't it? We've been pretending. Oh, Mother, I don't know how you stood it. How could you even bear to look at me after what happened to you? How could you bear to have me around?"

"Lucy! You must never say that again. You must never think it. I love you more than my own life. I always have, from the very beginning. I always will."

"But every time you saw me you must have been reminded—"

"Stop it, Lucy. All I ever saw was the beautiful daughter I loved so much. That's all I see now. Don't start imagining things, darling."

"I can't help it. The whole world's been turned upside down. Nothing makes sense anymore. . . . Today was the happiest day of my life. We were going to go to Bermuda for our honeymoon. We talked about it on the train coming home. Now Colin's gone and I'm—I'm alone." She fell back against the pillows, her legs thrashing restlessly. "I love him," she said.

"I know."

"What am I going to do, Mother?"

"Give yourself time, darling. You'll find the answers."

Lucy took the ring from her finger, cradling it in her palm. "There are no answers," she said.

The marriage was annulled, though nothing could be done for the pain Lucy felt. She wandered about in a daze, declining all invitations, seldom leaving the house. She was very pale, and there was hardly a week during the long winter when she did not have a cold or a cough or a sore throat. She had headaches and occasional dizzy spells. She ate little, sickened by the thought of food. Night after night she prowled her room, unable to sleep.

"You look perfectly dreadful," Josh said one afternoon early in March. "What are you doing to yourself?"

"I'm not doing anything."

"Aren't you? In case you haven't noticed, your mother is half crazy with worry. That's your doing. We're all worried, and that's your doing, too. I know it's been rough, but you can't spend the rest of your life moping around. Do you want to get sick?"

"I'm all right, Josh. I wish people would stop fussing."

"What do you expect? These black moods of yours have everyone on edge."

"I can't help my moods."

"Of course you can. At least you can try. I'm not suggesting you go out dancing. I'm saying you shouldn't cut yourself off from the world. You've turned inward and that's not good." Josh crossed the drawing room, his dark head bent in thought. "It's been two months," he declared. "Now it's time to start easing back into life. And whether you like it or not, I'm going to give you a push."

"I don't."

"Too bad, Lucy, because that's the way it is. When we were little and went on outings, I always had to hold your hand and make sure you didn't get lost. We're not little anymore, but you still need a guardian."

"And you've appointed yourself?" Lucy asked, tossing her mane of golden hair. "You're only five years older than I am, Josh. I don't have to listen to you."

"You have to listen to someone. It might just as well be me. I can handle you. I know when you need a swift kick in the derriere."

"Is that so?"

"Yes," Josh replied, smiling. "Go get dressed. We're lunching at the Plaza."

"I'm not going anywhere."

"You're going if I have to carry you. There's too much tension in this house. Everybody's angry at everybody else. I recommend a change of scenery."

"You can recommend all you like. . . ."

"We're going, Lucy. I mean it. You've been cloistered here for two months. That's enough. We're going, but first you have to make yourself presentable. A pretty dress and some lipstick will work wonders. Scoot."

"You really have a nerve, Josh. I told you I don't *want* to go."

"If the Plaza doesn't suit, you can name another place. Not too far though. I have to get back to the Galleries at a decent hour. I've been late twice this week and Dad gave me hell."

"Good!"

"Do I see a smile?" Josh asked, smiling himself. "Well, that's a beginning. Come on now, Lucy. Change your clothes and fix your face and we'll be off."

She stood. "Have it your own way," she said. "But you won't enjoy my company. I promise you that. Don't expect polite conversation, and don't expect me to laugh at your silly jokes."

"Agreed." Josh watched her stalk out of the room. He lighted a cigarette and sat down, rising a moment later when Sarah entered from the library. "Success," he said. "I'm taking Lucy to the Plaza. I bullied her into it."

"However you did it, I'm glad."

"You look tired, Aunt Sarah."

"I haven't been sleeping well."

"Lucy will be fine. Once she starts getting out, she'll stop all this brooding."

"That's the problem. She refuses to go anywhere. She's had lots of invitations. . . . She seems so disinterested in everything."

"Does she talk about Colin?"

"Not anymore. It's been weeks since she's even mentioned his name. I don't know whether that's good or bad. I don't know what's going on in her mind, Josh. The whole situation is delicate. We're walking on eggs."

"Maybe that's what's wrong. No offense, Aunt Sarah, but you're all giving in to Lucy. And to her moods. I took a different approach. I told her she needed a swift kick."

"Did you?" Sarah asked, surprised.

"It wasn't the first time I told her that. . . . Of course what she *really* needs is someone else to be in love with. He'd have to be a certain kind of fellow. Steady, determined, but the kind of fellow who can laugh at the world. Lucy is too serious."

"Any candidates?"

"I was thinking of Bill Landis," Josh replied. "He was a drinking buddy at Harvard. He's a broker now, and a strong possibility."

Sarah met Josh's earnest gray gaze. She smiled. "You're very like your father," she said. "You see a problem and set out to solve it logically. You cut to the heart of the matter."

"A Cameron trait, or so I've heard. Do you think I'm on the wrong track? About Lucy, I mean?"

"No, I wouldn't say that. But it may be a bit soon for Lucy to fall in love again. She's been hurt, Josh. The hurt runs deep and to so many different levels.

She's confused as well. You must remember she's struggling with a new identity. Until a short time ago she thought her natural father was a man named Griffith. Now she knows the truth, including the circumstances of her birth. It's not easy to accept."

"Brooding about it doesn't do any good, Aunt Sarah."

"We don't always do what's good for us, do we? I'll leave you now, Josh," she said, walking to the door. "I can't miss my train. I have a meeting in Philadelphia."

"The Markham porcelains?"

"Enid Markham is ready to part with her treasures. I got the call this morning. . . . Oh, Lucy, how pretty you look! I hear you're having lunch with Josh."

"It was his idea. He's appointed himself my guardian."

"Think of him as your guardian angel," Sarah laughed. "They're handy to have around."

"Handy for jaunts to the Plaza," Josh said. "Come on, Lucy, let's get out of here. Who knows, you might even enjoy yourself!"

Tony Jennings was enjoying the bright, blustery March afternoon. "Smell the air," he said to Jim Cleeve, his Harvard roommate. "Spring is coming. I love spring in New York."

"Exams are coming too."

"The hell with exams. Smell the air. You have to learn to relax, Cleeve. All this worrying will make you old before your time. Old and boring," Tony added, his robust laugh startling passersby on Fifth Avenue. "Loosen up, for Pete's sake."

"Easy for you to say. You're sailing through your courses. I don't know how you do it. I never see you

271

crack a book. It's damned annoying."

"You don't see me because you're always at the library. I put in my hours. Of course, I'm not the grind you are. I allow myself some fun."

"Like sneaking down to New York for two days. I must have been crazy to tag along."

"Crazy, eh? You didn't think it was so crazy last night when you were kicking up your heels with Mamie Powell. Now that was a sight to see, Cleeve," Tony laughed again. "A sight not seen often enough."

"Mamie Powell is quite a gal. Your date wasn't bad either."

"Poetry in motion."

"But that was last night. All I want to do today is get back to Cambridge. It's getting late, Tony."

"There's plenty of time. We'll catch the—" He stopped, his attention diverted by a lovely young woman in a vivid red coat and hat. "It really is a small world," he said, as if to himself.

"What are you looking at?" Jim Cleeve followed Tony's gaze to the entrance of the Plaza. "Oh, I see. The blonde or the brunette?"

"The blonde."

"Who is she?"

"Just a girl I kissed in the rain . . . Jim, why don't you go on ahead to Grand Central? I'll meet you there. If I should happen to miss the three o'clock, I'll catch the six-thirty."

"The six-thirty is a local. You'll be stuck on the train half the night."

"I don't mind. You go on, Jim."

"Well, if you're sure . . ."

"I am." Tony thrust his hands into the pockets of his coat. He crossed the street, bounding up the steps of the Plaza. He passed through the crowded lobby, his eyes fixed on the red-clad figure moving toward the Palm Court. "Lucy," he called. "Josh?"

Josh turned. "Look who's coming this way," he said. "Tony Jennings. I wonder what he's doing in New York in the middle of the week."

"I wonder if you wonder. You asked him to be here, didn't you?"

"Certainly not. You have a suspicious mind, Lucy." Josh held out his hand as Tony neared. "Good to see you again," he smiled. "Is Harvard in recess or have you been expelled?"

"Neither. I decided to take a couple of days off. I'm glad I did," Tony went on, his eyes sweeping over Lucy. "Chance encounters are such fun. Don't you think so? No, I guess you don't," he laughed, noting her sudden frown. "What am I doing wrong, Josh? Your cousin is giving me a fishy look."

"My cousin is in one of her moods."

"Is that it, Lucy? I hope it is. You wouldn't want to hurt my feelings. I'm very sensitive, you know."

"Hah! You're a lot of things, Tony Jennings, but sensitive isn't one of them. You're fresh. . . . Josh, our table is ready."

"Yes."

"Well? Aren't we going to sit down?"

Josh did not hear. He stared thoughtfully at Tony, at dark blue eyes filled with laughter, with deviltry, and he nodded. "Have you eaten?" he asked. "If you haven't, you and Lucy can lunch together."

"Now wait a minute. . . ." Lucy began.

"I haven't eaten," Tony interrupted, "and I'd be delighted to take your place, Josh. I'll even promise to be on my best behavior."

"Don't *I* have anything to say about this? If you suppose I'm going to be passed around like . . ."

"That's enough, Lucy," Josh said. "Stop fussing.

I'm going back to the Galleries and you're staying here with Tony. It's settled. And mood or no mood, you might at least *try* to be pleasant."

"All right, all right. You don't have to raise your voice."

"You're lucky I don't take you over my knee. You deserve a paddling. Tony, she's all yours, God help you."

"Have you been giving him a bad time?" Tony asked when Josh had gone. "I thought you only did that to me."

"Oh, Josh is so bossy. He's always telling me what to do. If I dare to disagree, he bites my head off."

"He means well."

"Everybody means well," Lucy replied, following the maitre d' to a small corner table. "I wish everybody would leave me alone."

"No, you don't. You know the old saying: Be careful what you wish for. No one should wish for loneliness."

Lucy glanced up, surprise clear in her eyes. "That's the first serious remark I've ever heard you make," she said.

"I have a serious side. It isn't often on display but it exists. . . . I even have a serious question to ask. Do you really dislike me, Lucy? The truth, please. I hate polite lies, comforting though they may be."

"I'm sorry. I haven't been very nice to you, have I? I don't know why. I suppose it's because I don't understand you."

"That doesn't answer my question."

"I don't dislike you, Tony. I . . . the truth is, I always feel a little lost around you. You're all the things I'm not."

"What things?"

"Confident and funny and popular. It's an

attitude. Wherever you are, you seem to be having a marvelous time. You seem happy."

"I am. Aren't you?"

Lucy shook her head. "I was happy for a while," she said. "Now I just feel empty." She took the menu the waiter brought and hid behind it, embarrassed by her admission. "Maybe there's something wrong with me," she murmured.

"There is." Tony pushed the menu away, gazing into Lucy's green eyes. "You're too pretty for your own good," he declared. "And too spoiled."

"You're teasing me again."

"It works. You're smiling. My ambition is to get a laugh out of you."

"Not much of an ambition, Tony. Why do you care? Why should you?"

"Well, let's see. You're the prettiest girl in New York. That's a reason, of sorts. I think the real reason is that you intrigue me. There's always been something different about you, Lucy, something elusive. That's an attractive quality. It is to me, at any rate. I love the unexpected and I love puzzles. You, missy, are a puzzle. . . . I'm writing a play about you."

"A play!"

"It's called *Shadow Dance*."

"It's foolishness, Tony. Your father will never allow you to be a playwright."

"Allow me?" he laughed, his eyes twinkling. "I'm past the age for asking permission. It's my life, isn't it?"

"But all the men in your family are bankers."

"Not quite all. An uncle escaped to Wyoming and bought a ranch. He was perfectly happy breaking horses and mucking out the stables. And I had a cousin who ran a charter fishing boat in Key West.

During the off season he was perfectly happy to bum around, doing nothing. Not everyone is meant to go into banking. I'm not. I'd die of boredom."

"Won't your father be angry?"

"Oh, he's a good sport. He won't be pleased, but once he's convinced I'm serious, he won't stand in my way. . . . He may tie up my trust fund for a few years," Tony laughed. "That's all right. I don't mind earning my own money. Last summer I worked on a construction crew, just for the hell of it. I made a lot of mistakes, but I learned. I also learned I'm not afraid of work."

"You're not afraid of anything, are you?" Lucy asked.

"What are you afraid of?"

"Life," she said quietly. She said no more, for the waiter came to take their orders. When he left she raised her eyes to Tony. "You must think I'm awfully silly."

"Do you want an honest answer, Lucy? I think your grandmother is the original dragon lady. I think she's made you afraid of things. What do you say to that?"

"I don't know. I guess I have to agree. Everything Gran does causes trouble. She . . . hurts people. She may not mean to, but she does."

"You've been hurt," Tony said. "I can see it in your eyes. Pretty as you are, you look a little frayed around the edges. Do you want to talk about it?"

"No." Lucy glanced away, color rising in her cheeks. "Let's change the subject. I don't like this conversation."

"Okay. Shall I tell you about my wild doings at Harvard?"

"I don't doubt they're wild. You have a reputation, Tony."

276

"Scandalous, I hope."

"You're impossible. Don't you care what people think?"

"People think what they want to think," Tony replied. "That's life. Why care about what you can't change? Anyway, despite the stories you hear, my doings really aren't all that wild or unusual. . . . Unless you count the time a campus cop found me buck naked, trying to start Jim Cleeve's Nash."

"What!" Lucy cried, erupting in laughter. "Naked on the campus of dear old Harvard?"

"There's a reasonable explanation."

"I bet."

"There *is*," Tony insisted, laughing too. "It was snowing, you see, and . . ."

Sarah hurried up the stairs, unbuttoning her coat as she went. She looked at her watch and then knocked softly at Lucy's door. "May I come in, darling?" she called.

"Yes, Mother."

She opened the door and walked inside. "My train was late," she said. "Some kind of trouble on the track. I was afraid you'd be asleep. I was so anxious to hear about your lunch with Josh. Did you have a nice time?"

"No thanks to Josh. We ran into Tony Jennings, and the next thing I knew, Josh was leaving. Tony and I had lunch together. It was fun," Lucy conceded. "Tony makes me angry a lot of the time, but he also makes me laugh. Does that sound strange?"

"Not at all. Tony's good humor is contagious."

"I guess it must be. I was in a gloomy mood when we sat down. He just kept talking and talking. Some of his stories are absurd. I couldn't help laughing."

"Tony is a charming boy. Perhaps you should ask him to dinner."

"Oh, no, Mother. I don't want to . . . encourage him. He'd get the wrong idea. I don't want to have a date or anything like that." Lucy put her book aside. She drew herself up on the pillows and stared at Sarah. "I can't even think about dating now," she said. "And if I have Tony here, Gran will be sure to invite Jonny Melvile."

"Is she still pushing Jonny on you?"

"Well, not as much as she was before—before Colin. But he's still in her plans. . . . Do you know what Tony calls Gran? The dragon lady."

Sarah smiled. She draped her coat over the back of a chair and sat down. "An interesting description," she said. "I must remember to tell your father."

"When is he coming home?"

"Not for weeks. He's running all around South America, and when he's done he'll take a little holiday. I can't blame him. It's going to be chaos here when they start putting in the elevator. All that drilling and hammering. I suppose he'll be back in time for Raymond's retirement party. This house will seem strange without Raymond."

"This house *is* strange."

"Yes," Sarah laughed. "I'm so glad you can joke again, darling. That's a good sign. Josh was right to insist you have an afternoon out. You even look better."

"Don't read too much into signs, Mother. I had a nice day but nothing's really changed."

"Oh, I think you're wrong. For the last two months you've practically been a recluse. Today you got out and enjoyed yourself, and now the world doesn't look quite as bleak. *You* don't look quite as bleak. I call that progress, Lucy. You just can't spend the rest of your life mourning."

"Mourning?"

"That's what you're doing. Mourning for lost dreams."

"Is that what you did, Mother? After Sir Roger and everything?"

"Yes, in a way. But after a while there were new dreams and I stopped mourning the old. That's how life is. If it weren't, it would be unbearable."

"I've lost more than dreams," Lucy said, her hands tightening on the satin quilt. "I've lost part of myself. I don't know how to get it back."

"Well, perhaps it's time we began filling in the missing pieces. We could start with your grandparents. . . . I'd planned to go to Europe this spring. That's been changed. I'm going next year instead, and I think you should go with me. Don't worry, there won't be any need to visit Aldcross. I'll bring your grandparents to London. . . . You don't have to decide now, Lucy. But I wish you'd consider it."

"Why did you change your plans?"

"This didn't seem a good time to go. Then, too, we're all keeping an eye on the situation in Europe. If war becomes a real possibility, I'll be needed to help at the London Galleries. Everything will have to be inventoried, and safe storage will have to be found for our treasures."

"I don't want to think about war, Mother. It's frightening."

"I know, darling. I hope to God it doesn't happen, but if it does, you should see Europe while there's still something to see. Besides, a trip will lift your spirits. Just planning for a trip is fun."

"I'd like to see Europe," Lucy said with a small smile. "And I'd like to meet my grandparents. But not now. I'm not ready now. It's hard to explain, Mother. I have to get myself straightened out. Maybe if I had something to do . . . Not parties or dates, but something . . ."

"College . . ."

"No, not college either. I might take a few courses though. Art courses, and maybe one in photography. I have that marvelous German camera Daddy brought me. I might as well learn how to use it."

"That's a fine idea, Lucy."

"What will Gran say?"

"Never mind Gran," Sarah replied. "I promise you this is one time she won't interfere. And if she tries . . . well, we'll gang up on her. The important thing is that you make a fresh start. If you want help, I'm here. I don't think you'll need help, Lucy. The worst is over."

"I hope so, Mother. I hope so."

Chapter Fourteen

Sarah felt life returning to normal as 1939 drew to
an end, for tensions had eased in the Cameron house
and tempers had quieted. Her time was her own now
and most of it she gave to the Galleries, planning a
series of major auctions. In the winter of 1940 she
began planning her trip to Europe. Memories came
flooding back—memories of a snug cottage on
Winding Lane, of a garden scarlet with geraniums,
of a china dog sitting atop the hearth. All these
things meant home to her, but she knew she would
not see them again; she would see London and Paris,
but Aldcross would remain a place of memory.
Aldcross is the past, she told herself, and that seemed
to settle the matter. "The past can't hurt me
anymore," she said to Janet one soft April afternoon.
"When I realized that, I was able to let go. It's a relief,
after almost twenty years. It's a relief to be done with
secrets and lies."

"Is Lucy all right now?"

"Yes, I think so. She's taken a great interest in
photography, and that's helped. She has her classes
to keep her busy. She's even fixed up a darkroom at
home."

"Elizabeth must be thrilled," Janet said dryly.

Sarah smiled. "Elizabeth is treating this like a passing fancy," she replied. "And it may be. Lucy's only eighteen, after all. The important thing is that she has an interest, *any* interest."

"I'll drink to that."

"So will I," Sarah laughed, raising her glass to her lips. "Schrafft's serves a good martini," she said. She glanced around the restaurant, seeing women with packages from Saks and Bonwit's, secretaries on their lunch hour and young mothers with children in tow. "I'm glad we came here. Mary Margaret won't feel out of place. It's hard to get her to go anywhere. Of course with six kids to worry about . . ."

"Six kids! Hal and I tried for years. We would have been happy with one. She's a lucky woman."

"We've all been lucky, Janet. You have Hal. Mary Margaret has Mike and the kids. I have Lucy. And Ned," Sarah added hastily, though her thoughts, as always, went to Patrick. "We've all done pretty well for ourselves."

"I know. I'm not complaining. I wouldn't really trade my life for Mary—oh, here she comes now. This way, Mary Margaret," Janet called. "Here we are."

"Ah, I never thought I'd make it. Two buses passed me by, and the third was so crowded I wanted to scream." Mary Margaret settled her plump form on a chair, exhaling a breath. "That's why I'm late," she said. "Blame the buses."

"How about a drink?" Sarah asked.

"I wasn't going to have a drink in the middle of the day, but I've changed my mind. Besides, it's a celebration, isn't it? It's your bon voyage lunch, and I'll be wanting to drink a toast. I think I'll have a pink lady. . . . A pink lady, please," Mary Margaret said to the young Irish waitress. "And maybe some of those little sandwiches to nibble on. You know, the little tea sandwiches."

"You'll spoil your lunch."

"Ah, not me, Janet," she laughed, patting her stomach. "A trencherman's appetite is what I've had ever since little Francis was born. I'm getting big as a house and that's the truth."

"You look fine," Sarah said. "I like your new hairstyle."

"New hairstyle!" Mary Margaret hooted. "The Gerrity kids came over to play this morning," she explained cheerfully, "all of them squirting me with their water pistols. Dripping wet I was. I had to put up my hair with pins. *That's* my new style. And cheaper than going to the beauty parlor . . . But that's enough of my stories. How are you, Janet? Is your Hal president of the bank yet?"

"Vice-president. We both know he won't go any farther, but it's all right. Hal's happy being a vice-president and I'm satisfied."

"You should be. It's an important job. My Mike was promoted to head of the Receiving Department at the Galleries. Did you hear? He's happy as a lark. We're thinking next year we might be able to buy our own home. Nothing fancy, you understand. We're looking in Brooklyn. . . . The borough of churches," Mary Margaret laughed again. "That's perfect for Mike! Ah, here's my drink. . . . And here's to you, Sarah. You've come a long way since the *Royal Star*. You were so quiet and frightened. Remember?"

"I remember how kind you were. I don't think I ever would have come out of my cabin if it hadn't been for you. That was a miserable time in my life. I was glad they retired the *Royal Star*. Such awful memories."

"Well, you'll have better memories of this trip,"

Janet said. "By this time tomorrow, you'll be off on an adventure. I hope . . . no, I *know* you'll enjoy every moment."

"Let's drink to it," Mary Margaret suggested, raising her glass. "To Sarah, our dear friend."

"To Sarah," Janet echoed. "Godspeed."

Baskets of flowers filled Sarah's large, elegant stateroom aboard the *Ile de France*. Stewards served canapés and champagne, deftly replenishing empty glasses. Somewhere music was playing, and everywhere was the sound of laughter. Sarah felt the excitement; she felt giddy with anticipation, as if she were a schoolgirl going off on her first holiday. Paris, she thought, and her heart beat faster. "Is it everything they say?" she asked suddenly turning to Elizabeth. "Paris, I mean. Is it really as special as they say?"

"It is indeed. Particularly for women with romantic natures. That would include you, my dear. I'm sure you'll have a lovely time. You and Patrick both. How fortunate he was able to get away. It will be nice to have a shipboard companion."

"Yes, it will. But we have work to do, too, Elizabeth. I brought a briefcase stuffed with reports, and so did Patrick. Don't forget we have the London inventory ahead of us, not to mention the directors' meeting."

"I'm pleased you've found a way to mix business and pleasure."

"I'm rather pleased myself," Sarah replied. "Get all your little digs in while you can," she laughed. "Nothing's going to upset me today."

"Upset you? Why, I have no desire to upset you, my dear. I *am* pleased you're taking this trip. It's long overdue. I would have preferred you to travel alone, but of course that was your choice."

"Patrick and I are traveling on the same ship, *not* in the same stateroom. All the proprieties are being observed. There won't be any nasty gossip. Though why it should matter at this late date, I can't imagine. . . . Besides, I'll be joining Ned in London."

"See that you do."

Sarah sipped her champagne, her eyes twinkling as she regarded Elizabeth. "You're a wonder," she said. "Still worrying about proprieties. I do believe you're the last of your kind."

"And what kind is that, my dear?"

"The uncompromising social arbiter." Sarah saw Lucy, and her smile widened. "Excuse me, Elizabeth," she murmured, slipping past numerous Cameron relatives to reach her daughter. "I'm so glad you're here, darling. I was afraid you weren't coming."

"I had to make a stop," Lucy explained. "I bought you a present, Mother. I had to wait while they finished the engraving."

"But you didn't have to buy—"

"I wanted to. It isn't every day you go to Europe. I wanted everything to be just right." Lucy opened her hand to reveal a delicate filigreed locket. "It's antique," she said. "Bend your head a little and I'll put it on."

"It's beautiful, Lucy. What a sweet thought."

"Bend your head. . . . There, that's better. . . . Oh, it looks so pretty on you, Mother. My picture is inside . . . so you don't forget me," she laughed. "Two months is a long time."

"It may not be that long, darling. If I finish the London inventory sooner, I'll be on the next ship home."

"I was only joking. I want you to enjoy yourself. . . . Give Daddy my love. . . . And promise you won't worry about me."

"Worrying is a habit."

"Promise, Mother."

"Very well. But you must make me a promise in return. Don't let your grandmother take over your life. Don't let her talk you into anything."

"I won't. I'll be fine, Mother. I'm not a child, you know."

"Yes, I know. My little girl is all grown up. I'll miss you, darling."

"Don't even give me a thought. Just have a good time." Lucy threw her arms around Sarah. "A *marvelous* time," she said. "Will you do that?"

"I'll certainly try. . . . What shall I bring you back from Paris?"

"Surprise me."

Sarah was about to reply when she heard the call for visitors to go ashore. "This is the part I don't like," she said. "The good-bye part."

"It's a French ship," Lucy smiled, "so you can say *au revoir* instead."

Sarah turned, almost engulfed by the wave of departing guests. *"Au revoir,"* she said over and over again. *"Au revoir,* Elizabeth," she said, clasping a cool, jeweled hand. "I suppose these next two months will be a holiday for you as well. Two months without arguments."

"It's true I won't miss our disagreements, but I'll miss your company. I wish you a most happy trip, my dear. You're not to worry about anything. You deserve to have a good time. You've earned it."

"Thank you, Elizabeth. I'll keep that in mind." Sarah followed her into the passageway. Quickly she bent and kissed Lucy's cheek. "Run along now, darling," she said. "Hurry, or I'll start to cry. You know me and my tears."

"Come, Lucy," Elizabeth said. "If we wait any longer, the crowd will be impossible."

"Yes, Gran."

Sarah watched them go. After some moments her eyes moved to the other end of the passageway, where Patrick was bidding good-bye to his guests. She turned and went through a door to the sun-splashed deck. She saw flags and streamers billowing in the wind, heard voices rising in laughter as people gathered at the rail. The ship's horn sounded then, two loud, long blasts answered by a chorus of whistles from tugboats drawn alongside. She found a place at the rail, her gaze skipping past the tugs to the boisterous crowd beyond. She caught sight of Lucy and she waved. "Lucy," she shouted.

"You don't expect Lucy to hear you in all this?" Patrick asked, joining her. "It's bedlam."

"It's exciting. Look how happy everyone is."

"I'm too busy looking at you. . . . I was beginning to wonder if we'd *ever* get to Paris. But now it's all right. I have you all to myself. We're going to have a wonderful time, my darling."

"We always do," Sarah replied softly.

"What did you say? You have to speak up. I can't hear in the noise."

"Later," she laughed. "I'll tell you later." She took the bag of confetti Patrick offered, tossing the bits of colored paper into the air. "We're off," she cried as the ship glided out of the harbor. Her face was radiant, her eyes brimming with tears. "Oh, Patrick, we're off on our adventure."

It was a romantic adventure for them both, their days filled with sunshine and swimming and shipboard games, their nights with dancing and moonlit strolls on the deck and love. In public their behavior was necessarily restrained, but during more private times they gloried in each other, in the unquenchable flames of passion and desire. They were each other's world, and for them both it was a world without beginning, without end.

They had six magical days in Paris, and not a moment was lost. They were together in the dark, smoky cafés of the Left Bank and in the splendor of lavish Right Bank ballrooms. They danced until dawn, breakfasting on champagne and croissants, making love on scented silk sheets. On their last day they picnicked in the *Bois,* holding hands while the misty blue-gray light closed about them. "I don't want to leave," Patrick said. "Let's stay. Let's chuck everything and stay."

"You mustn't tempt me."

"Why not? Lucy is grown. My boys are grown. Why not stay and be happy?"

"But we wouldn't be happy. It's true, Patrick," Sarah smiled, lifting his hand to her lips. "We're not the kind of people to chuck everything. If we were, we would have done it long ago. Perhaps someday . . . Someday when we're old, when we have no more responsibilities."

"Do you promise?" Patrick laughed. "I'll look forward to growing old if you'll promise."

"I promise. Cross my heart."

"I'll hold you to it, you know. I'll be gray and stooped and waving two tickets to Paris in your face. What will you say then?"

"I'll say 'Paris, here we come.' And I'll say it so fast, your poor old gray head will spin. . . . Oh, Patrick, we're happy *now.* That's what matters. I've never been happier. How many people have their dreams come true? We're so lucky."

"Yes, we are. I'm being greedy. I want all your time

and attention, my darling. That's asking too much. Especially when we already *have* so much."

Sarah leaned closer to Patrick, nestling her head on his shoulder. "We have everything," she murmured. "Everything."

Ned met Sarah's plane in London, whisking her through the terminal into a shining gray Rolls-Royce. "Welcome to England," he said as the car drove off. "How does it feel to be back?"

"I don't know yet. My hands are shaking. That must mean something. . . . Did you speak to Mama and Papa?"

"They're here," Ned replied with a smile. "They decided to come a day early."

"But why didn't you tell me?"

"Because you would have cut your holiday short and there was no need for that. I picked them up at the station and took them to the house. They're fine. They left at the crack of dawn to see the sights. Of course they're anxious to see you, too," Ned laughed, "but I suggested you might want a little time to rest and catch your breath. They understood. They're charming people, dear heart. It's been fun getting to know my in-laws after all these years."

"I wonder what they'll think of me. I've changed, Ned."

"Who hasn't?"

"You," Sarah said. "Apart from a sprinkling of gray in your hair, you've hardly changed at all."

"Well, if you're talking about looks, you look like a million . . . in pounds, not dollars."

"Nineteen years. It's been nineteen years. I hope they aren't expecting to see a young girl."

"You're not the only one who can count," Ned

laughed again. "Besides, thirty-six isn't ancient. It's a wonderful age for a woman. There's that air of experience, of knowing. And before you get your hackles up, I meant that in the nicest sort of way. You're damned attractive, Sarah. Mama and Papa will be delighted with you."

"I hope you're right. You—you didn't say anything about Patrick? Not even as a joke?"

"Certainly not. I have more sense than that. Enough sense to mind my tongue around proper country folk. As far as your parents are concerned, we're an ordinary, happily married couple. We'll be sharing rooms during their visit. I didn't think they'd understand separate bedrooms."

"No," Sarah said, "they probably wouldn't. You won't be able to come and go at all hours, Ned. It would raise questions."

"Well, that's all right. They'll only be here a couple of weeks. I can behave myself that long. It's the least I can do. The family honor and all that."

"Not family honor, family secrets. And I thought I was done with secrets."

"This particular secret is quite harmless. Why trouble them with something that can't be helped? Why spoil your reunion? It isn't worth it, Sarah. Honesty isn't *always* the best policy. You have to pick your spots. I should know. For every noble truth I've told, I've told a dozen obliging lies. . . . Perhaps that's wrong. If it is, I don't care. What the hell, a few sins more or less."

"You'll be forgiven."

"I wouldn't bet on it. But I've had a damn good time, so that's all right, too." Ned lighted a cigarette, exhaling a cloud of bluish smoke. "Your parents should be back at five," he said. "I'll disappear for a couple of hours and give you a chance to talk. Cook will have dinner ready at seven.''

"Thank you, Ned. That sounds perfect. You've been terrific about everything. Really you have. I warn you Mama can be a bit . . . wordy. Unless she's changed.''

"She hasn't. It's rather charming. Stop worrying, dear heart. I have a way with older women.'' He grasped Sarah's hand and a rare frown crossed his brow. "You *are* worried, aren't you?" he said. "You're still shaking.''

"Oh, it's nervousness. Once I see them . . . Once the ice is broken, I'll be fine.''

"A drink and a leisurely bath, that's what you need. We'll be at the house soon. It's a nice house. Not as large as Mother's, but very comfortable. And we have a small but marvelous staff.''

"Mama isn't used to servants.''

"Isn't she?" Ned smiled. "One would never know. She has Cook and the others dancing to her tune. They don't seem to mind. Quite the contrary. They seem to have taken to her. She has a natural air of authority.''

Now Sarah smiled. She turned her head to the window, staring out at the quiet London streets, at graceful three and four-story dwellings with windows draped in silk. She saw a street sign marked Eaton Place, and there the car came to a purring halt. "Are we home?" she asked.

"Home sweet home.''

"It's lovely," she said as the driver opened the door. She looked at the handsome gray house, the brick and stone weathered by time, and she smiled. "It's exactly the house I would have chosen.''

"The plumbing's a little tricky. I keep meaning to do something about it. On the other hand, there's a *superb* wine cellar. It's my pride and joy.'' Ned took

291

Sarah to the door, which was opened instantly by a middle-aged woman wearing a plain blue dress with white collar and cuffs. "This is Mrs. Porter, the indispensable Mrs. Porter," he explained. "And this is my wife."

"Welcome, madam."

"Thank you. I'm very glad to be here."

"Would you like to go to your rooms, madam? Or would you care to look about first?"

"I'll give Mrs. Cameron the tour," Ned said. "Perhaps you'd send up a bowl of ice. We could do with a cocktail."

"Yes, sir. Straightaway."

Sarah's gaze traveled from the hall to the gleaming black walnut staircase. In the curve of the staircase was a brocade settee, and opposite the settee were hand-carved double doors. The dark wood floors were polished and buffed. A porcelain urn held masses of bright yellow forsythia. "Papa brought the flowers, didn't he?" she asked, starting up the stairs with Ned. "Wrapped in butcher paper?"

"Why, yes. I'll never know how he managed on the train. He had huge bundles of those . . . whatever they are."

"Forsythia. Papa was always proud of his early forsythia. He used to take them to the neighbors, wrapped in butcher paper. It's all coming back to me now."

"The English are so serious about their gardens. So devoted, I should say."

"Papa was. Obviously he still is. It's comforting to think some things haven't changed."

"Well, you probably won't want to change anything here. You can, of course. . . . The sitting room," he said, throwing open a door. "Lots of chintz and a few good Sheraton pieces. And sunlight.

This room gets the morning sun. . . . The drawing room," he went on, opening another door. "Lots of silk and Queen Anne . . . And here's the library. It's my favorite room. I like the clutter of English libraries."

"Yes."

They crossed the hall, inspecting the family dining room and then the formal dining room. "We haven't had any formal dinners, thank God. . . . That's this floor. The bedrooms are upstairs. There are three small suites. . . . What do you think so far?"

"It's lovely, Ned. I wouldn't dream of changing anything."

"I had a feeling you'd approve. It's really *very* English."

"Very comfortable," Sarah laughed. "Even with all the elegance it looks a bit worn, just a bit faded. It looks as if people actually live here."

"We do. You and I and Mrs. Porter, anyway. The two housemaids don't live in. Nor does Cook . . . Your parents have the suite at the end of the hall," Ned said when they reached the landing. "This is our suite. Sitting room, bedroom, and dressing room."

Sarah entered the sitting room, nodding happily as she sank into a chair. She glanced around at the flowered chintz sofa, at the array of small tables and lamps and glass-fronted chests. A Windsor rocker sat near the hearth, almost bracketed by polished brass andirons. "It reminds me of the vicar's sitting room," she said. "Only he had coal scuttles."

"The vicar!" Ned exclaimed, amused. "You aren't going to turn provincial on me, are you?"

"I've always been a country girl at heart."

"Would you like a martini, country girl?"

"Touché. And yes, I'd *love* a martini."

Ned went to the liquor cabinet, pouring ice, gin,

and a trickle of vermouth into a crystal pitcher. He stirred the clear liquid for a moment and then poured two drinks. "You'll notice the glasses are chilled," he said, giving one of them to Sarah. "Mrs. Porter thinks of everything."

"I'm impressed."

"Shall we have a toast? To England. May the sun never set."

Sarah took a sip of her drink. "Perfect, as usual. But if you don't mind, I'll finish it in the bathtub. Is there hot water?"

"Most of the time," Ned chuckled. "You may hear some banging or sputtering. The pipes are temperamental."

Sarah rose. "Which way?" she asked, glancing around.

"I'll show you. Follow me." He opened the bedroom door and walked inside. It was a pretty room, the wallpaper a design of yellow rosebuds, the chairs and quilts and rugs colored soft shades of green and ivory. A large vase of forsythia decorated the marble mantel; smaller bouquets decorated the night table and the highboy. "I didn't have a chance to do anything about the bed," he explained. "It's a good size. Quite spacious, but still I don't suppose you'd want company."

"No," Sarah replied with a smile. "You can have the bed. I'll be fine on the couch."

"That's an affront to chivalry. I'll take the couch. . . . The bathroom's through there, Sarah. Holler if you need anything."

Sarah carried her drink into the dressing room. She saw that her bags had been unpacked, her things neatly put away; she continued into the bathroom and turned on the taps. She soaked in a hot tub for twenty minutes, smiling as her thoughts drifted back to Paris, to moonlit walks along the banks of the Seine and blue-gray mornings filled with love. The sudden sharp clanging of the pipes interrupted her reverie. She blinked, taking another sip of her martini. She heard a clock striking the hour and reluctantly she stepped from the tub.

It was four-thirty when she rejoined Ned. Her honey hair had been brushed into loose waves about her face, her lips tinted a clear coral. She wore a simply cut beige Chanel dress, a gold shell brooch at the shoulder. Her earrings were circles of gold and pearls, a recent gift from Patrick. "What do you think?" she asked. "I didn't want to look too showy, but I didn't want to look too plain either."

"You're gorgeous, dear heart."

"Be serious. Is this dress all right?"

"Very stylish. Stop worrying. Your parents aren't going to grade you on your clothes. They won't have any idea what that little outfit cost."

"They wouldn't believe it, even if they did."

"More courage?" Ned asked, lifting the pitcher. "A short one?"

"No, thanks. I just rinsed my mouth and I don't want them to smell liquor on my breath."

He laughed. "They're not teetotalers, Sarah," he said. "Your father likes his port, and your mother can be talked into an ale now and then. They both take a drink before dinner."

"I know I'm being foolish. I can't help it. I'm *so* nervous."

"Come, let's wait in the library. It's especially cozy this time of day." Ned took Sarah's arm, walking with her to the stairs. "There's really nothing to be nervous about," he said. "You must try to relax. Enjoy their visit. It's the only enjoyment you're likely to have for a while. We have a lot of work ahead.

You're going to be in the thick of it."

"Is everyone assuming there's going to be war?"

"Some people are more optimistic than others. I don't see any reason for optimism, not with crazy Adolf running wild. I think the real horror is just beginning. . . . But that's enough depressing talk. This is a happy occasion. A reunion!" Ned opened the library door, stepping aside to let Sarah pass. He crossed the room and parted the draperies, smiling as sunlight streamed through the windows. "Nice, isn't it? There have been only two days of rain since I arrived. . . . Sit down, for heaven's sake. Be comfortable."

"What time is it?"

"They'll be here soon. You've waited all these years, Sarah. Another few minutes aren't going to make a difference."

"That's just it. I *have* waited all these years. Now I want it to be over." Sarah dropped into a chair, then sprang up again. She started to pace, stopping whenever she heard a car go by, whenever she heard an errant sound. "They're here," she cried when finally she heard a sound on the stair. She dashed into the hall, her heart pounding. "Mama! Papa!"

The packages fell from Hilda's arms. "Sarah," she said, "is it you?"

But Sarah could not speak, for her throat was dry, choked with tears. She ran to her parents, her arms flung wide. She felt Hilda's embrace and in that moment the years seemed to slip away. She was Sarah Griffith again, innocent and carefree and seventeen years old. "Mama," she whispered. "Papa."

They went into the library. John and Hilda settled themselves on the couch, glancing uncertainly at each other. There was a silence, and then the murmur of John's quiet voice. "It's hard to know where to

296

begin," he said. "It's been so long. . . . You look well, Sarah. Very well indeed."

"You look like a picture star!" Hilda declared. "Not that I'm surprised. You were the prettiest girl in Aldcross. Did you know that, Ned? All the boys were after our Sarah."

"Mama's exaggerating."

"I'm not. Ask anyone and they'll tell you the same thing. Why, I remember as if it were yesterday."

"Sarah's the prettiest girl in New York, too," Ned laughed. "At least *I* think she is. And I'm said to have a keen eye. Isn't that right, dear heart?"

"He's famous for his keen eye."

Ned stood. "Also for my sense of timing," he said. "I'll leave you to your reunion now. . . . There's sherry on that table. If you want anything else, ring Mrs. Porter."

"Thank you, Ned."

"See you at dinner."

The door closed and Sarah's gaze returned to her parents. She felt a twinge, for while Hilda appeared to have changed little, John appeared older than his fifty-nine years. In the bright afternoon light she saw that his hair was thinner, completely gray. Deep lines were etched on his brow and about his eyes. He was pale, his lips almost colorless. He's never been strong, she thought, and her heart tightened with pain. "I'm so glad you're here," she said. "I've missed you both so much."

"We missed you," Hilda said. "Of course we had your letters and the pictures you sent. We saved them all. Sometimes we'd get out the box and read them through from the start. . . . But we knew you were having a fine life in America. That was what mattered. That's the way I saw it."

"America's been good to you, Sarah," John said.

297

"Have you—have you been happy?"

"Oh, yes, Papa. Very happy. Lucy is a wonderful girl. You'll meet her one of these days and you'll be so proud. She isn't a bit spoiled or uppity. She's a *nice* girl."

"And Ned?" John asked. "He seems a fine fellow. Have you been happy with Ned?"

"Yes, Papa. Our marriage was rather sudden. I suppose I had my doubts. You may have sensed that in my letters. . . . But everything's worked out very well. We've had lovely times together. Ned is . . . he's such a lighthearted person. He enjoys life."

John lowered his eyes, studying his veined hands. "Then it was the right thing?" he asked softly. "Sending you to America? It was the right thing to do?"

Sarah went to him, gently touching his pale cheek. "Oh, Papa, it was exactly the right thing," she said, anxious to ease his distress. "You mustn't think about it anymore. You mustn't blame yourself. I—I haven't a single regret."

"You've been happy? That's the truth?"

"The truth, Papa," Sarah replied, forcing herself to meet his gaze. "I didn't know you'd been worrying all these years. There was no need. I've had a marvelous life, really I have."

"I tried to tell him," Hilda said with a sigh. "A thousand times I tried to tell him. . . . Well, love, now you're seeing our Sarah for yourself. Doesn't she look happy? She does to me."

"I expect I should have listened to you, Hilda," John conceded, a sheepish grin edging his mouth. "But perhaps it was necessary to see for myself."

"Well, they say seeing is believing."

"There are lots of things I want you to see," Sarah said. "I want you to come to America for a nice, long visit. Autumn might be a good time. New York is so pretty then."

"I couldn't get away from the school, Sarah. My classes . . ."

"Never mind your classes. You ought to think about retiring, Papa. Money isn't a problem. I'll take care of that."

"Oh, money has nothing to do with it," Hilda chuckled. "We've more than enough already. Your papa refused to touch a shilling of the money you sent us over the years. Not a shilling! It's all been sitting in the Marbury bank. Collecting interest, too. Eighteen years worth of interest. We have a tidy nest egg by now."

"Yes, quite," John agreed.

"But why didn't you spend the money when I sent it? I wanted you to have some pleasures, a splurge once in a while."

"We have our pleasures, love. And we aren't really the sort to have splurges, are we?"

"Papa, don't you want to retire?"

"I like my work. It's a great comfort."

"Of course it is," Hilda said. "A man needs work to do. That doesn't mean we can't have a holiday in America. A holiday might be just the thing. We'll think about it, won't we, John?"

"Yes. Yes, indeed."

"Right now we want to hear about you, Sarah. Letters are all well and good, but they're not the same as hearing your own words."

Sarah's words were carefully chosen, painting an idyllic picture of her life. She had only kind things to say about Elizabeth, about the years spent in the Cameron house and the years spent as Ned's wife. She spoke of her friends, of her work, of the city she now called home. She spoke of Lucy's childhood and adolescence, describing the coming-out party but omitting any reference to Colin Averill. She spoke for more than an hour, saying nothing that might upset or alarm, nothing that might raise suspicions. Of Patrick she said nothing at all. "So you see," she smiled, bringing her recitation to an end, "it's been a very happy time."

"There now, John," Hilda said. "You can put your mind at ease."

"Yes, I expect I can. It's a relief, you know. . . . I was never sure, all those years. I couldn't be certain I'd done the right thing. It's a great relief."

"I'm glad, Papa. And we're going to make up for all those years. We're together again and we're going to celebrate. Ned's been busy hatching plans. We're taking you on the town."

"On the town?"

"Starting with a shopping spree at Harrods, Mama. That's just the beginning. For the next two weeks, London is yours!"

"Oh my," Hilda said, glancing at John. "Oh my. Imagine London being ours."

"A gift to the Griffiths."

And in the weeks that followed, the Griffiths felt they had indeed been given London as a gift. They were taken to the best stores, gaping in amazement while the Rolls filled with packages. Each night they were taken to late suppers at the city's most exclusive restaurants. They were taken to exotic Soho clubs and avant-garde Chelsea galleries. There was a formal luncheon at the American Embassy. There was a midnight cruise on the Thames, a gala affair with champagne and caviar and grilled lobster served on gold-traced Meissen plates. "It's like we've living in a fairy tale," Hilda commented, and an awestruck John hastily agreed.

"I'm afraid you've spoiled us, Sarah," he said as they waited for the train back to Aldcross. "We aren't used to such luxury, after all."

"It's done you a world of good, Papa. You look so much better."

"That's right," Hilda said. "You look ten years younger. You've had a nice rest and a bit of pampering. That's just what you needed." She reached out her hand, brushing a speck of lint from his new tweed jacket. "Ten years younger," she said once more.

"You're looking rather girlish yourself," Ned laughed. "You'll have to be wary of mashers. Here," he said, giving her a wicker hamper, "you can beat them off with this."

"Sandwiches for your trip," Sarah explained. Her next words were lost in the roar of the train pulling into the station. The doors slid open. The crowd moved forward, carrying John and Hilda toward the platform. "I'll telephone, Mama," she shouted over the noise. "Don't forget we'll see you again in June. . . . Good-bye. Good-bye, Papa . . . Safe home."

Ned put his arm around Sarah's shoulder. "Easy," he said. "It will be June before you know it. They'll be back."

She nodded, wiping away a tear. "Yes," she sniffled. "But I have the oddest feeling."

"What feeling?"

"That I'm never going to see them again . . . Odd, isn't it?"

April stretched into May, but now Sarah had little time to enjoy the beautiful English spring. She was working long hours, arriving at the Galleries before

301

...ly leaving before seven. Alone in the cavernous storage area she numbered and catalogued thousands of porcelains—bowls, vases, decorative plates, figurines, trays, lamps, tea sets, and entire dinner services. It was slow, tedious work, interrupted only for meetings with the executive staff. The subject of these meetings was war, war that seemed more inevitable every day.

War was also the subject of conversations in the house on Eaton Place. Sarah and Ned were both forced to change their travel plans, extending their stays to accommodate the needs of the Galleries. Sarah had to postpone her parents' June visit, suggesting they come in July. But war changed those plans, too, for in July of 1940 the Third French Republic ceased to exist and the Battle of Britain began.

It was known as the Blitz, an aerial war waged swiftly, violently, by Hitler's *Luftwaffe*. Night after night bombs rained from the sky over British cities, the lightning raids cutting wide paths of death and destruction. Night after night people fled to the shelter of basements or Underground stations, emerging hours later to streets filled with rubble, to air thick with smoke. It was a desperate time, but the new Prime Minister, Winston Churchill, rallied the nation and the world with a speech vowing "blood, toil, tears, and sweat," vowing victory.

England was at war and the face of London was transformed. Now blackout curtains were seen at many windows. Fire wardens and rescue workers were seen patrolling the dark streets, while plane spotters, binoculars in hand, patrolled the skies. Rationing was put into effect, thinning store shelves, thinning city traffic. Ships and planes had been requisitioned by the government, restricting access to docks and air terminals. Young men in uniform were everywhere, enjoying a last brief holiday before joining their units. At train stations, anxious parents sent their children off to the safety of the countryside; at hospitals, trucks delivered extra supplies to staffs preparing for the worst.

All these sights moved Sarah to tears, though like everyone else, she grew used to them. She grew used to shrill sirens in the middle of the night, to shouts of "Fire!" echoing through the deserted streets. Like everyone else, she grew used to her own fear. "At least Mama and Papa are safe," she said one late night in September. "Bertie went down to see them. He assures me they're fine."

"Did you two have a nice lunch?" Ned asked.

"Very nice, everything considered. He's gone back to Edinburgh to settle some business matters. . . . And then he's planning to volunteer. He's made up his mind."

"I envy him, in a way. He'll be *doing* something, and that's better than hiding in cellars while the goddamned Nazis bomb the hell out of us. Not that this is such a bad cellar," Ned added, glancing around at the chairs and cots that comprised their makeshift bedroom. "All the comforts of home. And we're so close to the wine. I think I'll open the Mumms tonight."

"Good. I'm in a champagne mood."

"Are you? This may be the time to get you drunk and spirit you away to Aldcross."

"Don't start that again, Ned. I'm not leaving. You know I won't go without you. I'd feel terrible."

"Dear heart, I feel terrible enough for both of us. I should have sent you back to New York with Patrick. Instead I kept you here. The inventory! Thanks to the damned inventory, you're in the middle of a war."

303

"So are you," Sarah replied. "Neither of us had any idea war would come so soon. But it's all right. The RAF is putting up a great fight."

"Great fight! I hope the RAF blows those bastards out of the sky. . . . Were you able to get a call through to Lucy?"

"No, but I wrote her this morning. I sent Elizabeth a note, too. Just a few lines to say we were alive and well."

"And drinking champagne in the cellar," Ned laughed. He popped the cork, deftly filling two glasses. "Here you are," he said. "What shall we drink to?"

"Peace?"

"To peace. To no more sirens in the night."

"Come sit down, Ned. Are you hungry? Mrs. Porter left some sandwiches before she went to her sister's. Chicken and tomato. She's coping nicely with rationing."

"The English always cope. That's why Hitler doesn't stand a chance. And when America gets into it . . . Enough about war. Let's talk about us."

"Us?"

"Well, what we're going to do with the rest of our lives. Do you suppose Evelyn would give Patrick a divorce? Because if she would, I think you ought to divorce me and marry the man you love."

"Ned, you know I love you."

"And you know what I mean. . . . It's a crazy world, Sarah. An uncertain world. There's a lot to be said for seizing the moment."

"What moment? What in heaven's name are you talking about?"

"The reasons we married are no longer valid. Lucy's grown, and I came into my trust four years ago. There isn't a single thing Mother can do to either of us now. This is *your* moment, dear heart. I've been thinking lately that you should make the most of it. Marry Patrick. Ride off with him into the sunset."

Sarah laughed, taking Ned's hand. "You're sweet," she said. "You always were. But you mustn't worry so much. I'm happy with things as they are."

"You'd be happier married to Patrick."

"Perhaps. Perhaps not. In any case, Evelyn will never give him a divorce. I knew that from the start. It was hard at first, but it doesn't bother me anymore. It hasn't for years. Besides, I don't want to divorce you. You're my dearest friend, Ned. . . . When I was telling Mama and Papa about all the lovely times we'd had, I realized it was the truth. We've had great fun. I don't regret any of it. Do you?"

"I'm not the type to have regrets. But if I were, you wouldn't be among them. You saved me from myself."

"Did I?" Sarah smiled.

"If not for you, I'd be on my fourth marriage by now. Trapped by scheming females. Think of the strain. Christ, think of the alimony!" Ned poured more champagne, leaning back in his chair. "You saved me from all that," he said. "I have no complaints. And you're right. . . . We've had fun. That's the icing on the cake. So if you're content to let things go on as they are, I am too."

"I'm content," Sarah replied, sipping the champagne. "Of course it's a woman's prerogative to change her mind."

"I wouldn't have it any other way. I enjoy the twists and turns of women's minds. That's the challenge."

"And you never refuse a challenge."

"Or a woman," Ned laughed.

Sarah laughed also. She raised her glass and touched it to his. "Another toast," she said. "To us."

"To us."

They drank, merrily hurling their glasses against a wall. The sharp crash of crystal was the last sound they would ever hear, for in the very next instant a bomb dropped by the *Luftwaffe* leveled the house on Eaton Place.

A young rescue worker digging through the rubble would later discover their bodies. "Holding hands, they were," he would say in sorrowful description. "Holding hands till the end."

Lucy

Chapter Fifteen

Eight hundred people attended the double funeral at St. James Church. Elizabeth was seated in the front pew, her head bowed, her face hidden by a heavy black veil. Beside her was Lucy, so pale and still she might have been carved of stone. Beside Lucy was Josh and at the end of the pew was Patrick, his red-rimmed eyes fixed on the mahogany casket that held Sarah's remains. Prayers were spoken, hymns were sung, but the Camerons took no part in the service. They seemed utterly drained, oblivious to the sounds and sights around them. When finally the service concluded, they rose and made their way from the church into waiting limousines.

Fifty people were present at the cemetery and afterward at a cold buffet lunch. They offered condolences in hushed tones, murmuring the words and phrases that were expected and that did no good. They were not sorry when the time came to leave, nor was the stricken family sorry to see them go. "I'm glad it's over," Lucy said quietly, sinking into a chair. "Why did we have to have all those people? All those stupid rituals?"

"Rituals are supposed to ease the pain," Josh

replied. "Shared grief and all that."

"But they don't. They don't change anything. It's just a lot of pretending. There wasn't anybody here I wanted to see."

"Not even Jonny Melvile?"

Lucy sighed, slumping deeper into her chair. "No matter what happens," she said, "Gran's matchmaking goes on. It was silly for him to come all the way down from Yale. Sillier for Tony to come from Harvard."

"He wanted to be here, Lucy. He called and asked to be invited. He was concerned about you. So am I. You haven't cried yet. You might feel better if you did."

"That's what Mother . . . Mother used to say that. But I don't seem to have any tears. I don't know why. . . . It's as if they're trapped inside me. The night the telegram came . . . That was such a terrible night, Josh. I heard the scream. Gran's scream. I ran to her room and she was just standing there. Standing like a statue. 'You must be strong,' she said. 'You must be very calm.' And then—then I read the telegram. . . . I couldn't cry. I couldn't."

"Maybe you're afraid to."

"Oh, I'm always afraid," Lucy murmured, lifting her eyes to her cousin. "I'm alone now, Josh. There's Gran but she's . . . I haven't anyone."

"You have me, and Dad. You know he'll do anything for you, anything at all."

"There's nothing to do. And even if there were, I wouldn't bother him, not now. I've never seen Uncle Patrick so upset. He looks awful."

"None of us looks very well, Lucy. You're looking rather frail yourself. When's the last time you had a decent meal?"

"I have no appetite."

"I understand that, but you still have to eat. Force yourself."

"No," Lucy said, shaking her head. "Then I'll be sick to my stomach. Just looking at food makes me sick."

"You're a stubborn girl."

"Don't lecture me, Josh. This isn't the time."

"Sorry. I can't help worrying about you, that's all. You can't crawl back into your shell. I know you, and when you start brooding you turn inward. You shut people out."

"What if I do?" Lucy said wearily. "Maybe I don't want people to get too close. I don't want to be hurt anymore. I loved Colin and look what happened. I loved Mother and Daddy, and now they're gone. . . . Oh, Josh, I feel so empty. I don't want to feel this way ever again."

"You can't stop living."

"That's a cliché." Lucy stood, steadying herself against the chair. "I'd better see how Gran is," she said. "Today must have been a strain."

"She's a tough old bird. She'll be all right. I'm not so sure about you. I can never tell what's going on in that mind of yours."

"Dark thoughts," Lucy said as she walked to the door. "Very dark thoughts." She entered the hall, spinning around when she heard a noise on the stair. "Tony," she exclaimed. "I thought you'd gone."

"I walked Mother and Dad to the car. I just came back to say good-bye. To say how sorry I am. I liked your parents, Lucy. They had . . . I don't know how to put it, exactly. They had a generosity of spirit, if that doesn't sound pompous."

"It doesn't. Thank you, Tony."

"Is there anything I can do? Any way I can help?"

"No, I'm fine. I was going up to see Gran. But

311

thank you for asking." Lucy looked at him, a faint smile shadowing her pale mouth. "I'm glad you're here," she said. "I don't know why, but I'm glad."

Elizabeth stood at the window, watching the tangle of traffic on the avenue below. She remembered a time when horse-drawn carriages traveled this avenue, remembered the gentle, rhythmic sound of horses' hooves on the cobblestones. But that was long ago, she thought to herself, long before all the deaths. She closed the draperies. Slowly, she walked across the sitting room to the mantel. She gazed up at Jasper's portrait, at the smaller portraits of her children. She turned and walked to an oval table upon which were dozens of silver-framed photographs tracing her family through the years. "Family portraits," she murmured, a moment later sweeping them to the floor. With trembling hand she poured a whiskey. She swallowed the fiery liquid and poured another. "Come in," she called, hearing a knock at the door. "Has Josh gone?"

"Yes, Gran. He's dropping Tony at Grand Central." Lucy looked around, her eyes settling on the overturned photographs lying amidst broken glass. "What happened?" she asked. "What happened to all your pictures?"

"An accident," Elizabeth replied. "Never mind. Dorothy will clean it up."

"Shall I ring for her?"

"No, not just yet. We must talk, my dear. We haven't really talked since—since the tragedy. Come and sit down. Tell me how you are."

"I'm all right, I suppose. It hurts, Gran. There's an ache that won't go away. . . . I don't know how else to describe it."

"There's no need. I believe I know what you're feeling. Years ago I lost Jasper. Then one by one I lost my children. And Sarah. I always thought of Sarah as my own. Always. She was a lovely woman. A bit headstrong perhaps, but a great credit to the Cameron name. I see you're wearing her locket."

"I gave it to Mother before she sailed. She was wearing it when—"

"Yes, yes, I understand. Of course Sarah had quite a lot of jewelry. Some of it disappeared in the tragedy. Most of it is still in her safe. It's yours now, you know."

"Please, Gran, I don't want to talk about that."

"It does no good to avoid unpleasant subjects, my dear. Facts must be faced. It's a fact that you're going to be a very wealthy girl one day. The wills haven't been read yet, but I'm privy to certain details. Aside from several bequests to friends and charities, everything comes to you. And naturally when I die—"

"Please, Gran."

"You may think it's the wrong time to discuss such matters. It's precisely the right time. I'm past sixty, and I have no delusions of immortality."

"Gran, I don't care about wills or jewelry or money."

"Don't you?" Elizabeth smiled. "You've never had to care, because you've always been given what you wanted. You would change your tune if you were forced to earn your living. If you were forced to work."

"Mother worked."

"Indeed she did. But it was a question of choice, not necessity. Those are vastly different things, Lucy. You were born to wealth. You are accustomed to a way of life. And you will have that way of life,

313

providing you're not foolish."

"Foolish?"

"There will be few restrictions on the inheritance from Sarah and Ned. Too few, in my opinion. Young girls of means often make foolish mistakes. The wrong diversions, the wrong men. It happens all the time, even to sensible girls. That's why you must give proper thought to your future. I would like to see you settled, my dear. Oh, not immediately. You need time to recover, to adjust. You may also want some time for yourself before you consider marriage."

"Marriage!" Lucy cried. "Marriage! Gran, I'm no more ready to get married than I am to—to join the circus."

"You were ready enough last year."

"That was different. I loved Colin. I still love him."

"You tell yourself you do."

"I don't tell myself anything, Gran. I know what I know."

"Well, all that is behind you now. You must start looking ahead. Jonny Melvile is a fine boy from a fine family. The same can be said of Tony Jennings, although he seems to have a wild streak. There are the Vanderbilt grandsons. I'm afraid they haven't turned out as I might have wished. There's Philip Colinge, a very nice boy. There's the Woodward boy. He seems to have an unfortunate taste for night-clubs."

Lucy stared in astonishment at Elizabeth. "I don't believe this," she said after a moment. "I don't believe this conversation. Today, of all days, to be thinking about matchmaking. How can you?"

"Life goes on."

"If I hear one more cliché, I'll scream. I swear I will."

"There's truth in clichés, Lucy. Life *does* go on. Life isn't always fair or kind, but it's all we have. We must accept what comes."

"I can't. Nothing makes sense anymore. Don't you see it's useless to go on with your matchmaking? I'm not interested."

"I'm simply suggesting you give thought to these young men. It's wise to have a plan in mind."

"I have my photography, Gran. Next month I'm going to begin a special class at NYU. Max Kazimov's class. Uncle Patrick helped make the arrangements. It wasn't easy. Everybody wants to study with Kazimov. He's the best. You've probably seen his photographs in *Life* magazine. He's done a few books, too. . . . Mother thought I had a talent for photography. I wasn't sure at first, but now I think she was right. I'm getting better. I can see that. My pictures have a certain . . . kind of style. Anyway, that's what I'm going to do."

Elizabeth was silent, studying Lucy. She saw the sudden flash of her eyes and then the rush of color to her cheeks. She smiled, thinking that, unlike Sarah, Lucy would not risk outright defiance. "I don't doubt you're talented, my dear," she said finally. "And photography is an excellent hobby. I approve of hobbies, as long as they don't interfere with more serious matters. Of course you won't let that happen."

"Oh, no, Gran," Lucy replied, anxious to avoid an argument. "It's just that for now I want to concentrate on my class. I want to learn all I can."

"A worthy ambition. In some ways, you remind me of Sarah. You have something of her spirit. Of course, spirit can be carried too far. We wouldn't want that, would we, Lucy?"

"No, Gran."

"You were always a sensible girl."

Lucy heard the implicit criticism of her mother. Her hands tightened in her lap but she said nothing. She stared down at the polished floor, feeling guilty, feeling ashamed.

"I'm so glad we had this talk," Elizabeth said. "I think things are much clearer and that's to the good. Don't you agree?"

"Yes, Gran." Lucy rose, glancing again at the welter of picture frames and broken glass. "I'll ask Dorothy to get a broom," she said.

"Don't bother, my dear. I'll call her when I'm ready. Run along now. It's been a difficult day, after all. I'm sure you're tired. You must rest."

Lucy went to the door. She looked over her shoulder, trying to read the expression in Elizabeth's cool, dark eyes, then went silently into the hall. I'll never understand Gran, she thought, her brows drawing together as she walked to her room. It occurred to her that perhaps she did not want to understand, that perhaps there were truths she did not want to know. "Coward," she murmured, flopping down on the bed.

She closed her eyes. She drowsed, and in that limbo between sleep and wakefulness her mind whirled with strange, garbled images from the past. She saw herself as a child skipping around the fun house at Coney Island. Colin was there, his face hideously distorted in a vast mirror; Tony was there, his head thrown back in laughter as the mirror shattered into thousands of tiny pieces that became raindrops. She saw the rain splashing a ship's empty deck. She saw bright streamers flurrying in the wind, and then a great burst of fireworks exploding in the sky. She saw a curtain of black smoke; when the curtain parted, she saw the sprawled and lifeless bodies of Sarah and Ned.

Terror brought her sharply awake. She sat up, feeling the thumping of her heart, feeling the tears that would not fall. After some moments she rose, wandering about the room. She stopped at her desk, staring down at the candid portraits of her parents, stopping again at the cabinet that held her many cameras and lenses. Atop the cabinet were three of Max Kazimov's books and these she carried back to the bed. She stretched out and began to read. The words blurred but she forced herself to concentrate, for she dared not sleep.

Max Kazimov was a big, burly man with tufted white eyebrows and a mane of unruly white hair. He was a flamboyant man, given to boisterous laughter and grand gestures and a certain unconventional style of dress, his usual outfit being a black turtleneck, black trousers, and a polo coat thrown jauntily over his shoulders. His usual attitude was one of exhilaration, for he took an almost childlike pleasure in life.

Kazimov, as he often referred to himself, had thirty students in his class. The young men and women were awed by his reputation, confused by his accented English, and utterly devoted. They listened to his impassioned lectures, hanging onto every word. They sought his advice. They accepted his judgments without question or complaint. "*Da*," he would cry when one of their photographs caught his fancy. "This is not good," he would declare at other times, offering vivid and lengthy criticism.

Lucy was the youngest member of the class and the shyest. She observed the freewheeling classroom debates, making notes but saying nothing. When she had to present her work she blushed beet-red and hurriedly returned to her seat. It was three weeks before she found the courage to ask a question, four weeks before she felt she might have a place amongst Kazimov's students. In that fourth week they were all given an assignment, the quirky task of telling the stories of their lives in two pictures. "When Kazimov is seeing these pictures," he explained, "Kazimov is seeing the soul."

Lucy thought about presenting a collage, but in the end she presented two separate photographs, one a somber study of the Cameron house at twilight, the other a moody study of the Central Park carousel, deserted and strewn with fallen leaves. There was not a trace of sentimentality in either photograph, not a trace of what Kazimov called "cheating." He lavished praise on her work, giving conspicuous display to the mounted prints. If privately he wondered why the beautiful young woman should be so unhappy, he made no comment. "Truth," he shouted to the assembled students. "Miss Cameron is telling here the truth. The eye, the camera, the soul, they are all one. And with the joining there is truth."

Lucy seemed to blossom under Kazimov's tutelage. Her appetite was restored and her nightmares were fewer, disappearing for weeks at a time. Now she did not hesitate to voice her opinions and to take part in her classmates' impromptu discussions. Eagerly she completed her assignments, and day by day her confidence grew. "I'm really getting better," she said to Josh during one November lunch. "I've learned *so much*. And it's all Kazimov. He's a genius."

"He's damned good."

"A genius. I don't know what I'll do when the class ends. I can't stand to think about it. These past two months have been . . . I feel *useful*, Josh. I have a talent and that's something no one can take away from me."

"I assume you mean Aunt Elizabeth. How is she

coping with all this?''

"Oh, she hates it when I quote Kazimov. She gets that icy look of hers. So I'm careful what I say. I don't want to rock the boat. As long as she thinks it's just a hobby, it will be all right.''

"She doesn't suspect you have something more in mind?'' Josh asked.

"I haven't said a word. And I won't, until I'm sure. I have a way to go before I can start talking about a career. I'll have to catch her by surprise. If Gran had any suspicions . . . well, you know how she is. She'd be hatching plots.''

"There isn't a lot she can do, Lucy. You'll have your own money.''

"Money is only part of it. I don't want to be at war with Gran. It's hard for me to oppose her. I try, but I'm not good at it. It's always been easier just to go along.''

"That may change when you're feeling more independent,'' Josh suggested. "That's where money comes in. I know it's not your favorite subject but—''

"No, it's not. It's ghoulish to talk about money so soon after Mother and Daddy . . . I asked to be excused from the reading of the wills. I practically begged. Gran said I had to be there. I don't know how I'll get through it.''

"At least you haven't much longer to wait,'' Josh replied, glancing at his watch. "It's almost two o'clock. We're expected by three. Do you want coffee or shall I get the check?''

"I want to finish my wine. Dutch courage, isn't that what they call it?''

"These things are never pleasant, Lucy. Best to have them over with.''

"Let's talk about something pleasant. How's Sallie?''

"She's terrific,'' Josh said, a sudden smile lighting

the gray of his eyes. "I'm thinking of popping the question. It's time I settled down."

"Oh, that's marvelous. I'm happy for you, Josh. I like Sallie. She's so friendly and high-spirited. . . . Imagine you marrying a southern belle. I always thought you'd wind up with a staid Bostonian."

"Did you? Why? I'm not staid."

"No, but you're orderly. Your life is planned. And you like tradition."

"Guilty on all counts," Josh laughed. "Though I have a wilder side. It's genetic. Dad has a wilder side, too."

"Uncle Patrick? I don't believe that. He's a perfect gentleman."

"Of course he is. All the Camerons have perfect manners. So what? There's more to us than manners. You have to learn to look beyond externals. Look into the soul, that's my advice."

"And Kazimov's." Lucy drank the last of her wine. She stared at the empty glass and shook her head. "Well, I don't suppose we can put it off any longer," she said. "I hope there won't be a lot of people."

"Everybody who's mentioned in the wills. There may be quite a crowd. Just grit your teeth and tell yourself it will soon be over."

"Yes, I'll try."

Josh paid the check and they left the restaurant. He hailed a taxi, giving the driver the address of the Cameron house. There was little conversation on the way. Lucy fidgeted, plucking at the lacy edge of her handkerchief. The house came into view and she stiffened. "I'm all right," she said as Josh's hand closed over her hand. "I'm fine."

Wilson, the new butler, opened the door. "Good afternoon, Miss Lucy, Mr. Cameron. They're waiting for you in the library."

"Thank you, Wilson," Josh said, taking Lucy's arm. "Come, the stairs are quicker than that ridiculous elevator."

They climbed the stairs, pausing at the top of the landing. "I won't have to say anything, will I?" Lucy asked.

"Don't worry. The lawyer will do all the talking." Josh opened the library door, then stood aside. "Don't worry," he said again.

Lucy did not hear, for she was looking around at the faces turned in her direction. She saw Patrick and his younger son Sam. She saw Mary Margaret and Janet and the ancient Amelia Boyce. She saw Raymond and Tully and all the maids who had served the Cameron household. Sitting some distance apart was a woman unknown to her, a striking, flashily dressed redhead who would later be identified as Nola O'Rourke. "I—I'm sorry to be late," she murmured.

"Come in, my dear," Elizabeth said. "Mr. Holcomb is ready to begin."

Lucy took the chair next to Elizabeth. She lowered her gaze to her clenched hands and drew a breath. She listened as Randolph Holcomb read the long preamble to the wills, listened to the legal phrasing that made no sense to her. I'll never get through this, she thought, fighting an impulse to run, to hide someplace where she would not be found. Dear God, she silently prayed, just let it be over.

But the lawyer's quiet voice droned on and on. There were explanatory remarks; there was something about "death in a common catastrophe." Ten minutes after he had begun, he read the first group of bequests. These were to the servants, and as had been arranged, they left the room moments later. The next bequest, in the amount of fifty thousand dollars, was to Nola O'Rourke, and then she too made her way from the room.

"Who is that woman, Gran?" Lucy asked, craning her neck toward the door. "I've never seen her before."

"No one important, my dear."

Randolph Holcomb set one document aside and picked up another. "'To my mentor and friend Amelia Boyce,'" he continued, "'I leave the sum of ten thousand dollars. To my cherished friend Janet Munroe Rawly, I leave my furs.' . . . There is a list here, Mrs. Rawly. With rather full descriptions, I'm afraid. Will it suffice for now to say there are eight furs of various kinds?"

"Yes, Mr. Holcomb."

"Then I will proceed. 'To my cherished friend Mary Margaret Culhane O'Connor, I leave the sum of twenty thousand dollars.'"

Lucy heard a loud gasp. She turned, jumping to her feet, for Mary Margaret had fainted. She rushed to help, joining the circle around the prone woman. It was Miss Boyce who furnished a vial of smelling salts. "Mary Margaret," Lucy cried, waving the vial back and forth. "Mary Margaret, open your eyes."

"Oh, it's you, Lucy."

"Are you all right? Did you hurt yourself?"

"Only my dignity."

Patrick and Sam helped her up. "That's better," Patrick said. "Your hat's a little squashed," he added with a smile, "but that hardly matters now. You're an heiress, Mary Margaret."

"It's true," she sniffled, tears slipping down her cheeks. "For Sarah to remember me like that . . . Ah, Sarah always was the kindest girl, God rest her."

"If I may return to the business at hand," Randolph Holcomb interjected. "If everyone will be seated . . ."

"Come along, Mary Margaret," Janet said. "A walk in the air will do you good. Perhaps we'll stop at the Plaza for tea. Miss Boyce, won't you join us?"

"I would enjoy that, Mrs. Rawly. Thank you."

The women left and the Camerons took their seats. "Do I have to stay for the rest of this, Gran?" Lucy asked.

"Certainly you do. Mr. Holcomb is just now coming to the heart of the matter. . . . Please continue, Mr. Holcomb."

"The remaining bequests concern family members only," he explained. "It's necessary to again point out that Edmund Lindsey Cameron, otherwise known as Ned Cameron, made his will in favor of his wife, Sarah Griffith Cameron. But here the 'common catastrophe' clause applies. If that's understood, I shall proceed. . . . 'To my cousin, Samuel Forbes Cameron, I leave the sum of seventy-five thousand dollars and a one-third share in Cameron Galleries Inc., Cameron Galleries Ltd. voting stock. To my cousin, Joshua Grant Cameron, I leave the sum of seventy-five thousand dollars and a one-third share in Cameron Galleries Inc., Cameron Galleries Ltd. voting stock. To my cousin Patrick Reynolds Cameron, I leave a one-third share in Cameron Galleries Inc., Cameron Galleries Ltd. voting stock, and a fifty-percent share of the Cameron Trust established by my father. In addition, I leave him all personal possessions, with the wish that appropriate mementos will be selected and given to my friends.'" Mr. Holcomb paused, taking a sip of water. "Are there any questions?" he asked.

"Please continue," Elizabeth replied.

"Lucy, we come now to you. Your mother's will states the following: 'To my dear parents, John and

Hilda Griffith of Aldcross, England, I leave the sum of twenty thousand dollars. To my brother, Albert Griffith of Edinburgh, Scotland, I leave the sum of twenty thousand dollars. To my dear mother-in-law, Elizabeth Lindsey Cameron, I leave my diamond sunburst brooch.' Ah, here we are. . . . 'To my beloved daughter, Lucy Griffith Cameron, I leave the sum of ten thousand dollars, this sum to be transferred immediately upon my death. In addition, I leave her all my jewelry, save for the brooch otherwise specified.' There is a detailed list of the jewelry in question, Lucy. There is also the appraisal, which values the collection in excess of one million dollars."

"A million dollars," Lucy murmured.

"That is correct. Your father's will states the following: 'To my beloved daughter, Lucy Griffith Cameron, I leave a fifty-percent share in the Cameron Trust, these funds to continue in trust until she reaches the age of thirty. In addition, I leave her all stocks, bonds, and cash reserves, these to be transferred outright in three equal installments: one-third when she reaches the age of twenty-five; one-third when she reaches the age of thirty-five; one-third when she reaches the age of forty.'" Again Mr. Holcomb paused. "I should add," he said after a moment, "that Patrick has been named executor and your trustee. As of today, your father's holdings are worth three million dollars. Exclusive of the Cameron Trust, of course."

Lucy had not known what to expect, but never had she considered that her inheritance would run into millions. She felt unaccountably embarrassed, ducking her head as she tried to compose her thoughts.

"Does that conclude my son's will, Mr. Holcomb?" Elizabeth asked.

"Well, there is one final bequest. You might prefer it be read in private, Mrs. Cameron. The bequest is of a rather . . . shall we say, whimsical nature."

"I don't doubt it. My son was often whimsical. Please proceed."

"As you wish." There was a rustling of papers, and then a quiet, reluctant voice. " 'To my mother, Elizabeth Lindsey Cameron, who took infinite pleasure in calling the tune for us all, I leave my antique Chinese flute.' That . . . er . . . concludes the will."

Elizabeth smiled, though something hard and cold came into her eyes. "Thank you, Mr. Holcomb," she said. She rose, her gaze settling on Lucy. "Wilson has cocktails ready in the drawing room, my dear. Perhaps you will be hostess. I want a word with Mr. Holcomb."

"Yes, Gran." She turned, gesturing to the others. They followed her into the drawing room, where pitchers of martinis and whiskey sours reposed on silver trays. "That was odd, wasn't it, Uncle Patrick?" she said when he brought her drink. "About the flute, I mean."

"I don't think it was odd at all. It was a nice touch. Very like Ned. He had a sly sense of humor. And he had the last word, didn't he? I'll bet he's laughing about that now."

"Who was that woman? The one in the silver fox?"

"A friend of the family," Patrick replied.

"But that couldn't be. I've never seen her here. I never heard her name before today. . . . Besides, she isn't the type. She's beautiful, but in a showy kind of way. Gran wouldn't have let her through the door."

"Yes, you're probably right. As a matter of fact, she was a friend of your father's. He had a great many friends, Lucy. He didn't bring them all here."

"What sort of friends?"

"You're full of questions today, aren't you?"

"There have always been things I didn't understand, Uncle Patrick. There have always been undercurrents in this house. I felt them again today. . . . Who is Nola O'Rourke? I know Gran won't tell me."

"Let's just say she was a special friend."

Lucy glanced away, sipping her sherry. "Yes, I thought it might be something like that," she murmured. "When I was growing up I . . . heard things about Daddy. . . . Daddy and other women."

"What difference can it make now?"

"Did it make any difference to Mother?"

Patrick did not know how to reply. He gazed into Lucy's green eyes, slowly shaking his head. "You must take my word that it didn't," he said. "Your parents loved each other. They understood each other. When you're older, you'll realize how important that is. Your father was a good man, Lucy. A noncomformist in some respects, but a good man. And Sarah," he went on, his voice breaking, "well, there was no one quite like her."

Lucy saw the look of pain flash across Patrick's face. She saw the grief, the sorrow. "Why, Uncle Patrick, you loved her too."

"Yes."

"I'm glad," she said, clasping his hand. "I'm glad."

Lucy returned to class the next day, and during the next three months it was the center of her life. To please Elizabeth she accepted dinner dates with the young men who called, but these evenings, pleasant as they were, meant little compared to Kazimov's class. She needed the challenge, the praise, and the criticism, for in these things she found escape. She found a sense of herself, an identity separate from the Camerons. In her own way, she found a measure of peace.

Mother would be proud, she often thought, and indeed she longed to share her feelings, her small triumphs, with Sarah. Her longing grew more intense as the Christmas holidays approached. The sight of festive holiday decorations brought an ache to her heart, a sadness that touched the deepest part of her. Elizabeth insisted she attend the usual Christmas parties and reluctantly she did so, making an appearance, murmuring a few words, and then making a hasty departure. After such events she walked for hours, losing herself in the crowds of shoppers and bewildered tourists. "Walking is good exercise," she explained to a curious Elizabeth, refusing to say any more.

Now, on a cold and raw December afternoon, she walked briskly up Fifth Avenue, clutching at her hat as the wind threatened to carry it off. The cold burned her cheeks but did not slow her pace. She started to cross the avenue, stopping only when she heard the squeal of brakes. She heard her name and she turned. "Tony," she cried, looking through the windshield at his scowling face. "You scared me."

He poked his head out the window, his hand waving her closer. "Get in," he said. "Get in before someone runs you over. *Now*, dammit."

Lucy rushed around the side of the car and slipped inside. "What's the—?"

"Are you crazy?" Tony demanded as he started the engine. "You could have been killed. You didn't have the light, you know. You're just lucky I was paying attention. If I'd been daydreaming, you'd have tire tracks running across your back."

"I'm sorry, Tony. I guess *I* was daydreaming. Don't be angry. . . . I've never seen you angry before. I didn't think you had a temper."

"I don't. Except when I see deliberate cruelty or deliberate stupidity. You qualify for the latter."

"I'm sorry."

"Where the hell were you going in such a hurry?"

"I was escaping. It's true," Lucy smiled. "I left Meg Wyland's tea early and I was afraid her brother was going to follow me out. Jeff's sweet, but he's awfully persistent. You know him, don't you?"

"We were at Choate together. He means well."

"I didn't even want to go to the party. I keep trying to tell Gran it's too soon after . . . She won't listen. She says my spirits need lifting. So I go to all these things and leave early."

"I hate to agree with your grandmother, Lucy, but she isn't entirely wrong. It may be too soon for parties, but it isn't too soon to get on with your life. Max Kazimov's class is a great beginning. Still, you know the old saying about all work and no play."

"How do you know about Kazimov?"

"I have my sources."

"Josh, I suppose."

"Among others," Tony laughed. He nudged the car into a parking space and switched off the engine. "Let's talk," he said.

"Let's not. Tony, I'm fine. Really I am. A little at loose ends perhaps, but that's because class is recessed for the holidays. I've been doing some work on my own. Or trying to, in between these silly parties."

"I'm glad you've found an interest, Lucy."

"Oh, it's more than that."

"A serious interest then. But what else are you doing?"

"Nothing," Lucy replied quietly, glancing away. "I miss Mother and Daddy. And it's worse now, with the holidays. . . . Daddy traveled so much. I can pretend he's just on another business trip. I can't pretend about Mother. I *miss* her, Tony. I can't get it out of my mind that I didn't even say good-bye. I didn't say half the things I should have. . . . I've—I've thought about going to the cemetery. . . . But I know I won't do it."

"Why won't you?"

"I'm not good at facing up to things. I'm a coward."

"Maybe you just need some moral support. I'll go with you, Lucy. I'll drive you out there. We could take flowers. Better yet, a Christmas wreath. What do you say?"

"I don't know. It's very kind of you, Tony, but I don't know. Why would you want to do that?"

"'Tis the season for doing good deeds."

"Don't joke. Tell me why."

"Let's say I don't want to see you walk into traffic again. That's no joke, Lucy. I mean it. There are things you haven't resolved. They're distracting you. If I can help clear the cobwebs away, I'm happy to oblige."

Lucy gazed into the dark blue of Tony's eyes. She expected to see amusement but instead she saw something she could not define, something that brought a blush to her cheeks. Quickly, she lowered her eyes. "Thank you," she said. "I—I never know quite what to make of you. You're fresh, but you can be very nice when you want to be."

"High praise. Careful, or you'll turn my head."

"What day do you think we should go?"

"I'm ready to go now," Tony replied.

"Now?"

"Why not? If we wait, you may change your mind. And then you'll have a sad Christmas. Now is the time."

Lucy took a breath. "Yes," she murmured. "Yes, all right."

Tony started the car and they drove off. They stopped at Constance Spry, selecting a holly wreath dressed with red ribbons and tiny red bows. Ten minutes later they were on their way to Woodlawn Cemetery.

It was a quiet ride, Tony watching the road, Lucy tearing her handkerchief to shreds. Her heart began to race as she thought of once again confronting the reality of her parents' death. She forced the thought away, moving closer to Tony. "Don't be nervous," he said. "I'm here."

He stayed with her, clasping her hand as they walked across the winter-scarred grounds of the cemetery. Together they entered the Cameron mausoleum. "Are you okay?" he asked.

"Yes . . . Yes, I really am," she said, relieved, for she knew now the things she wanted to express. She felt a sudden easing of the pain she had carried with her, a sudden easing of her heart. She took a step forward, holding out the wreath like a present. "It's Christmas, Mother," she began, "and I have so much to tell you. . . ."

Chapter Sixteen

Kazimov's class resumed in the second week of 1941 and Lucy was once more his devoted student. She listened closely to his long, detailed critiques. She asked questions. She continued to learn, further refining her style to the bare elements of truth. Her work was much admired by Kazimov, for it had the kind of moody clarity he appreciated. It had a hard-edged nuance that surprised him, coming from one so young. "This is not pretty pictures for calendars," he would cry, pointing to her mounted enlargements. "This is seeing the soul."

He followed her progress, and on the day his class ended he asked her to remain behind. "Sit down, sit down," he said, gesturing grandly to a chair. "I am wanting to talk to you. I am having a brilliant idea for Miss Lucy Cameron."

"Yes, sir."

"Kazimov is not sir. Kazimov is Kazimov. *Da?*"

"Da," Lucy smiled in reply. "I—I can't tell you how much your class has meant to me. It saved me."

"You are needing saving? Such a beautiful young girl like you? Once Kazimov is needing saving. In Russia, when comes the revolution. But a beautiful

American girl?" He shook his head, his bushy white brows shooting upward. "Some things even Kazimov doesn't understand."

"It's not easy to explain. . . . I didn't know what to do with my life."

"Marrying with a nice young American boy, that is something to do."

"Yes, but I want something more. Something all my own. Photography isn't just a hobby, a pastime. I want to go on with it."

"*Da*, that is what I am waiting to hear. I am now telling you my brilliant idea. You come to work in my studio. I have already many assistants. For you, you will watch. You will do the few things I say. You will learn from Kazimov. This is my true idea. It is safe, Miss Lucy Cameron," he added, laughing loudly. "Downstairs in my studio is my wife. She keeps her eye on me like hawk. I am not young, but she thinks I am chasing all the pretty girls. She is Russian woman, very suspicious."

"You want me to work for you?" Lucy asked, astonished. "You really want me to work for you?"

"You also have the eye like hawk. Only it is the artist's eye. From Kazimov you will learn to be true artist."

Lucy's heart skipped a beat. Her eyes shone with happiness, with the sheer joy she felt. "Yes," she cried. "The answer is yes."

"Good. Now we are talking about money."

"Oh, no, money doesn't matter. I'd work for you for nothing. I'd *pay* to work for you."

"In the Bible it is saying 'a man is worthy of his hire.' For women too. *Da?*"

"But I couldn't take money from you. I couldn't. The opportunity is enough. I'm—I'm honored."

"Is a great honor," Kazimov heartily agreed. "But

is also business. You are doing work and you are being paid money. You are being worthy of your hire. Twenty-five dollars a week. Is not a lot, but I am giving a fair salary. And I am making you earn it, Miss Lucy Cameron. With Kazimov you are working hard."

"I promise I will. I'll work day and night."

"Then we are shaking on it," Kazimov declared, extending his hand. "In America there is always shaking."

Lucy took his hand. "Thank you," she said. "Thank you so much. I'm very grateful."

Kazimov fished in his pocket and withdrew a business card. "On here is printed my address," he explained. "Monday morning is good for beginning. Ten o'clock of Monday morning."

"I won't be late. Shall I bring my camera?"

"I have already hundreds of cameras. All kinds. You bring with you your artist's eye. For beginning, that is enough. After that, we decide maybe other things. *Da?*"

"I can't believe this is really happening," Lucy laughed. "I hope I'm not dreaming. Am I?"

"You will know when comes Monday. Ten o'clock, Miss Lucy Cameron. Kazimov will be waiting."

Lucy hesitated at the door of Elizabeth's study. She knocked lightly and went inside. "Gran, I was wondering if I could talk to you," she said.

"Certainly, my dear. Come and sit down. Has something happened? You're looking very pleased."

"I am. I don't quite know how to tell you but . . . well, the thing is . . . the thing is I have a job, sort of."

"A job?"

"Yes, sort of. Max Kazimov asked me to work in his studio. It will be like—like an apprenticeship. He's going to pay me twenty-five dollars a week, but the most important thing is that I'll be learning. It's a wonderful opportunity, Gran. I'll be learning from the best. And it's really an honor. Kazimov doesn't usually offer to train his students."

"May I assume you've accepted his offer?"

"Oh, yes. It's *such* a wonderful opportunity."

"To what end, Lucy? Where will this wonderful opportunity lead you?"

"I haven't thought that far ahead."

Elizabeth smiled. "No? You aren't being completely honest, are you, my dear? You must have something in mind. I would like to know what it is. A career perhaps? Marriage is all the career a woman needs. It's the most satisfying way of life for a woman."

"I'm not ready to get married, Gran. Until I am, I want something to do. Something I'm good at. I have a talent and I want to use it."

"But you have many talents. In music, in art. In languages. Your tutors always considered you gifted. They said so."

"You were paying them, Gran. What else did you expect them to say? All the girls I grew up with had the same tutors. They were all told they were gifted. . . . I can play the piano. I can draw. I speak French. That's very nice, but it doesn't mean anything. Not to me. My photography means a great deal."

"There's nothing wrong with photography," Elizabeth replied. "I've often said it's an excellent hobby. If you will remember, I raised no objection to your studies with Mr. Kazimov. Those studies have now ended. You've learned quite a lot, I'm sure. I see no point in continuing . . . unless, of course, you are viewing this as a career. That is a different matter."

"Women do have careers, Gran."

"Some women are forced to work. Unfortunate women without husbands to care for them. Don't delude yourself that they're happy. They do what they must. We all do what we must. In this case, I feel I must keep you from making a foolish mistake."

"I don't see the harm in working with Kazimov for a while."

"The harm is that it separates you from your friends," Elizabeth said. "It makes you different."

"Is that so terrible?"

"It could be, my dear. I'm speaking of your future. The actions you take now may well affect your future. It wouldn't do to have you thought of as one of those independent-minded females. It wouldn't do at all. Spirit is a fine thing, Lucy, but it can be carried too far. No man wants too much spirit or independence in a wife."

"I'm not anyone's wife yet, Gran."

"And you may never be if you persist in these modern notions of a career. It's a man's world, Lucy. Women weren't meant to compete in a man's world. It's unnatural."

"Are you saying I should know my place?"

"I wouldn't put it exactly that way, but that's the essence of it, yes. And why not? It's quite a splendid place, after all. You're a Cameron. You're young and lovely, and you can have your pick of the most eligible men in New York. If I were you, I would count my blessings."

"You make me sound ungrateful."

"At times you are," Elizabeth replied, smiling again. "All young people tend to take things for granted. . . . Ned was like that. When he was your age he had some idea about being a writer. Ridiculous, of course. He soon came to his senses. He had a duty to the Galleries and he did it."

"My duty—"

"—is to marry well," Elizabeth interrupted. "To be a good wife and mother."

"A credit to the Cameron name," Lucy murmured.

"Sarah used to make light of the Cameron name also. She missed the point, which is that our name stands for something. We're respected. That may seem a small thing to you. It isn't."

"I know. I'm sorry. It's just that I want this chance with Kazimov very much. It means everything to me. . . . I don't want to upset you, Gran, but I can't turn it down."

Elizabeth folded her hands atop the desk, gazing calmly at Lucy. "You say Mr. Kazimov's offer means everything. I wonder if that's true, my dear. I wonder what you would do if I forbid you to work. Remember, the first portion of your inheritance is six years off. You have no other resources. You have Sarah's jewelry, but you're not of age and a sale might be difficult to arrange."

"I wouldn't sell Mother's jewelry," Lucy said, horrified at the thought. "That's all I have left of her."

"You have nothing else."

"I have ten thousand dollars, Gran."

"Ten thousand dollars is two years salary for most people. You're not most people, Lucy." Elizabeth opened a desk drawer, removing a file folder. "I rather expected we would have this conversation," she said, "and so I am prepared. . . . This folder contains your bills from last year. Look through it and you will see that ten thousand dollars is hardly more than a trifle. There is another matter as well. Before you declare your independence, consider how unprepared you are to be on your own. You've never cooked a meal, never made a bed, never even sewn on a button. You have talents, my dear, but housekeeping isn't among them. You weren't raised to do chores."

Lucy glanced away, stung by the truth of Elizabeth's words. Gran's right, she thought to herself. I don't know how to do anything useful. And it's my fault because I never tried to learn. I've been pampered for nineteen years. I've been spoiled. And that's my fault, too, because I let it happen. "I can't disagree with you," she said, turning her head to meet Elizabeth's dark gaze. "But I can change. I don't have to be a hothouse flower all my life."

"Yes, that's the reply I expected," Elizabeth sighed. "Young people can be so determined. . . . I'll give you a year, Lucy."

"I don't understand."

"I'll give you a year to get all these odd notions out of your system. Work for Mr. Kazimov, if that's your wish. Do as you please. I won't interfere. In return, I want your promise that you will continue to have a social life. That you will continue to see your friends. Do we have a bargain?"

"Yes. Thank you, Gran."

"I have your promise then?"

Lucy nodded. "I can work and see my friends, too. I won't be able to stay out late, that's all."

"There may be many things you won't be able to do. The choice is yours, my dear."

"I've made my choice, Gran. Be happy for me, won't you?"

Elizabeth smiled. "I always have your best interests at heart," she said. "Always."

Lucy looked up, her eyes suddenly troubled. Let me worry about my own interests, she wanted to say. "Thank you, Gran," she said instead.

Max Kazimov's studio was a spacious, airy loft on Bleecker Street in Greenwich Village. Huge photo enlargements were mounted on the white walls; lights and reflectors and tripods were clustered in various groups. There were two darkrooms, both of them constantly busy. There was a staff of six, including secretaries, stylists, and assistants. There was Kazimov's menagerie—a red parrot in a silver cage, two white Angora cats, and a shaggy black dog named Ivan. "So how you are liking it?" Kazimov asked Lucy now, his arm sweeping toward the vaulted ceiling. "Is what you imagined?"

"It's wonderful. I don't know what I imagined, but this is wonderful."

"Come, I am introducing you to Miss Alice Trimble. She is the real boss here."

"Your secretary?"

"My secretary, *da*, and also the boss . . . Alice," Kazimov called across the studio. "Alice, here is our new girl."

"In a minute."

"See?" Kazimov laughed. "The boss is making us to wait."

Lucy turned, looking at Alice Trimble. She was a young woman, perhaps twenty-five, with very fair skin and short, wispy brown curls. Her face was small and heart-shaped. She wore little pearl earrings and a simple blouse and skirt. "She's pretty," Lucy smiled. "So delicate."

"But a will like iron."

Alice put down the telephone and left the desk,

338

Ivan trotting along at her heels. "Hello," she said, holding out her hand to Lucy. "I'm Alice Trimble, and this is our mascot Ivan."

"I'm happy to meet you. You, too, Ivan," Lucy added, patting his head. "I can't believe I'm really here. It's very exciting."

"It's a madhouse," Alice declared. "You won't have a moment's peace. But that's the way Kaz likes it."

"*Da*, the hustle and the bustle. It is keeping us on our toes."

"I'll show Lucy around now," Alice said. "You have that ten-thirty appointment at Condé Nast. You better get going. And *please, please* be back by twelve."

"What is at twelve?"

"Lassie. The trainer says they're on a tight schedule. If the *Good Housekeeping* cover is going to be done, it will have to be done at twelve."

"A dog on a tight schedule," Kazimov snorted.

"Not just a dog . . . Lassie. Go on now. You don't want to be late."

"Is Lassie really coming here?" Lucy asked when Kazimov had gone. "The movie Lassie?"

"Everybody comes here sooner or later. Man, woman, and beast. That's why it's a madhouse. Kaz is booked up a year in advance. But I make exceptions for movie stars. . . . I suppose we'll have to do something about Ivan and the cats. How are you with animals?"

"Oh, I love animals," Lucy replied. "I never had one of my own. I wasn't allowed. But I wanted to."

"Your nice wool dress will be white with cat hairs," Alice warned.

"I don't mind. I'm so happy to be here, I don't mind anything."

"I'll be honest with you, Lucy. You're starting at the bottom and that means you'll get a lot of the dirty work. You'll help out in the darkroom when need be. You'll straighten up the studio, run errands, that sort of thing. It won't be glamorous. It will be months before you even touch a camera."

"I'll do anything you want, Miss Trimble."

"Alice. We're all on a first name basis here. It's a friendly place. Kazimov is just Kaz, if you were wondering what to call him."

"I was. Thank you, Alice. I want to get off on the right foot."

"You'll be fine. Everybody's nervous their first day. I broke out in hives. But then I got the hang of things and I was okay."

"Kazimov says you're the boss."

"Well, I run the studio. And by that I mean I keep him to his schedule. I also keep people from bothering him. The worst are the society ladies who want their portraits done. I practically have to beat them off with . . . Oops," Alice said, a sheepish smile lifting the corners of her mouth. "I'm sorry, that wasn't very tactful. You're a society lady, aren't you? I've seen your name in the columns."

"Society is really my grandmother's world. She cares about all that. I don't. . . . Alice, I don't want you to think I'm here on a whim. I'm not one of those bored society girls looking for amusement. I'm here to work and to learn."

"Fair enough. You didn't have to explain, by the way. Kaz's judgment is very good. He's a softy about some things, but *not* about his work. If he didn't think you were serious, you wouldn't be here. So that's that. Ready for the tour now?"

"Ready."

Lucy spent the next half hour following Alice

340

about. She saw the extraordinary collection of cameras and lenses, the sophisticated darkroom equipment, and the models' dressing rooms. She saw the kitchen, where everyone took turns fixing lunch. She saw the office, a sunny room cluttered with shelves and file cabinets and cork boards holding scores of scribbled notes. One of the cats lounged on a windowsill; the other lounged on Alice's desk, which was a jumble of papers and directories and proof sheets. There were two telephones, each with a row of push buttons. There was a large two-year calendar and a smaller daily calendar marked in red ink. "Sit down," Alice said, plopping into an old red leather chair. "Coffee?"

"No, thank you."

"We drink gallons of it around here." Alice leaned back, running a hand through her wispy curls. "Do you have any questions?" she asked.

"No, I don't think so. . . . Would you like me to start straightening up in here?"

"God, don't do that," Alice cried in mock horror. "I wouldn't be able to find anything. I know it looks bad," she laughed, "but it's my own system."

"I understand."

"There are just a couple of other things you should understand. About Kaz, that is. I guess there are really only two rules. Don't ever disturb him while he's shooting—not even if the place catches fire. And don't ever holler at the animals. You'll be tempted, believe me. They're all good-natured, but they're spoiled rotten. Especially the cats," Alice continued, stroking the Angora named Anna. "But Kaz is nuts about them. Be warned."

"Is there anything else I should know?"

"Well, there's Mrs. Kazimov," Alice replied slowly. "She comes upstairs every once in a while. Try to stay out of her way. She's a jealous woman. Not that she has reason. Kaz isn't a chaser. But she has all these suspicions. She'll probably faint when she sees you. You could be one of the models."

"Thank you," Lucy said, ducking her head in embarrassment. "Thank you for explaining everything. Have—have you been here long?"

"Five years. My husband used to be a subway mechanic. There was an accident and now Jerry's in a wheelchair."

"Oh, I'm so sorry, Alice."

"He gets a small pension from the city. It isn't enough. This job's been a lifesaver. I didn't start out as a secretary. I didn't even know how to type then. Kaz hired me to answer the phones and do errands. I guess we hit it off, because he sent me to business school. I've been his secretary for three years. Three crazy years," Alice laughed again. "I'm not complaining, Lucy," she said after a moment. "This is my second home and Kaz is like the grandfather I wish I'd had. He takes people under his wing."

"I'll try not to disappoint him," Lucy said. "I promise. And if I do something wrong, please tell me. Maybe you can't holler at the animals, but you can certainly holler at me. I want to learn."

"You will. You'll make a lot of mistakes, too. That's all part of it. . . . I think you're okay, Lucy. I admit I had my doubts. I mean, your background and everything. But you're one of us now, and that's how you'll be treated. Agreed?"

"Oh, yes. Yes, that's exactly right."

"Let's get started."

Lucy was introduced to the rest of the staff and then assigned to one of the two darkroom assistants. She was given film to process, later discovering that it had been a test of her work and that she had passed.

At noon she was given Ivan's leash and for forty-five minutes she walked the dog around Greenwich Village, returning him after Lassie had gone. She was sent uptown to deliver proofs to *Look* magazine. She was sent to a costume company to select props for the next day's shooting. Back at the studio once more, she found herself helping Kazimov, following his instructions as she repositioned lights and ladders and balky models. At the end of the afternoon she was left to tidy up.

"I wish Gran had seen me sweeping the floor," she said that evening to Josh. "I did a good job, too. You have no idea how much litter there is after a day of shooting. I filled a whole wastebasket."

"Did you?" Josh smiled. "I must say it's hard to picture you wielding a broom. Even for Kazimov. Is it safe to assume there are better things ahead?"

"Of course, silly. I'm starting at the bottom and working my way up. I don't mind that. It's an education, you know. This afternoon I had a chance to see how Kazimov works with light. Just being around him is an education."

"I'm proud of you, Lucy. You're showing some spirit. But you have to remember there's more to life than Kazimov's studio."

"Meaning?"

"Meaning work shouldn't be a substitute for love."

"Love! What are you talking about, Josh?"

"I'm glad you've found something you enjoy. But don't go overboard. Don't make it *every*thing in your life. That's my advice and also the end of my speech."

"Thank heavens. It's bad enough Gran is trying to marry me off. I couldn't bear it if you two joined forces."

"That's not very likely."

"No, I suppose you just have love on the brain.

How's Sallie?"

"Terrific," Josh said, his gray eyes twinkling. "Terrific. She's the reason I wanted to see you tonight. Can you keep a secret?"

"Try me."

"I will. Sallie and I are going to announce our engagement in June. We do want to keep it a secret until then. . . . But between now and then I'd like you to give a party for her. She doesn't know many people in New York, Lucy. She has her friends at Vassar and that's about it. If you gave a party, it would sort of get the ball rolling."

"I'd be happy to. Are you sure I'm the one you want? Gran is better at these things than I am. So is your mother."

Josh sipped his drink. He smiled. "You're right," he said finally. "But if I ask Aunt Elizabeth, it will be a very boring party. If I ask Mother, it will be a very strange party. And all the other relatives are ancients or drunks or both. That leaves you."

"Thanks."

"Will you do it, Lucy?"

"You know I will. I'll plan a cocktail party. A Sunday cocktail party here in the drawing room. About thirty people. All right?"

"Don't forget to ask Tony Jennings."

There was a flickering in the depths of Lucy's eyes. "Then I'll have to ask Melinda Craig, too," she said. "Tony's been seeing her. . . . Melinda Craig! She has the IQ of an eggplant! . . . But if that's what you want, I'll do it." She rose, turning toward the door. "And now I'm going to kick you out. I'm tired, Josh."

"It's still early."

"Not for me. I'm a working girl."

*   *   *

Lucy worked hard in the ensuing months. She did everything she was told to do, cheerfully running errands, climbing ladders to untangle wires, crawling about the floor to drape and pin the models' clothing. She spent long hours in the darkroom, often staying late. She toted equipment around during location shootings. She watched Kazimov and she learned.

Her work was rewarded when Kazimov finally put a camera in her hands. "You are ready, Miss Lucy Cameron," he declared. "Now you are taking pictures." She started by doing models' test shots, filling their portfolios with striking images so truthful they seemed to leap at the eye. Pleased, proud of his own judgment, Kazimov began turning over the studio's minor fashion assignments to her. The next month he allowed her to work with him on a photo story for *Look*. At the end of that month he sent her out on a solo shooting—a cover portrait of the Washington Square Arch for the small but prestigious *Architect's Monthly*. "God, I hope I got what they wanted," she said now, bending to pack away her tripod. "What Kaz wanted."

"There's no worry on that score," Alice smilingly replied. "You've never let Kaz down."

"There's always a first time."

"You slay me, Lucy. When are you going to get it through your thick head that you're *good*?"

"I know my work's good. It's being on my own, without Kaz looking over my shoulder, that's scary."

Alice picked up the spare camera and film bag. "C'mon," she said. "This is a red-letter day and we're going to have a celebration. My treat."

"You're sweet, Alice. Now that you mention it, I wouldn't mind a drink. A drink with a friend," she added as they turned up Fifth Avenue. "You've been true blue," she smiled. "Encouraging me all these months, rooting for me . . . Let's promise we'll always be friends."

"To the death."

"We'll drink to it!"

They crossed the street, walking another block to a quiet, pretty café. "It's too bad we can't make a night of it," Alice said, "but I have to get back to Jerry and you—"

"I have Gran. I told you about the bargain I had to strike with her."

"To keep up your social life?"

"If that isn't the most revolting thing you've ever heard."

"She's a tough cookie, all right."

"And a sharp bargainer."

Lucy, busy as she was, managed to keep her bargain with Elizabeth. She dated Jonny Melvile and Philip Colinge and the other young men who telephoned. She went to Sunday tea or cocktails with her old girlfriends. She went to parties and pretended to enjoy herself.

She was present at the gala party celebrating Josh's engagement to Sallie Leland. She was asked to be a bridesmaid and she accepted. Now all her spare time was given to wedding preparations—to fittings and shopping and endless dinners in honor of the happy couple. She saw Tony at these dinners, usually in the company of Melinda Craig. The sight of them laughing together, dancing together, left her strangely disturbed. She could not explain her feelings, but she wondered about them. Lying in her bed late at night, she wondered why she should care so much about Tony Jennings and his girlfriends. "Tony Jennings, of all people," she muttered at such times. "He must have a hundred girlfriends, a thousand."

In summer she noticed that Anne DeWinter had replaced Melinda Craig on his arm. When autumn came there was yet another girl, someone she had never met. The next girl was her old Brearley classmate Louise Archer, and it was Louise who saw Tony off when the wedding party left for Richmond. "Shameless," Lucy said, settling in her seat aboard the train. "You're shameless, Tony Jennings."

"What terrible thing have I done now?"

"You've been leading every female in New York a merry chase. Really, you ought to be ashamed of yourself. You're the only fellow I know who changes girls with the seasons."

"Keeping tabs on me, are you?"

Lucy colored. "Of course not," she replied, though too quickly. "Why should I?"

"A good question."

"Well, I'm *not* keeping tabs on you. I couldn't help noticing the parade of females, that's all."

"I see."

"I mean, it isn't as if it were a secret. You've been so obvious."

"I guess I'm just a hopeless case," Tony laughed. "But in my own defense, I'd like to say that no one's been hurt. I'm on excellent terms with all my lady friends, past and present. Feel free to ask around. They'll tell—"

"Oh, you're impossible." Lucy snapped the newspaper open, hiding her face behind it. I'm making a fool of myself, she thought, and I don't know why. I'm the one who's being impossible. "I'm sorry," she murmured after several moments.

"What did you say?"

Lucy lowered the newspaper. "I said I was sorry. . . . It's just that you make me so angry sometimes."

"I wonder why that is."

"I don't know, Tony, but I'd like to change the subject. I feel silly. And I don't want to spar with you all the way to Richmond. This is supposed to be a happy occasion."

"It is. Weddings bring out the best in people. Your grandmother was sweetness and light before she disappeared into her compartment. She gave me her brightest smile."

"Gran's in a good mood. She approves of Sallie. She thinks it's a suitable match."

Tony's black brows rose in amusement. "A suitable match," he said. "How Victorian. What suitable match is she planning for you? Jonny Melvile? You two have been all over town together. The Stork. El Morocco. I *have* been keeping tabs, you see. I've been reading the columns."

"Gran and I have a bargain," Lucy explained. "She'll let me work for Kazimov if I continue with my social life. . . . She's anxious for me to get married."

"Before you come into your money, I'll bet."

"Oh, Gran's afraid I'll start doing stupid things."

"Like what?" Tony asked.

"I don't know. Buying up playboys, *à la* Barbara Hutton. Buying impoverished princes. I'm not that type at all."

"What type are you?"

"Oh, no," Lucy replied, laughing suddenly. "You're not going to trap me into a serious discussion. I'm on vacation. Serious thoughts are forbidden, at least until Sunday."

"What shall we talk about?"

"Anything frivolous. But don't you want to join the other ushers in the club car? The party must be going great guns by now."

348

"It will still be going later on. Besides, I've seen enough of those guys. This is my third wedding in four weeks. I've spent more time in church than I have in class. I'm glad Christmas break is coming soon. I need the time to hit the books."

Lucy smiled, lifting her eyes to Tony. "Since when do you use the Christmas break for studying?" she asked. "You've always used it for fun and games."

"Not this year. I graduate in five months, Lucy. I promised Dad I *would* graduate, and with a respectable record. The least I can do is keep my promise. He's been pretty good about things."

"You mean about your career as a playwright?"

"Ah," Tony laughed, "I sense a nonbeliever in the audience."

"It just seems an odd thing for a Jennings to be."

"Odder than a Cameron being a photographer?"

Lucy laughed too. She leaned her head back, resting her hands lightly in her lap. "You win," she said. "Game, set, and match. I concede."

"Without an argument? That's a first."

"I don't want to argue. I'm on vacation and going to a wedding. I just want to have a nice time. No, a *wonderful* time. Okay?"

"Okay."

And Lucy did indeed have a wonderful time. With Tony she explored Richmond, the charming port city that had once been the capital of the Confederacy. With him she went to teas and receptions and an informal dinner given by the parents of the bride.

The wedding took place on Saturday. The bridesmaids wore gowns of rose-colored taffeta and matching picture hats trimmed with ivory ribbons. Sallie wore a gown of ivory satin and lace, the bodice scalloped and sewn with pearls. Her gossamer veil flowed from a pearl coronet atop her upswept black hair. Her long train, scalloped at the edges, was embroidered with lace and tiny brilliants. She seemed to glide down the aisle, utterly serene and untroubled. Her voice was clear as she repeated her vows; her face had the sheer glow of love.

Lucy watched, her throat choked with tears. She was happy for Sallie and Josh, but inevitably her thoughts strayed to Colin. She remembered her own wedding ceremony, remembered the brief moments that had brought her so much joy, so much pain. Colin, she silently cried, her reverie interrupted by the first loud strains of the recessional. She turned, looking up to find Tony at her side. "Wasn't it beautiful?" she whispered as they crossed into the aisle. "Josh never stopped smiling."

"He's a lucky man."

"They're both lucky. They're in love."

The reception was held at the Leland house, a gracious antebellum structure that had been in the family for generations. Lucy mingled with the guests, charmed by their elaborate courtesy, their honeyed accents. Several times she felt Elizabeth's eyes on her but she paid no attention. She danced and drank champagne, and when the newlyweds departed for their honeymoon, she showered them with rice. She watched the car drive away, and once again she thought of Colin.

"Come on," Tony said, "let's go back inside. It's getting chilly. You'll catch cold."

"More champagne. That's what I want."

"All right, but let's go inside."

"I've had lots of champagne, you know. *Lots.* And I want more."

"Eat, drink, and be merry—for tomorrow you'll have one hell of a hangover."

Lucy laughed, but the next morning she awoke

with a pounding headache and a churning, queasy stomach. It was a while before she dared lift her head from the pillow, a while before she dared move from the bed. She rose slowly, slowly making her way across the room. She managed to bathe and dress, though no matter how many times she rinsed her mouth, the stale champagne taste remained. "Never again," she grumbled, throwing her clothes into a suitcase. "Never again."

An early breakfast was served, but Lucy could not look at food. She said her good-byes to the Lelands and then slipped out to the pillared verandah. She sank into a chair, holding her head. "Oh, it's you," she said when Tony appeared. "You were right. I have a hangover. My first."

"First and last, if you're smart."

"Who said I was smart? God, I feel awful."

"Don't worry. Hangovers aren't fatal. You'd better pull yourself together, Lucy. Everybody's getting ready to leave. You don't want your grandmother to see you sitting in a heap."

"No, I don't. I'd never hear the end of it." She stood, shielding her eyes as she gazed at the wide lawns beyond the verandah. She watched a chipmunk scurry up a stately old willow tree and she smiled. "It's so peaceful here," she said. "The South is very beautiful."

"Yes, if you can get past the 'Whites Only' signs."

"What?"

"Nothing . . . Get your purse, Lucy. They're bringing the cars around. Vacation's over."

The trip back to New York was quiet. Patrick and his family relaxed in their compartments, Elizabeth in hers. Tony and Lucy sat together once again, though she dozed part of the time, her head falling onto his shoulder. Later, he persuaded her to have a light lunch and a few sips of a Bloody Mary. "Hair of the dog," he laughed. "Good for what ails you."

It was almost evening when they arrived at Penn Station, and almost immediately they sensed that something was wrong. The crowds were larger than usual, the faces of passersby strained and anxious. There was palpable tension in the air, an anger just barely suppressed. "Robbins," Elizabeth said as the new chauffeur hurried up to them, "has there been an accident on the tracks?"

"It's a worse thing than that, madam. Haven't you heard the news? The Japanese bombed Pearl Harbor?"

"Bombed Pearl Harbor?"

"Yes, madam. The news is all over the radio."

Lucy glanced quickly at Tony, clutching his hand. "What is he talking about?" she asked. "What does it mean?"

"It means war."

Chapter Seventeen

Lucy, like millions of other Americans, stayed close to the radio that evening. Alone in her room she listened to horrifying reports of bombs blackening the sky, of battleships going down in flames, their crews trapped aboard, of chaos and destruction and death. Now there could be no doubt that America would enter the war. Now another generation of young men would be torn from their families and sent overseas to fight, to die.

Lucy understood these things, and in her understanding was a profound sadness, a sadness beyond words. She thought of Josh, married less than a day. She thought of Sam, less than a year out of Harvard. She thought of all the boys with whom she had grown up. At the last, she thought of Tony. Her hand flew to her throat. She felt a sudden twinge of alarm and she drew a breath. When a knock came at the door, she jumped. "Yes?" she called.

Elizabeth opened the door and entered the room. "I rather imagined you'd still be glued to the radio," she said. "Turn it off, my dear. They're simply repeating the same things over and over. . . . It was easier in the last war. We didn't have radios."

"But don't you want to hear?"

"Hear what? That the world has once again gone mad? I'm sixty-five years old, Lucy. I've heard it all before." Elizabeth sat down, clasping her hands in her lap. "The names change," she went on, "and the places, but it's all the same in the end. There will always be wars. It's the nature of man."

"Do you really believe that?"

"Yes, I do. But I'm not here to discuss the nature of man. . . . Lucy, we are all facing uncertain futures now. Given that, I must ask you again if you won't reconsider and write to your grandparents in Aldcross? I understand that it was too painful for you before. A reminder, perhaps, of Sarah and Ned's death. I do understand. But now—"

"No. No, I won't. And it's no use your nagging me about it. Mother told me about them. She spoke a lot of those days. I'm sure the Griffiths are nice people but—but it's *England*. Everything bad that's happened is all tied up with *England*."

"That isn't very reasonable, Lucy," Elizabeth sighed.

"It's the way I feel."

"Now that we're all in the war—"

"We're going to win this war, Gran. America, I mean."

"I'm sure we will. You're showing the proper spirit, my dear. I'm confident you will do your part—the Red Cross, the USO, there are many ways. But there's quite a long road ahead. I'm afraid you won't find it pleasant. All your young men will go off to do their duty. Some of them will die."

"Gran, don't say that."

"It's the truth. You must be prepared to face the truth. Too many people have romantic notions about war. That's a mistake. I wouldn't want you to get swept up in the fervor of the moment."

"I'm not getting swept up in anything. Right now I don't know *what* I feel. I'm tired, I know that. I'm also angry and sad and a dozen other things I can't put into words. . . . You're never scared, are you, Gran?"

"At my age there's very little to fear. There's very little to lose, you see. All the horrors have already happened. All the deaths . . . From a very young age I understood that life was unfair, even cruel. If one understands that, one is prepared. And that is what I'm trying to impress upon you. You can't be hurt if you expect the worst, can you? The trick is in finding ways to deal with things as they are, not as you might wish them to be. Young girls are inclined to get dewy-eyed over war. They forget the realities. That's why wartime romances are always doomed to failure. You must be on guard, Lucy."

"Now I see what this conversation is about. You're expecting me to do something stupid. You're *always* expecting me to do something stupid."

"You have Sarah's romantic streak," Elizabeth replied. "It's charming, of course, but given present circumstances, it could lead to difficulty."

"Do you think I'll run off with the first soldier I see?"

"I'm merely suggesting that young men in uniform exert a special appeal. They're facing danger. Their futures are unknown. It's easy to get swept up in the drama of it all, particularly if one has a romantic streak, as you do. I'm not wrong to urge caution. Nor am I wrong to consider your best interests. So many foolish mistakes will be made before this war ends. Mistakes of the heart."

"Maybe, but that has nothing to do with me. Colin is the only one in my heart."

"But not the only one in your life," Elizabeth countered. "Tony Jennings is obviously fond of you. He's an impetuous sort of fellow, my dear. Not at all like his father, I'm sorry to say. He's the sort who will rush to enlist in the Army. And the sort who will rush into a wartime marriage. I wish him well, but not with you."

"Me! Tony doesn't want to marry me. I doubt he wants to marry anybody. The idea is fantastic."

"Is it?"

"*Yes*. I wish you had just come right out and said what you were thinking. All this talk of romance and wartime marriages—it's just silly. Tony Jennings, of all people."

"Of all people," Elizabeth murmured, staring thoughtfully at Lucy. She rose a moment later, turning toward the door. "Believe what you wish," she said, "but believe this too: There will certainly be war, and young men will certainly die."

Much to Lucy's surprise, Jonny Melvile was the first of her friends to enlist. She was his date at all the parties given in his honor, and she was at the dock when his troopship sailed four months later. There were other farewells. Philip Colinge enlisted at the end of May, Jeff Wyland the following week. Sam, tired of waiting for his draft notice, enlisted in July. The young men were assigned to Officer's Training School and ninety days afterward were on their way to war, Philip and Jeff as Army lieutenants headed for Europe, Sam as a Navy ensign headed for the Pacific.

Now the war was real to her. The fear was real. In dreams she saw twisted and violent images of battle. She saw the bloodied bodies of those who had been her childhood playmates. She saw horror and death.

In her waking hours she sought distraction, finding it at Kazimov's studio. "I'm so glad to have my work," she said one August afternoon in 1942. "It keeps me from thinking too much."

"*Da*, thinking about the war is making a nervous strain on you. On not only you, on everybody. Is a terrible thing, war. You know why? Because wars are taking the best, the *young*. To Kazimov, this is not right. Kazimov's heart is breaking for the young peoples."

"Is it true you're going to Europe?" Lucy asked.

"It is true I am trying to get there. For *Life* I am wanting to go. The Army says I am too old to be soldier. So I am wanting to be war correspondent instead. Not for writing, for taking pictures. But the red tape is long. Even Kazimov doesn't understand the red tape."

"It's as dangerous for correspondents as for soldiers. I—I wish you'd think about it."

Kazimov laughed. "You are worried, Miss Lucy Cameron?"

"It's dangerous. And you don't have to go. There are lots of correspondents over there."

"Not like Kazimov."

Lucy had no answer to that. She turned from the light box, staring up at her mentor. "I still wish you'd think about it," she said. "Think of your wife. Your wife wouldn't want you to go."

"I am telling you a secret. My wife is good reason for going."

"Oh, you don't mean that," Lucy replied, hiding her smile behind her hand. "Not really."

"Maybe yes and maybe no. Is not for worrying now. Now work is done and I am sending you home. You stay here already too late. *Da*, two hours too late."

"But there are the prints for—"

"Tomorrow is good enough for prints. Is Kazimov a slave driver like in story?"

"No, he certainly isn't."

"Then you are going home."

Lucy switched off the light box. "All right," she said, "but I'll be here early tomorrow. Alice will have a fit if the prints aren't delivered by noontime."

"Alice is the real slave driver," Kazimov laughed again. *"Exactly* like in story."

Lucy removed her white cotton gloves and placed them on the desk. She went to the office, running a comb through her hair, then gathering up her hat and purse. "Good night, Kaz," she called at the door.

"Good night."

She started down the stairs, stopping when she saw Kazimov's wife Olga. She noticed the woman's angry expression and she shrank back a step. "Hello, Mrs.—"

"It is late."

"Yes, I know. I'm sorry if . . . We were sorting negatives, you see. All the negatives from the—"

"Go now, please."

"Yes. Yes, I'm going," Lucy said, slipping past Olga Kazimov. She hurried through the foyer into the sweltering street. It was still light and she glanced up at the sky, wishing for rain. She heard her name called then. She turned. "Tony!" she cried, startled. "What in the world are you doing here? What in the world are you *wearing?*"

"Don't you recognize the uniform of the United States Army?"

"No, oh, no, you didn't."

"But I did," Tony replied with a jaunty smile. "I'm a soldier now. An honest-to-goodness soldier."

"Oh, Tony, *why?*"

"In case you haven't heard, there's a war on."

"Were you drafted?"

"I would have been, sooner or later. I didn't see any point in waiting. Come on, we'll have a drink and I'll tell you all about it. Can you, Lucy? Do you have time?"

"Of course . . . This isn't one of your jokes, is it? If you've scared me for nothing, I'll kill you."

"Are you scared? Scared for me? That makes it all worthwhile. But in answer to your question, it's no joke. I report in three days."

"Three days? That's so soon."

Tony took Lucy's arm, guiding her across the street. "Will you miss me?" he asked. "Will you cry into your pillow every night? Say yes, even if you don't mean it."

Lucy did not reply at once. There was a tightness in her throat, a sinking feeling in the pit of her stomach. She looked at Tony, and for the first time she realized how handsome he was. "I wish you'd waited," she murmured softly.

"What's that?"

"I just don't understand why you were in such a hurry. The war isn't going to end tomorrow."

"I'm not sure I understand either," Tony admitted.

"Then *why?*"

"Who knows? Perhaps it seemed the right thing to do. In any case, it's done. I can't tell the Army I've changed my mind. Not that I have. Our guys are fighting for something important over there. I guess I want to be part of it."

"You could have waited."

"It's done, Lucy."

"Yes, it certainly is."

"Here we are," Tony said, stopping in front of a small restaurant. "The good old Minetta Tavern. Shall we?"

"By all means."

The Minetta Tavern was a favored gathering place of Greenwich Village artists and writers. It was a friendly, informal place, with a long oak bar, pressed-tin ceilings, tile floors, and cozy red leather booths. On the walls were scores of caricatures and cartoons, many of them drawn by neighborhood artists in exchange for drinks or for the famous minestrone. "I'll bet you don't know that *Minetta* is the Indian word for 'Manhattan,'" Tony said as they settled into one of the booths.

"I'll bet I don't care."

"You're in a fine mood today."

"What do you expect? You caught me by surprise. . . . Gran said you'd be quick to enlist. *I* thought you'd have more sense." Lucy glanced around, looking at the caricatures. She saw one signed "John the Mad Russian," another signed "Al of the Apes," and she smiled. "You fit in here very well," she remarked. "'Tony the Terrible.'"

"Is that any way to talk to a soldier?"

"No, I suppose not. I suppose I'll have to forgive you."

"That's better. What would you like to drink?"

"Something cool. Gin and tonic."

"Two gin and tonics," Tony called across to the bar. "With lime." He turned back to Lucy, lightly clasping her hand. "Tell me about you," he said. "How's the job?"

"Kazimov wants to go off to war, too. As a correspondent. It's ridiculous at his age. But it's what he wants. Men are all alike, aren't they? Rushing into the thick of things at the first opportunity."

"Wouldn't you?"

"Heavens, no. I'm a coward. I'd wait to be called. I'd wait till the last possible moment." Lucy smiled again, her eyes roaming over Tony's uniform. "What are you?" she asked. "A lieutenant?"

"I'm an ordinary GI, Private Jennings. Don't look so shocked. All the appropriate offers were made. The Army wanted to send me to Officer's Training School. Mother wanted to get me a cushy desk job in Washington. Uncle Bart wanted to get me assigned to a general's staff. I turned them all down. I decided that if I was going to be in a war, I might as well be *in* a war. In the thick of it, as you said. . . . I'm just another dogface."

"No, not you."

"Woof!"

Lucy laughed. "Thank you," she said as the waiter brought their drinks. She raised her glass, meeting Tony's dark blue eyes. "To Private Jennings. You'll probably come out of this thing a general yourself."

"I'd be happy to make corporal. I have no military ambitions. At least none beyond helping to bring down Hitler and Hirohito and Mussolini. Otherwise known as the Three Stooges . . . Christ, I'd like to see those bastards get theirs."

"Well, now that you're in it, they're done for."

"Will you miss me, Lucy?"

"Of course I will."

"I don't mean the way you miss Jonny and Phil and the others. That's too easy. Will you hate it that I'm gone? Or will you just be a little sorry?"

"You ask complicated questions."

Tony sipped his drink. His expression had not changed, yet there was a certain intensity about him now, a watchfulness. "It shouldn't be complicated. You should know how you feel. We're old acquaintances, Lucy. Old sparring partners, old allies, and perhaps quite a bit more."

"You've always been around when I needed

you, Tony."

"That's not exactly encouraging. The same could be said for the family butler or the family cocker spaniel."

"I—I don't know what you want me to say."

"Say what you feel. You must feel something. You can't be indifferent after all these years. I'm putting you on the spot, Lucy. I'd rather not, but there isn't much time left. Before I leave—"

"Don't talk about leaving."

Tony smiled. He reached out, twirling one of Lucy's golden curls around his finger. "The subject can hardly be avoided," he said. "I'm leaving. That's a fact. But before I do, I want to have things settled between us."

"Settled?"

"I want us to tell each other the truth, Lucy. I'll start. . . . I love you. I've loved you ever since I was twelve years old and stepping on your toes. I've waited. I've bided my time. But time is running out. There are so many uncertainties now. It's somehow very important to me to know what you feel. . . . That's why I was waiting for you outside Kazimov's. I'd made up my mind to have the truth. The truth," Tony repeated, "not a lot of pretty lies. Do you understand?"

Lucy nodded, for she could not speak. She felt the hammering of her heart, the quickness of her breath, and with shaking hands she gripped the table. He loves me, she thought, a sudden warmth sweeping over her. Tony Jennings, of all people. "Did you—did you say you . . . loved me?"

"I'll say it again. I'll say it until you're tired of the words. I love you. You're spoiled and moody and sometimes off in a world of your own. And I love you."

"Tony . . ."

"Surely you must have guessed."

"I—I knew you were fond of me. But there were all those other girls."

"I'm not a monk, Lucy. Nor will I be an obedient spaniel, trotting along at your heels. You're used to that, I know, but it's not my way. I decided to give you time to grow up, to cut the ties to dear old Gran. But Hitler and company put a crimp in my scheme. Speak now or forever hold your peace."

"Tony, I can't."

"Can't or won't?"

"*Can't.* I'm so confused. I don't *know* what I feel. I haven't thought about it, not that way."

"I don't believe you, Lucy. For years you've kept track of the girls I dated. You've accused me of breaking hearts, of changing girls with the seasons. Do you remember the train trip to Richmond? You were damned annoyed that Louise had come to see me off. You made a fuss about it. You did, and that was interesting. You were upset. Have you ever asked yourself why?"

A thousand times, thought Lucy. She gulped her drink, recalling that day on the train, recalling all the days and nights when she had been angered by Tony's gallivanting. In her mind's eye, she saw the almost endless stream of his girlfriends. She saw their faces smiling up at him and she felt a swift surge of annoyance. "All those girls had their caps set for you, you know," she sniffed. "Including Louise."

"Why do you care? Do you care when a girl goes after Jonny?"

"No. Actually, I'm relieved."

Tony laughed, his eyes twinkling. "Doesn't that tell you anything?" he asked. "Are you really so dense?"

363

Once again Lucy cast her mind back. It's as if I want him all to myself, she thought. That's what it is. I'm jealous. My God, I'm jealous. Because I'm afraid. . . . Afraid of losing him. But why should that matter? It wouldn't, not unless I . . . "You seem to have me figured out," she murmured, color flooding her cheeks. "You're very clever."

"I have *parts* of you figured out, Lucy. The rest is a puzzle and probably always will be. But you know my weakness for puzzles."

"And for jokes," she replied slowly. Now the color left her face and a frown wrinkled her brow. "This hasn't been a joke, has it? You haven't been teasing me?"

"Christ," Tony roared, his head thrown back in laughter, "what a suspicious female you are. I open my poor, battered heart to you, and still you're not convinced. What must I do to prove myself?"

"I'm sorry, but I'm never sure whether you're being serious. Everything is a joke to you."

"No, not everything." Tony's hand closed tightly over hers. "Not everything," he said again. "I'm serious about you, Lucy. Are you serious about me? Do you care at all?"

"You know I do."

"Say the words. The words will get me through the war."

Lucy gazed into his eyes, into smoldering blue fire. "I care about you very much, Tony," she murmured. "I think I always have. There are things I didn't let myself see, things I see now. It's confusing." She was quiet, holding his gaze. This is so strange, she thought. Do I love him? But how can I? How can I when it's Colin I . . . "I don't want to say any more, Tony. Don't ask me to go on."

"Poor darling. This hasn't been easy for you, has

it? I understand." And certainly he understood that she was not yet ready to talk of love. She's frightened, he thought to himself. She needs time. For now, it will have to be enough to know she cares. It's a start, and after the war . . . "Will you write to me while I'm away?"

Lucy's head had begun to ache. "But I don't *want* you to go away," she wailed, putting her hand to her throbbing temple. "Oh God, it's so confusing. Nothing makes sense. . . . I don't want you to go away, Tony. Can't you—can't you get leave or whatever they call it?"

"I'm *on* leave now," he replied with a smile. "This is it."

"But do you really have to go in three days? Can't you get more time?"

"It would be fun to ask, if only to see their stunned expressions. . . . There isn't any more time, Lucy. I expect to be shipping out very soon. I'm not much use to the Army here, after all. They spent their money training me. Now it's time for me to do my stuff."

"Well, where are we then?"

"In a better place than we were last month or last week, or even this morning. You know I love you. You do know that? You do believe me?"

"Yes."

"And I know there's hope. The enigmatic Miss Cameron says she cares. . . . Will you write to me? Long letters with all your thoughts?"

"Yes, I'll write," Lucy said quietly. "Do you know where you'll be sent?"

"Europe somewhere. Sam's in the Pacific, isn't he?"

"On a battleship. That's all we know, really. The censors keep blacking out parts of his letters. Josh is waiting to be drafted. At least *someone* has sense enough to wait."

"That's different," Tony declared. "Josh has a wife. If I had a wife, I'd wait too. Hell, they'd have to drag me away."

"I wonder."

"Don't."

"Tony . . . Are you scared?"

"Sure I am. It's scary to think people will be shooting at me. It's worse to think I'll be shooting back. I've never shot at anything alive. Dad sometimes goes to a hunting lodge in Canada. Duck hunting, if I remember correctly. I prefer the tamer pleasures of New York."

"Pleasures, yes. Tamer, I'm not so sure."

"Hmm. We'll have to do something about getting you to trust me."

"You'll have to start behaving yourself. Is there any chance of that?"

"In the right circumstances."

"For example."

"Well, I'd be a faithful, sober husband." Tony paused. He saw the change in Lucy's smile, the uneasy shifting of her eyes. "But perhaps I'm jumping too far ahead," he said. "Let's stick to the immediate future. Which for me is a foxhole somewhere in Europe. Even I can't get into very much trouble in a foxhole. . . . Would you like another drink, Lucy? Or how about dinner? I know what. Let's take a drive to Connecticut. I know a romantic little restaurant overlooking the water. And they have great lobster. Can I tempt you?"

"You already have. I'd better call Gran and tell her I'll be late."

"Will you tell her with whom? She doesn't approve of me."

"Neither do I."

Tony laughed, throwing up his hands. "I asked for that," he said. "I set myself up. I keep forgetting I have to watch my step around you. You're pretty quick, missy." He reached into his pocket, dropping a five-dollar bill on the table. "Shall we go?" Lucy nodded and he stood, helping her to her feet. "We'll find a phone booth so you can call dear Gran. Then we'll find my car."

The sporty red Packard convertible was parked two blocks away. Tony folded the top down and a moment later they drove off. It was a lovely evening, the sky so clear they could count the stars, the air growing cooler, sweeter, with each passing mile. Lucy leaned her head back, enjoying the gentle summer breeze on her face. Now and then she glanced at Tony, her eyes tracing the lines of his handsome profile. He loves me, she said to herself, and she realized that those three simple words changed everything. Whether for better or worse she did not know, nor did she want to know. She was happy, happier than she had been in a long time, and that was enough.

"A penny for your thoughts," Tony said, his hands steady on the wheel. "What's going on in that mysterious mind of yours?"

"Confusion. But it's a nice sort of confusion, like waking from a dream and feeling all cozy and snug." Lucy gazed up at the starry sky. She smiled. "Life is full of surprises, isn't it?"

"It is if we're lucky. Surprises are fun. I think I'll have to teach you about fun. First order of business after the war is over."

"Let's not talk about the war tonight, Tony. Not tonight. Let's not talk about anything serious."

"Agreed. Tonight is for us. It's an occasion. An

historic occasion," he laughed. "This is our first real date!"

"Something for my diary," Lucy said.

"Do you keep a diary?"

"Well, a journal. You wouldn't be interested. It's very dull reading."

"So far, that is. As you said, life is full of surprises."

"Yes," Lucy replied, smiling in the darkness. "I'll start a new chapter headed with your name."

And late that night she found herself doing just that. She filled six pages, recounting the conversation at Minetta Tavern, describing the drive to Connecticut, describing the charming restaurant overlooking Long Island Sound. She wrote at length about Tony, about his attentions to her, about his touch when they danced together, about the look in his eyes the instant before he kissed her good night. She thought about his kiss long after she closed the journal. She remembered the heady excitement, the sudden and feverish pleasure. "Tony," she whispered, thrashing restlessly in her bed. "Tony."

But when finally she slept, it was Colin who came into her dreams. She saw him with an almost perfect clarity—his golden head, his chiseled features, his smile. She saw him walking toward her and then she saw him turn away, as if in anger. She heard him speak Tony's name, though so bitterly it might have been a cry of accusation. It was that cry she remembered when she awoke the next morning; it was Tony's phone call that drove it from her mind.

With a start, she realized that Tony would be gone in two days. She realized how much she had taken him for granted, confiding in him, relying on him to joke her out of her moods and make her laugh. I never really appreciated him, she thought, fervently wishing she had the years to live over again. But if her first thoughts were of herself, her last, most an-guished thoughts were of the dangers he was facing now. It occurred to her that he could be injured, that he could die, and she felt pain squeeze her heart. "Not him," she murmured. "Oh God, not him."

These fears were with her even as she arrived at the Jennings house for Tony's informal farewell dinner. She was greeted by his parents—Sophie, a warm, stylish woman of forty-two, and George, a reserved, very handsome man of fifty—and then shown to the drawing room. There were thirty guests, a few of them family, most of them friends. There were two maids serving drinks and canapés. Gratefully, she took a martini from a silver tray. She sipped it, her eyes traveling across the room to Tony. He was his usual smiling self, at ease and surrounded by people awaiting the punch line to an intricate joke. She heard the loud burst of laughter, and in the next moment he was at her side. "It's a lovely party," she said.

"Just our nearest and dearest. Dad wanted to do something more ceremonial. We talked him out of it, Mother and I. Did you and Mother have a chance to talk?"

"Briefly. She seems to be taking things in stride."

"If you mean my imminent departure," Tony said, amused, "she's resigned to it by now. Are you?"

"No. But your mother's had longer to get used to the idea. It's still new to me. . . . And I still don't want you to go."

"I'll be back before you know it. Anyway, they say absence makes the heart grow fonder."

Lucy could not reply, for the other guests had begun crowding around. Tony was rightfully the center of attention and she drew away, fading into the background. She spoke with Sophie and then with

369

Tony's uncle Bart. She spent some time with Josh and Sallie, joining them for the buffet dinner in the dining room. After dinner she wandered out to the small terrace, beyond which was a small garden in full summer bloom. Lucy bent, plucking a yellow geranium and holding it to her cheek. She gazed across the courtyard at all the lighted windows and she sighed.

"A penny for your thoughts," Tony said, coming up behind her. "Of course that's not my final bid. I'm willing to go higher."

Lucy smiled. "I was just thinking how peaceful it is out here," she explained. "And how pretty. It's hard to believe that such terrible things are happening in the world."

"We made a bargain: No gloomy talk tonight."

"I know. That's the last of it for tonight, I promise. And I promise I won't say a single gloomy word tomorrow."

"There won't be a tomorrow, Lucy. I've never liked good-byes, especially in public. They're awkward. They're difficult for everyone."

"Do you mean you don't want me to see you off?"

"I'd rather you didn't. I want my last glimpse of you to be right here in the garden, with the moonlight shining on your face and the breeze ruffling your hair. That's a picture worth remembering. . . . You understand, don't you?"

"Yes, I suppose I do. But *why* did you wait so long to tell me you were going away? We could have had more time."

"That was the problem. I knew I couldn't go without telling you my feelings, but I knew I had to play fair." Tony smiled suddenly, stroking Lucy's cheek. "There's a lot of emotion in wartime," he said. "I could have turned it to my advantage. If we'd had a few weeks, I might have been tempted. I didn't want that. An easy conquest isn't what I'm after. I have bigger things in mind for you."

"What things?"

"You're not ready to hear, not yet. But I'll say this much. . . . I want more than a night or even a bunch of nights. I want a lifetime. No, don't look away. Look at me. . . . That's better. I guess I'm asking you to do some thinking while I'm gone. Will you?"

"Yes."

"And will you write?"

"Yes, I promise."

"Then there's just one more question. You won't run off with some dashing 4F while I'm off serving my country?"

"Oh, Tony, for heaven's sake. How can you joke at a time like this?"

"It's the best time." He clasped Lucy's hand, leading her across the brick path and onto the terrace. He paused, his eyes scanning the nearby apartment buildings. From one of the open windows came the sound of music. He listened, smiling as he recognized the lilting rhythms of "Isn't It Romantic." He turned and swept her into his arms. "They're playing our song," he said. "Shall we have a last dance?"

"Tony, I don't want you to go."

"Don't worry, my darling. I'll be back."

Chapter Eighteen

"Tony's always kept his word," Lucy said to Alice the next day, "so I know he'll come back. I know he'll be fine."

"Sure he will. And you can do your part by writing lots of letters. It must get awfully lonely over there. Loneliness can be worse than fear." Alice stood away from her desk. She scooped Anna into her arms, carrying the cat to a sunny windowsill, then resumed her seat. Frowning, she glanced through a stack of proof sheets. "You'd better have Kaz look at these," she said. "There seem to be shadows in the background. He may have wanted shadows, but you'd better check. I can never figure out what he's thinking."

"I'll take them in now. Things are quiet this afternoon."

"Enjoy it while you can, Lucy. We're booked solid tomorrow. We'll be lucky to finish by seven."

"I don't mind. I don't have anything else to do."

Alice looked up, running her hand through her wispy curls. "Have you thought about the USO?" she asked.

"What about it?"

"Well, they need hostesses. There are thousands of servicemen coming to the city, some of them with nothing to do at night. No place to go. That's what the USO is for. . . . And you said you wanted to be useful."

"Yes, but making small talk and serving doughnuts isn't really useful."

"It is to some scared kid about to be shipped overseas. A friendly face can mean so much. A beautiful face can mean even more. I'd consider it, if I were you. You have the time."

"With everyone away, I have nothing *but* time." Lucy gathered up the proofs. She left the office and walked into the studio. Ivan napped in a corner, his legs curled beneath him. Kazimov was alone, happily feeding salted crackers to the parrot. She waited until he finished and then dropped the proofs on the light box. "Alice is a little concerned," she said. "There are shadows."

"Shadows? Impossible!" He joined Lucy, holding a loupe to his eye. *"Da,* now I am seeing what she means. But is not shadows, not when I am being finished. Watch and you will see. . . . We crop here and here and here. . . . You understand?"

Lucy bent close to Kazimov. "Yes," she said, patting his arm, "yes, I see. It looks like smoke. There's just a suggestion of smoke swirling in the background. Kaz, you're wonderful!"

"What you are doing with my husband?"

Lucy jumped at the sound of Olga Kazimov's voice. She spun around, her lips parting as she saw the woman's furious expression. "Mrs. Kazimov," she said, "we were looking at proof sheets. Here, see for yourself."

"I see you and that is enough."

"Olga, you are being the jackass. There is nothing

here to worry about."

"There is *her*."

"Jealousy, always jealousy," Kazimov snorted. He moved toward his wife but too late, for she sprang at Lucy. "Olga!" he cried. "Olga, stop!"

Lucy was thrown backward, her head crashing into the wall. She felt hands tearing at her hair, her face, and she screamed. Kazimov tried to pull Olga away but he stumbled, tipping over a bank of lights. Now Ivan bounded onto the scene, barking and snarling. Alice came running, followed quickly by two darkroom assistants. It was a full minute before they were able to drag the enraged woman from Lucy, another minute before Kazimov was able to drag her from the studio. "My God," Alice cried, helping Lucy to her feet, "are you all right?"

"I—I think so. . . . I was just standing there and all of a sudden—"

"Never mind. Don't think about it. She's gone now. Come on, I have a first-aid kit in the office. Will you guys see to the dog? I'll take care of Lucy. . . . Come on, that's a nasty cut." Alice helped Lucy to the office. "Sit down," she said, pouring a glass of water. "And drink this."

"What's *wrong* with her?"

"She's crazy, that's what's wrong. Kaz has a bottle of Scotch around here somewhere. I'll get it."

"No, I don't want any. My stomach . . . I just don't understand, Alice. Why would she do a thing like that?"

"I told you she's crazy. No kidding, she is. A real loony bird. She gets away with it 'cause she's Kaz's wife. Why he takes it, I'll never know." Alice found the first-aid kit. She sat next to Lucy, carefully cleansing the bloodied patch of skin. "At least you won't need stitches," she said. "The old lady must have dug in with her fingernail, but it's not too deep. I'll just get this Band Aid on. . . . That's fine. Okay. Now for the scratches . . ."

Lucy's hands stopped shaking. She leaned back, taking a breath. "Has this sort of thing happened before?" she asked.

"Well, we've never had bloodshed. We've had screaming arguments. And I mean *screaming*. She once chased a model halfway down the stairs. We caught her before any damage was done." Alice finished her ministrations. She put the kit aside and turned to Lucy. "I'm sorry," she said. "I should have kept a closer eye on things."

"Oh, don't blame yourself. There's no harm done."

"No harm! You have scratches and a cut and you're probably missing some hair."

"I have a bump on my head, too," Lucy replied with a faint smile, "but still it could have been worse."

"That's what bothers me. Next time it might—"

"We are not having any more next times," Kazimov declared, striding into the office. "Is too dangerous. Lucy, you are all right?"

"Yes, perfectly all right."

"From my heart I am apologizing. Always, Olga is jealous. Always, from the old days. But now it is becoming sickness." Kazimov sat down. One of the cats jumped into his lap and he stroked its soft white fur. "Tomorrow I am talking to doctor. He knows her already. He knows the sickness. There is a place in Connecticut. A place for this," he added, tapping his head. "Olga will be going to there. . . . But all the doctors and the red tape is taking time. Overnight it doesn't happen. . . . Lucy, it is not good that you work anymore for Kazimov."

375

"Oh, Kaz—"

"No. It is not good, Lucy. But there is being a bright side also. Because Kazimov is having a bright idea."

"*NewsView?*" Alice asked. She leaned forward, relief and excitement mingling in her eyes. "Is it *NewsView?*"

"*Da*, you are too smart for me."

"What is *NewsView?*"

"Is small magazine," Kazimov explained. "But *good* small magazine. Owned by Mr. Donald Cullen, very nice man. Last month I show to Mr. Donald Cullen your pictures from my class and also my studio. I am telling him about you. He will hire you, Lucy. Tomorrow I am telephoning and you will be *NewsView* photographer."

"But, Kaz, I don't want to leave here."

"Soon everybody is leaving. In October I am leaving to be war correspondent. Then no more studio, except for Alice. Alice I need here to look after things."

"But it's not October yet. The studio is still busy. We're busier than ever."

"Lucy," Alice said, "haven't you been listening? Kaz has fixed it so you can be a staff photographer on *NewsView*. This is what you've been working for. You've worked hard. You've earned this chance. Grab it, for gosh sakes."

"The salary is the same," Kazimov pointed out. "Twenty-five dollars a week, like here."

"It's not the money, Kaz. I don't care about that."

"Don't you care about being a photographer?" Alice persisted. "Lucy, this really is your chance."

"I—I don't know if I'm ready. There's so much more I have to learn."

"Kaz thinks you're ready. Isn't that right, Kaz?"

"*Da*, is right. There is always the time for the chicks to be leaving the nest. So I am giving you push."

Lucy smiled. "I may fall on my face," she said.

"Such a pretty face," Kazimov laughed. He settled the cat on the leather couch and stood up. "Now I am seeing how is Olga."

"Can I help?"

"Is nothing to help, Alice. Maybe you can show to Lucy a copy of *NewsView*."

"Sure."

"Poor Kaz," Lucy said when he had gone. "And poor Olga, too, I guess. I feel sorry for both of them."

"Yes, but one good thing came out of it, anyway. *NewsView*." Alice opened a drawer, plucking a large folder from the file. "There's a copy of the magazine and the cover Kaz shot. It was their first cover, two years ago. He did it as a favor. They don't have much money. They're kind of a high-class news magazine. A monthly. They do a lot of commentary and— what's that word—analysis. I have to admit they're a little over my head."

"Do you mean they're boring?"

"Well," Alice replied, shrugging, "I'm a *Look* girl myself. The important thing is they have a good reputation. The important thing for you is you'll get lots of work. . . . I don't understand why you're not excited."

"I'm scared, Alice."

"Scared? What are you scared of?"

"Falling on my face."

"Lucy, you're talented. Kaz says so. He wouldn't have talked you up to Cullen if he didn't think you were ready for this. You weren't ready when you first came here. Now you are."

"We'll find out, won't we?" Lucy glanced at the

377

magazine, then glanced away. "*NewsView*," she murmured. "God, I wish Tony were here."

Lucy felt a familiar apprehension as she arrived home. She thought about facing Elizabeth and she wondered how she could explain her abrupt exit from Kazimov's studio, how she could explain her new job. Slowly, she walked through the hall, rehearsing what she might say. After some moments she drew a breath and knocked at Elizabeth's door. "Gran?"

"Come in, my dear."

"Am I interrupting you?"

"Not at all." Elizabeth was seated at a graceful antique secretary. In front of her was a sheet of monogramed writing paper; to her right was a large whiskey and soda. She looked up, her dark gaze settling on Lucy. "What have you done to your forehead?" she asked.

"Oh, it's nothing. I tripped. It's just a little cut."

"Sit down, Lucy. I want to talk to you. Patrick telephoned earlier. I'm afraid it's bad news. They've had word that Sam was killed in action. . . . There's no mistake, I'm sorry to say. We've been in touch with Washington. It's confirmed."

"Sam," Lucy gasped. She gripped the arms of her chair, staring in horror at Elizabeth. "But it can't be," she said when she was able to speak. "He—he's only twenty-two."

"Wars always take the young."

"But I had a letter from him only last week."

"Yes, we all had letters."

"Oh my God. I just can't believe—"

Elizabeth sipped her drink. She set the glass aside and folded her hands in her lap. "Josh now plans to

378

enlist immediately," she said. "He—"

"No, no, he mustn't!" Lucy cried, leaping up. "I couldn't bear it if . . . No, he mustn't do that. There's Sallie. And she's going to have a baby. He has to think of her. He has to. Gran, you can't let him enlist."

"Calm yourself, my dear. And do sit down. Josh has made his decision. A proper decision, in the circumstances. Certainly an inevitable decision. There is no choice but to accept it."

"How can you say that? How can you act as if nothing has happened?"

"One can't always judge by outward appearances," Elizabeth replied. "Sam's death is a terrible tragedy, of course. But tragedy is part of life, and no stranger to me. That may seem cold. When you've lived as long as I, you will understand. . . . Where are you going?"

"I want to change my clothes. Then I'm going to see Uncle Patrick and Aunt Evelyn."

"We'll go together after dinner. Although I wouldn't count on seeing Evelyn. She's been put to bed and heavily sedated."

"How is Uncle Patrick?"

"Bearing up. He's a Cameron, after all." And perhaps the last of the line, thought Elizabeth, unless Sallie has a son. "There are other matters to discuss," she said. "I'll come straight to the point, Lucy. It's time now for you to end your association with Mr. Kazimov. If you feel you must work, then you may do so at the Galleries. Patrick will need your help."

"The Galleries!"

"It's time to consider family interests. The Galleries—"

"I won't do it, Gran," Lucy said quietly. "Uncle Patrick may need help, but not mine. I don't know anything about the Galleries. I don't know anything about business. I'm good at only one thing, and that's photography. It's all I have."

"All you have? What a foolish, ungrateful remark! You will end your association with Mr. Kazimov and at once. Is that clear? You've had your adventure. Your fling, if you will. Now it's time to consider the family."

Lucy was startled by the angry edge in Elizabeth's voice. She sank onto the couch, fighting the anxiety she always felt when she found herself at odds with her grandmother. "I didn't mean to sound ungrateful," she said. "And I don't mean to be selfish. But there's nothing I can do at the Galleries. I wouldn't be a help to Uncle Patrick. I'd be a hindrance."

"You're a very stubborn girl, Lucy. I offer you the Galleries yet still you prefer Mr. Kazimov's studio."

"Well, not exactly. Kazimov is closing his studio. That's what I came in to tell you. *Life* is sending him to cover the war. I—I have a new job. At *NewsView* magazine. I'll be on staff there, Gran. I'll be a staff photographer."

"And just when did all this come about?"

"Today. It was a surprise to me, too."

"A happy surprise, I take it," Elizabeth said.

"Sort of. I hate the idea of leaving Kazimov's, but this is a wonderful opportunity."

"And you have accepted? Without consulting me?"

Lucy shifted around on the couch, twisting her fingers together. "Yes," she said, swallowing hard. "I accepted."

"Very well. I won't belabor the subject. You have obviously made up your mind . . . as have I. If you go ahead with your plan, you had better be prepared to live on your salary. This is your home and you will remain here, but your bills will no longer be paid. Nor will your allowance be paid. You will be forfeiting five hundred a month. Is *that* clear?"

"Yes, Gran. I have the ten thousand Mother left me."

"Indeed you have," Elizabeth icily replied. "We will see how long it lasts."

"Gran, I—I wish you wouldn't be angry. I'm not doing this to spite you."

"Perhaps not, but you're spiting me nonetheless. You're letting the family down. I had hoped Sam's death would bring you to your senses."

Lucy swallowed again, color flooding her cheeks. "That's not fair," she said. "It's not fair to use Sam's death that way."

"I've been more than fair with you. I've been more than patient. If you persist in these ridiculous notions, you do so without my blessings. I suggest you think about it, Lucy." Elizabeth rose, turning toward her dressing room. "Will you?"

"I know what my decision is going to be, Gran."

"Then there is nothing further to say. Excuse me, my dear, I must change for dinner."

Lucy started work at *NewsView* late in September. She looked frail, for Sam's memorial service and the nightmares that had followed had been a great strain on her. She was nervous, though when she walked into Donald Cullen's office she forced herself to smile. "I'm Lucy Cameron," she said, holding out her hand to the thin, balding publisher. "It's so nice to meet you at last."

"I'm sorry we couldn't get together before now. It's been a busy time for us. We're a small magazine, as you know. We have a small staff. . . . Please sit down, Lucy. Tell me about yourself."

"There isn't much to tell. I studied photography at NYU, and then I took Kazimov's class. When it ended, he asked me to work for him. It was a kind of apprenticeship. Of course I jumped at the chance. I learned a lot. . . . Then he told me I had a job here. I'm very anxious to have the job, Mr. Cullen, but if you want to have a—a trial period, I certainly understand. I mean, it's unusual to get a job without even an interview."

"It would be, except for Kazimov. When he says he's found a fine young photographer, I have to pay attention to that. What he didn't say was *how* young you were. I simply assumed you'd be a bit older. I need someone who's responsible, you see. We carry only one photographer on staff. We take most of our photos from the wire or from free-lancers."

"I'm twenty, Mr. Cullen. I never missed a day's work at Kazimov's, and I did everything I was asked to do. And I . . . well, I've been reading your magazine and I have an idea."

"Oh? Let's hear it."

Lucy bent, unzipping her portfolio. "I noticed you've been running articles on the war effort here at home. I thought . . . that is, I was wondering if you might be interested in a regular photo feature called 'Home Front.' A different photo each month," she explained, blushing bright red, "but each with a home front theme." She removed a large black-and-white print from the portfolio and laid it on the desk. "I shot that at a USO club. I'm a hostess there four nights a week."

Donald Cullen picked up the photograph. He studied it for a moment and then swiveled around in his chair, holding the print to the light. "Extraordinary," he said after a while. "These young sailors in the foreground. It's as if you went behind their smiles to their fear. It's really a very . . . naked photograph. It's extraordinary."

"I remember those sailors," Lucy replied. "They were about to leave for California, on their way to the Pacific. I knew they were scared, but they kept making jokes and flirting with all the girls. They pretended everything was wonderful. I was touched."

"This shot will touch a great many people."

"Thank you, Mr. Cullen."

"Call me Don. No need to be formal now that you're working here."

"Do you mean it?" Lucy cried. "You'll give me the job?"

"You're damn good. Young, but damn good. You see things with your camera. Kazimov showed me examples of your work. There was one photo in particular—a photo of one of those Fifth Avenue mansions. It was a magnificent house, yet somehow uninviting, *cold*. There again a very naked photograph. I'm honestly impressed with your work."

"Thank you, Don."

"I like your idea for a home front feature. And we'll kick it off with your USO shot. . . . Did Kazimov tell you the salary? We can't pay much. Twenty-five dollars a week to start." He paused, his glance sweeping over her simple and expensive gray tweed suit, her simple and expensive jewelry. "If it matters."

"It does," Lucy smiled. "But twenty-five dollars is fine."

"Then welcome to the family. I'll show you around now. We're not fancy around here. We can't afford to be. We *are* serious about our work. When we write the news we write it straight, no interpretations. When we write analysis we try to consider the

383

total picture. When we write editorials everybody knows exactly where we stand. In other words, we don't cheat. . . . We argue with each other, Lucy, but we respect each other. Fair enough?"

"Oh, yes. It sounds like a terrific place to work."

It was, at the very least, a friendly place to work. Lucy followed Don through a maze of small offices, some of them cluttered, some of them Spartan, but all of them filled with staffers eager to put her at ease. She noticed that doors were always left open, that telephones were answered by anyone who happened to be in the vicinity. She noticed the energy, for people were constantly popping up and down behind desks, moving through the narrow corridors, striding to an enormous coffee urn to replenish their cups. Yes, she thought, a terrific place.

She was assigned a desk, a telephone, and a file cabinet in an area just steps away from the darkroom. She was given a key to the darkroom and to the ladies' room down the hall. "I guess I'm all set," she said. "Is there anything else I should know?"

"Our hours are ten A.M. to whenever. It's usually a five-day week, though you'll be expected to be here one weekend a month—the weekend we go to press. Your first editorial meeting will be tomorrow morning. Since you're the new girl on the block, you can come in a little earlier and make the coffee."

"I make great coffee," Lucy replied with a smile. "Strong and hot. That's another thing I learned at Kazimov's. He trained me well."

And during the next months she began to see how valuable Kazimov's training had been. In his own way he had accustomed her to the pressure of deadlines, of last minute changes in plans. He had taught her to work amidst chaos and the erupting crisis of the moment. Perhaps most importantly, he

384

had treated her like any ordinary young woman, making no concessions to her lofty family background. This last proved especially useful, for at *NewsView* no one cared that her name was Cameron.

She took her turn fixing coffee and filling lunch orders at the neighborhood delicatessen. She took part in good-natured office bantering, and she was sometimes the butt of office jokes. Personally and professionally she was judged on her own merits, and on both these levels she was successful. Lucy made friends at the magazine, casual friends with whom she went to movies and inexpensive restaurants. She worked hard, and in November her work appeared in print for the first time. "I did it!" she wrote in a long letter to Tony. "Gran is barely speaking to me, but I did it!"

Work continued to be Lucy's distraction, though nothing distracted her from the war. Along with millions of other Americans, she knew moments of great optimism and moments of great despair. She cheered major American victories at Midway and the Coral Sea, mourned major American losses at Corregidor and Bataan. Certainly she mourned the casualties, for Jonny Melvile was killed at Guadalcanal in February of 1943 and Jeff Wyland at Salerno three months later.

Their deaths stunned her. It was many weeks before she could accept the truth, and when finally she did, she felt a terrible emptiness. Their deaths brought the reality of war ever closer, and now she gave all her free time to the USO, to clothing drives and bond rallies. Returning home late at night she tuned in BBC broadcasts on the shortwave, trying to match the dispatches to the maps she kept on her desk. She listened for any hopeful sign, but she listened in vain. Hitler's forces were occupying Poland, The Balkans, Holland, Belgium, Norway, Denmark, and Greece. Mussolini's forces were battling the Allies in Italy and North Africa. France had fallen to the collaborationist government at Vichy. England was under siege. And somewhere in the middle of this horror, she thought to herself, were Josh and Tony.

She wrote to Josh every week, to Tony almost every night. Some of her letters to him were brief, but most ran to several pages. She poured out her thoughts, her feelings, her fears, and she did so with an honesty she would have found impossible face to face. She opened her heart in these letters, keeping only one secret to herself. The secret was Colin, for still she could not bear to probe that time in her life.

Tony kept no secrets. His letters to Lucy were by turns funny and tender and passionate. Occasionally he wrote about the war. She read his thoughtful musings so filled with sadness and anger, and in them she saw other sides of him. She saw his decency, his grace; she sensed his stubborn courage and she was moved. In the small hours of night she read his letters again and again, treasuring certain passages in particular:

> . . . I've seen terrible things over here. Ugly things. I've seen what happens to men when they're scared and tired and hungry and shivering in the cold. The ones who come out all right are the ones who have something to hold onto. I hold onto you, my mysterious Shadow Dance girl in all her glory. Memories, darling. Memories are keeping me alive. I see us as we were the night before I sailed away to this mess. If I close

my eyes, I can see the moonlight dancing in the gold of your hair. I can hear the music playing. Remember? The song was "Isn't It Romantic," and I guess that really *is* our song because you are the great romance of my life. God, how I love you.

I love your letters, darling. When things are at their worst here—when this damned war seems hopeless—your letters are my courage and my strength. In your last letter you wrote "Hurry home to me," and now I know I will. With those four words I can take on the whole Nazi army. With those four words I'm invincible.

We have a crack unit here, top to bottom. Our sergeant, a lyrical kind of Irishman named Cornelius Doyle, tells the guys to forget about politics and remember what we're really fighting for. "Home," he says in his Barry Fitzgerald voice, "you're fighting for home and what's in your heart." *You're* in my heart, Lucy. I'm fighting for that part of the world that still has beauty and joy and dreams. That still has you, the center of my world.

Until next time, my darling.

Tony

Lucy read these passages so many times she lost count. Always she could hear his voice, see his laughing blue eyes, and at such moments her heart swelled within her. At such moments she knew the depth of her love for him, and that knowledge was like a bright flame, warming her, lighting the way.

"It's very strange," she said to Alice one snowy day in 1945. "I've known Tony all my life but I don't think I *really* knew him until I started reading his letters. Reading them . . . well, it's as if I've seen into his mind, his *soul.*"

"Do you like what you see?"

"Oh, yes," Lucy replied with a blush. "I do. I just wish it hadn't taken me so long to realize how I feel. It all seems so obvious now. I can remember when we were little. Even then I felt something special for him. Anger, most of the time," she laughed. He was an impossible little boy. Tony's still impossible, but in a marvelous kind of way. You'll see what I mean when you meet him. And you will. He *is* coming back, Alice."

"Sure he is. They say the war won't last much longer."

"They've been saying that for six months. Ever since Normandy."

"Yes, but Normandy was the final blow. The Germans are beaten. They're just hanging on." Alice tossed her crumpled napkin on her plate, glancing around the busy Automat. She heard the tinkle of coins as they were pushed into slots, the sharp clicks as food was taken from little glass cubicles, the rattle of trays as they were slapped down on tables. "God, I *hope* it's over soon," she said. "We sit here all safe and warm while people are dying. I feel so damn guilty sometimes. The worst we have to cope with is rationing, and I've heard complaints about *that.* As if it's a big deal. They're starving in Europe, yet some people here have the nerve to complain!"

"Mother used to say Americans are spoiled. I think we're just so used to having everything, we take it for granted. Or some people do, anyway. Some of Gran's friends have been buying extra ration books on the black market. I was tempted to dip into the black market myself when I ran out of nylons. But then I changed my mind. I had a twinge of conscience. So instead I bought leg makeup and felt *very* virtuous."

Alice smiled. "Are things better with you and your grandmother?"

"Not much. She realizes *NewsView* isn't a passing fancy. After all, it's been three years. But she still hates the idea. Last month the wire services picked up one of my photos. I was thrilled. There's—there's even been talk it will win an award. I wanted Gran to be happy for me, Alice. I really did. She used the occasion to remind me that I've had to borrow money to pay my bills. She wasted no time cutting me down to size."

"I'll bet I know which photo it was. The one of the Gold Star mother standing at a window. Her face was blank, but there was such pain in her eyes. It was heartbreaking. It made me cry."

"Yes," Lucy said quietly. "The woman in the picture is Mary Margaret O'Connor. She was a friend of Mother's. . . . Her oldest son was killed at Anzio. Mike Junior was twenty."

"Poor woman."

"Speaking of heartbreaking photographs, have you heard anything from Kaz?"

"I had a letter a few days ago. He seems to be in great spirits, I guess because he feels he's doing his part. And he is. He's showing us what war's all about. I'll tell you the truth, Lucy. His pictures from St. Lo gave me nightmares. Those young soldiers with blood streaming down their faces. War isn't like that in the movies. In the movies it always looks so . . . tidy."

"I know."

"God, I hope it's over soon."

Lucy finished her coffee. She pushed the cup away, lifting her eyes to Alice. "Has there been any word of Mrs. Kasimov?" she asked. "Is there any change?"

"She's not getting better, if that's what you mean. I

doubt she'll ever leave the sanitarium. The doctor says it's—let's see if I can get the name straight. He says it's delusions."

"I'm sorry."

Alice nodded, running her hand through her curls. "A very sad thing," she said. "But what isn't, these days?"

What isn't? thought Lucy as she walked back to the offices of *NewsView*. But, in truth, she saw many happy sights along the way, normal city sights. There were vendors selling hot roasted chestnuts on street corners. There were lines of people waiting to get into movie theaters. There were shoppers and noontime strollers. There were the inevitable tourists in search of the Empire State Building. There were the usual traffic tangles, cars and trucks and yellow and orange taxicabs maneuvering around buses whose signs read "Welcome to New York." It was wartime, yet the life of the city went on much as before.

"We don't realize how lucky we are," Lucy complained at the afternoon editorial meeting. And at her suggestion, the next issue of *NewsView* ran contrasting photographs of peaceful New York and war-scarred London. It was a startling series, widely discussed. The last page, which was a pledge form for war bonds, was said to have raised many thousands of dollars.

Lucy continued her efforts, even in the waning months of the war. She continued to initiate dramatic photo essays, to run clothing drives, to raise money. She worked harder than ever, often spending weekends in her office. She was in her office when George Jennings called to tell her that Tony had been wounded, and she was there an agonizing week later when he called to say Tony was all right. She was there on a May day she would remember all her life, for on that day a jubilant radio voice announced the unconditional surrender of Germany.

The news spread rapidly through the city, and everywhere people stopped what they were doing and joined the celebrations. Elizabeth was hostess at a gala, if hastily planned, champagne supper. It was the first great social event at the Cameron house since the beginning of the war, but Lucy made only a brief appearance and then left to meet her friends for the celebration at Times Square. She had never seen anything quite like it—a million people jamming the streets and avenues in all directions, a million people laughing and crying and hugging strangers and waving flags. There were party horns and swirls of confetti. Every neon sign on Broadway blazed with light. Lucy had not brought her camera but she knew there was no need of pictures, for this night, too, she would remember all her life.

Walking home hours later, she stopped at the first church she saw and gave thanks. Dear God, she prayed, let this be the *last* war.

When the celebrations ended there were sober truths to be faced, for war still raged in the Pacific and Europe lay in ruins. Perhaps the most horrifying truth of all was the revelation of Hitler's death camps. Ten million men, women, and children had been exterminated by the Nazis, six million of them Jews. A stunned world learned of Hitler's "Final Solution," of the grotesque plan that had sought nothing less than the elimination of the Jewish race. In newsreels and newsmagazines, a stunned world saw pictures of the survivors—skeletal figures who had been starved and beaten and tortured, who had

391

watched their loved ones marched into Nazi ovens. It was considered a testimony to the human spirit that there had been any survivors at all, but to Lucy, viewing Kazimov's photographs of Nazi atrocities, it was also a testimony to the evil lurking in the human heart. It was incomprehensible to her that such things could have happened. For the first time she began to understand the nature of hatred, the corrupt and poisonous nature of racial hatred. She recalled her trip south for Josh's wedding. She recalled her comment on the beauty of the South and she recalled Tony's curt reply: "If you can get past the 'Whites Only' signs." He's always understood, she thought. Always.

The ringing telephone interrupted her thoughts. She snatched up the receiver. "Lucy Cameron," she said.

"Hello, Lucy Cameron. Guess who?"

"Tony!" she cried. "Oh, Tony, I've been wondering when you'd—"

"Minetta Tavern. Three o'clock."

"Tony, wait. I—"

"Minetta Tavern. Three o'clock."

Chapter Nineteen

Lucy hurried along MacDougal Street, glancing nervously at her slim gold watch. She was early, but that fact did not seem to slow her pace. She thought of Tony and she felt the hammering in her chest, the weakness in her legs. Now she quickened her pace yet again, smiling to herself. She had almost reached Minetta when she saw a tall, handsome young man coming from the opposite direction. "Tony!" she shouted, running toward him. "Tony!" She ran into his waiting arms, holding him close. "You're home," she murmured. "Thank God, you're really home."

"Let me look at you, darling. . . . What a beautiful sight you are. You'll never know how many times I imagined this moment. . . . Seeing my girl in a soft summer dress, sunlight in her hair . . . You're my girl, aren't you, Lucy?"

"All yours."

Tony kissed her. He stepped back an instant later, clasping her hand in his. "Come," he said. "We have a lot of catching up to do. I want to hear everything. . . . I want to sit and look at you, the prettiest girl in New York. *My* girl."

"I like the sound of that."

"You'd better."

Holding hands, they walked to the restaurant. Tony opened the door and followed Lucy inside. "Two gin and tonics," he called to the bar as they settled into a booth. "Comfortable?" he asked.

"I'm fine, Tony. I want to know how *you* are. Your father called me the day he got the telegram saying you were wounded. We were half crazy until we heard you were all right. That was the truth, wasn't it? You're all right?"

"In the pink," he laughed. "It wasn't much of a wound. A bullet through the shoulder. They kept me in a field hospital for two days and then sent me back to my unit. End of war stories."

"Don't you want to talk about the war?"

Tony's blue eyes darkened; the smile left his face. "It was ugly and dirty and hard," he said. "I saw a lot of guys die, Lucy. I saw one of our guys blown apart when he stepped on a mine. Another guy . . . well, you get the general idea. I didn't come back with many funny stories. I was damned lucky to come back at all, and I know it. . . . We won. I suppose that's the only thing that really counts in war. I'm sorry Roosevelt didn't live to see it."

The waiter brought their drinks. Lucy sipped hers, gazing quietly at Tony. "When did you get back?" she asked. "Why didn't you let me know you were on your way?"

"I didn't let anybody know. I didn't want to send a wire and then have my jeep turn over en route to the plane. Stupid accidents like that happen all the time. The families get a double jolt." Tony laughed again. "But I made it," he said. "I showed up at home last night. Dad was breaking out the champagne, the hundred-year-old brandy. All I wanted was fresh orange juice and *real* eggs. You have no idea what a treat that is after years of the powdered stuff."

"Last night? But why didn't you call?"

"If I had, I wouldn't have slept. And I was beat. Besides, I was looking pretty scraggly. If you'd seen me that way, you might have run screaming to some well-kempt 4F."

"Tony, how can you say that? Even as a joke."

"It happens, you know," he replied, stroking Lucy's cheek. "Wartime romances unravel. I saw quite a few Dear John letters in my unit."

"But that's cruel."

"That's life. Women are born to break men's hearts. . . . Tell me, have you guessed why I wanted us to meet here at Minetta?"

"I think so," Lucy smiled. "This is where you first said you—you loved me."

"I still love you. Very much. The war is over and I still love you. Not that that should come as a surprise. I wrote it in every letter. But I want you to know, really know, nothing's changed. As far as you're concerned, I'm still twelve years old and head over heels."

"You're awfully tall and handsome for twelve."

"Don't slip around the subject, Lucy. The subject is love."

"You want to hear me say the words."

"Yes."

Lucy gazed into his eyes and now she felt no reticence, no lingering confusion. "I do love you, Tony," she said softly. "I do. It scares me a little, but not as much as it used to."

"Why should love scare you?"

"Oh, everything scares me."

Tony leaned closer, tilting Lucy's face to him. "Am I included in that?" he asked. "Do I scare you too?"

"You make me feel happy and safe. . . . And when you're this close, you make me dizzy. I may just swoon in your arms."

Tony smiled, brushing his lips to hers. "In my arms is exactly where I want you," he said.

"Is it? Strange, that's exactly where I want to be. How did you know?"

"I didn't. It was a hopeful guess." Tony drew away. He took a swallow of his drink and put the glass down. "You certainly aren't what I'd call an open book," he said, smiling. "Mystery is part of your charm. You keep me guessing."

"Guessing?"

"There are some things I've always known about you and some things I may never know. . . . I've always known you loved me, Lucy. But I've never known why you fought so hard against it." He paused, his expression more intent. "I don't know why you still feel some small hesitation," he continued. "I just know it's there."

Colin flashed through Lucy's mind. She glanced away, but in the next instant she looked back at Tony. "You're wrong," she declared. "I'll admit it took me a while to figure things out. What's the cliché—to see the light? Well, I've seen it. I haven't the slightest hesitation now. I'm all yours."

"Say that again. I love hearing it."

"I'm all yours." They gazed at each other, turning suddenly toward the bar where the radio was playing. "Isn't It Romantic." "See," she laughed, "the Fates are with us."

"Where are you going?" Elizabeth asked one humid July evening a few weeks later. "Have you forgotten we're expecting guests?"

"I haven't forgotten. I told you, Gran, Tony has a lead on an apartment and he's asked me to look at it with him. It has to be tonight. You know how hard it is to find apartments these days. He was lucky to hear about this."

"Come into my sitting room, Lucy. I want a word with you."

"But I'll be late."

"I want a word with you nevertheless."

Lucy followed Elizabeth inside. She perched at the edge of a silken chaise, nervously tapping her gloves on her purse. "I hope we aren't going to argue, Gran," she said. "There will be fifty people here tonight. I won't be missed. I'm not very good at these things, anyway."

"These things? Tonight's dinner is in honor of Josh's homecoming. I would hardly put that in the category of 'these things.' It's a family occasion, my dear. A most happy occasion. Surely you don't want to hurt Josh's feelings."

"I had a drink with Josh yesterday, and I talked to him just an hour ago. He understands, Gran. He's not at all hurt that I won't be here. . . . And it's only important to you because you've invited Philip Colinge. You're still matchmaking . . . or trying to. Poor Jonny is gone now, so you've moved on to Philip."

"Nonsense. Philip and Josh were in the service together."

"Tony was in the service, too, Gran."

"Yes, I rather expected we would get back to the subject of Tony. Your favorite subject."

"Gran, please let's not go through this again. I thought you'd be glad. You've been trying to pair me off ever since I was eighteen. And you probably started planning long before that. I know things haven't turned out exactly as you'd wanted. I mean, the war changed things. But I'm happy now, truly happy, and you should be glad."

"The war had very little to do with what we're discussing. There was always an unfortunate attraction between you and Tony. You denied it, of course, but it was there. Make no mistake, Lucy. It *is* unfortunate. Tony is the wrong fellow for you. I'll grant you his charm. I will even grant you his courage. He has the courage of his convictions. I'm afraid you'll find that a mixed blessing at best. He has ideas—foolish ideas—and he'll see them through, no matter the consequences."

"What consequences?"

"Tony's refused to take his place at the bank," Elizabeth replied. "With that act he's thrown away part, if not all, of his trust fund. Financial considerations aside, he's thrown away his future. And why? To chase some ridiculous dream."

"It isn't ridiculous. He wants a career in the theater."

"What do you want, my dear? I suggest you think about that, because Tony won't. Tony will go his own way. I had an interesting talk with George Jennings only last week. George admitted that Tony can't be swayed, once he's made up his mind. Do you know what that means? You would be living *his* life and on *his* terms. . . . A life very different from all this," Elizabeth added, her hand sweeping about the serene and elegant sitting room. "Philip hasn't Tony's charm, but he would give you the life you know."

"You must think I'm awfully shallow."

"Not at all. I simply think Tony is wrong for you. I believe that, Lucy. There can't be any question I have

398

your best interests at heart."

"You don't always know what my best interests are, Gran."

"I'm sorry you feel that way." Elizabeth rose. "Certainly I've tried to give you the benefit of my experience. I've tried to protect you. Perhaps I've tried too hard."

"Please don't be angry. I didn't mean . . ." Lucy rose also, going quickly to Elizabeth. "Gran, I didn't mean to upset you. Sometimes I say things without thinking. I appreciate all you've done for me, really I do. But you have to understand I love Tony. I need him. It took me a *long* time to realize it, to admit it. Now I have, and there's no turning back."

Elizabeth was silent, staring at Lucy. She was reminded of Sarah, of the disagreements they had had, of the conflicts. I always did what was best for Sarah, she thought to herself. I did what had to be done. And I will do what has to be done for Lucy. One way or another, this foolishness will end. "Have you told Tony about Colin?" she asked.

"No, I—I will, when the time is right."

Elizabeth smiled. "Run along now," she said. "I'll make your apologies to Philip and the others."

"Thank you, Gran."

"Where is this apartment of Tony's?"

"Oh, it isn't his yet. He has to find out about the rent and all that. He's going to be working for a living, you know. Watching his pennies, or so he says."

"Where is the apartment?"

"On Bleecker Street," Lucy replied, hurrying to the door. "It's not far from Kazimov's studio. Isn't that a funny coincidence?"

"I don't know how funny it is, but it's an odd place for a Jennings."

"That won't stop Tony. He's at home anywhere. And he really wants this apartment. Keep your fingers crossed, Gran." Lucy paused in the doorway, glancing at Elizabeth. "You do understand, don't you? About Tony and me?"

"I do indeed. Good night, my dear. Don't be too late."

"I won't. Good night, Gran."

Elizabeth heard Lucy's footsteps fade in the hall. Smiling, she turned toward her dressing room. Colin is the key, she thought to herself. Yes, Colin will prove useful after all.

Tony moved into his new apartment on the fourteenth of August. It was a date he would remember, for on that date the unconditional surrender of Japan was announced. Once again there were joyous celebrations. Once again prayers were offered in thanksgiving, in hope of a lasting peace. General MacArthur, accepting the surrender aboard the battleship *Missouri*, offered the hope "that peace be now restored to the world, and that God will preserve it always."

Once again there were truths to be faced, because in 1945 one kind of world ended and another began. President Roosevelt was dead, Hitler was a suicide, and Winston Churchill was voted out of office. The United Nations was founded in New York. The independent republic of Vietnam was formed, with Ho Chi Minh as President. The atom bomb was a reality, its lethal threat haunting mankind.

The bomb was a topic of heated discussion amongst the friends who gathered at Tony's apartment. Over plates of spaghetti and jugs of cheap Chianti, his friends debated a wide range of subjects—politics, sports, the economy, the existence of God. It was, he often said, like being back in college, where informal bull sessions went on late into the night. Lucy found herself more a listener than a participant during these sessions. Much to her annoyance, she found herself joining the other women in the kitchen, where the talk was usually of clothes and weddings and parties. "I'm getting tired of this," she said to Tony one cool October evening. "We all are. I've been appointed a committee of one, and I'm registering a complaint."

"Appointed by whom?"

"Sallie and Meg and Grace and the others. Sitting in that little kitchen night after night isn't a whole lot of fun. We feel exiled."

Tony smiled, settling down beside Lucy on the couch. "Nobody's chased you into the kitchen," he said. "You're all welcome to put your two cents in."

"But they won't. And I feel silly being the only woman. Anyway, the conversations are *boring*. It's the same conversation all the time. Don't you ever have enough of politics and the New York Giants?"

"Of politics, yes," Tony laughed. "Of the Giants, never."

"I'm serious."

"Then I'll be serious too. There aren't going to be many more of these get-togethers, Lucy. I have a job. Two jobs, in fact. One to feed my stomach, the other to feed my soul."

"Really? Have you been keeping secrets from me?"

"I wanted to wait until everything was set. Now I can do some bragging. Are you ready to hear?"

"Ready."

"I start Monday at Hunts Point Market," Tony explained. "I'll be loading and unloading crates and trucks. The hours are midnight to six A.M. Perfect,

401

because that gives me days and evenings to do my other job—which is an Off-Broadway play."

"A play! Tony, that's wonderful! I'm so happy for you."

"Well, it's *way* Off-Broadway," he laughed again. "But it's a start. I'm going to direct a play called *Strangers*."

"Direct? Lucy asked, her head snapping up. "You're going to direct? But you always wanted to write. What happened to *Shadow Dance?*"

"It's still around here somewhere, torn and smudged and dog-eared. I took it with me overseas. There were lulls in the action, you see. When it got quiet there, it really got quiet. I must have read the play through a hundred times. It's just no good, Lucy. The construction is terrible. The dialogue rambles. There's only one decent character in the entire script—your character. I suppose that's because it was written from the heart. . . . So I discovered I was a lousy playwright but a damned fine editor. In the theater, that's what a director has to be. He has to edit the script, the actors, has to cut the bad parts and bring out the best. I can do that, and well. I'll prove it with *Strangers*."

"I know you will, Tony. Oh, this is *so* exciting. We ought to celebrate."

"Precisely what I had in mind. Tonight is for us. I even bought champagne. The good stuff, too. Mushroom omelets and champagne. How does that sound?"

"Marvelous. But let's have the champagne first."

"You're learning to read my thoughts," Tony said. He leaned close to Lucy, taking her face in his hands. He kissed her brow, her lips, the hollow of her neck. Her arms slid around him, but at that moment he drew away, rising from the couch. "I'll be right back," he said.

She watched him go, an uncertain smile flickering about her mouth. After a while her gaze moved across the room. It was a comfortable room, oddly stylish, furnished with a combination of thrift shop bargains and Sophie Jennings's cast-off antiques. There were handsome English drum tables and faded, lumpy wing chairs. There were twin chinoiserie cabinets and twin ottomans frayed at the seams. Atop the mantel were several exquisite Staffordshire china dogs. Bracketing the fireplace were tall bookcases, the sagging shelves crammed with every volume Tony had ever owned. Magazines and newspapers were scattered around. A chess board was set up on a glass coffee table. On the beige walls was a collection of framed sporting prints, a gift from George Jennings. "It's very cozy here," she said as Tony returned. "Have I told you that before? I was just thinking how homey it is."

"Perhaps a bit messy for your tastes? You'd better get used to it. This is the real me. My room at home was always a mess. The rest of the house was always in perfect order."

"Yes," Lucy laughed, "we both grew up in museums. I wasn't even allowed a messy room. Gran was strict about that."

"Poor darling. *Gran* was strict about everything." Tony opened the champagne, aiming the spray in Lucy's direction. "Have to save the carpet," he said with an innocent smile.

"By all means."

Tony filled their glasses. He sat next to Lucy, gazing into her eyes. "What shall we drink to?"

"To your first play, of course. To *Strangers*. You're going to make a brilliant debut. I can feel it. Will you let me read the script?"

"If you promise to be kind."

"I'll love the script, Tony. I'll love anything

403

you do."

"That's my girl." His gaze remained on Lucy as he sipped the champagne. He seemed to be studying her, moment by moment his eyes growing more intense. "You're very beautiful," he said quietly.

"Beautiful enough to kiss?"

"Do you want to be kissed?"

"I want you to stop pulling away from me, Tony."

"That's just it. If I kiss you now, I won't stop."

Lucy's arms wound around him. She felt the wild pounding of his heart against her own. She felt the fire of his lips as his hands slipped beneath her sweater to her breasts. "Tony," she whispered, drawing him closer. "Tony."

They fell back on the couch. Slowly, he undressed her. Now she lay naked under him, and the sight he had imagined so many times left him breathless. "My darling," he murmured hoarsely, his mouth caressing her swelling breasts, his hands stroking the lush curves of her body. He swept her into his arms and carried her to the bedroom. His own clothes were flung away and he was beside her on the bed, their bodies pressed together, their soft cries lingering in the air.

She moved against him, her back arching as once again she felt his lips, his seeking hands. She was trembling, almost faint with pleasure and desire. She felt his hand slip between her legs and her cries grew louder. In a frenzy her hands moved over him, and hungrily her mouth found his. Their bodies joined, driven by the sweet, urgent rhythms of passion. As if with one voice they murmured to each other, and for both of them there was nothing but this time, this place, this love.

*   *   *

The room was silvery with moonlight when Lucy opened her eyes. It was an instant before she remembered where she was, but then she saw Tony staring down at her and she settled back on the pillows. "I fell asleep," she said.

"I hope you had happy dreams."

"Very happy." She reached her hand to Tony's shoulder, rubbing the soft terry cloth of his robe. "I love you."

"I love you, darling. When are you going to marry me? I approve of marriage," he went on, seeing Lucy's smile. "So much nicer for the children."

"Children!"

Tony laughed. "Are you still drowsy?" he asked. "Surely you've heard of children."

Lucy turned her head, gazing off into space. Once she had wanted children, but that was before she had learned the circumstances of her own birth, before she had learned what her father really was—a drunk and a rapist and probably crazy, too, though no one had said so. In her closed, quiet way she had despised him; in her closed, quiet way she had decided she would never have children, for they would be the grandchildren of Roger Averill. Now she knew she had not changed her mind. Maybe it's irrational, she thought, but I can't help it. I can't.

"Lucy? What's wrong?"

"Nothing," she said, coming slowly out of her reverie. "It's just . . . we don't have to think about all those things yet. Children and marriage and all that. You're just back from the war. I'm just starting to get somewhere at *NewsView*. . . . I finally talked Don into letting me do photo features. Whole stories in pictures, Tony. He's agreed to give me three full pages a month. Four, if the story is really unusual. I had to fight hard to get that much space."

Tony smiled at her earnestness. "He couldn't very well turn down an award-winning photographer, could he?"

"Oh, that was just a press association award. Hardly the Pulitzer Prize. Anyway, I don't care about awards. All I want is a voice in my own work. I want to be allowed my own choices."

"That's fair enough. . . . But don't you want me to make an honest woman of you?"

"Soon."

"Soon when?" Tony asked with a smile.

"I have to get Gran used to the idea of you as husband material," Lucy replied, stifling a laugh. "I'm not going to say anything to her. That wouldn't work. She always has a thousand arguments to my one. But I'm going to go on seeing you, being with you. . . . She'll get the idea after a while."

"Darling, you're not a child anymore. Why do you let dear old Gran upset you? If it's money—"

"No, it's nothing like that. She's always frightened me, Tony. She's a strong woman. She wears people down until they do as she wants. I've seen it. I saw what she did to Mother. . . . Mother learned to fight back. But I—I don't know. For as long as I can remember, Gran's made me feel useless and dumb. I wasn't supposed to have any thoughts of my own, any plans. I was just supposed to look pretty and do as she wanted."

"That was then, Lucy. That was a long time ago. Things have changed."

"Gran hasn't changed. There's no end to her schemes."

"Nor to mine," Tony laughed, pulling the sheet aside.

Lucy snatched it back. "Tomorrow," she said. "It must be after two. I have to get home."

"Gran again?"

"She never waits up for me but she always knows what time I got in. She has spies. I want to stay, Tony. God, I want to stay, but Gran would just go crazy."

"Well, we don't want that. She's crazy enough as it is."

"You're terrible," Lucy said, laughing. She stretched, utterly relaxed and restored and content. "I'm so happy," she sighed. "Deliriously, deliciously happy. Aren't you?"

Tony bent, lightly kissing her lips. "Of course I am," he said. "I'm a man in love. All those years of waiting, of wanting you . . . You were worth the wait, my darling."

"Thank you," Lucy laughed again. "So were you . . . I guess," she added, eyes twinkling.

"You *guess?*"

"Well, I have no basis for comparison, have I? I was pure as the driven . . ." Lucy said no more, for Tony swatted her with a pillow. She scrambled out of bed, giggling as he chased after her. She ran into the bathroom, a moment later opening the door a crack. "Can I have my clothes?" she called. "Please?"

"Let me think about that. We have an interesting situation here."

"Please?"

"Well, all right. Since you asked nicely, I'll bring your things."

"My purse too."

"On the way."

Lucy washed and dressed and brushed her hair. She put on lipstick and cologne, and then returned to the living room. Tony, clad now in faded corduroys and a Brooks Brothers shirt rolled to the elbows, was seated on the couch. "You don't have to take me home," she said. "I'll get a taxi."

"Not a chance. You're much too pretty to be running around alone this time of night. My car's just downstairs." Tony grabbed his keys from the table. He stood, slipping his arm about Lucy's shoulder. "Come," he smiled. "Your chariot awaits."

They walked into the dim hallway and started down the stairs. Lucy glanced at him, a tiny frown wrinkling her brow. "There's—there's something I wanted to . . . I mean, I wanted to ask. . . . Tony, I'm worried about getting pregnant. Not for tonight. Tonight was probably all right on the calendar," she continued with a blush. "But . . . well, you know . . . you understand what I'm trying to say."

"Trying and just barely succeeding," he replied, amused. "You mustn't be embarrassed, darling. It's really very simple. I'll take you to the doctor and he'll give you—"

"Dr. *Westerman?* Oh, I couldn't. We'd *both* die of embarrassment."

"Not Dr. Westerman. A gynecologist. You'll have to say you're *Mrs.* Cameron, or better still, Mrs. Jennings. And of course you'll have to find the right doctor. Some of them still believe a woman should have a baby a year, no matter what."

"But where will I find a doctor? I don't think Sallie would know. She's pregnant again. They're hoping for a girl, a little sister for Scotty."

"Ask Meg Wyland," Tony said as they reached the foyer. "You two are old friends."

"Meg! She wouldn't know."

"Ask her."

Lucy stepped into the cold night air. She drew on her gloves, looking thoughtfully at Tony. "I suppose I'm a bit slow," she said. "Are you suggesting Meg's had experience in these things?"

"Would that surprise you?"

"I'm going to be a bridesmaid at her wedding next month."

"Well, if she wears white, she's fibbing."

Lucy slid into the car and slammed the door. "Is this firsthand information?" she asked, an edge to her voice. "Or are you guessing?"

Tony made no effort to hide his smile. "Neither," he replied, turning the key in the ignition. "But I had you going for a moment, didn't I? Guys talk, Lucy. That's the answer to your question. There's never anything explicit, you understand. That sort of talk is frowned upon. It's just locker room talk after squash or tennis."

"And what do the *guys* say about Meg?"

"That she's not exactly a nun."

"What else?"

"You won't like it, darling."

"What else?"

"They say she has great tits."

"God!" Lucy exclaimed. "A bunch of grown men having high school conversations!"

"I warned you you wouldn't like it," Tony said between bursts of laughter. "You're such a sensitive girl. I'll bet you're blushing to your fingertips."

"I'm wondering how *I'll* fare after the next squash game."

"You're quite safe. I don't talk much in locker rooms. I listen and learn. . . . But if I *were* to talk—"

"Don't you dare, Tony Jennings."

"Don't worry. I have no intention of sharing you with anyone. You're my girl. My girl and my love."

Love was immensely becoming to Lucy. She seemed to bloom with health and color, with radiant light. Her sunny smiles mirrored her mood, for she had never been happier. She went about in a heady daze, her step so light she might have been floating on air. She had kind words for everybody and everything. She had energy to spare, energy that saw her through long days and nights without the slightest trace of fatigue. She had a new assurance and she wore it like a badge, proclaiming the rightness of her world.

Elizabeth, observing these changes in Lucy, drew swift and accurate conclusions. She was not surprised but neither was she pleased, for still she disapproved of Tony Jennings, of his maverick ways. I must put an end to this, she thought to herself, and soon.

It was a frosty December afternoon when her limousine glided to a stop outside Tony's building. Robbins helped her from the car, then stood away as she entered the old brownstone. She located Tony's apartment number in the foyer and, with a sigh began climbing the three flights of stairs. She was close to seventy now, but if age had slowed her pace, it had had no effect on her resolve. She reached the third floor and went directly to apartment 5, lifting her hand to the bell. Seconds later the door burst open. "Good afternoon, Tony," she said. "I do hope I haven't come at a bad time."

"Mrs. Cameron. You're the last person I expected to see."

"No doubt. May I come in?"

"Of course." Tony smiled, closing the door behind Elizabeth. He watched her sweep through the living room and his smile widened. "Not quite what you're used to, is it?"

"It has a certain charm. Are you happy here, Tony?"

"Yes, I am." He took her coat, draping the dark

410

sable on a chair. "Please sit down, Mrs. Cameron," he said. "Would you like a drink? Some sherry?"

"This really isn't a social call. I've come to have a talk with you. I had hoped it wouldn't be necessary, but now there is no choice. I'm very concerned."

"About Lucy?"

"You come straight to the point, Tony. I've always liked that about you."

"All compliments gratefully received. Thank you, Mrs. Cameron."

"You needn't be so formal. You're old enough to call me Elizabeth."

"Thank you, Elizabeth." Tony sat opposite her. He was at ease, though his eyes were wary. "I don't see any reason to play games," he said. "Lucy is probably the only subject we have in common, so we might as well get to it. I love her, and she loves me. I want to marry her. . . . I'm sure you know that the terms of my trust have been changed. I can't support her in grand style, not yet. But I do have a job. I have prospects. I admit we may have some lean years ahead. That's all right. We'll survive them."

"You speak as if the matter were settled. Has Lucy agreed to marry you?"

"No, not exactly. She seems to be worried about your reaction."

"My reaction hasn't kept Lucy from doing other things of which I disapprove. Please don't misunderstand me, Tony. I'm certain that the lean years, as you describe them, wouldn't trouble her. I'm certain that money wouldn't be a factor, one way or another. In that regard, she is like Sarah. No, I think we may safely eliminate both my reaction and money as causes for her hesitation."

"I said nothing about hesitation."

"It was implied. If Lucy has not yet agreed to

marry you, there is a hesitation of some sort."

"Perhaps," Tony conceded. "But I wouldn't read too much into that, Elizabeth. Lucy decides things in her own mysterious ways and in her own time. We love each other. There's no hesitation about that. There's no doubt."

"I wonder."

Tony smiled. "That won't work," he said. "If you think you're going to *plant* doubts in my mind, you're mistaken. The only thing I wonder about is why you find me so unsuitable. At the risk of sounding immodest, Lucy could do a lot worse. . . . You've known three generations of my family, all upstanding citizens. There may be a drunk or two on the old family tree and my great-grandfather married the Irish scullery maid, but there aren't any criminals. There aren't any crazy aunts hidden away in the attic."

"I don't question your background," Elizabeth replied, laughing despite herself. "The Jenningses and the Camerons have been friends for many years. And whatever you may believe, I've always been fond of you. Having said that, I must also say you're the wrong fellow for Lucy. You have a wild streak, Tony. That's not a good thing in a husband. That's not a good thing for Lucy. She needs someone prudent and settled."

"Someone like Philip Colinge?"

"Yes, Philip would be an excellent choice."

"The choice isn't yours to make."

"I'm considering Lucy's best interests, you see."

"So am I," Tony said. "Love is in her best interests, don't you think?"

"Love is a very easy word, especially when one is young. There is the presumption that love is the answer to everything. When you've lived as long as I have, you will realize it's no such thing. Compatibility is far more important in marriage. Understanding is far more important, and acceptance." Elizabeth paused, her dark gaze narrowing on Tony. "Love certainly won't solve the problem of the career you've selected," she went on. "Are you still determined to pursue this theater foolishness? Are you determined to waste your life?"

"You have a way with words, Elizabeth. The theater isn't foolishness to me. It's what I want to do. Dad tried to make a banker of me, but it was no use."

"That is your final decision?"

"It is."

I've given him every chance, thought Elizabeth. Now I must do what has to be done. "I'm afraid we've strayed from the point," she said. "The point is that you and Lucy will not be happy together. There are things you don't know."

"What things?"

"Has Lucy ever mentioned a young man by the name of Colin Averill?"

"No," Tony replied, his eyes suddenly watchful. "Who is Colin Averill?"

"He was, for a brief time, Lucy's husband."

Tony did not move. He stared at Elizabeth. "Her husband!" he cried after some moments. "Her husband! Have you gone mad? Do you really expect me to believe a lie like that?"

"It's the truth," Elizabeth said, calmly opening her purse. She removed a folded sheet of paper, holding it out to Tony. "That is the marriage license," she explained. "Of course the marriage was annulled."

Tony took the paper, the words blurring before his anguished eyes. There was a terrible clanging in his head, a pounding in his temples that matched the pounding of his heart. "I don't understand," he

413

murmured. "Lucy never—she never told me."

"She rarely speaks of Colin. But he's with her, in her thoughts. Thoughts too private to share."

Tony crumpled the license and hurled it to the floor. "You're wrong," he declared. "I don't know what this is all about, but I know you're wrong."

"Am I? A woman always remembers her first love. And when first love ends in heartbreak, it's all the more compelling."

"Go on."

"I'm afraid the story is rather complicated."

"Go on," Tony said again, the coolness of his gaze matching Elizabeth's own. "Let's have it."

"Very well. It's quite possible you met Colin at Lucy's coming-out party, although the trouble began long before that. It began with Sarah. . . ." Succinctly, dispassionately, Elizabeth related the circumstances of Sarah's departure from Aldcross, of Lucy's subsequent birth. She related the deceptions that had marked Lucy's childhood. At the last, she related Lucy and Colin's unexpected meeting and their elopement to Maryland. "They learned the truth when they returned to New York that night," she continued. "It need hardly be said that Lucy was devastated. She was seventeen then, a young seventeen. Not only had she lost the boy she loved, she'd lost her identity."

"My poor darling," Tony murmured.

"But she isn't yours. Don't you see? Colin will always be there between you. He will be the unspoken presence in both your lives."

"Lucy loves me."

"Perhaps. She loves Colin also. Are you prepared to deal with that, Tony? Are you prepared to accept that? I think not. Compromise isn't in your nature. For you, it's all or nothing, and you will never have

414

all of Lucy."

He tensed, feeling the sharp sting of Elizabeth's words. "I don't believe that," he said quietly. "I don't believe your interpretation of things. Frankly, I don't trust your motives."

"You will never have all of Lucy," Elizabeth repeated, unruffled. "The fact that she's made no mention of Colin proves my point."

"And just why did you decide to enlighten me? What did you hope to accomplish?"

"I hoped to prevent a most unfortunate mistake. There is nothing personal in this, Tony. As I've said, I'm fond of you. But you're wrong for Lucy. It's that simple. . . . Someone like Philip will give Lucy the life she knows, the stable life she needs. Philip accepts things the way they are. It won't matter to him if part of Lucy's heart is elsewhere. He's a pleasant, unassuming fellow who will always do what's expected of him and who will never expect too much in return."

"You make him sound like a kindly spaniel."

"That was not my intention."

"No," Tony said, his blue eyes flashing. "Your intention was to scare me off. Because you disapprove of the way I live. Because you disapprove of me . . . You have a right to your opinion, Elizabeth. But you've no right to come sneaking behind Lucy's back."

"I'm trying to spare her."

"Spare her *what?*"

"More heartbreak. Lucy has much of Sarah's spirit, but she hasn't her strength."

"If she hasn't, it's thanks to you. I'm sorry to be so blunt, but you raised her to be fearful and unsure. Even as a child she always worried about things. Silly things, like getting her dress dirty or playing

415

jump rope with the chauffeur's daughter. Because *Gran* would be upset. Well, she's come a long way since then. Bit by bit, she's loosening your hold on her. . . . That's the real problem, isn't it? That's why you want her to marry a Philip Colinge, a kindly, obedient spaniel of a man. You'd have control again, and that's what you want."

Elizabeth rose, gathering up her purse and gloves. "Think what you will," she said, "but include Colin in your thoughts. Lucy's kept him a secret from you. Ask yourself why. Ask yourself if you can live with the answer. If you can, then by all means marry her." She turned, folding her coat over her arm. Her glance went to the marriage license crumpled on the floor. "Just a piece of paper," she smiled. "Tear it up, burn it in the fireplace. That's the easy part. Memories are much harder. Memories are with us always."

Tony heard the soft click of the door as Elizabeth left the apartment. He reached down and retrieved the license, smoothing it on the table. Over and over again he read the words; over and over again he imagined Lucy in another man's arms. His eyes flickered with hurt, with pain, with anger. His mouth twisted and quickly he struck a match, watching as the license turned to ashes. Moments passed. The telephone rang, but he paid no attention. After a while he rose from the couch. He went to the bedroom, the bedroom he had so often shared with Lucy, and slammed the door.

Chapter Twenty

"Has Tony seemed subdued to you lately?" Lucy asked. "Has he seemed a little different?"

Alice frowned. "Different? No, I don't think so." She turned her head, looking at the ice-glazed window of Minetta Tavern. "It's probably the weather," she said. "All this snow and sleet. It must be the coldest December on record."

"No, it's not the weather. . . . Maybe I'm imagining things."

"Maybe he's just tired. It can't be easy for him, working all night, then rushing to rehearsals bright and early every morning. How's the play coming along?"

Lucy sipped her drink. She smiled. "It's an awfully good play, Alice. But it wouldn't be nearly as good without Tony. He's given it a moody, almost Gothic interpretation. The actors are having the time of their lives, and he is, too. You should see him when he's at the theater. *Bursting* with ideas. With enthusiasm. And I've got it all on film! Which gave *me* an idea. I sold Don on a feature layout called "Off-Broadway Odyssey." By Lucy Cameron, of course. He's going to run it in the next issue. In time

417

for the opening."

"That's great."

"What's really great is that he didn't fight me on it. I outlined the idea and he said okay."

"Don isn't giving you trouble, Lucy?"

"No, not trouble exactly. But he interferes sometimes. I want to make my own choices. . . . I mean, my work is the only part of my life where I have any control, so choices are important to me. . . . Sometimes I fantasize about having a little studio of my own."

"Good for you!"

"It's only a fantasy," Lucy laughed. "I'm not ready for that yet. I'm still learning. But maybe someday. Who knows, maybe someday I'll even do a book. And you'll edit it."

"I have the time right now. The war took a lot out of Kaz. The war and his wife. Then, too, he's getting older. He's cut his schedule way down. There are days when all my work is finished by noon."

"Oh, I have plans for you, Alice. For after Kaz retires. First Tony becomes a famous director. Then he opens an office. Then he hires you to run the whole thing."

"Have you been looking into your crystal ball? If you have, tell me if you two will be married by then."

Lucy took another sip of her drink, gazing at Alice over the rim of the glass. "Maybe before then," she said quietly, a smile playing at her mouth. "Gran won't like it, but at least I've given her time to absorb the idea. . . . It's been a while and she hasn't made any trouble so—"

"Forget about her," Alice said, clasping Lucy's hand. "And let me be the first to congratulate you."

"Well, it's not official yet. I have to wait for Tony to ask me again. . . . I have to wait for *Strangers* to open, for his work to get sorted out. Right now, Tony's work comes first."

"Then I'll say a prayer for Tony's work."

Lucy's eyes twinkled. "And if you could mention *Strangers*," she said. "A plug, I think it's called."

Strangers opened in January. It was a modest production, befitting the budget and the surroundings—a converted garage on Hudson Street. The first night audience was filled with friends and family of the cast, but two glowing reviews in local newspapers soon brought theatergoers from all over the city. Both reviews hailed the young playwright Walter Nash, praising his "honest vision," his "authentic and powerful voice." Tony was hailed as a "brilliant new director," a director whose "flawless pacing and risky choices keep the audience on the edges of their seats."

Lucy could scarcely contain her pride. She carried the reviews in her purse, happily showing them to one and all. She telephoned everybody she knew, everybody she had ever known, urging them to see the play. She started a scrapbook for Tony, keeping a duplicate in her room at home. "Next stop Broadway," she said on a rainy evening some weeks later. "I told you you'd be a hit. I felt it. Did you see what *Variety* called you? 'A savvy young director with—'"

"I saw it," Tony laughed. "But I wouldn't count too much on Broadway. I'm still unloading lettuce crates in the Bronx."

"Not for long."

"I wouldn't count on that, either. Nothing happens overnight in the theater. . . . I've had another offer, though. Summer stock at Truro. I've been offered a season's contract. I'm going to take it, Lucy. I want you to come with me, as my wife."

She smiled, snuggling her head on Tony's shoul-

419

der. "That isn't the most romantic proposal I've ever heard. Where are the hearts and flowers?"

"Hearts and flowers don't seem to work," Tony replied. "God knows I've tried. I've tried everything." He turned, his fingers stroking Lucy's cheek. "Tell me what will work and I'll do it."

"You're in a serious mood tonight."

"It's time to be serious. There are moments when I feel I don't understand you."

"But that's silly."

"Damn it all, Lucy, you know what I mean. What goes on behind those green eyes of yours? What do you think? What do you see? Are you happy? What makes you happy? Are you ever sad?" Tony paused. His glance moved to the table where, months before, had lain the charred ashes of a wedding license. "Talk to me," he said quietly. "Tell me your secrets."

Secrets, thought Lucy, her breath catching. She thought of Colin, swiftly dismissing him from her mind. "I have no secrets," she murmured. "I love you, Tony. That isn't a secret anymore."

"If you love me, then marry me. I don't want to play house. I don't like all this sneaking around. Marry me."

Lucy gazed into his eyes and suddenly she was afraid, for suddenly she realized she could lose him. She felt as she had during the war, a little lost and utterly alone. "You're frightening me," she said.

"Fear is a good, honest emotion. We could stand some more of that around here. Marry me, Lucy."

"Are you sure? Very sure? I won't be the kind of wife Sallie is. Sallie and the others . . . I'm always doing the wrong thing. I can't really cook, and I when I make a bed it comes out lumpy. . . . And I'm hopeless about money."

"Is that all?" Tony asked, wondering if she would

420

offer any word of Colin Averill. "Is there anything else you want me to know?"

"No. That's enough, isn't it?"

"Will you marry me, Lucy?"

"Yes. Oh, yes, Tony, I will." She threw her arms about his neck, holding him close. "I will, I will, I will."

It seemed to Tony that he had waited all his life to hear those words. He savored them, though even now he felt faint and shadowy doubts stirring in his mind. "Tell me the truth," he said softly. "Did I bully you into saying yes? The truth."

"You're not a bully. You're very firm sometimes and I'm *so* glad. I *want* to be your wife, Tony. I'll try—I'll try not to disappoint you. . . . I'll buy a cookbook," she added with an earnest smile. "I'll learn to do all the wifely things."

He laughed. "Some wifely things interest me more than other wifely things," he said.

"You're a naughty boy."

"You bet." Tony left the couch, returning moments later with a small velvet Tiffany box. "I bought this before I went overseas," he explained. "I carried it around from North Africa to Normandy. It was my good luck charm." He opened the box, revealing a perfect diamond solitaire set in white gold. "May I?"

Lucy held out her hand, watching as Tony slipped the ring on her finger. "It's beautiful," she said. "The most beautiful ring I've ever seen." She lifted her hand to the lamplight. "Look how it sparkles, Tony."

"Your eyes are sparkling too. Are those tears I see?"

"Tears of joy. But they won't fall. They never do. I can't cry. Strange, don't you think?"

"I'm delighted. You won't be able to use tears to

421

get your way."

"Oh, I wouldn't do that," Lucy protested.

"Famous last words. And speaking of famous last words, shall we set the date?"

"You pick the day. I'll pick the month—June. I'll be a June bride. . . . Tony, there's just one thing. I don't want a big wedding. We all have to agree. You and I and your parents . . . and Gran," she sighed. "I wish I could lock her in her room until it's done. I can imagine the kind of wedding she'll want."

"Are you sure? Remember, she's not getting the bridegroom she wants."

"But *I* am. That's all that matters." Lucy leaned back, snuggling again in Tony's arms. "Mrs. Tony Jennings," she murmured.

"Louder."

"Mrs. Tony Jennings."

"I'm engaged, Gran," Lucy said, thrusting her hand into Elizabeth's view. She paused, bracing herself for the inevitable argument. "It's official," she added.

"Oh? And who is the lucky fellow?"

"Tony, of course."

"I see." Elizabeth smiled slightly, thinking that she had underestimated Tony, thinking that she was getting old. "Sit down, my dear. You must tell me all about it."

"There isn't a lot to tell, Gran. Tony's asked me before. Tonight I said yes. I suppose I always knew I would. You knew too, didn't you?"

"I knew there was a certain feeling between the two of you. Naturally I hoped you would get over it. Such feelings are no basis for marriage." Elizabeth folded her hands atop her desk. She smiled. "How did Tony take the news of your first marriage?"

Lucy stiffened, her gaze sliding toward the floor. "I didn't tell him," she admitted. "I couldn't. I've thought about it, Gran. I—it's very hard. I'll tell him, but the time has to be right."

"If you don't trust him to understand—"

"It's not that. Certainly I trust him. But I should have said something months ago, maybe years ago. I didn't, and that makes it hard."

"Have you asked yourself *why* you didn't?"

"I don't like to talk about Colin," Lucy replied. "I don't like to talk about any of it. I mean it isn't just Colin, is it? It's Mother and Roger Averill and that terrible night. . . . I was born because Mother was . . . raped. I've never said that out loud. Never. But it's haunted me."

A frown crossed Elizabeth's brow. "That's past history," she said. "It does no good to dwell on the past."

"But I've *hidden* the past from Tony. Well, not hidden, not exactly. I've . . . omitted it."

"Indeed you have. You must believe it would make a difference. It wouldn't to Philip, you know."

"Gran, I wish you'd stop talking about Philip. I love Tony and I'm going to marry him."

"Has he asked any questions about the past?"

"No. Why would he? He hasn't any idea that . . . He's never even heard of Colin or the Averills."

Elizabeth recalled her meeting with Tony. She recalled the anguish in his eyes, and reluctantly she credited his strength of character. Yes, she thought, I've underestimated him. He didn't say a word to Lucy. He knows the truth and still he said nothing. "I don't doubt he loves you," she conceded. "You will find, however, that love in itself isn't enough. You won't be happy together, Lucy."

"Why are you always the voice of doom?"

"The voice of experience, my dear. Sometimes they are one and the same."

"Not this time."

"As you wish."

"Gran, I told you these things because I want your promise."

"Promise?"

"Yes. Promise me you won't go to Tony. Promise you'll let me handle things my own way."

"You're a grown woman," Elizabeth replied. "If you want to cast your lot with his, if you want to throw both your futures away, I can't stop you. Nor will I try. One day you will come to me and admit your mistake. Of course it will be too late by then."

Lucy sighed, slumping deeper in her chair. "I didn't expect you'd be glad," she said. "I did hope you might at least offer a kind word."

"Has the date been set?"

"June. I'm going to be a June bride."

Tony and Lucy were married on the last day of June 1946. They had resisted Elizabeth's plans for a large society wedding, arranging instead a simple and romantic candlelight ceremony in the chapel of St. Thomas's Church. Fifty guests watched the radiant bride walk to the altar. She wore a summery gown of white organdy and lace, a matching organdy picture hat pinned atop her upswept curls. Clasped about her neck was a single strand of pearls; at her ears were Sarah's antique pearl clips. Her lace-trimmed bouquet was a charming mixture of daisies, white roses, and baby's breath. Her smile was luminous, filled with exultation, with love.

After the ceremony the newlyweds ran through a

shower of rice to the first car. Twenty minutes later they were greeting their guests in the handsome dining room of Minetta Tavern. There, beneath a vast mural of Greenwich Village sights, the wedding party dined on prosciutto and melon, cold tarragon chicken, and fresh berries in cream. The wedding cake was brought, a beautiful three-tier creation of vanilla cream and glacé rosebuds. Tony and Lucy cut the cake, laughing as Kazimov's camera recorded the moment. "I guess it's official now," Tony said, turning to his bride. "We're married."

They spent their wedding night at the St. Regis, leaving early the next morning for Cape Cod. "It's a long drive," Tony warned. "Are you sure you don't mind?"

"I don't mind *anything* today," Lucy replied with a dreamy smile. She settled back in the car, watching the summer breezes ruffle Tony's hair. Gently, she stroked his shoulder. "I have a wonderful husband," she went on, "and we're going to have a wonderful honeymoon. What more could I ask?"

"I'll be working, too, don't forget. That is if I can concentrate. I left a whole theater company waiting for me and I haven't given them a thought. It's your fault," he laughed. "You're a very distracting female."

"I try. . . . You aren't really worried, are you? You've only been gone three days."

"No, I'm not worried. We were in pretty good shape before I left. But the opening is two days off, and there are always last minute problems. I still haven't seen a dress rehearsal straight through."

"Everything will be fine. You're the brilliant new director Tony Jennings."

"Am I?" he laughed again. "I'm impressed."

"Tell me about Truro."

"You'll love it, darling. It's beautiful. The rest of the company is staying at a boarding house, but I rented a little cottage for us. It's on a cliff overlooking the ocean. I want you all to myself."

"Can we afford it, Tony?"

"Well, it isn't exactly grand. It isn't Dad's idea of a cottage, which is sixteen rooms in Newport. This is a sweet little tumbledown place. Living room, kitchen, bedroom. And spectacular views, of course. Later in the season we'll rent a sailboat. I expect to be able to steal a day here and there."

"If you don't, I'll kidnap you. How's that?"

"Hmm. Kidnapped by a gorgeous, sexy woman who happens to be my wife. Sounds good to me."

"Me too."

"I hope you won't be lonely," Tony said, taking his eyes briefly from the road. "I'll be working long hours."

"I packed my cameras. While you're working, I'll be roaming around snapping pictures. I don't suppose I'll get anything *NewsView* can use, but I'll keep an eye out. They were so nice about my leave of absence."

"I can promise you won't run out of scenery."

"Tell me about it. Tell me about Truro."

"You'll love it, that's all I'm going to say. It's . . . special."

To Lucy it was magical, a place of cliffs and moors and hills and moonlit beaches. During her first week in Truro she was a tourist, exploring the steepled Town Hall, the Meeting House, the old Congregational Church with its Paul Revere bell and its windowpanes of Sandwich glass. She strolled through the quaint cemeteries. She rode her bicycle to the splendid isolation of the Highland Light, an eighteenth-century lighthouse standing sentry over the Atlantic. She scrambled up and down the cliffs, gazing out at the Peaked Hill sandbars, at the curling bands of surf that had once sent tall sailing ships to watery graves below.

After the first week she settled into a happy routine. She spent her mornings at one or another of the beaches, photographing children and sandcastles and waves breaking on the shore. Each noon she rode to the theater for lunch with Tony. She often stayed to watch rehearsals, slipping out later to photograph the sunset over Corn Hill or Gull Pond. She returned to the theater for the evening performance, waiting backstage until Tony was ready to leave.

The nights were theirs and they treasured every moment. They had picnic dinners on the lawn of their small cottage. Hand in hand they walked down the steep path to the ocean. They swam; they played in the surf, splashing each other, chasing each other through the white-capped waves. In the shadow of the Truro moon they made love.

It was an idyllic summer, though all too brief. July seemed to fly by, as did August; almost before they knew it, Labor Day had come and gone. Lucy began packing their things for the return to New York. Carefully she packed the seashells she had collected, the wildflowers she had dried and preserved between sheets of cellophane. She packed dozens of rolls of film, as yet undeveloped. She packed programs and ticket stubs from each of the plays Tony had directed during the season. She gazed at these odds and ends of their summer and she felt a kind of emptiness. She sank down on the bed, wishing she could cry.

Hours later Tony found her walking in the garden. He saw her pale, strained face and he took her into his arms. "It's all right, darling," he said. "We aren't leaving forever. We'll be back someday. Perhaps next summer."

"Oh, I hate leaving. I do. . . . But it's more than that. Alice called a while ago. . . . Tony, Kazimov is dead. It happened this morning. He was shooting on location and he—he collapsed. By the time the ambulance arrived, he was gone."

"Darling, I'm so sorry."

"He was such a good man."

"I know."

"And now he's gone." Lucy buried her head in Tony's shoulder. "God, I can't believe it," she said. "I don't want to believe it."

"He had a great life. The end was quick, Lucy. You can be thankful for that. You wouldn't want to see him dying inch by inch in some hospital."

"No, that would be horrible. I guess it was best this way. At least he'll be remembered. His work will be remembered."

They started back toward the cottage, Tony's arm circling her waist. "On the subject of work," he said quietly, "I've had some news myself. Is this the wrong time to talk about it?"

"Of course not. Tell me your news."

"Well, I got a call at the theater. *Strangers* has been doing such big business it's going to move to the Provincetown Playhouse. I'm going to sign on to restage it, freshen it up a bit."

"Tony, that's marvelous! The Provincetown Playhouse, of all places. That's just a block from Minetta Tavern."

"It really is a small world."

"I wish we could stay in our own small world right here."

"We can't stay, but we can visit. Or we could if we had our own cottage. Let's sit down a minute, Lucy. Let me tell you what I've been thinking."

428

"Do you have a plan?" she asked with a smile. "I'll say yes to anything that will bring us back here."

"Remember when Mother and Dad told us to choose whatever wedding present we wanted? I think Dad had it in mind to buy us an apartment in New York. But we can manage in my apartment for a while. It's fun bumping into each other," Tony laughed. "So instead of an apartment, what if he were to buy us a summer place? For ten or fifteen thousand, we could do very well."

"Could we buy this cottage?"

Tony glanced around, amused. "Perhaps something a little more substantial," he said. "Something roomy enough for kids and dogs and chaos."

Kids and dogs and chaos, thought Lucy. She felt Tony's eyes on her and she looked away. "You're talking about a family," she said.

"Not right now, but in time. When we've fattened up the old piggy bank. I like children, darling. I'm a former child myself." His smile faded, for Lucy's expression troubled him. He had seen that expression before, but still he wondered what lay behind it. He wondered, as he too often had, about Colin Averill. "Anyway," he said, "shall I tell Mother and Dad we've decided on our present?"

"Oh, yes, Tony. It's a wonderful idea. I think Gran wanted us to have Broadmoor, but I'd much rather have our own place here on the Cape. I love it here."

"That's good, because if she gave us Broadmoor, she'd have to give us a staff of twenty to keep it up." Tony stood, his glance falling on the suitcases packed and waiting near the door. "Are we all set?" he asked. "I have to leave the keys with Mrs. Purdy."

"I'm ready. . . . No, I'm not ready. I don't want to go."

"We'll be back. Maybe we'll drive up in a few

months and do some house hunting."

"Let's walk down to the beach one last time. Can we?"

Tony held out his hand. "Come, we'll say good-bye to the gulls."

"Just what I was thinking." She took his hand, gazing into his eyes. "You won't mind if it's just the two of us for a while, will you? I mean the two of us alone, without kids and dogs and chaos."

"Two is my favorite number, darling." At least for now, he silently added. At least for now. "I love you, you know."

"And I love you."

"Then two is my favorite number."

"Of course Tony wants a family," Josh said, sipping his drink. "Does that surprise you?"

"Tony was always such a playboy," Lucy replied. "I didn't give the idea of family much thought. And when I realized he was serious about a career in the theater, I put the idea completely out of my mind."

"Theater people have been known to have families."

"Yes."

Josh's gave moved around the cluttered living room. He smiled, observing the mismatched furniture, the welter of newspapers and magazines, the cartons of wedding presents still unpacked. "I'll grant you this doesn't seem a very likely place to raise a family," he said. "I used to think it was the perfect bachelor apartment. Even now it fits that description."

"Well, we've been back from the Cape only two months. There hasn't been any time to worry about redecorating. There hasn't been any money, either."

"Don't be silly. If you need money, Dad will be glad to—"

"No loans," Lucy declared. "Not from my family, not from Tony's. He made the rule and we're sticking to it."

"Admirable."

"Tony's determined to succeed on his own. That's the admirable part. He's working so hard. And I'm working. Between his schedule and mine, we don't see a lot of each other. He gets home from his night job just as I'm leaving. By the time I get home, he's at rehearsals. We have to steal moments here and there. But things should be easier now that *Strangers* is opening."

"I'm looking forward to it," Josh said. He finished his drink, an instant later checking his watch. "I hope we don't miss the curtain. Sallie should have been here by now."

"Why didn't you wait and come together?"

"I wanted some time alone with you, Lucy. We haven't talked in a while. Besides, Sallie likes to sit with the baby before she goes out for the evening. She's absolutely nutty about our daughter."

"I can see why. Ellen is a little doll. Tony's in love with her."

"And you?"

"Fishing for compliments, Josh? You know very well she's bewitched the whole family."

"But what about you? Don't you want a child of your own? Children?"

"The grandchildren of Roger Averill? He was a drunk and a rapist."

Josh was startled by the sudden bitterness in Lucy's voice. He frowned. "The facts are the facts," he replied quietly. "I won't make light of them. But you mustn't let them color your life. Whatever Roger

431

was, it isn't hereditary."

"How do you know? How can anyone know what he's passed on?"

"You're the proof, Lucy. You aren't a drunk. There isn't a shred of violence in your nature. . . . Roger wasn't insane, after all. As I understood it, he was undone by the war."

"Yes, that was the story."

"Lucy, I realize it's been painful for you. Your long silence on the subject was indication enough. But you've moved beyond all that now. You have a husband who loves you deeply. The past doesn't matter to him."

"Tony doesn't know."

"I beg your pardon?"

"He doesn't know, Josh. I've never told him about it, any of it."

"Do you mean to say he knows nothing of the Averills? Nothing of *Colin?*"

"That's right."

Josh could not hide his astonishment. He gaped at Lucy, his mouth opening and then clamping shut. "How could you have been so foolish?" he asked when he found his voice. "Tony is your husband. How could you have deceived him like that?"

"I'm not proud of myself. I have a habit of putting off unpleasant things. The more unpleasant they are, the longer I put them off. . . . At first I couldn't think of a way to tell him. I had the chance before he went overseas, but I couldn't do it. I wrote to him every day during the war. I had hundreds of chances, but I still couldn't do it. I promised myself that I'd tell him as soon as he got back. I didn't. There were any number of chances before the wedding. I let them slip by. After we were married, it just seemed too late. I've come close, Josh. I've had the words on the tip of my

432

tongue. But then . . ."

"You don't doubt that Tony loves you?"

"No."

"Do you love him?"

"Oh, yes. Oh, yes, very much."

"In that case, what's stopping you? What are you afraid of, Lucy?"

"I don't know."

"You must know. Has it something to do with Tony? Surely it couldn't have anything to do with Colin, not after all these years."

Lucy looked down at her hands, twisting her wedding band around and around. "I don't know," she said again. "Part of me—part of me will always love Colin. Maybe that's what I'm afraid of. Because that's what I can't tell Tony. He'd never accept it. I'd lose him, and if I lose him I'll die."

"If you lose him, it will be your own fault," Josh said. "You're risking your marriage, Lucy. And for what? A memory."

"It's more than that."

"Like hell it is. You were seventeen and in the throes of first love. An elopement, a forced separation, that's all very romantic stuff. The stuff of memories, but not of life. *Tony* is real life. And if you love him, you'd better take care. Secrets rarely *remain* secrets. Tony is bound to learn the truth sooner or later. It should come from you."

"I can't, Josh."

"Then you're a fool."

"I wish you'd try to understand. I'm scared."

"The longer you postpone this, the harder it's going to be. You're simply digging a deeper hole for yourself, Lucy. You're not a child anymore. You must see how Tony will interpret your silence. How would you interpret it if situations were reversed?"

433

"That's why I'm scared."

"Talk to him. Do it soon. At least promise me you'll try."

The doorbell rang then and Lucy rose to answer it. "That will be Sallie," she said. "It's late. We'll meet her downstairs."

"Lucy—"

"Not now, Josh. The curtain goes up at eight."

"Lucy—"

"Not now."

Strangers, in its new home at the Provincetown Playhouse, was a great success. There were more reviews, superlative ones praising both author and director. There were sold-out performances and heavy advance sales, assuring a long run. It was said, correctly, that Tony's career was launched. He did another Off-Broadway play, followed by another season of summer stock. He spent the year of 1947 commuting to Washington, where he was the director of a repertory company. The next year he was again doing summer stock, but in 1949 he was offered his first Broadway play.

Lucy started a new scrapbook. "Look what I bought," she cried, showing off the large red leather album. "Look, I had your initials stamped in the corner. In gold!"

"I hope that's an omen," Tony laughed. "Aren't you tired of scrimping and saving?"

"Oh, it hasn't been so bad. Artists are supposed to have lean years. It's something to look back on. Anyway, it's for the cause, for the *theatuh.*"

"That's my girl."

"Of course if you'd let me use just a little bit of my trust fund money—"

"Nope. It stays where it is, collecting all that lovely interest. Much better than making a kept man of me."

"A kept man! Really, Tony, that's silly."

"I wonder how I'd do as a gigolo. I'm in pretty good shape," he said, patting his flat stomach. "I can still turn on the old charm. What do you think?"

"I think you'd better turn your charm in my direction or else turn it off. I'm the jealous type."

"I'm glad."

Lucy smiled, nestling in the crook of Tony's arm. "This is a special time," she said. "We should celebrate. Once you start rehearsals you'll be too busy. And once the play opens you'll be deluged with new offers."

"Well, maybe not exactly deluged. *Count to Ten* is a very slender comedy. I'm only doing it because it's a chance at Broadway, and because of Maggie Meredith. She's going to be a big star."

"So you've said."

"She's beautiful," Tony went on, "but that's the least of it. She has marvelous timing and a marvelous throaty voice. She has presence. When you meet her, you'll see what I mean."

"I'm not sure I want to meet her. Remember I'm the jealous type."

"Maggie's an actress, darling. A damned good actress. My interest in her begins and ends there. . . . My interest in you is endless."

"Even after three years of marriage?"

"Especially after three years of marriage." Tony ran his fingers through Lucy's golden hair. He gazed down at her, his expression thoughtful. "Do you recall all those puzzles you sent me during the war?" he asked. "Crosswords and jigsaws and anagrams? Then there were all those mystery stories. Well, I solved the puzzles. I solved the mysteries long before the end. But you, my darling, are still a challenge. I keep wondering if there isn't a piece missing, a vital clue."

Lucy stirred uneasily, her hands rising and falling in her lap. "I wish you wouldn't say things like that, Tony," she sighed. "Why do you?"

"I don't know. You sometimes seem to retreat into a world of your own. You're here, yet you're not here. You look as if something's troubling you. A veil drops over your eyes." Tony paused, hoping Lucy would speak, hoping her ghosts would be exorcised at last. "What's behind the veil?" he asked softly. "Tell me your secrets, darling."

Lucy was quiet. This is the time, she thought to herself. Just say Colin's name and the rest will come. Just *say* it, for God's sake. "I love you, Tony," she said instead. "I love our life together. I admit I'm moody, but it has nothing to do with us." She lifted her head, slowly meeting his gaze. "It has nothing to do with us," she repeated. "You have to believe that." She took a breath. Her heart had begun to race, and there was a familiar throbbing in her temples. She glanced away, fighting a sudden panic. In that moment she felt Tony's arms close about her; she felt the warmth, the comfort of his embrace, and she took another breath. "All these questions," she murmured. "They—they scare me."

"It's all right. It's all right, darling," he said, stroking her hair. "There won't be any more questions, I promise. I didn't mean to upset you, Lucy. That's the last thing I wanted. I was clumsy. We're all entitled to our . . . moods. What I'm trying to say is that I worry about you. But you're a big girl now, aren't you? And I'm a clumsy fool."

Lucy smiled, relaxing against him. "No," she said.

"You're wonderful. I'd be so miserable without you."

"I'm not going anywhere."

"You're going to be famous. All the beautiful women in New York will be chasing you."

"I'll remember to wear my track shoes," Tony replied with a laugh. "But *Count to Ten* isn't going to make me famous. That will have to wait a while. Until Wally Nash finishes his new play. I've read parts of it. It's an extraordinary piece of work. It's pure gold. Unfortunately, it's a year off."

"That's the play with the odd title, isn't it?"

"Not so odd. *Ghost Stories in the Dark*. I like it. No, I love it, because it's going to open all the doors."

"What doors?"

"The doors to our dreams, missy. To a snazzy new penthouse. To snazzy cars and clothes, and champagne by the case . . . To a family. We'll be able to start our family, darling. Kids and dogs and chaos. Ain't life grand!"

Kids and dogs and chaos, thought Lucy, ducking her head. "Yes," she said. "Grand."

Chapter Twenty-One

Count to Ten opened in the autumn of 1949. It opened on a Tuesday and closed the next day, a flop, or in the phrase of one disgruntled critic, a floparoo. The closing was hardly noticed, for that was the season of *Death of a Salesman, Detective Story, Gentlemen Prefer Blondes,* and the Rodgers and Hammerstein smash musical *South Pacific.* But if the closing went unnoticed, Tony and his young leading lady did not. The otherwise gloomy reviews applauded their work. Tony was said to be a gifted new director of sure instinct; Maggie Meredith was said to be Broadway's loveliest new ingenue.

She was indeed lovely, a slender lemonade blonde with delicate features and porcelain skin. She was the picture of innocence, though her throaty voice, her dimpled smile, her almost feline grace stirred men's imaginations. She seemed to light up the stage, on cue moving an audience to tears or laughter, to great affection. Tony saw all these things; his director's eye saw a young actress on the brink of stardom. "Maggie is the only choice for *Ghost Stories,*" he said to Wally Nash. "She'll be a memorable Christina."

"I agree. Now all you have to do is convince our

beloved producers."

"Leave them to me, Wally old boy. You keep hammering away at your typewriter. I'll keep hammering away at Frank and Lee. I can handle Frank. Lee's the stubborn one."

Frank Elliot and Lee Rothman were both in their forties, longtime friends and recent partners, with a string of modest successes behind them. Like most producers they were considered pennypinchers, but they were serious about the theater and about the quality of their productions. Frank, quiet and bespectacled, was considered the creative partner; Lee, bald and exuberant, the businessman. Their arguments were few, and about *Ghost Stories in the Dark* there were no arguments at all, for they felt they had a hit. They had faith in Wally Nash and in Tony. If they had reservations about Maggie Meredith, they nonetheless bowed to Tony's judgment and signed her for the lead. "You better be right," Lee said to him shortly before rehearsals began. "If you're wrong, we're all in the sewer."

But Tony knew he was not wrong. He was confident as he guided the cast through the first cold reading, confident as he staged the first dress rehearsal weeks later. Lucy often slipped into the theater to watch him work. When the company left for out-of-town tryouts, she took another leave of absence from *NewsView* and went along. Their first stop was New Haven, where reviews were decidedly mixed. "We'll pull it together in Boston," Tony promised. "Wally's already revising the second act."

In Boston, Tony's hotel suite was filled with the tension, the nervous uncertainty that accompanied the tryout of every play. Tempers flared and then were soothed, only to flare again. Telephones rang constantly, regardless of the hour. All the doors were

439

open, people rushing in for scripts or drinks or sandwiches brought by harried room service waiters. There was always someone pacing back and forth. There was always someone sprawled on the couch, eyes closed, trying to steal a few moments of sleep. There was always someone mixing a Bromo-Seltzer. Late at night, when Wally tore the latest revisions from his typewriter, there were calls for more coffee—"hot and black."

Tony thrived in this chaotic atmosphere. He slept less than three hours each night and never seemed tired. He listened to everyone's complaints and never seemed to lose patience. He calmed Wally, reassured Lee, encouraged Maggie. He was firmly in control, raising his voice only to be heard above the noise. For Lucy it was not that easy. The lack of privacy made her uncomfortable; the constant ringing of the telephone, the constant squabbling, made her head ache. She resented the round-the-clock demands on Tony's time. Perhaps most of all, she resented Maggie Meredith. "Why are you always at her beck and call?" she asked one early October morning. "I think she takes advantage."

"Who? Maggie?"

"Who else? She must have been in here a dozen times last night. When she wasn't here in person, she was telephoning. What's wrong with her?"

"Nothing," Tony replied, laughing. "Maggie's an actress, darling. She's high-strung, and she has a certain flair for the dramatic. In other words, everything's a crisis."

"*Your* crisis."

"If necessary, yes. I'm the director of this circus, Lucy. That means I have to be part traffic cop, part boss, and part shoulder to lean on."

"Is that why she calls *you* darling?"

"Theater talk." Tony sat at the edge of the bed, stroking Lucy's tangled golden hair. "A lot of actresses," he said quietly, "fall a little bit in love with their leading men. Some fall a little bit in love with their directors. It's harmless. And in my case, it's not reciprocated."

"I can't stand the way she looks at you. Those big cow eyes of hers. She's flirting."

"Of course she is. That's all part of the game. But it really is harmless. You haven't seen me flirting back, have you?"

"No," Lucy said.

"Then what are you worrying about? My sole interest in Maggie is as an actress. I intend to bring a hit play into New York. I'm close, darling, but there's still work to be done. The second act still isn't right. Maggie's uneasy with it, and she's looking to me for support. That's my job. One of them, anyway."

"Sometimes I wish you'd gone into the bank. *No*body falls in love with bankers."

Tony laughed again, wrapping his arms about Lucy. "You're stuck with a director," he said. "For better or worse. Just remember that we'll be home soon. Our lives will return to normal."

"I know, Tony, and I know I shouldn't complain. You have enough on your mind. I promise I won't say another word about it. Or her."

He glanced around at the cameras and lenses covering the bureau. "I was hoping you'd come to the theater today, after your shooting. We're making some more changes."

"I'll be there. It won't take me long to get what I need at Harvard. How many ways are there to photograph the Yard and the ivied walls?"

"You manage to find new ways."

"Not this time," Lucy said. "It's a silly assignment. A three-page spread on Harvard."

"What's wrong with Harvard?"

"Nothing, but *Life* did it a couple of months ago."

"That was Yale, darling."

"Same thing. The point is, Don's started to play safe. He used to let me do those wonderful mood pieces. Now that *NewsView* is getting so successful, he's lost his nerve."

"Have you told him that?"

"Tony, you know how I hate arguments. I have my full quota with Gran."

"But if you're unhappy there . . ."

"Oh, I suppose I'm restless." Lucy turned, looking up. "Joan Cleeve was an editor before she married Jim. Did you know that? She's suggested I put together a book. Around a central theme. Alice thinks it's a good idea."

"So do I. What's stopping you?"

"I'd have to leave *NewsView*, Tony. If I did a book, I'd want to give it all my time."

"Then leave *NewsView*."

"I don't know if I'm ready."

"Of course you are. Just do it."

Lucy could not help laughing. "Easy for you to say. You're a director. You're used to bossing people around. I'm used to being bossed."

"Faint heart never won fair book contract."

Now Lucy groaned, burying her head in the pillow. "And on that note . . ." she said.

"And on that note I take my leave. I'm off. See you later, darling."

"Yes, later." Lucy stretched her arms over her head. She decided to sleep for another hour, but as she closed her eyes the phone began ringing. "Damn," she said. "Damn, here we go again."

* * *

Ghost Stories in the Dark opened to brilliant reviews. The play was acclaimed as a "modern classic," "a gripping drama that builds to a shattering climax," "a stunning achievement in American theater." Tony was called "a director of great vision and strength." Of Maggie one critic wrote, "Make no mistake about it, Miss Meredith is a star."

Three months after the opening, Tony bought a nine-room apartment on Sutton Place. He had a gold latchkey made at Tiffany's and this key, engraved with the date, he gave to Lucy. "We're home," he said, stopping in the middle of the empty living room. "Just think, darling. No more crowded closets. No more plaster falling from the ceiling. No more clanging pipes."

"I'll miss the old place."

"It was time to move on, Lucy."

"I know." She turned, her glance roving over the shining parquet floor, the brick fireplace, the slim and graceful staircase that seemed to be suspended in midair. She took a step, looking at the glass panels of the terrace doors, at the majestic sweep of blue sky beyond. "It's lovely," she said. "A bit cool. We'll have to add those little touches that make it a home."

"I'll be glad to add some clutter," Tony grinned. "As much as you like."

"Save that for your office. Really, I don't know how you find anything there. If you didn't have Alice working for you, you'd *drown* in clutter."

"A happy death."

Lucy smiled, shaking her head. "I can see you're not going to be any help," she said. "The next time I see Sophie, I plan to tell her what a sloppy son she has."

"We'll raise *our* sons to be neat. Or our daughters. I'm quite sure sloppiness isn't hereditary."

"No, I'm sure it's not," Lucy replied. Her smile

wavered and she looked away, fixing her eyes on the skyline. "Shouldn't you be getting to your office?" she asked. "The moving men will be here any minute. Alice is coming, too. She volunteered to pitch in."

"Why can't I pitch in? Remember, I'm the guy who used to unload fifty-pound lettuce crates."

"Oh, no. Oh, no, that will never work. First you'll start a conversation with the moving men, and then you'll all wind up sitting on the floor, drinking beer and arguing politics. I'm on to you, Tony Jennings. Off you go and not another word."

"You're a hard woman, spoiling all my fun. . . . But I think you ought to know something else is being delivered. A piano."

"A piano?"

"A baby grand," Tony smiled proudly. "I ordered it last month. See, it will fit right in by the windows. It's a beauty. It will be great for parties."

"Tony, aren't we getting in over our heads? A baby grand must have cost—"

"Money is no object," he laughed. "I have a dozen scripts piled up on my desk. I'm in demand, as the expression goes. Besides, I have another surprise for you. Dad's finally accepted the fact that I won't be joining him in the bank. He's going to release my trust fund next year. On my thirtieth birthday! However you look at it, happy days are here again."

Lucy did not reply immediately. She walked with Tony to the door, all the while wondering what this change in their fortunes might mean. Money had been her excuse for not starting a family, but now she knew things were different. She felt trapped, as if the walls were closing in. "Anything else you forgot to tell me?" she asked, managing a small, wan smile.

"Any other surprises?"

"Well, let's see. . . . A piano and my trust fund. No, that's all for the moment."

Lucy waited at the door until the elevator came. She watched Tony go and then she turned away, wandering through the empty rooms. The moving men arrived at ten, Alice at ten-thirty. Together they began unpacking cartons and barrels. They took a break at noontime, sitting down to a lunch of chicken sandwiches and coffee from a nearby luncheonette. "Not very festive, is it? I'm sorry, Alice. I should have planned ahead."

"With all this going on? Moving day is always a big mess. And you have so much stuff."

"A lot of the cartons are wedding gifts we never opened. We never had the room."

"You have now. What a place! It's great, Lucy. I'm happy for you."

"Thanks. I guess I'm not used to it yet. Things seemed simpler on Bleecker Street. God knows it was cozier."

"Oh, you'll make it cozy. Like a nest. My mom used to say every woman wants a nest. And when you add some baby chicks . . ." Alice smiled. "I bet you can't wait to have kids running around here."

"I can wait," Lucy replied, her voice brusque. "Sorry again, I didn't mean to snap at you. It's just that I'm tired of the subject. . . . I'm not ready to have children, Alice. The theater is really a crazy life, you know. The constant confusion, the weird hours. And the out-of-town tryouts! My God, they're nerve-racking. There's never a moment's peace. There's never enough time. . . . The hours. Did I mention the hours?"

"Take it easy, Lucy. You don't have to explain to me. If you're not ready, you're not ready. It's a big

445

step, having kids. You probably want to settle in first."

"Yes, that's it. That's it exactly."

Alice was quiet, considering Lucy's eager, almost grateful response. Something's going on, she thought to herself, and whatever it is, it's not good. "Let's change the subject," she said. "How's everything at *NewsView*?"

"I've decided to quit. If I don't do it now, I never will. So I'm going to put in a darkroom here, sort through thousands of negatives, and then try my hand at a book. There, I said it."

"Hallelujah! Somewhere Kaz is smiling."

"I don't know. . . . It's going to feel strange."

"But *nice* strange. You'll have control over your own work; that's what you've wanted. And you've earned it, Lucy. You've paid your dues."

"We'll see, won't we? Anyway, Gran will be pleased."

"Is she still as feisty as ever?"

"Amazing, isn't it?" Lucy laughed. "She'll be seventy-five next year. She walks with a cane now, but otherwise she hasn't changed. She certainly hasn't mellowed. She still runs her household in grand style. Everybody complains about the servant problem. It doesn't seem to be a problem for her."

"They don't make 'em like your grandmother anymore."

"I wonder if that's such a bad thing. I don't know, Alice. These steely matriarch types can be awfully hard on their families. They always scared the hell out of me. Of course, I scare easily."

"You shouldn't keep saying those things about yourself. You're stronger than you think."

"Hah!"

"It's true," Alice insisted. "Your grandmother

446

didn't want you to work but you went to work anyway. That was one way you stood up to her. And she didn't want you to marry Tony but you went ahead and did it. That's another way. If you look back, you'll see you stood up to her when it counted."

"Maybe."

"There's no maybe. You became a photographer, didn't you? You married Tony, didn't you?"

"Thank God."

"So she didn't win after all."

"It isn't over yet," Lucy said with an odd smile. "Gran's old, but she knows the final score has yet to be tallied."

The Jenningses' first big party in their new apartment was a gala celebration of Elizabeth's seventy-fifth birthday. Lucy spent weeks planning the event. She fretted over every detail, no matter how small, for she wanted the evening to be a success. She hired the caterer, the waiters, the musicians. She selected the food that would comprise the cold buffet and she wrote the guest list, writing in the names of a hundred Cameron relatives, friends, and a few privileged employees of the Galleries. She bought a new gown, a simple bare-shouldered column of black velvet. At the last moment she went to the bank and took Sarah's diamonds from the vault.

Patrick was struck once again by Lucy's resemblance to Sarah. He watched her moving about the crowded room, chatting with her guests, and he remembered other parties, other times. Happy times, he thought, finding comfort in his memories. He made his way across the room, stopping at Lucy's side. "You look beautiful," he said. "Your mother would be very proud."

"Thank you, Uncle Patrick. I'm wearing her jewels tonight. They always give me confidence."

"It's a lovely party."

"I hope so. I haven't been this nervous about a party since my debut. I keep waiting for Gran to come and tell me what I've done wrong."

"I wouldn't worry about that. The old girl seems to be enjoying herself."

Lucy smiled, studying Patrick's face. He was sixty now and still handsome, with thick silver hair immaculately barbered and wide gray eyes that still missed very little. "What do you think of the apartment?" she asked.

"I like it. A bit modern for my tastes perhaps, but I like the way you've mixed in the antique pieces. It's all quite comfortable and relaxed. Of course the terrace is wonderful. I understand you cook out there."

"Tony does. He barbecues. We went to a few barbecues on the Cape this past summer. That was the beginning. Ever since then he's been dragging home different kinds of grills. Oh, and bird feeders, too. His two current goals in life are to find a grill that will make a perfect hamburger and to find a bird feeder that the birds will actually use."

"It sounds as if Tony is enjoying country life," Patrick laughed. "I wouldn't have thought him the type. Though I suppose it must be nice to get away from all the pressures. The theater isn't an easy business, is it?"

"It's bedlam."

"Then the Cape offers an excellent change of pace. I hear Scotty is going to spend part of next summer with you and Tony."

"Scotty?"

"Do I have that wrong?" Patrick asked. "I was

certain Josh said something along those lines. Something about Scotty going to camp in July, and to you and Tony in August. . . . I must have it wrong," he added, seeing the confusion in Lucy's eyes. "My memory isn't what it used to be."

"Your memory is fine, Uncle Patrick. It's Tony's memory that needs work. He sometimes forgets to tell me things. But I'll be glad to have Scotty. Your grandson is a charming little boy."

"He's a little devil."

"That's why he and Tony get along so well. They know each other's tricks." Lucy took a glass of champagne from the tray of a passing waiter. She sipped the bubbly liquid, listening as the pianist began playing "Isn't It Romantic." Her gaze traveled across the room. She saw Tony surrounded by six or seven people; she heard the laughter when he finished one of his stories. "They're kindred spirits," she said, "Tony and Scotty. Tony and children in general."

"He wants a child of his own. You know that, don't you?"

"Everybody knows that. It isn't a secret." Lucy finished her champagne. She put the glass down and turned back to Patrick. "There are other secrets though," she murmured.

"You haven't told him?"

"I waited too long. There isn't any way to tell him now."

"You're wrong, Lucy. You're making a terrible mistake. I wish . . ." Patrick stopped speaking, his attention drawn to the arched entryway. "Isn't that Maggie Meredith?" he asked.

Lucy followed his glance, seeing an exquisite blonde in shimmering white satin. "Yes," she said. "Straight from the evening performance. You think she'd at least have the decency to look tired. Not our Maggie. Watch her, she's about to make a grand entrance."

Patrick laughed, for Maggie had flung out her arms, crying *"Darling"* as she ran prettily to Tony. Conversations in the room ceased, heads turned, and even the pianist stopped playing. Everyone watched Maggie fling her arms about Tony's neck. *"Darling,"* she cried again, kissing him on both cheeks, "what a *marvelous* party."

"Isn't she something?" Lucy said. "You'd think she hadn't seen Tony for twenty years. Actresses!"

"Not your favorite people, eh?"

"Oh, they're all right, most of them. This one drives me crazy. Have you met her?"

"Briefly," Patrick replied. "On opening night. Of course it was a madhouse."

"Well, go on over and Tony will do the honors again. I'm going to see how Gran is holding up." Lucy found Elizabeth seated with a small group of friends. "Gran," she said, bending down, "are you having a good time?"

"Indeed I am. You're a lovely hostess, my dear. Come sit next to me. We haven't had a chance to talk."

Lucy plucked another glass of champagne from a tray and then took her place beside Elizabeth. "I didn't mean to chase your friends away, Gran."

"I see them every Wednesday for bridge. I suspect the Ryders cheat. They have signals, although signals are clearly against the rules. Tiresome people, the Ryders. Now tell me, is that blonde woman the one in Tony's play?"

"Yes, that's Maggie Meredith."

"She's very striking. I'd keep my eye on her if I were you. She's far too interested in your husband."

450

"They're friends, that's all."

"Men and women are rarely friends. Who are those other fellows hovering about her?"

"Well, there's Jim Cleeve. He's Tony's old college roommate. There's Paul Donner, an old classmate, Lee Rothman, his producer, Uncle Patrick, and cousin Andrew."

"Andrew should know better," Elizabeth sniffed. "Miss Meredith is young enough to be his granddaughter. But that's what happens when men get near that sort of woman."

"Gran, please. This is a party. *Your* party."

"It was thoughtful of you, my dear. I suppose seventy-five is something of a milestone. There can't be any question that I've seen a good deal of the world. I've seen women like Maggie Meredith. In my day, they weren't received."

"Things change."

"Yes. When I think of Elsie Woodward and that creature her son married. Naturally, poor Elsie makes the best of it. When I think of the Vanderbilts and all their divorces. Yes, things change."

"Perhaps you ought to change the subject, Gran. Elsie Woodward is headed this way."

"Is she? Oh, yes, so she is. . . . Elsie, my dear. How very nice to see you."

Smiling, Lucy went off to mingle with the other guests. At one minute to twelve, she dimmed the lights and an enormous birthday cake was wheeled in—five square tiers of mocha cream with pink and white icing and spun sugar violets. "Happy Birthday" was sung, and then Elizabeth rose to blow out the seventy-five candles. She raised her hand, silencing the applause. "I have a few words," she said in her clear, cool voice. "I'm an old woman now and there are people from my life I would like to remember. To mention by name . . . My late husband Jasper, the finest man I have ever known. My late children Anne, Charlotte, and Ned. Ned's wife Sarah, whom I always thought of as my own . . . I'm an old woman, but not a foolish one. My granddaughter reminded me tonight that things change. Indeed they do. The world is now in the hands of the younger generation. The generation of Josh and his lovely Sallie, of Lucy and her husband Tony. What they will make of it remains to be seen. I would urge them to respect the past and to learn from it. I would urge strength. . . . My generation did not do what was easy. We did what was right."

Applause followed Elizabeth back to her seat. Patrick, looking on, could only shake his head. She doesn't know what a hypocrite she is, he thought to himself. Josh, whose thoughts were similar, turned away in disgust. Tony glared at her, his eyes bitter with recollection. The old witch, he thought, the lying old witch. Lucy alone seemed to take Elizabeth's words seriously. She felt the rebuke, as she had so many times before, and she touched her hand to Sarah's necklace. After some moments she slipped out to the terrace, staring up at the frosty winter stars. "I can't do what's right," she murmured into the darkness. "I haven't the courage."

All the guests had gone and the Jenningses climbed the staircase to their bedroom. Lucy was quiet, clutching Tony's hand. Every now and then she looked at him, quickly looking away, "What did you think of Gran's little speech?" she asked finally. "You didn't say."

"You know very well what I think of dear old Gran. 'We did what was right,'" he mimicked.

"That's such bull. Oh, it struck a responsive chord in her friends. In all the other sainted old ladies of Fifth Avenue. Promise me you won't ever become one of them."

"There isn't much chance of that."

Tony opened the bedroom door, stepping aside as Lucy entered. He switched on a lamp and then removed his dinner jacket, tossing it in the direction of the nearest chair. "Missed again," he laughed.

Lucy picked up the jacket. "It was a nice party," she said. "Wasn't it a nice party?"

"It was great. I'll overlook the fact that every guy in the room had his eye on you."

"Until Maggie Meredith made her entrance."

"Ah, yes, Maggie. Does she still get under your skin?"

"'*Darling*, what a *marvelous* party.'"

"Meow, meow." Tony went to Lucy, catching her hand in his. "Come with me," he said. He led her across the room, stopping in front of the full-length mirror. "You have nothing to worry about, darling. Look at yourself. . . . Look at that," he added, unzipping her black velvet gown to the waist. Now his lips moved over her naked shoulders, his hands over her naked breasts. "Every man here tonight wanted to do this to you. . . . And this . . . And this."

"Tony," she whispered. "Oh, Tony."

"But I'm the one who's going to take you to bed." He stripped away the rest of her clothing and carried her to the large four-poster. "I'm the one who's going to make love to you. All through the night."

Lucy helped him undress, flinging his clothes to the floor. She gathered him into her arms, murmuring against his bare flesh, calling his name. She felt the fire of his touch. She felt wave after wave of sweet pleasure, and when she closed her eyes silvery lights leapt and whirled in the dark. "Tony," she cried, and it was a cry of joy.

Dawn was streaking the windows when Lucy awoke. She saw Tony smiling down at her, his black hair tousled over his brow. She smiled too, reaching for his hand. "I had the loveliest sleep," she said.

"Well deserved. You're fantastic, Mrs. Jennings."

"Don't tell the guys in the locker room."

"Never."

"Couldn't you sleep?"

"I've been thinking about something, darling. I've been thinking how wonderful it would be if we started a baby tonight. I know your reservations about theater life, but we can solve those problems. I have faith in us, Lucy. All the faith in the world." Tony said nothing more, for her eyes had clouded. The veil's dropped again, he thought to himself, wondering if even now Colin Averill was in her mind. Slowly, he swung his legs to the floor, fumbling for a cigarette. He watched the smoke curl toward the ceiling, then bent his head down. "Did I tell you I asked Scotty to spend part of the summer with us? I meant to tell you. I must have forgotten."

"Uncle Patrick mentioned it. It's a fine idea, Tony. He's a nice little boy."

"Well, the Cape is a good place for kids. And it's time Scotty learned to sail."

"He's only eight."

"Just the right age." Tony stood, tying the belt of his robe. "I'd like to have Ellen too," he said, "but a four-year-old may be more than we can handle."

"Have you decided whether you're going to do stock this summer?"

"No, I'm going to relax. It's the last chance I'll have for a while. It looks as if I'll be directing the Seaton comedy in the fall. Frank and Lee are raising the money. And then . . . well, I'd planned to surprise you, but you'll read about it in the papers. MGM's bought *Ghost Stories*. They bought a package—the play, Wally, Maggie, and me. We'll be going to Hollywood next year."

"Hollywood!" Lucy sat up, tucking the sheets around her. "Tony, that's so exciting. Your first movie."

"My last, if I mess it up."

"But you won't. You're the best director in the country, the world."

"The world's a big place, Lucy."

"You—you don't seem very happy about all this."

"Don't I?"

"Tony, can't you see how impossible it would be if we had a child now? Your career is just—"

"Yes, my career." He turned. They gazed at each other and in that moment they read each other's thoughts. They both knew that something had been lost between them, that a part of them had been damaged. They both knew that the subject of children would not be mentioned again. "Hooray for Hollywood," he said.

Chapter Twenty-Two

Tony and Lucy arrived in California at the close of 1953. The Korean War had ended but the Cold War raged on, as did the Communist witch hunts that would destroy so many innocent lives. In Hollywood that meant the blacklist; it meant fear and suspicion and, sometimes, friend turning against friend. "Everyone's scared," Tony wrote in a letter to Josh. "It's contagious. I've been here a week and I'm already looking over my shoulder."

There were other pressures in Hollywood during the early 1950s, for the film industry was coping with the enormous popularity of television. "Movies Are Better Than Ever" was the industry's rallying cry, but still millions of Americans sat down each night to their favorite television programs, to *Burns and Allen* and *I Love Lucy* and *The Jack Benny Show*.

Hollywood was changing. In time, little would be left of the old Hollywood and nothing of the old studio system, though to Tony this system was a miracle unto itself. He marveled at the armies of set designers and makeup artists and wardrobe women and prop men who were almost instantly available. He marveled at the armies of contract players who had been trained and nurtured by studio personnel. His eyes were as wide as a child's when he drove through the acres of back lots, for there he saw scenes of New York, of Paris, of London, reproduced in perfect detail. He saw scenes of small-town America, too, taking special and childlike pleasure in the sight of Andy Hardy's house. "The whole thing is simply incredible," he said to Lucy. "Sound stages big enough to land a plane. All the technical assistance in the world. Actors who can do anything on cue— ride, fence, dance a gavotte. Special effects people who can give you an earthquake or a tornado or a talking horse. It's simply incredible!"

Lucy had her own studio tour, accompanied by Alice. She saw the sights Tony had seen and she understood his enthusiasm. "There's magic here," she remarked. "It's everybody's fantasy come true." She lunched a few times with Tony at the studio commissary, trying not to gape at the stars who sat at nearby tables. She watched the first day's shooting of *Ghost Stories in the Dark*, but she felt she was in the way and did not go back after that. She felt out of place, disoriented; quietly, she retreated to their rented Malibu house.

She spent her days alone, for Tony left every morning at six and seldom returned before dark. She filled the time as best she could. She took her cameras to the beach, photographing golden California children at play, photographing splendid sunsets over the Pacific. At night she fixed martinis for her exhausted husband, then put steaks or shrimp on their fancy new grill. On weekends they went to parties, lavish parties at lavish mansions in Beverly Hills and Brentwood. She was charmed by Jimmy Stewart, awed by Clark Gable, impressed by the glacial beauty of the young star Grace Kelly. She was treated kindly, but again she felt out of place. She was aware that she was only "the wife of," an accessory who had no role of her own. "All wives are extras in this town," she was told by another Hollywood wife. "You're expected to dress well, entertain well, overlook hubby's flings, and keep your mouth *shut*."

She repeated the conversation to Tony. He laughed, but she was not reassured. She sensed a threat, and as always her thoughts turned to Maggie Meredith. "They spend so much damn time together," she said to Alice one breezy evening in January. "They're together at the studio all day, but that's not enough. Oh, no. Three out of five nights she calls here asking Tony to come over. He has yet to refuse. He jumps into his car and off he goes."

"That's his job, Lucy. Maggie's nervous. She puts up a good front, but I watch her on the set every day and I can tell you she's a bundle of nerves. There's a lot riding on this picture for her. She wants to be a movie star."

"So?"

"So she's relying on Tony. She needs him. And right now he needs her. He's getting a great performance out of her, Lucy. He's managed to keep her calm, to make her feel secure. Don't forget it's the first movie for both of them. It's not easy."

"I know it isn't. I just can't help thinking that she sees Tony as something more than her director."

"If she does, it'll pass when she starts her next picture or her next play. You're silly to worry. She doesn't mean anything to Tony. Haven't you ever noticed how his eyes light up when you come into the room? After almost eight years of marriage, that's pretty good."

"You always find the right thing to say, Alice."

"I say what I think. There were times I had to fudge

458

a little when I was dealing with Kaz's clients. I guess there've been times at the studio, too. You have to be careful what you say out here. But with friends it's different."

"I'm afraid I take advantage of our friendship," Lucy sighed. "I tell you all my problems and never ask about yours."

"Oh, everything's okay with me. Tony's a great boss. I like my job. At first I thought the traveling would be a problem, but Jerry doesn't mind. It makes him proud that he can look after himself. He's doing wood carving now," Alice went on. "He carves duck decoys. They're beautiful. The best part is he's talking about maybe starting a little business. A business from home. I'm all for it."

"You're quite a couple, Alice. I don't know many people who could have made the adjustments you and Jerry made. I've never heard a single complaint, either."

"Well, we both realized dwelling on the past wouldn't do any good. You can drive yourself crazy thinking of what might have been. . . . It's harder for Jerry. He's the one in the wheelchair. The worst of it was that we couldn't have children. He's from a big family and we'd planned a big family of our own. But once he accepted the truth, the rest was easy."

Lucy was quiet, gazing across the beach to the moon-flecked waters of the Pacific. She watched the rolling waves, the foamy surf lapping at the shore. "Men always want children, don't they?" she said, sipping her drink. "That's just how they are."

"Not always. My father would have been glad if none of us had been born. There are more of him than the other kind. Kaz told me he never wanted children. He wanted to be free. A free spirit," Alice added with a smile. "And I guess he was. I wonder what he'd make of all this. Hollywood, I mean."

"He'd love the glamour and the extravagance. It's fun. Watching Joan Crawford make an entrance at a party is fun. She's even better than Maggie. At least so far."

"Do yourself a favor, Lucy. Stop worrying about Maggie."

"As a matter of fact, that was my New Year's resolution."

"Stick to it."

Lucy smiled. She stood, sliding open the glass doors. "Let's go inside," she said. "Aren't you starving? I certainly am. We'll get dinner started."

"Don't you want to wait for Tony?"

"He can catch up with us. . . . I'm never really sure when to expect him these nights. He's a busy man."

"Another drink?" Maggie asked, slipping behind the bar of her rented Beverly Hills house. "A little one?"

"No, thanks," Tony replied. "I'm driving."

"You're such a good boy. You don't mind if I have another?"

"If the camera doesn't mind, I don't mind."

"Oh," Maggie wailed, "that's mean. You mustn't be mean to me, darling. You'll make me cry and then my eyes will be all red and awful. I'll look a fright."

"Not very likely."

"Is that a compliment, darling?"

"I suppose it is. You look lovely tonight."

Maggie twirled around, showing off long, graceful hostess pajamas of creamy white satin. "I knew you'd approve," she said. "I bought this outfit just for you."

"Sorry, not my size."

"You're being mean again," Maggie said, sinking down beside Tony on the couch. "Why don't my feminine wiles work on you? Tell me why."

"I love my wife. You know that."

"Do I? I've been paying attention, darling, and I've had the strangest feeling that there's trouble in paradise. I can't quite put my finger on it," she said, putting her hand on Tony's arm. "But something is *just* a wee bit out of kilter."

"You're wrong, Maggie," he declared, though to himself he admitted the truth. Things aren't the same between us, he thought. Maybe I realized I couldn't fight Colin Averill's memory anymore. Maybe Lucy realized that, too. The past. It's so damned hard to fight the past. . . . And yet I love her. "I love her," he murmured.

"Yes, of course you *love* her. But it's as if you're *sad* about her in some strange way. And it's as if *she's* sad about you. It's all *terribly* fascinating. If this were a play—"

"It's not. You're wasting your time looking for hidden meanings. You're wasting your time on me. Not that it matters. The picture wraps next month and then I head back East. You, on the other hand, stay here and become the new Carole Lombard."

"Carole Lombard?" Maggie cried happily. "Is that what they're saying?"

Tony laughed. "Among other things," he replied. "The word is you have a very bright future here in tinseltown. Don't pretend to be surprised. You've seen the rushes. You know you're giving one hell of a performance. You know the camera loves you."

"But what about the Carole Lombard thing you said?"

"Well, you can do both drama and comedy. You're as beautiful as she was. Classy, but not forbidding.

And you make men wonder."

"Wonder what?"

"Does she or doesn't she? Put out, that is."

"Why, Tony Jennings, I should wash your mouth out with soap."

"First you have to decide which character you're playing tonight. The seductress or the innocent ingenue."

"Both. Or I would, if you'd give me the chance. . . . Darling, why are you going back to New York? I know Metro wants to sign you for another picture. Everybody knows that."

"Perhaps, but I don't want to do another picture right away. I'm tired. I've been working ridiculous hours. Really ridiculous hours when you add in all the driving time. I'm not used to being so tied to a car. I'd like to come out to do a picture every once in a while. I don't want to live here. This town is rough on marriages."

"Rougher than *New York?*"

"No contest," Tony said, smiling. "The film community is a very small world, and everybody in it talks, eats, and sleeps pictures. Wives are irrelevant. There are just too many pressures, Maggie."

"Pressures never bothered you before. Are you sure that's all there is to it?"

"Let's say I miss the easy give-and-take of New York. I miss sitting around with my friends, arguing politics to all hours."

"Politics! That's *so* boring. Are you afraid John Wayne or Ronald Reagan will call you a pinko?"

"No," Tony laughed again. "I'm not the pinko type. Besides, I actually fought for my country in a war. John Wayne and Ronald Reagan did all their fighting in the movies. . . . No, Maggie, it's not any one thing. I've enjoyed myself here but it's time to go home. End of story."

"You're deserting me."

"You won't even remember my name once the picture opens. You're going to be a very big star, Maggie my girl. I knew it when you read for *Count to Ten*. I know it now."

"You discovered me, darling."

"You can thank me when you pick up your Oscar."

"Honestly, Tony, aren't you *ever* serious?"

"Only on alternate Thursdays."

"You're in luck," Maggie said. "This happens to be an alternate Thursday." She twined her arms around his neck, drawing him to her. She kissed him, drawing him closer still. "I want you," she murmured. "Don't you want me?"

Quite suddenly his hands were in her hair, his lips on her throat, her mouth. He felt her breasts straining against the creamy satin of her pajamas; he felt the wild beating of his own heart. "Maggie," he said uncertainly. He watched as she pulled the pajama top over her head and tossed it aside. Now she was rubbing against him like a cat; now he was kissing her, kissing all the warm, willing curves of her body. "Do it," he heard her say, and it was as if her voice awakened him from a dream. His hands fell away. He sat up, taking a great breath.

"Tony?"

"No, we can't."

"I don't understand. I thought—"

"I'm sorry, Maggie. Truly sorry. This was entirely my fault and I apologize."

"A gentleman to the end."

With a sigh, Tony rose. He retrieved the pajama top and brought it to Maggie. "You'll catch cold," he said.

"Okay, but you don't know what you're missing."

"Maggie, I love my wife. I love her. There are times when I wish I didn't, God help me, but all that is beside the point. I'm sorry, and now I'm going home."

"This will happen again, darling. When it does, I won't let you stop."

"No. No, it won't happen again. Because it's not the answer to anything. For either of us. We don't need easy conquests, Maggie. We're better than that."

"Easy conquests!" She cried, leaping to her feet. *"Easy conquests?"*

"Sorry," he smiled. "Poor choice of words." He was still smiling when Maggie's hand shot out and slapped his face. "I guess I deserved that," he said quietly.

"Get out!"

"I'm going. Good night, Maggie."

"Bastard! Get out and don't come back!"

Tony picked up his briefcase, making his way to the paneled hall. He opened the door, stepping out into the breezy night. He heard the trees rustling against the house. He turned, and in that moment he heard the sound of china hurled against the door. Sighing again, he got into his car. It's going to be fun on the set tomorrow, he thought. *Damn*, it's going to be a battle royal.

He had driven a couple of miles when he realized that Maggie's perfume was all over him. He stopped the car at the nearest motel, washing away the scent, the blotches of pink lipstick. "Like a guilty schoolboy," he muttered, returning to the MG. He gunned the engine and drove off toward home.

Lucy was at the door when he arrived. If she sensed that something was wrong, she made no comment. "Did you miss me?" she asked.

"You'll never know how much," he replied, taking her in his arms. "You'll never know how glad I am to be home."

Rumors followed Tony back to New York that winter of 1955—rumors of open hostility between him and his star Maggie Meredith, of shouting matches on the set, of costly production delays. But these rumors were forgotten when the picture opened, for it was a huge success with both the critics and movie-going public. He was immediately offered another picture, an offer that he declined. He did a play instead, a comedy that ran a respectable six months. He had a flop the next fall and then two smash hits in a row. By the winter of 1958 he was an established and respected director, a "money director" whose work was said to guarantee long runs.

Lucy's scrapbooks now filled a whole corner of the study, for proudly she clipped every word written about Tony. She had a collection of theater programs and of opening night ticket stubs. She had posters from each of his plays and from his movie. "I think we'll have to call this the Tony Jennings Museum," she said one spring morning. "We can charge admission."

"To Mother and Dad perhaps," Tony laughed. "They're pushovers."

"Don't be modest. You have your fans."

"I'd rather my *fans* spend their money at the theater. That's the idea, you know. . . . Come," he said, holding out his hand. "Elsa has breakfast on the table and I'm hungry. Blueberry pancakes today. Doesn't that make your mouth water?"

"I don't know if my waistline can take any more of Elsa's breakfasts."

"I love your waistline," Tony remarked. "And all your other lines, too. Yum, yum," he said, brushing his hand lightly across her breasts. "Delicious."

"You're so fresh. What will Elsa think?"

"She'll think I'm crazy about my wife."

"Or just plain crazy," Lucy laughed.

They walked into the sun-splashed breakfast room and sat down at the table. Tony glanced briefly at the morning paper, then set it aside. "Anything interesting in the mail?" he asked.

"Bills and invitations . . . Do you want to spend Easter weekend with the Cleeves in Westport?"

"I'd rather spend it with you on the Cape. We can take the whole week, the whole month."

"Don't you have to start casting the new play?"

"There's plenty of time," Tony replied. "Let's take the month, darling. Let's be beachcombers." He drank his juice, gazing at Lucy over the rim of the glass. "We've earned a vacation, don't you agree? I haven't stopped working since we got back from California. And you've been busy putting together the pictures for your book. Your masterpiece. When am I going to be allowed a peek?"

"Soon, I promise. At least I finally figured out what was wrong. I had too much stuff and no focus. . . . Now I'm thinking about calling it *Coastlines*. I can use my photos from the Cape and Maine and Malibu and Big Sur. How does that sound?"

"They're spectacular photos, Lucy."

"Yes, they're good. The lighthouse pictures . . ." Her thought was interrupted by the telephone. "I'll get it," she said. "I'll get it, Elsa."

"Yes, missus."

"Hello? Oh, hello, Josh. It's rather early. . . . No, I haven't. Why? I mean . . . Yes, he's here. . . . But . . .

466

What did you say? I don't . . . Oh, my God. My God, are you sure?"

"What is it, darling?" Tony asked. He saw her back stiffen. He saw her hand clench the counter and he frowned. "Lucy, what's wrong?"

"Nothing . . . Josh, I'll call you later. . . . Yes . . . Yes . . . I'll call you later." She replaced the receiver, turning slowly away. "It's—it's something about the Galleries," she murmured. "There's some sort of problem. Josh . . . well, he wants me to sign some papers."

"You're white as a sheet, Lucy. What's going on?"

"Nothing. Nothing important anyway. It's about the Galleries." She sank into her chair, hiding her nervous hands in her lap. "You know I never understand a word Josh says when he talks about the Galleries."

"You look ill."

"I'm not. I'm fine, Tony. Really I am. My stomach is a little upset, that's all. I should have taken something."

"I'll fix you a Bromo."

"No, don't bother. I'll—I can fix it. Have your breakfast." Lucy stood, rushing from the room. "I won't be long," she called.

Tony's frown deepened. He knew that Lucy had lied, though he could not imagine why. He rose, thinking to call Josh, then sat down again. He did not appear to notice the tray of pancakes Elsa set before him, nor did he hear her pleasant chatter as she returned to the kitchen. He sat very still, trying to piece together Lucy's part of the telephone conversation. Again he thought about calling Josh and again he changed his mind. After several moments he picked up the newspaper, glancing idly through the sports section. He was turning to the business section when a name on the obituary page caught his attention. He folded the paper and began to read: "Sir Colin Averill, noted British historian and sportsman, died Tuesday in England after being thrown from his horse during a point-to-point race. He was thirty-nine years old and resided in London and Aldcross Village."

Tony lighted a cigarette. Once more he lowered his eyes to the paper, reading about Colin's achievements at Oxford, in the RAF during the war, and later in the field of history. He read of cups won in various racing events. At the end of the obituary he read: "Sir Colin is survived by his mother Lady Mary; his wife Lady Helen; three sons, Charles, William, and David; and a brother Harry, all of England."

Quietly, Tony closed the paper. He could take no pleasure in Colin's death, but he wondered if now Lucy would be freed of the memories that had haunted her for so long. We have a second chance, he thought, and with the thought, a weight seemed to lift from his shoulders. He looked up as Lucy came back into the room. "Are you feeling better?" he asked.

"Oh, yes. I'm fine."

He gazed at her pale, strained face, her veiled eyes. He reached across the table and took her hand. "Are you up to a little breakfast? How about some toast?"

"Maybe later. You go ahead. Don't wait for me. The pancakes look wonderful."

"I think your stomach ache is contagious. I'm not hungry now either." Tony dropped his napkin on the table. He smiled. "I can stay home today," he said. "Or do you feel like being alone?"

Lucy heard the concern in his voice. She looked at him and then swiftly looked away, assailed by guilt. Tell him the truth and have it over with, she silently urged herself. *Tell him.* "I . . . there's something . . . I mean I . . . Tony, I wanted to . . ." She shook her head, staring vacantly into space. "I don't deserve you," she murmured after a moment.

"Lucy, what's wrong?"

"Nothing."

"You sounded as if you were about to tell me something. I'm here, darling. I'm listening. You know you can tell me anything, anything at all. What's troubling you?"

"Oh, I'm in one of my moods today. I don't seem to be making much sense. Don't worry, Tony, it will pass."

"Then there isn't anything you want to tell me?"

"I was just babbling."

"I see." He stood, pushing his chair back. "I might as well get to the office," he said. "Shall I get us out of Tom Cantrell's party tonight?"

"No, don't. Frank and Lee want us there. Isn't Mr. Cantrell one of their biggest backers?"

"One of the *world's* biggest idiots, too."

"I don't mind going, Tony. I promise I'll pull myself together."

"All right, we'll go." He bent, kissing her cheek. "See you later."

Lucy watched him walk from the room. As soon as he had gone she picked up the paper and turned to the obituary page. "Colin," she whispered, her chaotic thoughts leaping back and forth in time. She remembered her very first glimpse of him and her last. She remembered the euphoria of first love and the sorrow of parting. She remembered a boat ride on a foggy day, a kiss stolen in the darkness, a tiny blue silk butterfly hidden between the pages of a book. All these memories she had carried with her for years, but now she knew she had to say good-bye to the past, to

Colin and what had been. She put her head in her hands, feeling both sadness and relief. It's over, she told herself. It's finally over.

Tony, his face impassive, stood in the doorway. He watched Lucy, pondering the changes in her expression, in her every gesture. He saw her drop her head to her hands, a gesture he could only interpret as despair. Abruptly, he turned on his heel and left the apartment.

"Tell me when you want to leave," Tony said later that night, "and I'll make our excuses to Tom Cantrell."

"We have to stay a reasonable length of time, don't we?"

"We don't have to do anything. Cantrell is a pain in the ass. He's a bore, he's grabby with women, and he's usually drunk. Keep your distance, Lucy."

"Gladly."

"And there's one more thing. His ancestors were part of the Old South. Whatever you do, don't let him get started on the Civil War and Reconstruction. Especially if he's been drinking."

"Touchy subjects?"

"In a way," Tony replied. "He'll tell you, in all sincerity, the the Ku Klux Klan was really a civic association and that slavery was really in the best interests of the Negro."

"Why on earth do Frank and Lee put up with him? Money?"

"Cantrell's been a major backer of most of their shows. But there's more to it." Tony opened the taxi door, helping Lucy out. "He doesn't interfere, you see. He signs checks and then fades into the background. All he wants for his money is a set of choice opening night tickets . . . and our attendance at his damned parties."

Lucy was quiet as she walked with Tony through the marble lobby of the apartment building. She glanced curiously at him, for there had been no mistaking the sharpness in his tone. "If Mr. Cantrell upsets you so . . ."

"He doesn't upset me. He's a fool and fools make me mad, but that's life."

"*Something's* upsetting you," Lucy persisted, stepping into the elevator. "Tell me."

Tony looked at her. She seemed tired, and beneath the skillfully applied makeup, pale. Mourning dear Colin, he thought to himself. "We all have our moods," he said. He said nothing more during the ride to the penthouse. When the elevator doors opened, he took Lucy's arm and steered her into Tom Cantrell's foyer. He gazed at the sea of guests in the vast living room beyond, sniffing the mingled scents of flowers and cigarette smoke and liquor and women's perfume. A wry smile edged his mouth, for somewhere in the crowd a pianist was playing "Isn't It Romantic." He shook his head, looking again at Lucy. "Let the games begin," he murmured.

"Tony . . ."

"Good evening, Matthew," he said to the Negro butler. "Where is our beloved host?"

"Coming this way, sir."

"Ah, yes, so he is. . . . Good evening, Tom. Wonderful party. Lucy, may I present Tom Cantrell? My wife, Lucy."

"A great pleasure, Mrs. Jennings. I'm delighted you were able to be here tonight."

"Thank you. Please call me Lucy."

"Delighted. Come along, you two. You probably know most of the people here. Probably know them

471

better than I do. Theater folk."

"We *love* theater folk," Tony said.

Lucy pinched his arm but he did not appear to notice. Confused, she turned back to their host. "You have a charming apartment, Tom. What marvelous views."

"That's why I bought it. Of course it's spacious, too. I needed room for my collection."

"Collection?"

"Well, I fancy myself something of an historian," Tom replied, slipping his hand under Lucy's arm. "I have a collection of Civil War relics. My people were from the South. They would say the War Between the States."

"I was once interested in history myself."

"Were you?" Tony asked. "Twelve years of marriage and I'm still learning things about you."

"Oh, it was long ago."

"Tony, may I borrow your wife? I think Lucy might enjoy my collection. Historian to historian."

"What do you say, Lucy?"

"Well, maybe just a little look."

Tony watched them walk off. He turned, plunging into the crowd to exchange a few words with the people he knew. After a while he went to the bar. "Double Scotch," he said, carrying his drink to where Lee Rothman stood. "Having fun?" he asked.

"I hate these parties like the plague, but what can I do? Where's Lucy?"

"Viewing Tom's collection. She and Tom make a nice couple don't you think? They're both so blond and pretty. . . . The bastard's going to make a pass at her before the evening's out."

"And you didn't warn her?"

"I warned her," Tony replied. "But dear Tom said the magic word."

"What magic word?"

"*Historian.*"

Lee frowned, studying Tony's closed face, his brooding blue eyes. "There's something bothering you, kid," he declared. "I can tell. You're not yourself tonight. What's the matter?"

There's been a death in the family, thought Tony. He sipped his drink, glancing around the room. "I've been mulling an offer," he said finally. "A two-picture offer from Universal. A Rock Hudson soap opera and the Inge screenplay. I'm going to take it, Lee. I want to get away. We open *Yesterday's Children* in October, and then I'm on a plane west."

"Sure, we say October, but if we have trouble on the road . . ."

"There won't be any trouble on the road, not with this play. It's a solid domestic drama. You'll be up to your ears in theater parties. And I'll be in sunny California."

"Maybe that's not such a bad idea. Make peace with Maggie. We want her for Wally's new play."

"*Winter Moon* is two years off, Lee. I'm not going to worry about it now."

"You have better things to worry about?"

Tony swallowed the last of his drink. "Ghosts," he said. "I'm worried about ghosts." He went to the bar and got another Scotch, sipping it as he moved from group to group. He heard the latest gossip, laughed at the latest jokes, and told a few jokes of his own. He flirted harmlessly with the women who came his way, looking around for Lucy but in vain. It was past midnight when he wandered out onto the terrace. He heard a muffled cry and he turned. In the shadowy light he saw Lucy struggling with Tom. "Let her go," he called, his voice cold and hard. He grabbed Tom by the collar, swinging him around. "Bastard," he said, his fist crashing into Tom's chin. "Want some more?" he asked. "Get up and we'll do it again."

"Tony," Lucy said, "don't. I'm all right. Everything's all right now."

"Is it?"

"Please, Tony."

"This wasn't what it looked like, old man," Tom managed to say. "You misunderstood."

Tony pulled him to his feet, and once more there was the sickening sound of a clenched fist finding its target. "Another word and I'll break your jaw," Tony warned. "What it looked like was *exactly* what it was. Now apologize to my wife."

Tom pressed his handkerchief to his bleeding mouth. "I'm very sorry, Lucy," he said, sober now. "I'm afraid I . . . had too much to drink. I do apologize. I meant no harm."

"Tony, please let's go home. *Please.*" She took his hand, pulling him toward the door. "Tony, for heaven's sake."

"Thanks for a lovely evening, Tom. We must all get together soon again." He straightened his tie, following Lucy back into the living room. He saw that the other guests had not noticed the commotion and he smiled. "No fuss, no muss," he said.

"Tony, I really would like to get out of here."

They said their good-byes, several minutes later entering the elevator. There was silence as they rode downstairs, relief as they settled into a taxicab. "Quite a night," Tony remarked.

"You scared me to death. I've never seen you that way before. I've never seen you so angry."

"I suppose I'm tired of seeing my wife in another man's arms."

Lucy's head snapped up. "Tired of seeing . . .

474

What in the world are you talking about?''

What *am* I talking about, thought Tony. That was a slip, a Freudian slip. "I meant," he corrected himself, "that seeing you struggling with Cantrell was the last straw. He's a pig when he drinks. I wish you'd listened to me."

"So do I. But he didn't seem drunk. He sounded all right. He looked all right. . . . We were having a perfectly pleasant conversation, and then the next thing I knew he had me cornered. I'd just reached behind me for a flower pot when you appeared on the scene. My knight in shining armor . . . I can see you're still angry, Tony. I'm sorry. . . . I keep thinking this is the kind of thing we used to laugh about. We're not laughing now, are we?''

Tony had no ready answer. He lighted a cigarette, turning his head toward the window. He felt Lucy's hand creep to his shoulder and he turned back to her, smiling, but still he said nothing. Her hand dropped wearily to her lap. She lowered her eyes, her silence matching his own.

There were other silences between them in the weeks that followed. Tony was busy with a new play, though he seemed to take small pleasure in it. He seemed tired, distracted, lost in thoughts he did not share. Lucy was busy also. She spent long hours in her darkroom and later at her desk, where she wrote the text for her forthcoming book. She accompanied Tony to the New Haven tryout, but she left before the company moved on to Philadelphia and Boston. Her abrupt departure fueled rumors of trouble in the Jennings marriage, rumors that began to see print in Broadway gossip columns. These rumors she denied to Elizabeth and Josh and her friends; she did not deny them to herself.

Her nightmares returned. In her sleep she saw a shadowy figure pursuing Sarah along a darkened road. She saw stark black trees with branches like arms reaching out to ensnare the terrified young woman. She saw swirling black mists, a blackened sky. Again the shadowy figure appeared and now she saw his face—Colin's face—his features frozen in death.

She awoke screaming from these nightmares but there was no one to comfort her, for Tony was in California. They spoke on the telephone twice each day, having strained conversations in which nothing was really said. She made several trips to see him, quick trips that did more to keep up appearances than to help their marriage. To friends and family she continued to deny any problem, denials belied by her hollow eyes, her unsteady hands. In her private moments she faced the truth, though this truth she could not put into words. She could not define what had gone wrong, could not affix a name to it. Unless the name is Colin, she thought, wondering if Colin had always stood between them.

Tony came home to attend the publication party for her book *Coastlines*. He seemed truly proud of her achievement but he seemed distant, too, as if he were viewing events from across a wife gulf. His manner weighed heavily on her, eclipsing the happiness she should have felt, eclipsing any sense of triumph or success. She was relieved when the party ended. Arriving back home, she tossed her coat and purse aside and fell into a chair. "Well, that's that," she said.

"Yes," Tony quietly agreed. "Did you hear what people were saying? They were calling you another Ansel Adams. I'm glad your work is getting the respect it deserves."

"At least with my work I know where I stand."

"Meaning?"

"Tony, what's happened to us? Ever since that night at Tom Cantrell's we've been drifting farther and farther apart. I remember you were in an odd mood even before we got to his place. Then there was that awful scene. And then . . . well, we just haven't been the same since."

"You've noticed."

"Of course I've noticed."

"You haven't said anything until now."

"No," Lucy sighed. "At first I made excuses. I told myself you were preoccupied with work. When that wore thin, I told myself you were tired from all the traveling you were doing. I even used your uncle Bart's death as an excuse. . . . But I suppose I knew it wasn't any of those things. I'm frightened, Tony."

"Why?"

"Why? We're in trouble, aren't we?"

He sat down and lighted a cigarette. His face was somber, and his eyes, moving slowly around the bedroom, were dimmed with worry. He had not been able to forget Lucy's despairing expression when she read of Colin's death, nor could he forget it now. He was tempted to blurt out the truth but this he knew he could not do, for he was frightened also—frightened of rash declarations, of words that, once spoken, could never be taken back. "I can't explain it," he replied after a long silence. "I don't feel . . . There are times when I don't feel close to you, when I don't feel I know you. . . . Maybe it's just some mood I'm going through. Maybe it has something to do with turning forty. . . . Yes, I guess we're in trouble."

Lucy felt a sudden chill. She clasped her hands together, hunching her shoulders as if against an icy wind. I have to stay calm, she warned herself. I have to stay calm or I'll go crazy. "Tony," she said, her voice unnaturally high, "I'm closer to you than anyone on Earth. I've given you all I have to give. I *love* you. You must know that."

He ground out his cigarette. "Yes, I know that."

"Then . . ."

"Sometimes you're like a child, Lucy. You think that if you say I love you, everything will be all right. This isn't a fairy tale or a movie. This is that complicated thing called marriage. Two people against the whole damned world. But when one of those people feels shut out—"

"I don't shut you out, Tony."

"Not often, but often enough. I can look at you and see you're a million miles away. I can see something in your eyes—some secret pain. And then the veil drops. . . . My mysterious shadow dance girl," he said with a bitter laugh. "I used to call you that. Remember? But we're grown up now and mysteries aren't what they used to be."

Lucy was shivering. Fear clawed her heart, for she sensed where this conversation was heading. Her eyes darted wildly about. She saw Tony rise and she flung herself from the chair, rushing to him. "Please," she said, her hands fast on his shoulders. "Please, Tony. Things will be different. I promise they will."

"I'm not sure that's a promise you can make. You're so used to turning inward, Lucy. You're so used to hiding."

"I'll change."

"You're doing it again, Lucy. You're deliberately missing the point. I don't want you to change. I want you to be who you are. Warts and all, without the evasions, the things you hold back. But that takes strength. The worst part of this is that you *have* strength. I see it in your work. I see it when you jolly Elizabeth along and then do as you please. . . . I *don't* see it in our marriage." He took her hands from his shoulders. He took a step, two, and then her hands were on him again. She kissed him, pressing her lips, her body, to his. He responded, but a few moments later he stepped back. "No," he said. "I want you, Lucy. I'll want you till I'm dead and buried in my grave. But we can't solve our problems that way."

"Then where are we?"

"I don't know."

Lucy searched his face. Slowly, very slowly, her hands fell away. "Oh, I think you do," she said in a flat, raspy voice. She walked unsteadily to the nearest chair and sank into it. "I think you do," she said again.

"All right, if you want the truth. It might be a good idea to take a break from each other."

"You mean a separation, don't you?" she asked, hugging her arms around her waist. "Who's being evasive now?"

"It doesn't have to be anything formal. Just a—"

"Just a separation."

Tony thrust his hands into his pockets. He gazed at Lucy's pale, stricken face and he sighed. "A separation then," he conceded. "We need time to sort things out. If we go on this way, we'll lose it all."

"You've made up your mind?"

"I don't know what else to do." He went to where she sat, lightly stroking her cold cheek. "It can't be a surprise to you, Lucy. You said yourself we've been drifting apart."

"I should have kept my mouth shut. I would have, if there hadn't been all that champagne at the party. . . . What—what do we do now?"

"I'll go to the club for a while."

"I see."

"Lucy . . ."

"No, please don't say anymore. I—I couldn't bear it."

"Do you want me to call someone to come stay with you? Sallie? Alice? Maybe you shouldn't be alone. . . ." He saw her flinch, as if from a blow, and he bit down on his lip. "I'm sorry, Lucy," he said, his own voice catching. "I just don't know what else to do."

She said nothing, for she knew there was nothing more to say. The silence deepened, broken only by the ticking of a clock. She stared straight ahead and she could almost hear Sarah's voice saying, "Old sins cast long shadows." And old lies, she thought, cast the longest shadows of all. She felt a terrible heaviness in her arms and legs, a lethargy that rooted her to her chair. She saw Tony start toward the dressing room, but neither with word nor gesture did she try to stop him. She heard a closet door open; she heard the sliding of drawers, the thump of a suitcase as it was thrown down. With great effort she pulled herself out of the chair and made her uncertain way across the room. She snatched up a pretty blue afghan from the foot of the bed and tossed it over her shoulders. "Do you have everything?" she asked when Tony reappeared.

"Lucy, I don't want to leave this way."

"What way?"

"With you huddled in a blanket, looking like death. I'm not going to Mars, only to the club. And it isn't forever."

"I know."

"Will you—will you be all right?"

"I'm tired. I want to sleep."

Tony drew a breath. "I'll call you in the morning."

"I'll be here."

She watched him go. Tears burned behind her eyes but would not fall; her lips parted but no sound came. Moments passed and still she stood there, staring at the door. When finally she admitted to herself that Tony had gone, she ran to the bathroom and was sick.

They did not see each other during the next three months. Tony went into rehearsals for *Winter Moon*, the play that would mark Maggie Meredith's return to Broadway. Battling with his star and besieged by the press, he worked sixteen-hour days, losing himself and his problems in work.

For Lucy, work became an obsession. She left the Sutton Place apartment early each morning, taking her cameras all over the city. She photographed the many splendors of Central Park, the snug serenity of Gramercy Park, the expanse of Washington Square. Parks, she decided, would be the theme of her next book.

She arrived home each evening in time for Tony's phone call, but then she retreated into her darkroom, remaining there until well past midnight. She was tired when she crept into her bed, but sleep did not come easily. Often she rose before dawn, thinking of Tony, longing for him. She wanted to run into his arms, to tell him the truth and make everything right, but the irrational fear that had held her hostage for so many years was with her still. In defeat as much as in despair, she paced her lonely room, turning first one way and then another until it was time to pack up her cameras and go out again.

She had no life outside her work. She declined invitations to parties and dinners. She avoided Josh and Sallie and the Cleeves and other, more casual, friends. She saw little of Alice, busy now with the opening of *Winter Moon*.

Lucy chose not to attend the opening, though she stayed up to read the rave reviews, clipping them as always for her scrapbooks. There were scores of clippings that season, for Tony won every award there was to win, Maggie was named Best Actress, and the play itself won the Pulitzer Prize.

"Do you know that Tony's moved to a suite at the St. Moritz?" Elizabeth asked one cool, cloudy spring afternoon. "Do you know—"

"Yes, Gran," Lucy replied. "I know all about it. We're in touch. As a matter of fact, we had lunch together last week. No, don't bother asking me about it. Nothing was settled. Nothing's changed."

"How long do you expect to go on this way?"

"I don't know, Gran. Tony seems . . . less pressured. Perhaps that's a good sign. Perhaps—"

"Perhaps! Is that the best you can do, Lucy? With your marriage in ruins you—"

"*Stop it.* I won't talk about it anymore. I can't. If I talk about it, if I say the words, I'll die."

Chapter Twenty-Three

Divorce was not mentioned, but it was a subject much on everyone's mind. Certainly it was on Elizabeth's mind as she arrived at Tony's hotel suite. Wrapped in sable and clutching a gold-headed cane, she swept past him, her eye selecting the most comfortable chair. "We can dispense with the amenities," she said, sitting down.

"We've already dispensed with one," Tony replied. "You might have called before you came over, Elizabeth."

"And if I had? I strongly suspect you would have found some excuse not to see me. I wasn't about to be put off. We must talk. We must make sense of things while there's still time."

"I'm sorry to say it isn't that simple."

"Perhaps not, but I'm sure you agree it's worth the try."

Tony exhaled a breath. "Sherry?" he asked.

"Thank you."

He brought her drink and then sank down on the couch. "I really thought you'd be glad about all of this, Elizabeth," he said. "You opposed our marriage from the start. You did everything you could to prevent it. I remember your visit to the old Bleecker Street place. I remember the conversation almost word for word."

"Then you will remember that I told you it was nothing personal. I've always been fond of you, in my fashion. At the same time, I felt you were a poor choice. I still do. But that's quite beside the point."

"Just what *is* the point?"

"Seventeen years of marriage. Are you prepared to throw seventeen years away?"

Tony rubbed his hand across his eyes. "I don't know what you mean by *prepared*," he said. "It's the last thing in the world I want. Oddly enough, it's the last thing Lucy wants, too. But there's a wall between us and we both keep crashing into it."

"Walls can be torn down."

"An interesting comment, considering that you supplied the bricks."

"I merely told you the truth, Tony. I warned you you'd never have all of Lucy."

"Congratulations, you were right."

"That is also beside the point. You entered into this marriage with your eyes open. You knew very well about Lucy's troubled past."

"From *you*, Elizabeth. I knew about it from you. I've waited years to hear it from Lucy herself. I gave her so many openings. After Averill died, I gave her a perfect opening. Still she kept silent. That doesn't say much for trust or anything else."

"And so you're throwing in your hand? Have I overestimated you?"

"*Over*estimated me," Tony laughed. "Since when?"

"I give credit where it's due. Your choice of career was irresponsible, but I respect your accomplishments nonetheless. You've made a success, Tony. I

484

respect success. It's a sign of strong character."

"Don't forget about luck, Elizabeth."

"Strong men make their own luck. Whatever your faults may be, you've never lacked strength. That's why I expect you to fight for your marriage."

"I learned something about fighting during the war," Tony replied slowly. "I learned that the battlefield can make all the difference. . . . Well, the battlefield isn't here, Elizabeth. It's in Aldcross."

"Aldcross!"

He shrugged. "It began there," he said. "That's where it must end. If Lucy is ever to get rid of her ghosts, Aldcross is the place."

"Impossible. I've often urged her to visit England. She's flatly refused. Why, she's even refused to be in touch with Sarah's parents. The Griffiths write to me and I to them, but Lucy hasn't sent so much as a Christmas card. She's closed her mind to Aldcross and everyone in it."

"That's precisely what she *hasn't* done, Elizabeth. She's haunted by things she should have been made to face years ago. Instead of facing them, she locked them inside herself. And they've been eating away at her ever since. She can't cry, you know. That's part of it, too. Even her tears are locked inside. Aldcross is the key to the lock."

Elizabeth sipped her sherry, her dark eyes thoughtful. "How do you propose to use this key?" she asked. "Assuming it *is* a key? Obviously you would have to get her there. A most unlikely possibility."

"You may be right. I haven't any kind of plan, not yet. I don't intend to kidnap Lucy. Nor is this something she'll do on her own. So I'm afraid we're nowhere. We're in limbo. We've been there a long time."

"All marriages have their difficult moments.

You're not a child, Tony. You know marriage isn't perfect. Good marriages survive, no matter what."

"Good marriages don't sleep three to a bed."

Elizabeth put her glass down. She was still, her cool gaze studying Tony. "I once told you," she said, "that you would never have all of Lucy. What I didn't tell you was that Colin wouldn't have had all of her either. She cared for him, yes. A youthful infatuation that may or may not have lasted. But what she saw in him was escape. . . . Lucy wasn't a happy girl. She wasn't entirely comfortable with her social obligations. She wanted to rebel. Of course she didn't have the courage. And then Colin came along. Quite a handsome young man. A romantic like herself. A romantic who could take her thousands of miles away. The result was inevitable."

"Love at first sight," Tony snapped.

"Only in a manner of speaking. It was like calling to like, blood calling to blood. They shared the *same* blood, Tony. They looked at each other and saw opposite sides of themselves. Is that really so hard to understand?"

"*You're* hard to understand. Why the big pitch? Why are you suddenly on my side?"

"There has never been a divorce in the Cameron family. My late husband Jasper didn't approve of divorce. Neither do I."

"Well, that's honest, anyway. But your interpretation of events—"

"—is the correct interpretation," Elizabeth said. "Lucy and Colin cared for each other, yes. That aside, there was no . . . spark between them."

"Oh?"

Elizabeth smiled. "They returned to New York immediately after the wedding ceremony," she continued. "In similar circumstances, I rather imagine you and Lucy would have delayed long enough for a honeymoon. There was another train, after all. There's always another train."

Tony's lips parted. He stared at her, his eyes bright with surprise and amusement and, at the last, a certain respect. "I, too, give credit where it's due," he said. "You're a witch, Elizabeth, but you're a perceptive witch."

"You have the benefit of my perception. Put it to good use."

"When the time is right."

Elizabeth rose, gathering her furs about her. "Mind you don't run out of time," she warned.

Indeed the year seemed to pass quickly. Tony and Lucy remained apart, their lives revolving around work. He made several trips to California; she started devising an outline for her new book, a moody photo album of parks and trees in different seasons. She spent her days in the study, cluttered now with hundreds of prints and negatives, with light boxes and magnifying glasses and red marking pencils. She was in the study on a November afternoon when Elsa appeared suddenly at the door. "Is something wrong?" she asked, regarding the woman's pale face. "Did the garbage disposal explode again?"

"Terrible news, missus. I was listening to the radio, and the radio says the President has been shot. In Texas," Elsa added, wiping her anxious hands on her apron. "Dallas, Texas."

"Shot? You must have misunderstood."

"No, missus, I heard it."

Lucy hurried across the room and switched on the television set. She watched for a few moments, then fell into a chair. "My God," she murmured. "Oh my

God, it's true."

"Yes, missus."

Lucy grabbed the telephone, dialing Tony's hotel. He was out and she left a message. With a sigh, she returned to her chair. "You don't have to go, Elsa," she said. "Stay if you want. We'll watch together. It's no time to be alone, is it?"

"Such a fine man. How can this happen, missus?"

"I don't know, Elsa. I don't know."

The two women did not stir from the television set during the next half hour. They listened to the same news repeated over and over. They listened to wild rumors almost instantly discredited by harried reporters. They saw the chaotic scenes outside the hospital; they saw the chaos everywhere, for the nation was in shock. Tony entered the study just as the President's death was announced. Lucy ran to him, falling into his arms. Tears burned at the back of her eyes but she could not cry. "They killed him," she murmured. "My God, they killed him."

Tony said nothing, for there was nothing to say. There were no easy words, no comforting phrases; certainly there were no explanations. He took Lucy to the couch and sat her down. He noticed the housekeeper then. He turned. "You probably want to be with your family, Elsa," he suggested. "At a time like this . . ."

"Yes, mister," she agreed. "A time for family."

Tony reached into his pocket, pulling out a crumpled twenty-dollar bill. "The doorman will get you a cab."

"Thank you, mister."

He heard Elsa's heavy footsteps fade away. He sat down, reaching for Lucy's hand. "Do you want a drink?" he asked.

"I just want to know why."

"I suppose they'll tell us. All we can do is wait."

"You'll stay with me, Tony, won't you? You won't leave?"

"Of course I'll stay. Suddenly our problems don't seem very important. Not compared to what's happened."

"But we don't *know* what's happened."

"We know the President is dead," Tony replied grimly. "We know the nightmare's begun."

No one would ever forget the nightmare of that long weekend. A stunned and grieving nation watched Air Force One arrive in Washington, watched the President's casket taken from the plane, watched the President's widow, so pale and dazed in her blood-stained suit. The nation watched as the President's assassin was taken into custody and then, incredibly, was himself assassinated. The nation and the world watched the President's funeral, a solemn pageant whose images were etched in memory—images of a riderless horse, of a courageous widow, of a young son, his hand lifted in salute, of an eternal flame burning into the night, remembrance of the years that had been known as Camelot.

At the end of that weekend, when the television set had finally been turned off, when overflowing ashtrays had finally been emptied, Lucy again asked Tony to stay. "We haven't solved anything being apart," she said. "We haven't been any happier. At least," she added quickly, "I haven't been any happier. . . . Can't we try, Tony? Can't we try together?"

His arms went around her. He felt the fluttering of her heart against him. Like the fluttering of bird's wings, he thought. "But will you really try?" he asked, seizing the opening. "If I asked you to—"

"I'll do anything you ask, Tony. I promise."

"Come and sit down. I want to talk to you about something." He led her to a chair in the living room, sitting opposite. "I haven't stopped loving you, wanting you, Lucy. But our problems are real."

"I know. All these months I've been hoping for a miracle, hoping I'd wake up one morning and find everything the way it used to be."

Tony gazed into her eyes. "A miracle like a second chance?" he asked.

"Exactly like that. Silly, isn't it?"

"Perhaps not. I've had an idea. . . . Actually, I've been offered a script. A movie script that's going to be shot in London . . . London is a wonderful place for a second honeymoon. A second honeymoon, a second chance."

"Tony, we need more than a change of scenery. I . . . somehow I have to be different."

"Oh, we were both at fault. We stopped talking to each other. We talked, but we didn't say anything. I was always rushing off to the theater or the airport. You were busy with your work. Dear old *Gran* was constantly sniffing around. . . . Don't you see, Lucy? We need to go away from here. Far away. We need time to ourselves, just the two of us. We were so happy once. . . . Remember?"

"It breaks my heart to remember."

"We need time to find each other again. The people we were, once upon a time. There are too many distractions here. Gran is here. Wouldn't you like to get away from her meddling?"

"It's easy to blame everything on Gran," Lucy replied, her shoulders rising and falling in a sigh. "The truth is that I'm the problem. . . . I saw things in your eyes, too. Sadness, disappointment. I put those things there all by myself."

Tony stood, pulling her up into his arms. "Listen

490

to me," he said. "I don't care about blame, and neither should you. The future is what matters. It's time to find out whether we have a future, Lucy. We can't do that here."

"We could go to the Cape."

"The Cape!" he exclaimed. "With Lee telephoning every ten minutes? With Mrs. Purdy dropping by at the crack of dawn? With the local bird watchers tramping back and forth over the cliffs? That isn't what we need now. We need time for ourselves. We need to go away from here."

"But you never have any time when you're on a picture."

"Ah, you forget this is a British picture. Working over there is a lot more civilized. I'll have all my nights free. I'll have Sundays. And when the picture wraps, I'll have all the time in the world. Just imagine it, Lucy. A real holiday in London . . . It's changed, you know. It isn't prim and proper anymore. It's *swinging* London now."

It's England, she thought wretchedly, old fears, old hatreds prickling her spine. It's Aldcross and the Averills and the memories that haunt my dreams. "I—I don't know," she murmured.

Tony's hands dropped from her shoulders. He stared at her, his face as hard and impassive as stone. "I'm asking you to go away with me," he said. "I won't ask again."

She heard the warning in his voice and it occurred to her that all the years of their marriage finally came down to this one moment, to the sudden discussion of a trip, to his sudden insistence, to her decision. "I don't understand," she said slowly, "but if London means so much to you . . ."

"It does, Lucy."

She swallowed. "Then of course I'll go." She saw

491

something very like relief in his face. She saw the light return to his eyes, an infinitely gentler, brighter light. "Tony, what do you expect to find there?"

"Our marriage."

"I—"

He kissed her, his strong hands tangling her hair, his body pressing closer and closer. Absence had fueled the fires of their passion, and soon they were walking toward the stairs. "I love you, darling," he murmured, sweeping her up into his arms.

"Oh, Tony, I love you."

"Our second honeymoon begins today."

"And then London?"

"And then they all lived happily ever after," he smiled, nuzzling her ear. "Just you wait and see."

Lucy, Tony, and Alice arrived in London in the spring of 1964. They went directly to their rooms at the Connaught, an old and elegant hotel on Carlos Place in Mayfair. Lucy had been very tense during the flight, but her nerves calmed as she stepped into the hotel's paneled lobby. She glanced around, seeing Oriental rugs, upholstered antique chairs, and a magnificent staircase, its patterned carpet bordered in brass. To the right was the reception desk and the small elevator, to the left the desk of the hall porter, a cheerful, smiling man dressed in a navy-blue tailcoat. It was a formal setting, yet so cozy that she breathed a deep sigh of relief. "I love it," she said, squeezing Tony's arm. "I feel better already!"

Alice was shown to a room on the third floor, Lucy and Tony to a small suite at the opposite end of the hall. Both the sitting room and bedroom were papered in soft yellow traced with white. The couch and the deep, comfortable armchairs were upholstered in bright chintz. In the bedroom was an antique secretary and a wall of windows overlooking a leafy side street. "Do you approve?" Tony asked, flopping down on the bed. "The housekeeper will be in later if you want anything changed."

"Oh, it's charming. I really do love it."

So far so good, he thought. "You know," he said, folding his hands behind his head. "I have almost a week before production meetings begin. Why don't we hire a car and driver and go out on the town? We can do all the tourist things first, get them out of the way. Then we can have tea at Brown's. And then we can go to the theater and afterward make the rounds of all the clubs. We'll have ourselves one mad whirl."

"You're in a good mood today."

"I'm in a *great* mood," Tony laughed. "'Ah, to be in England now that spring is here.'"

"You're excited about the picture, aren't you?"

"Well, it's a marvelous comedy. It's a marvelous cast. David Niven, the suave man of the world. Tony Curtis, the not-so-innocent abroad. Two old pros with perfect comic timing. This picture will be a romp."

"Who gets the girl? Niven or Curtis?"

"It's a movie, Lucy. They both find true love just before the fade-out."

"Lucky them."

"Lucky us. We're here and we're going to have a wonderful time. We won't waste a moment. The world is our crumpet, missy."

She smiled. "I hope I can keep up with you," she said. "I'm not as young as I used to be."

"You're the prettiest girl in London."

"You haven't seen the girls in London yet."

"I don't have to see them. I see you."

493

"That's sweet, Tony. But I think I'd better do a little primping anyway, just in case. I wouldn't want some fair English beauty turning your head."

"You're a fair English beauty."

"Goodness, all these compliments! What do you have up your sleeve?"

"Don't be so suspicious," he laughed.

"But you've been *showering* me with compliments."

"And why not? That's what second honeymoons are for. That and—"

"Don't say it," Lucy laughed too, a blush coloring her cheeks. "I get the idea."

She turned, starting to unpack the smallest of the suitcases she had brought to London. After a moment she glanced back at Tony. She frowned, for she could not get it out of her mind that he was up to something. She could not understand why this trip was so important to him, nor why her acquiescence had wrought such a sudden and startling change in his manner. Once again she was beset by vague doubts, by vague and shapeless questions. Her heart began to thump, for quite suddenly she was afraid.

Her fears quieted as the lovely English spring lengthened into summer. Much to her surprise she felt at home in London, and during long walks about the city she came to know it well. She delighted in the old—in the historic churches and museums, the exquisite royal parks, the friendly pubs. She was charmed by the new—by the "swinging" London of short skirts and long hair, of Carnaby Street and King's Road, of youth and the Beatles. She moved easily between both worlds. At night she and Tony explored the latest restaurants, the latest discotheques; when Tony went off to Shepperton Studios each morning, she went off on her own. She took her camera, photographing the quaint bookstores on Charing Cross Road, the churning crowds at Piccadilly Circus, the laden flower carts around Covent Garden. She went often to St. James's Park, where she photographed the graceful fountains, the willow trees in their summer glory, and the ducks gliding upon the lake. She snapped dozens of pictures of the romantic footbridge, and one of them she had mounted and framed as a gift for Tony. "He *loved* it," she reported to Alice during lunch the next day. "Of course he's loved everything lately. He's so easy to please, it scares me. Has he been that way at the studio?"

"The picture is on schedule and under budget," Alice replied with a laugh. "Does that answer your question? Maybe he's been a little keyed up the past couple of weeks. That's natural this close to the end of shooting. Six days on location and the picture wraps up. The time's gone quickly. I can't believe it's September already."

"Neither can I. It's been such a fantastic trip."

"I only have to look at you to see that. The color's blooming in your cheeks again, Lucy. You're smiling again. You've even gained a pound or two, thank God. You were so thin."

"Well, we've been to every restaurant in London. Every restaurant, every play, every party. Tony promised we wouldn't waste a moment. He's kept his word."

"You know I was worried about you and Tony for a while there. I'm so happy you two patched it up."

Lucy was quiet, her eyes clouding as she considered her reply. "I really can't explain it," she said some moments later. "We've had so much fun . . . not a single argument. Tony's his old self. *We're* our old selves. And yet there are times when I can feel him watching me. As if—as if he's studying me. He gets the oddest expression. That's when I can't help thinking there's something more to all this."

"Something more?"

"As I said, it's hard to explain."

"You're not still worried about Maggie?"

"Oh, no, nothing like that. Whatever happened to our marriage was my fault."

"It takes two, Lucy."

"Not always." She finished her tea and pushed the cup aside. "Not always," she said again. She rose, wandering across the sitting room to the windows. "I'm good at that. At telling myself comforting little lies. But not this time . . . That's why I don't know if we've really patched it up. I don't know what's in Tony's mind. I'm afraid to ask."

"Well, if you ask me, all that's on his mind is a second honeymoon."

"Yes." Lucy nodded, a dreamy smile touching her lips. "We've had a second honeymoon. We've had a grand time. . . . But I'm not sure anything's changed. What happens when we get back to reality?" She turned, glancing at the suitcases packed and standing near the door. "What then?"

"You have the wrong slant. *This* is the reality, right here and now. Okay, you and Tony had your problems. They're behind you now. Don't look for trouble, Lucy, just be glad."

"I'm trying."

"Try harder," Alice chuckled. "Think about spending six days in the beautiful English countryside. Everybody's been telling me it's beautiful. It should be a nice way to end the trip. . . . And that reminds me. Your tickets." She left the table and walked to the desk. With one swift motion she opened her briefcase and reached inside. "Here we are," she said. "You're on the 4:50 train. You'll be at the Three Swans Inn in time for dinner. And you won't be disturbed. The rest of us won't be arriving till tomorrow morning. So you're all set!"

"Thanks, Alice. I've put away my mini skirts and packed my tweeds. I thought tweeds would be better for Marbury if it's one of those old country towns."

"It is. Derek Cole, the set designer, says it's picturesque, whatever that means. But you're not staying in Marbury, you know. You and Tony are in the next village over. . . . Let's see . . . Yes, that's right. You're in a village called Aldcross."

Lucy spun around. "What did you say?"

"You're staying in a village called Aldcross. We're shooting in Marbury, but Tony said he wanted some privacy at the end of the day. So we set you up in Aldcross. It's only a ten minute drive between . . . Lucy, are you sick? You're white as chalk." Alice rushed to her, helping her into a chair. "What is it?" she asked. "Do you feel faint?"

"I'm not going."

"Not going? I don't understand."

"I can't go. To Aldcross. I can't go."

Alice touched her hand to Lucy's brow. "You don't seem to have a fever," she said. "Is your stomach upset? I hope you didn't get a bad shrimp."

"I'm all right," Lucy murmured, staring straight ahead. "I—I'd like to be alone, Alice."

"I'll just call downstairs for more tea. Tea is good—"

"No, don't bother. I'd really like to be alone now."

"Lucy, I can't leave you this way. You look ready to keel over."

"I'm all right. I probably ate too fast. . . . Please, Alice, let me be."

"Then I'll call Tony at the studio."

497

"*No.* Don't call anyone and don't do anything. . . . I'm sorry, Alice, but I'd like you to go."

"Okay, if you're sure. I think you ought to lie down. There's time," she added, walking to the door. "Tony was planning to leave the studio at three. . . . You're sure you don't want anything?"

Lucy shook her head. She managed a smile, a smile that disappeared the moment the door closed behind Alice. She sat very still, her thoughts rushing and tumbling one on top of another until she wanted to scream. "Aldcross," she murmured in the silence. "Aldcross." For an instant the room seemed to tilt, to grow dim. She grasped the arms of her chair. Her mouth tightened and it was as if her face had turned to stone.

"Darling?" Tony called out, entering the suite. "Oh, there you are. Alice said you weren't feeling well. I got here as quickly as I could. . . . You're very pale, Lucy."

"What do you know about Aldcross?"

He took a chair opposite her and sat down. "I know it's next door to Marbury," he replied.

"What else do you know?"

"I'm told it's a typical English village. Rather small, quiet."

"You read your line nicely. Have you been rehearsing?"

"Lucy . . ."

"I've been sitting here wondering about coincidences. Wondering about pieces of a puzzle, as you would say. This location shooting isn't a coincidence, is it, Tony? You planned it. . . . What do you know about Aldcross?"

He lighted a cigarette, watching her through a haze of gray smoke. He heard the ticking of a clock.

He heard the sudden blare of a car horn from the street below. He heard the beating of his own heart and he sighed. "Well," he said finally, "we've waited a long time to have things clear between us. I suppose this is the moment. I know everything about Aldcross, Lucy. I know about Roger Averill and what happened to your mother. I know about Colin and your marriage. There it is. I've waited all these years for you to tell me yourself. I've seen you eating yourself alive with things that couldn't possibly matter anymore. Or perhaps the word is *shouldn't*. In fact they seem to matter very much. That's why I had to get you here, get you to Aldcross. I hoped you would face your demons, Lucy. Face them and be rid of them once and for all . . . Because that's our only chance."

"How do you know these things?"

"Elizabeth told me shortly before we were married. She came down to the old Bleecker Street apartment. Just appeared at the door one fine day. Obviously she expected I would change my mind about you. I didn't, of course. I married you and I waited. I asked you about secrets. Christ, I tried to make it easy. But you didn't say anything. And after a while it really didn't make any difference. We were happy. At least I was . . . Then I saw your face the morning you read of Colin's death. I knew it was no good. I didn't know what to do about it. In the end, I realized the answers were here. I accepted the picture on condition that we could shoot locations near Aldcross. That's the whole story."

"You've lied to me all these years, Tony."

"*I?*"

"You knew and yet you acted as if . . . Was it a game? An experiment? Did you feel sorry for me? What was it? How could you do such a thing?"

Tony's eyes flashed. He leapt out of his chair,

angrily flinging his cigarette into an ashtray. "I don't believe I'm hearing this," he snapped. "A *game?* An *experiment?* An experiment in heartbreak! Before you climb on your high horse, I'd suggest you consider how *I* might have felt. It's no game, wondering if your wife is thinking about another man while she's making love to you. It's no game, competing with a memory. . . . Did I feel sorry for you? Yes, because I saw you throwing happiness away with both hands. And why? Did you think I'd give a damn about who your father was? Or how he happened to be your father? Did you think I'd give a damn about some stupid teenage marriage? No, Lucy. All I cared about was you. I've known a lot of women. I wanted only one—you. But you'd go off into your own little world. You'd go off to your memories, your precious Colin. I'm tired of fighting ghosts . . . in my bed and out."

"Tony, I never thought of Colin that way. He was never in our bed."

"Wasn't he? Well, I wouldn't know. Your silence on the subject was deafening."

"But I didn't know *how* to tell you. I couldn't find the words. I—I was afraid I'd lose you. I've always been afraid."

"Lose me? You could have wrapped me in burlap and dropped me in the river and I'd still have come back to you. It was that simple, that complicated. But you didn't know. . . . I wonder if we've ever really known each other."

Panic gripped Lucy now, for there was something in the depths of Tony's eyes she did not recognize, did not understand, something deeper than anger, deeper even than pain. "I'm sorry," she said. "So very sorry,"

"Not good enough."

"Tony, I—"

"Not good enough."

Her fingernails dug into the palms of her hands. She took a breath. "Do—do you want a divorce?" she asked.

"I don't know what the hell I want anymore. Perhaps it's time I found out."

"Where are you going?"

"Away from here."

"Tony, please."

"I'm sorry too, Lucy. And that's not good enough either."

She watched him go. She put her hands to her head, trying to quiet her throbbing temples. After some moments she rose and went to the windows. She watched as he emerged from the hotel. She watched until he was out of sight and then, unsteadily, she made her way to the telephone. "This is Mrs. Jennings," she said when the hall porter answered. "I want to hire a car and driver. . . . Yes, that's right. . . . I—I want to go to Aldcross."

Chapter Twenty-Four

"Have we much farther to drive, Robert?" Lucy asked, leaning forward in the car. "Will it be long?"

"No, ma'am, I wouldn't say so. We're three kilometers from Shepherd's Lane on my map. Now from Shepherd's Lane it's another kilometer to Crowhaven. That's the junction. After that, it's straight on to Aldcross."

"Thank you."

"Pretty country it is, too. 'Course there's the Developments springing up all over. What used to be farms is houses now. Good value for the price, they say, but if I was to live in the country, I'd like a nice bit of land. A garden, you know. And a kitchen garden for the wife. 'Course I'd like a nice yard for my boy Jack. And then . . ."

Lucy leaned her head back, wearily closing her eyes. She paid little attention to Robert's harmless chatter, for she was thinking about her own life, about the mistakes and misunderstandings that had left her life in ruins. Panic rose in her again, clutching her heart, cutting off her breath. She pressed her handkerchief to her damp brow. A moment later she rolled down the car window, staring blindly at the lush green countryside. As if from a distance she heard Robert's cheerful voice rambling on. In memory she heard Tony's voice, so cold, so flat, and she slumped against the seat. "I'm tired of fighting ghosts," she heard him say, and she knew that she, too, was tired. . . . Tired of secrets and lies and terrors in the black of night. "Face your demons," she heard Tony say, and now she had no doubt that was what she must do. "Excuse me, Robert," she said, interrupting his monologue. "Are we almost there?"

"We've just now come into Aldcross, ma'am. Passed the train station, we did. Up ahead is the square. We'll likely find the Three Swans on the square. The inn and the shops and all. Makes it easy, doesn't it? Everything in one place?"

"Yes, very convenient."

"Here we are, ma'am," Robert said, bringing the car to a smooth stop. "It's the Three Swans, all right."

Lucy gathered her purse and jacket, hesitating briefly before stepping out of the car. She glanced about, her eyes scanning the half-dozen small shops, the small post office, the tearoom with trays of muffins and frosted cakes in the window. "Thank you, Robert," she said, pressing several twenty-pound notes into his hand. "It was a lovely ride. Would you mind taking my bag to the desk? I'll check in later. I want to have a look around the village while it's still light."

"Yes, ma'am. I'll see to your bag straightaway. I hope you enjoy your holiday."

An uncertain smile flickered at the corners of Lucy's mouth. She turned, gazing off toward the ancient church. She crossed the square and soon she was outside the church, watching as a group of children burst through the carved wooden doors. Choir practice, she thought, recalling Sarah's descriptions of the Friday afternoon ritual. She walked around the back of the church to the cemetery, where generations of village families lay beneath simple white headstones. The names were unfamiliar to her, though the names of Emily Sparrow and Philip Burshaw again recalled Sarah's descriptions. At the far end of the cemetery she saw a fair-haired boy of eleven or twelve. She drew nearer, standing quietly by while he swept leaves from a headstone. He looked up after a moment and she smiled. "Hello," she said. "I didn't mean to intrude."

"That's all right. I'm finished now. Do you see the big oak just over there? It always sheds on Father's grave. Mummy says we can't cut it down. It's hundreds of years old."

"Well, you've done a fine job clearing the leaves away." Lucy glanced at the headstone. Her smile fled as she read the inscription: Colin Averill. 1919-1958. She bent, touching the cold marble. In her mind's eye she saw the golden hair and chiseled features of the young man she had once loved. I did love him once, she thought, but not the way I love Tony. No, never that way. It's Tony I've wanted and needed all these years. It's been Tony all along, but now it's too late. "Was Colin Averill your father?" she asked, rising slowly to her feet.

"Yes, I'm David Averill. I was little when he died. Just six. Sometimes it's hard to remember him. . . . Are you an American?"

Lucy nodded. "Here on a visit," she explained.

"Do you know any cowboys?"

"I'm afraid there aren't any cowboys in New York."

"I've been to New York," David said proudly.

"Mummy took us on the plane. We had a very nice time," he added, walking toward the gates. "But I like it better here."

"My mother was born here. Her name was Griffith."

"Griffith? That's the schoolmaster's name. He isn't the schoolmaster anymore. He's old now, like Grandmama. Is your name Griffith too?"

"No, I'm Lucy Jennings," she said, shortening her stride to match his. "And I'm happy to have met you. . . . Would you know where the Griffiths live?"

"On Winding Lane." The child jumped onto his bicycle, glancing over his shoulder at Lucy. "That's after Beechwood Road," he said. "It's not far."

"Thank you, David. I'm sure I'll find it."

"Good-bye then."

"Good-bye." Lucy watched him ride away. She turned and looked one last time in the direction of Colin's grave. "Good-bye," she murmured.

She walked past the ivy-colored vicarage, past the neat white brick cottages set behind herbaceous borders. She knew that very little had changed in Aldcross, that these were the sights her mother had seen, had left behind forever. She paused when she came to a sign marked Beechwood Road. She looked up at the sky, dark blue with twilight, and now her pace quickened. This is the road that's haunted my dreams, she thought, her heart thumping in her chest. She took a great breath and hurried on.

She had gone halfway when the shadows of night closed around her. Lucy thought about turning back; she wanted to, but she forced herself to continue. There was a roaring in her ears, a shiver rushing along her spine. All at once she was certain that she heard footsteps. She whirled around, seeing nothing but darkness. The footsteps seemed to grow louder.

She ran, her hair streaming out behind her, her breath coming in short gasps. She stumbled, quickly righting herself. Now the footsteps seemed almost upon her. She ran faster, running just as Sarah had run some forty years before. She was terrified, and in her terror she took the path through the wood. She saw the stark black tree trunks of her dreams. A branch touched her shoulder and she screamed. She fell to the moist ground, too frightened to move. She closed her eyes, for she was certain that somewhere in the darkness a shadowy figure waited.

But there was no shadowy figure. When finally she dared open her eyes she saw magnificent old trees silhouetted in moonlight. She saw a carpet of wildflowers and birds soaring gracefully toward the sky. She started to laugh, and in the very next instant she was crying. The tears she had held within her for so long coursed down her cheeks. Now the breeze seemed to quiet and the birds also, as if the whole earth was listening to the sound of her sobs.

Hilda Griffith put down her knitting and looked curiously toward the hall. "Did you hear a knock, John?" she asked. "Who do you suppose would be calling at this hour?"

"It's probably the shutter come loose again. I can't find the right sort of hook. Billy Clegg is no better than his father was. Sells me what he wants me to have, not what I need."

"No, it's not the shutter. I'm sure I heard a knock. Well, I'll have a look, shall I?" She rose, slowly walking the few steps to the hall. She switched on the light and then opened the door. "Sarah," she murmured, her eyes blinking behind the lenses of her glasses. "No, it's—it's Lucy, isn't it?"

"Yes, I'm Lucy. I'm so sorry to startle you this way."

"Not at all, love. Not at all . . . John," Hilda called, "it's our Lucy come from America."

"But—but aren't you surprised?" Lucy asked.

"I'll tell you the truth, love. We never knew when, but we always knew you'd come. It was a feeling, you see. Wasn't it, John? Wasn't it a feeling we had?"

"Yes," he replied, adjusting his own glasses. "Why, you're the picture of Sarah. . . . Come in, my dear. Come in and sit down. We must—we must get acquainted."

Lucy stepped into the hall. For a moment they all stared at each other, but soon they were in each other's arms. "I didn't know if you'd want to see me," Lucy sniffled, brushing a tear away. "I've been so awful."

"Now none of that," Hilda said. "Of course we want to see you. You're our granddaughter. Our only one. Your uncle Bertie has four sons. Big, strapping fellows they are, too. . . . Sit down, Lucy. The sofa's nice and comfortable. . . . That's it. Have you had your dinner?"

"Oh, I'm not hungry."

"A bit of sherry then. I'll get the good sherry I've been saving for a special occasion." Hilda bustled off to the kitchen, returning swiftly with a bottle and three fluted crystal glasses. "We'll have a toast, shall we?" she asked, pouring their drinks. "We'll have a toast to family. Family's all that matters in the end."

They had several more sherries before the night was over, talking for hours and trying to make up for all the lost years. Lucy was astonished at how much John and Hilda knew about her life. She was touched by the album they had kept, an album filled with pictures of her, with clippings from New York society columns, and even with the reviews of Tony's plays. Silently, she thanked Elizabeth. Gran has a good side after all, she thought to herself.

She felt at ease in the snug little cottage. From Sarah's descriptions, she recognized the china dog sitting atop the mantel, the polished brass coal scuttle, the reading lamp angled behind John's favorite chair. In John and Hilda she recognized kindness, an innate decency. Time had whitened their hair, lined their faces, but it had not diminished their spirits, and this too she found touching. It strengthened her to know that she was part of them, a Griffith with the hardy roots of ordinary people. "It's been a wonderful evening," she said as the clock struck twelve, "but it's late and I really ought to be getting back."

"You must stay the night with us," John said. "It's a bit of a walk to the Three Swans. I haven't a car to offer you. I never did take up driving. I was so used to my bicycle."

"We don't even have the bicycle anymore," Hilda added. "Not since John's fall. Of course you'll stay with us tonight, love. You can have your mother's old room. . . . There's no reason to go all the way to the inn. You said Tony wasn't coming down till morning."

"That's just it. I'm not sure when he's coming, not exactly. I mean, he could arrive any time. That's how it is when he's shooting on location. I'd feel better if I were there, just in case."

"Well, if you'd feel better . . ." Hilda reluctantly agreed. "We want to meet your Tony, you know."

"Oh, you will," Lucy replied, quickly averting her eyes. "He—he isn't really himself when he's on a picture. You'll have to take that into account."

"Men have their moods, love. We'll like him

whatever mood he's in. Won't we, John?"

"Yes. Yes, indeed we will."

They walked with Lucy to the door, once again enfolding her in their arms. "Now you want to go straight along on Beechwood Road," Hilda said. "When you come to the end, it's two turns left to the inn. And mind your step, love. They fixed the road last year, but you still want to keep an eye out."

"I'll be fine," Lucy smiled, pausing at the open door. "I'll see you tomorrow." She looked at her grandparents, tears glittering on her lashes. "I'm so happy I came," she murmured. "The bad times are over at last."

The night held no terrors for Lucy now. She walked briskly along the road, every once in a while glancing up at the starry sky. I have to make Tony understand what's happened here, she thought. Somehow I have to make him see that the ghosts are gone, that everything's all right.

Her thoughts were interrupted by the sudden roar of a car engine. She shielded her eyes, blinded by the glaring headlights. Hastily she moved to the side of the road, but as the car drew closer she recognized Tony behind the wheel. "Tony," she called, dashing to the black convertible. "Oh, Tony, I was just—"

"Get in."

"You're still angry and I don't blame you but—"

"Get in, Lucy."

She slid onto the seat beside him. "Are you too angry to listen to what I have to say?" she asked.

"The word is *furious*. Your little disappearing act had the desired effect. I was half crazy with worry. Alice was so upset she had to take a tranquilizer. We spent hours trying to track you down, Lucy. We phoned all over London, every place we could think of. Then I had a talk with the hall porter. He said you'd hired a car. Then I had to phone the car company to find out where they'd taken you. *Then* I drove down here . . . only to find that you'd left your bag at the desk but never checked in. Oh, it's been a *splendid* night."

"I'm sorry, Tony."

"And I'm tired of hearing that. Where the hell have you been for eight hours? Mourning at dear Colin's grave?"

"I saw his grave," Lucy replied quietly. "I didn't feel anything. I'm sorry he died, but that's all there is to it. I'm not mourning or grieving or any of those things. Whatever I felt for Colin ended a long time ago. The tragedy is that it took me such a long time to see the truth."

Tony turned the car around, shifting gears as he headed back to the Three Swans. "You were in love with him," he said.

"I think I was in love with love. Colin was different from the boys I'd known. A romantic stranger who magically appeared at my dance and swept me off my feet . . . Yes, I loved him. But I was seventeen and dreamy and looking for Prince Charming. . . . I don't know what would have happened if we'd stayed together. I suspect I would have realized that life wasn't a fairy tale and that he wasn't Prince Charming after all. . . . I suspect there wouldn't have been much left, once the dreams were gone. He was a wonderful young man, but he wasn't the man for me."

"Are you telling me what you imagine I want to hear?"

"No," Lucy cried. "You don't understand. I'm telling you the *truth*. In a way I've always known the

510

truth," she continued, her words coming in a rush. "But seeing it, admitting it, that was hard. It was *impossible*, because in my mind Colin was all tangled up with the *other* things I didn't dare face. Mother and Sir Roger and the lies and my nightmares. My demons, you called them. You told me to face my demons. You were right."

Now Tony pulled the car to the side of the road and cut the engine. "How was I right?" he asked.

"The past was destroying my life. What's worse, it was destroying our life together. But I'm such a coward. Or I was. I found my courage, Tony, thanks to you. When you walked out the door I knew I'd rather face all the demons in the world than face losing you. Demons, devils, fire-breathing dragons. It didn't matter. *You* mattered."

His hands relaxed on the wheel. He smiled, his first real smile in a long time. "Fire-breathing dragons, eh? Did you do battle with fire-breathing dragons?"

"Shall I tell you about it?"

"All about it."

Lucy described the terrifying journey along Beechwood Road, the terrifying sound of footsteps that was in reality the sound of her own heart, the terrifying detour into the wood. "When I opened my eyes I saw that the moon had come out. . . . There was no one hiding in the shadows. There was nothing to be frightened of. It was *over*, Tony. I started to laugh and then I was crying, actually crying. It felt so good. . . . After a while I tried to find my way back to the road. I must have stumbled around for an hour or more. I finally found a clearing. I saw a cottage in the distance and I walked toward it. . . . Mother had described that cottage a thousand times. I knew it belonged to the Griffiths, my grandparents."

511

"So you spent the evening with your grandparents," Tony said quietly. "I wondered if you'd wind up there."

"Yes. They're such nice people. They want to meet you. . . . Will they, Tony? You aren't going to leave me, are you? I couldn't bear it if . . ." She felt his arms surround her, felt the warmth of his lips. "You know," she sniffled, "they might start hinting around about wanting a great-grandchild. . . . And if they do, I think you should tell them we're working on it."

Tony held her away for a moment, gazing into her eyes. "Does that mean what I hope it means?" he asked.

"Well, we're a little past the age. People will laugh at us. But I won't mind, will you?"

"Mind? Darling, I'll be the happiest man on earth."

"Then why don't we find our way to the Three Swans and see what happens?"

"Is that a proposition, Mrs. Jennings?"

"It certainly is."

Tony started the car, slipping his arm about her shoulder. "Have I told you lately that I love you?"

"Tell me again."

"I love you."

"And I love you, very much." She stared up at the sky, smiling as the clouds parted. "Oh, Tony, look. The harvest moon. Make a wish. Everybody's allowed one wish on the harvest moon."

"I already have my wish, darling."

"Yes," Lucy sighed, snuggling against him. "Yes, so have I."